ANGELA R HUGHES

ARTHUR

AND THE

GOLDEN DRAGON

THE ONCE & FUTURE CHRONICLES
BOOK THREE

IMAGINE NOW PUBLISHING
www.angelarhughes.com

Editor Stephanie Cotta
Illustrations by Sindi Fatkoja, Instagram @sindifatkoja
Cover design by 100Covers, www.100covers.com
Images: Licensed Adobe Stock Photos

ISBN 978-1-7362443-2-6 (Paperback)
ISBN 978-1-7362443-3-3 (Hardback)
Library of Congress Control Number: 2024901929

IMAGINE NOW PUBLISHING

Dedicated to my sister Amanda…
You once told me that as you read the words of Merlin's song, you discovered
the meaning beyond the words. His magic unwound, and it was made clear to you
what his lyrics intended, as though written for you to understand. They were.
I will always appreciate you for hearing and understanding.
You cannot imagine what that has meant to me. Thank you for seeing my world,
and understanding the reason for the lines I have written on these pages.

And to BEDWYR & PEREDUR, heroes of old…
You chose to believe in something bigger than yourselves. To live and die for
another purpose. It is heroes like you that remind us all that brotherhood is worth
fighting for, and that *LOVE* is bigger than our own wishes and desires. Your
existence in stories makes me want to believe there is strength and courage that
extends beyond the reach of my own arm—an invisible hand that slays giants, and
defeats armies with the simplicity of *FEALTY & FAITH*.

CONTENTS

PRYDAIN
LAND OF
THE
BRITONS
PICTI LAND
CAER EOYN
King Bram
King Lot
GREAT WALL
naldin's village
THE HILL OF THE RINGS
CAER LIAL
dragon's cottage
CELYDDON
King Thul
CRYSTAL CAVE
ISLE OF AVALON
King Crioghcat
RIVER TOWN
dyfed
South Lands
NARROW PASS
CAER MYRDDYN
King Cormach
Lindonium
King Lugh
the forest of goll
LLYONESSE
N
W
E
S

THE SONG

Sweet…Are the healing days, when pain will find no way.
The earth will sing, for the Sun has made it day.
Sweet…As it will be proclaimed the new days of the Sun.
Its rays will rise high, setting thrones upon kings' holds,
The New Way coming, and the land set in gold.

Oh, Kingdom of the Sun, renew our land with grace.
Oh, Kingdom of the Sun, the warmth of its bounty upon our face.
Blood will stop dripping, as the oil of gladness is tipping.
The sword no longer killing, but its emblems triumphing.
A new day rising, with the old moons setting.
Sweet…days of the Sun are coming

"And the meaning of the rock cut from the mountain, though
not by human hands, that crushed to pieces the statue of iron, bronze, clay,
silver, and gold. The *Great God* was showing the king what will happen
in the future. The dream is true, and its meaning certain."
Daniel 2:45 NLT

PROLOGUE

IN THE YEARS BEFORE ARTHUR WAS KING

Arthur grimaced, brushing his golden curls from his ruddy, adolescent cheeks. With hesitance, he eyed the dirty stone archway suspended above his head, leading into the city of Lindonium. Already, the fumes of raw sewage wafted into his nose.

Merlin twisted his lips, grumbling with disgust, "Filthy city."

Arthur gave a facetious smile. "I thought you *loved* Lindonium?"

Merlin rolled his eyes. "I only come here when forced."

Arthur had no desire to enter Lindonium either. Though he had never been, he had heard enough to make him never want to step foot inside the city. While training to become a warrior, the battle chieftains often disregarded this citadel altogether as part of Prydain's realm. Yet, here they were at the city's doorstep, among the pulsing throng of people waiting to enter through the gate.

"Tell me again why you hate it so much?" Arthur asked.

"You mean, besides the stench? This city holds onto Rome like an orphan to the breast of its dead mother." Merlin faced Arthur with a repulsive glare. "They have no part in the world just outside their gates—leaving this city to drip with the depravity of a stagnant pool."

Arthur chuckled at Merlin's bitter rant.

Merlin went on, "With both Aurelius and Uther now dead, the realm is fracturing, with the lesser kings fighting over who should be high king."

Arthur sniffed. "You mean, Lugh and Croighcat?"

Merlin nodded, tsking. "There is a void that leaves us vulnerable, giving the Saecsans too much time to strengthen their forces. And these *fools*—" Merlin pointed through the gate—"still think Rome will save them."

"This is why we have come?" Arthur asked, feeling anxious. His broad shoulders tightened, and he dragged his feet through the dry dirt while they waited for the guard at the entrance to check them. Dust coated his boots and wafted through the air, creating a dank cloud that filled his teeth with grit.

Merlin glanced sideways at Arthur. "This is where the council of kings has been summoned. This city is neutral ground."

Arthur nodded, then smirked. "You told me you brought me here because I have come of age, but what does someone like me have to do with a kings' council? I am no one's son. You have been tight-lipped this entire journey. There is more you are not telling me."

Arthur eyed Merlin, who feigned ignoring him. A tense lump rose in Arthur's throat.

"Listen," Merlin said, narrowing his eyes at Arthur. "Perhaps I should have explained, but right now"—he flashed his papers to the guards who waved them through—"there is no time."

"Merlin," Arthur demanded, but with the crowd pressing through the gates, the conversation halted.

Merlin grabbed Arthur's arm and pulled him through the crowd. His face was tense and his hold firm. Arthur grimaced at his mentor's odd behavior.

Why is Merlin gripping onto me like I might try to escape?

Ever since they left from the northlands, Merlin's aloof and mysterious demeanor made Arthur uneasy. His strange manner only escalated the closer they got to Lindonium. Merlin had never brought Arthur along to a kings' council before. The opportunity to see the kings in action was an exciting prospect, but he was not high born. He didn't belong in a gathering like this.

Merlin glanced back, meeting Arthur's eyes, and his expression softened. "I need you to trust me."

Merlin's words only increased the suspicion building in Arthur's thoughts. What was it that he needed to trust?

Breaking through the entrance walls, they squeezed through the bustle, and Arthur peered back over his shoulder. The stone wall, along with the crowd of bobbing heads and pointed spears, shrouded his view of the forests and hills.

People dispersed down the citadel's widening avenues, and Arthur finally caught a waft of fresh air. He scanned the streets while Merlin rushed ahead—Arthur's arm still tight in his grip. Rodents scrambled in broad daylight; sickly, poor children begged for bread next to crippled beggars. But as Arthur lifted his gaze, he discovered rows of Roman columns with sleek empty-eyed statues—ghosts of the past. He gaped at their magnificence, and his feet slowed to take in the scene.

Merlin tugged his arm to keep him moving.

Arthur resisted. "Are we in a hurry? Why the haste? Have we not arrived on the appointed day?"

The druid shook his head. "We cannot delay. Some of the kings may already be within the citadel. I want *you* there before—"

"*Me?* Before what?"

Merlin's mouth tightened; earnest regret hovered in his eyes. Arthur's stomach pulsed with anxious swirls.

"We cannot delay," Merlin said. His hand clenched even tighter around Arthur's arm, and they started forward again.

If it had been anyone other than Merlin, Arthur would have put up a fight. The druid was his teacher, guardian, brother. Arthur's only constant.

Another pull aggravated Arthur's pride, and his jaw clenched.

If he keeps pulling me through the city like an obstinate child, I am going to bash him.

The lane opened into a cobblestone square surrounded by a circular colonnade. A Romanesque fountain trickled at the heart. Vendors lined the edges, their voices polluting the air as they shouted their wares.

Merlin took a deep breath and looked at Arthur with a distressed expression.

Arthur ripped his arm from Merlin's grasp. "I am *not a child* that you have to drag through the streets." Then he added sharply, "Have we arrived, then?"

"Yes." Merlin nodded, staring at Arthur's reddened wrist. "I am sorry, Arthur."

Arthur jutted his chin forward, well past ready for an explanation. He could tell Merlin's apology had layers, like he was amending for more than just his current brash behavior.

Merlin's eyes had moved on from Arthur's contentious lour, and he was now searching the square as if looking for someone.

"Listen," Merlin huffed, pointing to a large stone hall adjacent to a humble monastery. "The kings have been meeting here for the five years since Uther's death, fighting over who should be *high king*. I have been able to persuade them each time to defer the election…but now the time has come." He squared Arthur's shoulders, his eyes boring into him. "I have done all I could to prepare you for this."

Arthur's eyes widened. "Prepare me?" He leaned in close. "Merlin, what are you talking about?"

"Prepare you for what must happen next. The southern kings fight for high kingship—I think Lot would have it too. They will wait no longer. They would have already waged war against the north if it had not been for Igraine."

"Igraine?"

"Your"—Merlin bit his lip—"your mother."

Arthur gasped as though slapped in the face. His heart dropped, and his knees buckled. The secret of his parentage—he had sought answers for years to no avail.

Stunned, Arthur fought to regain his emotions. "You knew who my mother was? I thought—" He swallowed down the anger rising in his chest. "I thought my parents were dead."

His head swam. Confusion and betrayal flooded him. Bedwyr's father, and then King Ector after him, had been the men he looked to as Father.

He glared at Merlin. "My mother is alive?"

"No." Merlin shook his head sadly. "No…I am sorry, Arthur. That is why we are here. Igraine and I had a plan, and now that she has passed, it is time. There is now no boundary to hold the kings back. The tension will soon snap the last strand that keeps what Uther built together. You must be revealed."

Revealed?

Arthur's stomach churned. The name Igraine floated through his mind. He had heard her name before—

All at once, the connection unlocked in his mind. Arthur gasped.

She was—she was Uther's—

"Merlin! Arthur!" came a familiar shout from across the square.

The voice pulled Arthur from the shock, and he lifted his head.

There, scrambling across the cobbled stone, was King Ector with his son Cai. Arthur sighed, momentarily comforted at the sight of Ector's burly arms spread wide in welcome. His rugged, brown, leather-woven breastplate was buckled over his green tunic, and his ginger braided beard swung over his chest.

"Cai." Arthur met his red-headed brother with a hearty, relieved squeeze. Cai was a few years younger than Arthur but stood a head above him. "Brother," he said, slapping Cai generously on his back, "I did not know *you* would be here."

"Ai, my father had me come. It is my first year of manhood," Cai said with a proud gleam in his eye. "Father said this was the year for me to join him within the kings' council. Bedwyr will be here also. He comes with Thul."

Arthur could tell by the innocent luster in Cai's eyes that he knew as little as Arthur did. But Ector—he had the same suspicious, knowing look as Merlin.

Exasperated and desperate for answers, Arthur stepped toward Merlin. "Why did you not tell me my brothers would be here?"

Merlin looked at Arthur from the corner of his eye; a nervous twitch threatened the edge of his mouth. "You will need those who love you best to support you."

"What is he talking about?" Arthur asked Ector, baffled. "Merlin drags me here, tells me *nothing*, then reveals that he knew my mother? And that she—"

It couldn't be. His mind refused to believe it.

Ector raised his eyebrow at Merlin.

"Ah." Chagrined, Arthur's face heated. "I see it is not just Merlin keeping secrets from me."

Cai's brow furrowed. "What is Arthur talking about?" he asked his father.

Merlin gripped Arthur's shoulders, then pointed across the square to a stone rising out of a small patch of grass, nestled underneath shady oak trees beside the monastery. "That is Aurelius's sword embedded within that stone."

Arthur squinted. It appeared small from their distance. "Why is it there?" He clenched his jaw to suppress his rising angst. "Why would Aurelius be honored in Lindonium? This citadel has little to do with our world."

"No, Arthur. It was *not* put there to honor Aurelius. It is there for another reason. Igraine brought the sword here during the first council after Uther's death. And it was I who struck it into that stone as a sign before *all* the kings."

Arthur gritted his teeth. "I *do not* understand."

"Ai," said Ector, nodding his head. His eyes glimmered. "I remember the day."

Arthur lifted his gaze to meet Ector's.

"Sent fear into my very bones." Ector gripped Arthur's arm. "My boy, when Merlin stood before that stone, with the beautiful Igraine beside him, he declared before all the kings that blade's purpose. When he lifted the sword above his head, his voice shook the air. Then, to our amazement, he slid the sword into that stone, as though it were slicing through soft soil. Lightning struck!" Ector lifted his hands and clapped. "*BOOM!* The thunder sent us all sprawling onto the ground."

Arthur scanned Merlin's face. The reason—Arthur needed to hear it.

"I enchanted it," Merlin said, holding Arthur's stare. "Only Aurelius's heir can draw that sword from the stone. As high druid…*I* am the kingmaker. I declared that day that only the true king, as by mine and Igraine's design, could pull that sword free. Many have tried, and failed. Now the kings grow anxious and may disregard my law. It is time for you"—he tugged Arthur closer—"to pull the sword from that stone. *You* are the true heir. You are the son of Aurelius. And you will be named High King of Prydain, and silence the scheming kings of this land."

Merlin's words shook Arthur to his core. There it was. The reason. This was why Merlin had dragged him here. This was why all the haste. The kings would need to bear witness.

His mind wrestled to put all the pieces together.

Not Uther's, but Aurelius's son? How? Not possible. Merlin has not prepared me for this… Not to be king!

Arthur's eyes welled, and anger flared in his chest.

How can I be king?

Arthur's world spun. The crowded street around him blurred as his emotions tumbled.

Merlin reached for Arthur as though pulling him back from the edge of a cliff. He glimpsed the compassion in Merlin's gaze, but at that moment, it meant little. Arthur wanted to speak, yell, curse, but his boiling emotions clamped his throat, and his voice floundered.

WHY DIDN'T YOU TELL ME? He wanted to scream at Merlin.

Though hadn't he truly always known? Merlin had been so careful to keep him hidden. Merlin purposefully raised him at the feet of kings and chieftains. Arthur had always wondered why he was given such a prominent place as a child who belonged to no one. Merlin had told him he was important, but never why. Arthur had excelled as a young leader and warrior. He thought maybe this was what Merlin had meant. But now…now it all made sense.

He imagined himself wrapping his hand around the hilt of the sword in the stone. What guarantee was there that the blade would come free? Did he even want it to? What had Merlin done to him, keeping this from him all his life?

He fell to one knee and sank his head into his chest. The weight felt like a mountain crushing him, stealing his breath. Then a curious pair of feet came into view. Arthur looked up; the sun glinted behind the stranger's silhouetted countenance.

Then, slowly, his familiar face dispersed the mist surrounding Arthur's lost and reeling spirit.

Bedwyr. His best, and most trusted, friend.

Bedwyr offered his hand, a tether of escape from Arthur's spiraling thoughts. Bedwyr's brazen boldness rekindled Arthur's own strength.

Arthur steadied his heart and breathed out his turmoil into the echoes of the past. He clasped Bedwyr's hand, and then he rose.

PART ONE

THE GREAT DIVIDE

*Two seasons after the return of Arthur,
Merlin & Elanor from the Future time.*

Arthur stood on the steps of the Great Hall, gripping the hilt of Caledfwlch. The sticky leather fit perfectly against the ridges of his fingers. There had been a bustle of people rushing in and out of the citadel in the few short seasons since his return. Many chieftains and Cymry had traveled to see if their *high king* had truly come back from the dead, and now he watched another group of Cymry sojourners arriving through the main gate. Both joy and fear mingled in the atmosphere, and Arthur felt the burden of it in his bones.

He glanced at the woman standing near him on the stone steps. Her raven-haired child slid down from her hip, likely bored of watching the parade of people below. Elanor kissed the top of Gwendolen's head before her daughter leapt away. Elanor's lips formed a beautiful smile, and yet a sullen shadow dampened the sparkle of her blue eyes.

Samara, Elanor's handmaid, whisked little Gwendolen away, and Arthur watched until they disappeared into the hall. Turning back, Elanor's eyes met his for the briefest moment. Her smile faded, and her empty gaze turned away—back to the field.

Her dark hair and verdant dress fluttered in the wind. She stood silent without acknowledgement. Arthur could still feel her grief. It hung from her like chains. Guilt raked his gut over what happened in the Hill of Kings—the exchange of his life for her father's. It wasn't like he had any choice in the matter, but Elanor blamed him. He knew she did. They had hardly spoken since their return, nor had her eyes even glanced at his. This was a responsibility he had never known before.

Daughter.

He wanted to ease her pain and be a shelter from the oncoming storms, but she wouldn't let him. It gnawed at his heartstrings like a rat chewing through rope.

Why does she reject me? What did I do wrong?

Waves of resentment and anger swelled within him. He had only meant to protect her, but she begrudged his every move. And yet, if she only smiled, or looked his way, she would see what was in his heart. It would ease the rising tides between them. But she never did.

He clenched his jaw. "Why does she stand away from us? Always so forlorn."

Merlin shook his head. "Give her some time. She still mourns the death of her father. And you"—he turned toward the field—"seem determined to hold her like a honeybee under a glass."

Merlin's words grated on Arthur like coarse sand between his teeth. "She needs to learn," Arthur said. "She does not understand. She thinks she can go foraging outside the gate with your apprentice, then takes off with your child to the orchard without a guard—"

Merlin lifted his hand, halting him. "I understand why you keep her guarded, and forbid her the freedom to go where she wills. Though, you could extend some measure of grace. Keep in mind—she is different from others, and is stronger than you think she is. She bears a burden unlike the rest of us, and aims to distract herself.

"You know she dreams of the enemy, night after night. A battle rages between her and an invisible devil." Merlin pointed down to the warriors' fields. "We are all preparing for that battle, and tensions have never been higher since Osian left the heads of those twelve Cymbrogi on pikes."

Arthur sighed and watched Elanor a moment more before turning away. War was stirring, and he had arrived at few answers. He did not have time to consider whatever it was Elanor needed from him. "I have summoned the lesser kings, but I must know more before they arrive." He paused, collecting his thoughts. "You told me of the prophecy. The one of the two stars."

"Mmm." Merlin nodded, looking over at Elanor.

"The one who revealed the prophecy still lives?" Arthur asked, following Merlin's gaze.

Arthur knew Elanor was part of the prophecy, but he hoped to shield her from its unfolding events. Maybe her usefulness had passed when they brought him back from his cursed sleep. Maybe that was all the role she was meant to play. She could stay safely hidden behind the walls of Caer Lial. She was too naive of wars and what was required of Cymry in these times.

"He is called Marcus," Merlin said. "He lives not far on the eastern borders of the forests of Celyddon."

"Thul's lands." Arthur considered for a moment, then asked, "Could he have further prophecy? More words that could help us discover our enemy? The Great God is *not* silent. There *must* be more we could know."

"If Marcus knew something more about our enemy, he would have told us.

And…you are right. The Great God is not silent. He has revealed the many faces of our enemy through Elanor's dreams."

"That is not good enough! Knowing his face does *nothing* to stop him from killing my people. They are afraid, Merlin." He thrust his hand in the direction of the Southlands. "I cannot sit idly by and wait. I *will not!* This dark sorcerer," Arthur grumbled, "is *not* a god."

"No. In that you are right. He hides. That is his *one* power."

"We need to seek Osian out."

"Arthur, do you think we have sat here indolent? We have searched these lands." Then Merlin murmured with a rueful tone, "*I have searched…and found nothing.*"

Arthur's jaw rippled. "My gut tells me there is more we could discover. More this Marcus could tell us."

Merlin's shoulders sank. "It would be less than a day's ride to reach him."

Arthur rubbed his chin, drawing his thumb and finger together. Then he snapped his head up. "This we will do. You and I. Tomorrow." Arthur was firm on his decision as he spun on his heel and headed back into the Great Hall.

Merlin stood in Arthur's tense wake, wondering if there could possibly be any fruit in journeying to see Marcus. If it would appease Arthur, enabling him to feel like they were doing something useful, then he would go. He did relish the chance to see Marcus again. The thought of it lifted his spirit.

He glanced over at Elanor. Gwynevere had joined her, and Elanor's head now rested firmly on her shoulder, their hands clasped tight together. He breathed easily at the sight of them. If only Arthur could be patient, Elanor would come around. He would be known to her like Gwynevere had become. It was only right that Elanor be given grace to grieve. In truth, Merlin also felt the residual heaviness of the constant throes of darkness and death.

Still, the creaking rafters of the dead hanging in the stable of Haldin's village haunted him—staining his peace. He cringed in recollection. Even now, the starved animals and the dimly lit barn with the stench of the rotting innocent turned his stomach. Then there were those insidious scratch marks—a disorganized array of seven intersecting lines—that had become the sign of Osian's sorcery.

Merlin ground his teeth together, shutting his eyes against the memory. He had burnt the stable down, refusing to leave the villagers as lingering ghosts of Osian's evil.

And then the twelve heads, blindsiding them in the moment of their celebration. Merlin had expected it, especially after he had seen the eerie appearance of the falcon on the day of their return to the citadel. Elanor's dream confirmed what he already knew. Osian was now uncomfortably close.

The falcon in her dream had three faces: one of a falcon, one of Osian, and one of a woman. This third face unsettled Merlin more than the other two. He had not mentioned it to the others, as he wanted to be sure, but now Osian's specific aims made even more sense.

But how?

Merlin sighed and shook his head. Having no answers, he approached Elanor and Gwynevere. He slid his hand over Elanor's shoulder and glanced at her face. One crystal tear clung to the edge of her cheek.

Elanor quickly wiped it away. She always did that. She didn't like him seeing what she viewed as weakness. He wished she wasn't so worried about that. All he ever saw was her strength.

"Merlin," she said, lifting her sullen gaze.

"Are you alright?"

Her eyes were distant, as if staring far beyond the citadel. "I…I just can't stop myself from missing him."

"I know." He squeezed her shoulder. "And you will never stop missing him. Nor would you ever want to." He stopped short. Who was he to help or give explanation to grief? He walked through loss like a madman, only sobering because he was forced to. Elanor had more strength in grief than he did.

Gwynevere nodded with a mournful look of understanding and said, "The loss of Arthur nearly destroyed me."

Merlin dropped his head, knowing the heaviness of that sorrow. The trauma still lingered. It still did not feel real that he was alive.

"By some miracle Arthur is back in my arms," Gwynevere continued, "and that piece in me that died is slowly coming back to life. But the loss of my father…my brothers, is still a pain I have never found enough joy to resolve. As time goes by, my thoughts and memories of them become sweeter, losing their sting. I think often of my father's laughter, and my brothers"—Gwynevere gently smiled—"they were beautiful. The younger one, Dair, was so burly. His mouth always got him pounded by my older brother, Taeg. Taeg being the righteous, more serious one."

Gwynevere paused for a moment before her countenance brightened.

"I remember one particular day, Dair insulted Taeg. He was doubled over in laughter, proud of his clever slight—clueless to the wrath he had unleashed. He never saw Taeg coming. He barreled into him like a giant auroch, and pummeled him to the ground. The pair of them wrestled, trying to tear each other apart, when finally, Dair gasped through his bloodied lips, 'Taeg, stop tryin' ta kiss me. I ain't yer woman.'" Gwynevere chuckled. "Taeg popped up and punched Dair in the face, then they both fell to the ground in a fit of laughter."

A sad but peaceful luster entered Gwynevere's eyes. "I will never stop missing them. But I have learned to love remembering them."

Elanor gave a consoled grin. Gwynevere leaned over to kiss her forehead and squeezed her closer.

"I think Arthur feels left out of conversations like this," Merlin muttered. "He was just grumbling about it a moment ago." He smiled, lightly elbowing Elanor.

"Where is Arthur?" Gwynevere asked, glancing behind her.

"He is off making plans, determined to do something. You know how he is. He hopes to solve the riddle of Osian, and so we ride out tomorrow morning for answers."

"Tomorrow?" Elanor asked with a curious lift in her brow. "Aren't the kings on their way to Caer Lial?"

"We are not going far, and will not be gone long. Arthur thinks there is something more he can learn from Marcus. We only need to go the short way to Celyddon."

Elanor's eyes brightened. "Marcus? Oh, how I would love to see Marcus. Do you think I could come along? I have been aching to ride—get my mind off things."

Merlin stepped back and eyed her with apprehension. He knew what Arthur would say, and he also did not want her outside the walls. The last time, he had no power to protect her. The last time...

The memory of the arrow stole his breath.

"Why should I not come? I would be safe with you," Elanor said, as though guessing at his thoughts.

"It is not that I do not think you should come, it is only..." His words trailed off.

"Only what?"

Elanor's eyes narrowed, then flared with realization.

"Oh, I see. You do not think Arthur would allow me to come," she growled. "He stops me at every turn. Even Bedwyr and Peredur seem to not recognize me in his presence. And you—" Elanor pursed her lips and caught her tongue.

Merlin stood back and Gwynevere glanced away.

"This used to be my home," Elanor whispered.

Arthur was king. Something Merlin had struggled to get Elanor to understand. He now regretted telling Elanor so hastily about Marcus.

A rebellious spark rose in her countenance the longer she stood pondering. Her brows pressed together, her breathing sharpened, and her cheeks flushed.

Merlin knew that look.

"Elanor?" he warned.

Without a word, she spun toward the Great Hall. Merlin grimaced, baffled by her striking resemblance to Arthur as she stormed toward the entrance.

He shook his head to Gwynevere. "This is not going to end well if we let her go."

"Two horses are about to buck," Gwynevere agreed. She sprinted after Elanor, and Merlin followed directly behind.

Why am I so upset? Elanor honestly didn't know. Her frustration spurred her on anyway. With rising angst, she passed over the stone floor of the Great Hall, past the tables of Cymbrogi refreshing themselves with food and drink, and then continued by the orange glow of the hearth.

Seeing Arthur at the back of the hall sobered her anger. She stopped, studying the authority of his brow—his stature as king. Suddenly, she realized her own impertinence. Was he her father, or was he king? Could he be both?

What am I doing?

She sucked her lips in tight and pressed her hand to her forehead.

With a timid eye, Elanor watched Arthur converse with some footmen. He dismissed them and turned toward the doors leading into the courtyard.

She sighed, hearing the footsteps of Gwynevere and Merlin behind her. "*What?*" She twisted around, giving them an aggravated look.

Merlin scowled at her. "I know what is in your mind. You cannot—"

"There they are!" Cilaen called, trotting over with a happy smile plastered on his face.

Cilaen's sudden appearance was a breath of fresh air. His optimistic demeanor was often a hopeful light to Elanor against the pervasive darkness. He had been Merlin's apprentice for years, but now he was the Palisade's healer. His exuberance cut through Elanor's tense mood. Samara quickly followed, pulling Gwendolen along.

Cilaen wrapped his arm around Elanor and gave her a squeeze. Still irritated, she flashed him a smirking grin.

"What is that?" Cilaen said, grimacing. "Seems we are upset about something?" He raised an eyebrow and turned to Merlin.

"Yes, well," Merlin began, "it appears I touched a nerve with Elanor about—"

Elanor cut him off. "The king and Merlin are—" She didn't want to whine, so she swiftly changed her tone and the subject. "It does not matter."

She scooped up Gwendolen in her arms. "Were you playing with the hounds again?" she asked, noticing dirt smudged on her cheeks and clothes.

"Yes," Samara confirmed with a sigh. "I turned my head for one moment, and now she has mud all over her."

"Muma, Mara is gon'a make me take anover baf."

Merlin chuckled, tapping her nose. "Well, my little one, it appears your need to wrestle with the hounds after they have been in the field demands more bathing."

Elanor nuzzled her nose into Gwendolen's round cheek, enjoying the smell of apple jam and fresh dirt. Her scent was like a soothing balm.

"Come now," Samara said, holding her hands out to Gwendolen.

"Gwen," Elanor cooed into her daughter's ear. "Go with Samara. We will see you after you are bathed."

"Muma, I don' wanna baf," Gwendolen whined as Samara pulled her away.

"If I am quick, then I can help you build a mountain of suds before supper."

Gwendolen grinned with her sweet little teeth hanging over her bottom lip. Samara chirped in Gwendolen's ear while tickling her ribs and they walked away. In a fit of giggles, Gwendolen waved her hand at them, then called to Cilaen, "Bye, Laen."

"See you, little one," he said, winking. Then Cilaen turned his attention back to Elanor and Merlin. "I have to admit, I am half guilty for getting her in with the hounds. She gets so excited when they play, and I could not resist encouraging the game." He smiled but furrowed his brow. "Anyway, Arthur put a stop to the play on his way through."

Elanor's eyes widened. Her insides growled.

Why did Arthur need to be involved with her play? How was it a hindrance to him if she was wrestling with the hounds?

Cilaen touched her shoulder, drawing her attention back to him. "What is all the trouble? You stormed in here like you were ready to tear the walls down."

Elanor considered whether she shouldn't follow after Gwendolen right then—save herself from her own temper. Exhaling sharply, she said, "It was nothing. Just an overreaction. I just would have liked to see Marcus, that is all."

Cilaen peered at her, confused. "And why should you not see Marcus?"

Elanor caught Merlin shaking his head, clearly warning Cilaen from pressing the issue, but it was too late. Elanor already felt the heat rising back into her cheeks. She huffed and went on, "Merlin and Arthur are riding to Celyddon tomorrow to see Marcus. Arthur—he would not want me to come. He has already made it *very* clear he would rather I was bound to a post."

Merlin shook his head. "Elanor, you do not under—"

"Yes, I do!" she snapped. "I see in his eyes how much of a burden I am to him."

The more she said about Arthur, the more she noticed Merlin and Gwynevere tense up. This only fueled her fire. Their fealty to Arthur overshadowed her pain. Or so she felt.

Merlin's stare grew stern. "Elanor, you misunderstand."

"Maybe," she said, working to control herself. "Or, maybe, my eyes see what yours cannot."

Something changed that day she, Arthur, and Merlin returned to the caer. Arthur was suddenly *the king*. When she looked in his eyes, her magic revealed he was conflicted and afraid of her.

She knew he was *supposed* to be her father, but was that something he even wanted? Her insecurities triggered every time he peered at her, infuriating her. She started recognizing that familiar feeling. The way she felt with the Evanses, as though she didn't belong. Worst of all, Merlin was always defending him. She sometimes felt invisible to him now too. All of them. Gwynevere, and even Bedwyr's love for Arthur, made her resent him all the more.

She hadn't expected to feel this way. Prydain, and more specifically the Palisade, had always been more of a home than any other place in the world. Here, she was free. Accepted. Almost like a missing piece—she fit so well.

But now, *he* was here. Always so stone-faced, disrupting all she had known Prydain to be, and it intimidated her.

Did she really need to see Marcus that badly? Was it really worth pushing where she hadn't been invited? And yet, there it was. The real crux of her anger. She felt excluded from a place she had always belonged. Now she felt more like a stranger that needed permission for *everything*.

"I am sorry," she pleaded to Merlin. "I am not sure what has gotten into me." She ran her fingers through her hair and took a deep, calming breath.

Merlin pulled her to his side. "Let us go see my mother and Gwen. Our daughter is waiting for us. It is after midday. After Gwen's bath, Samara will have food brought up from the kitchen."

Cilaen bowed and turned to leave, but Merlin called after him, "Come now, my friend." Cilaen halted. "Do not tell me you are too busy with your medicines to join us. You know my mother would love to see you."

"Surely not," he returned with a smile. "I will never refuse seeing Adhan. I have not seen her come down in a few days—though, I have been rather busy and likely missed her. I owe her a visit." Cilaen winked. "After all, I am practically her second son."

Elanor offered him her hand. At least she still had Cilaen. She considered him part of their family, and he still looked out for her like the brother he had promised to be all those years ago. And he—unlike the rest of them—didn't have the same tie to Arthur, making him more understanding without her having to say anything.

Cilaen hooked his arm around hers and patted her hand. "Arthur will see you— he will come around. I promise."

She smiled up at Cilaen, feeling the warmth he offered. He gently tugged her arm, then led her forward with Merlin and Gwynevere beside them. They meandered through the courtyard, heading back toward the Palisade. Elanor was still bothered, but she forced herself to swallow the swells of pride that kept bubbling up into her chest.

This isn't a mountain to die on, she told herself. *Pick your battles more wisely.*

They opened the doors to the Palisade and there was Arthur. He stood upon the circle of tiles, speaking to Bedwyr and Peredur. Arthur paused as they walked across the echoing hall toward the staircase.

Elanor couldn't help but catch his eye. There was no acknowledgement in his gaze. He cleared his throat, then continued speaking to his men.

This dismissal snapped something inside Elanor. Something about his disregard, even as they passed, irked her beyond reason. He could have smiled, nodded— anything. But instead, he gave an empty glance.

Without thinking, she let go of Cilaen's arm and spun around. She felt Gwynevere's fingers grasp at her arm, but Elanor slid right through them. The blur of sudden anger blinded her, and she stormed across the vast hall toward Arthur.

What am I going to say? What am I even doing?

She didn't know, but she was already rolling like an unstoppable peel of thunder.

A KING FOR ELANOR

Elanor saw red. She blazed toward Arthur, heat surging up her spine. Why did he have the power to make her feel so angry? Words of resentment burned like embers on her tongue, vying to have their say.

Arthur turned, and his eyes widened when he noticed her storming toward him. He stepped back and held up his hand, pausing his conversation with Bedwyr and Peredur.

Elanor's heart leapt, and she stopped her mad dash. Again, the stern look on his face reminded her that she had no ground to stand on. Chills of embarrassment prickled her skin.

She had created a scene. All eyes were on her. She immediately regretted making this spectacle and turned to walk away.

"*Elanor.*"

She froze, wincing at the firmness in Arthur's voice. She didn't want to turn around. Instead, she looked pleadingly over at Merlin's stunned face, which only made her feel worse. She wished she could disappear, or better yet, rewind the moment she decided it was a good idea to truculently charge *the king*.

"Elanor?" Arthur called more gently this time.

Her stomach twisted hearing his approaching footsteps. He grasped her shoulder, and she jerked away. With a surge of defiance, she whipped around to face him. Hot tears blurred her eyes, threatening to spill over.

Do not cry.

She hated appearing weak.

I will not cry! Not this time.

She swallowed hard, averting her eyes to the floor. As long as she didn't look at him, she could hold it all together. She bit her lip to hold back the storm.

Befuddled, and appearing aggravated, Arthur said, "You are upset. Why? What has happened?"

His tone stoked her anger a little more, but she still preferred to retreat. She tried to soften her face, and again, glanced over at Merlin, then to Bedwyr and Peredur, who both wore baffled expressions.

Speak! she told herself, having lost her tongue. She felt suddenly very alone. Her heartbeat was hot in her ears. All the ones that had been with her were now disappearing under the length of Arthur's shadow. She wouldn't stand a chance if she confronted him. Not this time, anyway.

"Have *I* done something to upset you?" He waited a moment, then sighed, clearly exasperated. "Elanor, I am addressing my battle chieftains. I do not have time for this."

His dismissal snapped her right back into the boiling anger, only now, it broke free. "Yes," she hissed, lifting her face to meet his. "You *have*."

"Elanor. *Stop*," Merlin warned.

She dared not look at him this time.

"What have *I* done?" Arthur growled. His face contorted, briefly, then softened, and he addressed her more tenderly. "I would aim to mend whatever it is, and create peace between us."

Elanor sighed, collecting herself. "I...I was told you are leaving to Celyddon, and...I was made aware that you would not allow me to accompany you."

There was no hesitation in Arthur's reply. "This is true. I will *not* allow it. You will stay here in the caer."

"Could you not hear me out?"

"I will not. I am firmly decided."

"But—"

"I will *not* hear another word." Arthur turned away.

"Please...Arthur." Elanor struggled to keep her tone from rising. "Marcus...h-he is my...I would like to..." She glanced back at Merlin, hoping he might intercede for her. He evaded her gaze, and she swallowed down the bitter lump.

"*Enough*, Elanor!" Arthur scolded, his voice firm and rigid.

His brazen command sent fire through her veins. She stepped closer, and with a defying glare, she snapped, "How *dare* you." Her anger reached full bloom, sending tremors through her body. "How *dare you* dismiss me as though I were only a child!"

Arthur leaned in to meet her challenge and pointed at her face. "You are fortunate that only our friends stand here to witness this. *I* am king, and *you will* obey me."

"Oh?" she puffed, disregarding his prideful strike. She flicked her fingers at him and said, "Thank you for making it *abundantly* clear where we stand."

Gwynevere gasped at her words. Arthur's neck reddened, and his teeth clenched.

Elanor didn't care. Maybe she would regret this later, but she couldn't hold back the fury ignited on her tongue. "In case I was *ever* confused as to who I am to you, I now *clearly* understand."

Arthur's eyes narrowed. "What do you mean? What are you accusing me of?"

"To you, I am just an inconvenience. A *burden*. I get it. I am a peon in your way.

Chapter Two

Well, *you* may want to know—" She stepped even closer, her chin lifted high. "You are *not* my king."

"Elanor, that is enough," Merlin said, clipping toward her.

"I do not *need* a king. And I am not *your* subject. I do not come from your world of rules, and I am *not* a child."

Merlin grabbed hold of her arm, but she ripped it free. "At least now I can rid myself of any ridiculous expectation of being your daughter."

"Ridiculous?" Arthur snarled.

"I understand *now* how you see me."

"This is nonsense. You will s*top* this ranting. You have no idea—"

"No idea? You think you can order me to stop, as if I belong underneath your foot?"

Arthur's eyes widened. His shoulders broadened and his chest lifted, as if ready to assert his authority.

"What are you going to do?" She searched his face, and her fierce fire gave way to her first tear. "Y-you going to punish me for my insolence? Lock me in a cell? Execute me? To think"—she sucked in her breath, fighting back the tears—"I gave up a *true* father to rescue…*you*! You…You mean *nothing* to me."

Something inside her was beginning to break; she could feel it. The lump in her throat grew bigger the more she rebuked. She clenched her hands into fists in a final effort to stay strong.

Arthur stood trembling with his mouth agape. Silence hovered in the hall like a heavy fog, the atmosphere thick with tension. Finally, he sighed and shook his head, then lowered it to his chest.

His eyes wavered when he peered at her once more. She had wounded him. She could see it in his eyes. A chord she didn't know existed was struck, and her heart ached with regret.

Arthur hissed through his teeth, "What is it that you want from me?"

"I—" Her chin trembled as tears streamed from her eyes. "I do not know." Her anger now spent, she felt ashamed. She knew there was nothing more she could say, and the edginess surrounding her was already more than she could stand. Mortified, she dashed for the doors, wishing she could find a place somewhere—anywhere she wouldn't have to see the gawking faces that had just bore witness to her brazen display.

But she still felt so angry. So rejected.

"How could he?" She sobbed, racing up the stairs. When she reached the top, she came face-to-face with Merlin.

"Why…why wouldn't you defend me?" She paused, caught between a sob, then said, "You are all like *dogs* at his feet."

Merlin was not daunted. "I will not take that from you, Elanor. You cannot blame me, nor any of us for being disarmed. None of us could have known just how stubborn and bullheaded the two of you would become toward one another. You are both one and the same, blaming each other for your own insecurities."

"What?" Elanor huffed, stunned. "I am not insec—I am *nothing* like him."

"What possessed you, Elanor? He *is* king."

"He is *not* my king."

"That, you made very clear. However, that is not a choice you get to make. Not here. Not in these lands. You…" Merlin tightened his lips, and Elanor braced for the incoming rebuke. "Listen, if you attack him in front of his men, he may have to act against you. You will force his hand."

Merlin's words felt like a harsh slap across her face. Elanor's lip quivered. "But why…why could he have not just heard me out? Or treated me like I was worthy of his time. Why does he have to treat me like I am nothing? Do you need his permission to leave? I—" She covered her face. "I—"

Merlin sighed, sweeping his hand over his face, wiping free his frustrated expression. "I know he did not say it, but…he only wants to keep you safe. Not because you are an inconvenience, nor because you are a woman. Osian is closer than he has *ever* been. You know this. It is dangerous outside these walls. Arthur only aims to protect you." He lifted his hand and cradled her chin. "Even I would not have let you come." He paused. "You should give Arthur a chance."

Elanor jerked her chin away. "Me? Give him a chance? What about him giving me a chance?" She glared at Merlin. "Why do you always defend him? Why could you not have helped me? Spoken to him? Done *something*. You left me there *all* alone."

Merlin shook his head. "You were the one who chose to put yourself in a position where I could not help you. What was I to do, Elanor? I would have defended neither one of you in that moment. I was not abandoning you in support of him. Though, understand—and let me be very clear—while I know these recent days have been hard for you…Arthur *is* king, and I *will* honor him. And do not pretend," Merlin stated tensely, "that you do not understand that kind of honor. I have seen you give it to others. Even to your servant. Your real struggle…"

Elanor wanted to jam her fingers into her ears. She didn't want to hear it.

"…is that he is your…"

"*Enough*, Merlin!"

Merlin grimaced. He took a step back and folded his arms.

Elanor tsked. Dejected, she gripped her arms tightly and lowered her eyes to the floor. Merlin reached out to comfort her, but Elanor held up her hands to stop him. "I just need to be alone for a little while." She brushed past him, walking away.

"Elanor, please. Come with me. Come see Gwendolen. You promised her you would come."

She paused for a moment, then continued walking. She knew if she turned around, she would concede and go with him. She would have been comforted. But the words she had spoken to Arthur…*You mean nothing to me*…and then the sad look in his eyes played over and over in her mind. Regret was a hammer shattering the walls around her chest. She was still so angry—she wanted to hurt him. She wanted him to feel pain because he had made her feel small. Insignificant. Orphaned. And yet, she knew what truly upset her was that she had wounded him. In that one second, she saw in his eyes what she had desired from the start, and then she destroyed it.

JOURNEY TO MARCUS

Merlin and Arthur galloped toward the forests of Celyddon in the cool of the morning. Mist hung in the air, dulling the sunlight creeping above the horizon.

Arthur brooded in silence, fuming over yesterday's event, when Elanor had challenged his authority in front of their closest friends. He had to dole out a punishment—something to teach Elanor her place in his court. He couldn't let her get away with such defiance. But deep down, he wondered if she was right. That alone enraged him, and worse, shook his confidence.

He knew she resented him, but he never saw her outburst coming. He had mulled it over and over, and still felt justified in his decision. She would never leave the walls of Caer Lial as long as Osian waged his war of horrors. She, barely capable of wielding a sword, had no instinct. Whether she liked it or not, he would lock her in a cage if it meant her not falling prey to the enemy.

She can hate me for all I care. He pursed his lips. *I have only ever shown her kindness, and this is what I get for it. Cast aside. Berated. She has not even begun to see my authority. She may not think of me as her father…*he winced, then shook his head…*but I will not allow her stubbornness to put her in danger.*

He lifted a meager eye over his shoulder at Merlin, who rode just a little behind him. Arthur didn't know what Merlin's opinion was on the matter, and didn't care to know. Gwynevere had already given him an earful before he left, vindicating Elanor. Their earlier conversation filtered through Arthur's mind as he rode.

"I know Elanor should have never addressed you like she did, but you could have given her the grace to at least speak," Gwynevere said, rising from her bedside. The disappointment in her eyes was a scathing blow to his heart. "You could have reasoned with her more gently, instead of dismissing her outright. She caused a scene, but you were the one who willfully pushed her over the edge."

Bah!

Arthur tried to push the conversation from his mind. He didn't want to hear any of it. And the last thing he wanted was for Merlin to do the same, becoming an irritating mosquito buzzing in his ear. But he couldn't get away from Gwynevere's words. The conversation echoed inside his head—words that had irked him to his core:

"No…no…I am king. I have merit. Elanor needs no explanation from me. She just needs to obey," Arthur growled, struggling to resist the pleading in Gwynevere's eyes.

Through tightened lips, she said, "You have never ordered me into obedience."

"You clearly did what you wanted anyway," Arthur replied, strapping his sword to his hip. He didn't need this. Gwynevere's insistence made him eager to leave on his errand. "I told you to stay behind when the Saecsans raided Celyddon's shores—you did not listen. You wrapped yourself in leather, and painted yourself blue." Arthur stopped, enjoying the memory of his wife battle ready. He shot her an admiring smile, now wanting to pull her into his arms. "You were a fierce warrior. I gave up trying to keep you safe."

"Why then must you be so rigid with Elanor?"

"She is not like you," Arthur said, holding his wife's stubborn gaze. "She did not grow up wielding a sword, defending these lands. She is soft—inexperienced. The future time she came from is *fatuous*, and *indulgent*. The people there do not even *live*. But you…you knew what it was to be pounded by the enemy. Your foes would have never taken you down without you first leaving your mark."

"I think you assume too little of her," Gwynevere said, handing him his cloak. "You haven't bothered to understand what she is capable of."

"Oh, I saw." Arthur folded his arms across his chest. "On our journey back from the future time, I saw how hasty and emotional she could be under pressure. The arguments between her and Merlin. She proved that again yesterday, when she disgraced herself in front of everyone. She will *not* go to Celyddon."

Gwynevere's voice turned stern. "That is not fair. Elanor had just lost her father. And you know that the whole scene yesterday was not about whether or not she should have been allowed to go with you to Celyddon. You treat her like—"

"She must understand her place."

"Then she was right when she said what she did." Gwynevere's gaze hardened. "If you have chosen to place your thumb upon her and press her down, then you'll not have her as a daughter."

Arthur grimaced as the memory faded. It seemed to him that Elanor didn't want to be his daughter anyway. It was already such a strange thing—being a father to a grown woman who hadn't even been born yet, and was barely ten years younger than him. It defied all reason. Yet his heart could feel something real, and undeniable. He saw it in the familiarity of her eyes; they were tied by blood.

"Neither one of you is willing to understand the other," Merlin interjected, snapping Arthur out of his dark ponderings. It was disconcerting how easily the druid could read him. "You know, I have been watching you talk to yourself all morning. Your irritation has been tangible from the moment we set off."

Arthur grunted and stared gloomily ahead.

Merlin pulled his horse alongside Arthur's. "Whether you want to talk about it or not, you are only keeping the hound at bay."

Arthur could feel Merlin's eyes on him, waiting for his response. Arthur jutted out his lip and ignored him.

"You think I will defend her, but I will not," Merlin confessed. "She was not wise to confront you. The pressure and grief has made her intolerant."

Arthur's brows lifted in surprise, and he turned in his saddle toward Merlin.

"Oh, but I will not defend you either."

Arthur scowled and slumped forward.

Here it comes. The lecture.

"You see, she has this stubborn streak that very closely resembles that of her father's. One of you will have to humble yourself if you want to cross over the wall between you."

Arthur grumbled, "And I suppose you think that should be me?"

"Well, that all depends on what you want. If you would like to keep things strained, you do not have to do anything."

"I am king, and I—"

"Ah, yes, well, that is the trouble, is it not? You are king and Elanor *does not* care."

"She has to—"

"She could be forced...Or, maybe, she could be shown."

"Aaa!" Arthur shouted, swiping his hand in frustration. "Quit cutting me off with your superior words."

"The man with wisdom is not usually the one lost in the midst of the trees, but the one who can see the whole forest." Merlin raised one brow and provoked Arthur with a smile. "Arthur, I know more than most men, but even *I* lack wisdom when I am overwhelmed by the chaos of what is before me. I have been the purveyor of unwise and prideful choices derived by my emotions. You know this. You are not exempt from this, my brother, and you know it."

Arthur flinched, shutting his eyes as Merlin's words triggered a sudden stinging memory. His search for The Holy Cup. Overwhelming regret pierced his gut at the bitter reminder of the loss of time and near destruction of his kingdom. All for his stubborn persistence to seek something that apparently could never be found. It was not worth the price he paid with the lives of his men, nor the near murder of Gwynevere and Merlin. And he had been warned...warned by Merlin to stop. To let it go. To humbly surrender the search, but he had chosen not to. His pride had not allowed it.

Would he feel this same regret in regards to Elanor?

"Gah! Enough!"

Merlin lifted his hands. "I have said all I needed to say."

"Good," Arthur snapped, kicking the sides of his horse. He picked up speed, and left Merlin to trail behind.

The sun hung in the middle of the sky when the trees that gated the small village came into view. Most villages within the lands of Celyddon lay intentionally hidden amidst its dense forests. It was the way of Celyddon to protect their people, by nimbly hiding its warriors amongst the woods' boughs and branches, hindering any stranger from waltzing in uninvited. Their archers, the best in all of Prydain, were ready to rain terror on any who dared enter.

Merlin stopped his horse and whistled so the archers did not regard them as foes. Both he and Arthur knew the sacred call for entering unharmed into the green folds. Merlin paused, then whistled again, this time coupled with a cawing sound that lilted from low to high.

They waited in silence for a sign. Their horses gently stamped the ground. Merlin lifted his hand to his mouth to call again when, finally, several warriors clothed in green emerged through the thick tree line.

One by one they filtered out, perfectly camouflaged until they stepped free of the foliage. One archer stepped ahead of the other twenty and put his hand to his mouth, hailing them with a whistle. Merlin smiled at Arthur, enjoying their welcome call. They kicked their horses and galloped to meet them.

When the archers recognized it was Merlin and Arthur who approached, they each quickly dropped to one knee.

The leader of the archers said, "I…I cannot believe it…" His eyes misted, glancing up at them, then he contritely shot his gaze back toward the ground. "H-hail, Great Pendragon, and Emrys Wyllt. We had heard that you had returned to us, but to see you, High King…it is hope itself."

Arthur dismounted and approached the lead archer whose golden hair was twisted into a braid and streaked with the wild white clay of the Cymry. Arthur placed his hand upon the archer's shoulder, then addressed them all. "I have surely returned, and have come to declare strength back to my people. Archers!" he called to them. "Cymbrogi of Prydain! Rise!"

The archers stood, and Arthur smiled, staring each one in the eye as their heads lifted. A well of pride gleamed in Arthur's eyes when he gripped the leader's shoulder. "Your name?"

The archer lifted his chest. "Alun, my king! I am captain of this guard."

"Have you encountered the dark sorcerer's men in your woods?"

"No, my king. King Thul has positioned us on all corners of Celyddon, and we have seen nothing of the dark shadow or his men. But we are ready for them. We will not hesitate. We killed many of them the last time they tried to attack Celyddon, and we are ready if they should come again."

"The time for war is near!" Arthur declared.

At his words, the archers shouted, "Ho!" They pounded their chests and lifted their bows.

"I am proud to see that you are ready." Arthur beamed. "It gives me great faith to see that the strength of Prydain's warriors did not weaken while I was away."

Swells of emotion rushed through Merlin. He would never grow tired of witnessing the hopeful countenances of the Cymbrogi seeing their king returned. A beautiful mix of restored faith and wonder. Tales had spread as to how the king had come back from the dead. Most of the stories were false; the truth, more than many could grasp. Most remained unbelieving, until the sight of him made it real. All who saw Arthur marveled at the miracle.

"We have come to see the old druid, Marcus," Merlin began. "He lives among the people of the small village just west of here."

"Y-yes!" Alun quickly replied. He pointed behind him. "We will not hinder you." The captain bowed, and his men pulled back, strapping their bows back behind them.

Merlin and Arthur climbed back onto their horses. Merlin clicked his tongue and jabbed his heels against his horse.

As they passed, Arthur turned to Alun and said, "Thank you, Alun, and Cymbrogi of Celyddon, for your protection of these great forests."

The archers bowed, and Arthur and Merlin trotted past the trees. They followed a narrow path familiar to Merlin, delving deeper into the woods as dusk darkened the sky with shades of deepening blue. With the soothing chirp of crickets serenading them forth, the first few wooden huts of the village appeared. The homes sat scattered on the forest floor, while some perched high up amongst branches and boughs.

They were simple wooden structures—nothing extraordinary—that blended into the trees. The huts on the ground circled an open meadow, with a stone fire pit in the very middle. Its flames licked the air, the sparks floating up to meet the stars.

The villagers were eating at tables situated on the grass. They paused, startled at Merlin and Arthur's approach. The villagers studied the newcomers. Their faces drifted between them with hushed voices. After a long silence, a man rose from among them. He was a tall, lumbering man with short dark hair and a full beard.

"Please be at peace!" Merlin said, knowing the villagers could not clearly see their faces through the wan light. "I am Merlin, and I have brought with me the king, Arthur Pendragon of Prydain."

The people gasped and rushed to their feet.

With sudden haste, the burly man pushed through the people toward them. "M-my king! I am the elder of this village. T-Tomos. My name is Tomos. I welcome you. What has brought the lords of Prydain to our humble village?"

"We have come to seek your druid, Marcus."

"Oh," Tomos said, nervously eyeing Arthur who remained silent. "He-he's not here, my sires. He has gone to the forest to listen to the gods, or—" He paused. "I am not entirely understanding his druidic ways…b-but I know he will be back come morning. He has a young filidh whom I could fetch for you."

Arthur climbed down from his horse, approached Tomos, who fidgeted awkwardly, clearly not knowing how to compose himself in the king's presence.

Tomos mumbled, "We welcome you, s-sire…Great Pendragon."

"Please. This is your home," Arthur reassured him. "Be at peace, Tomos. We do not wish to interrupt your people as they sup."

Merlin slid down from his horse and joined Arthur who was observing the sea of sparkling eyes, highlighted by the fire. A certain sadness lingered in Arthur's glassy eyes, and Merlin knew in that moment Arthur still harbored deep regret at having left his people.

Merlin cleared his throat, then told Tomos, "Please help your people feel at ease."

Tomos nodded and turned to the unsettled villagers, waving them down. "It is alright. You can go back to your eating." He anxiously commanded a nearby boy to take care of their horses, and then shouted to a woman to fetch them food. "B-best ale for my lords." He called another child to his side. "Go fetch Gethin. Bring 'im here. Let 'im know the lords of Prydain are here. Quick!"

The child ran off at the orders of his elder.

"Please, my sires. Follow me. There is a more private place you can refresh yourselves, and wait for Gethin."

Tomos walked them around the people, who remained quiet. Their eyes followed the footsteps of their king. A few gaped as though seeing a ghost.

"Tomos," Merlin inquired. "Is Gethin Marcus's filidh?"

"Mm. Yes, my lord. Once he comes to ya, he may even be able to fetch Marcus for you. He might know where he goes." Tomos motioned to a table just off the side of one of the larger huts. He knelt at a small circle of rocks and heaved wood from an adjacent pile into its center.

Merlin held up his hand. "Please, allow me." Then he spoke, "Danau!"

Sparks sputtered and lit the kindling.

Tomos's eyes grew large. "Oh!" He jumped back, wiping his shaky hands on his shirt. "By the gods! Heh! To have the Great Pendragon and Merlin sitting at my table. I would nev'r believed it."

Arthur smiled. "We are happy to be given the blessing of your hospitality."

Tomos nodded humbly with a grin. "The blessing is ours to be sure. I-I will go prepare beds for you while you wait for Gethin. Y-you'll be needing a place to rest, I assume."

Arthur nodded. "Yes. Thank you."

Tomos bowed. As he walked away, he mumbled excitedly, "King Arthur lives, and has come to eat at my own table."

Grinning, Merlin elbowed Arthur, and they both chuckled.

THE FILIDH

A generous helping of steamy meat stew and a wedge of bread was delivered to Arthur and Merlin. Merlin's stomach groaned after their day-long journey, and he eagerly dove in, relishing each savory bite. Arthur perked up, sitting comfortably near the fire's warmth. He even grinned while gnawing on his bread and sucking down his frothy ale.

"Tomos"--Arthur tilted his head in the direction he had gone—"he is an unlikely leader for this village. A large fellow, but timid as a rabbit."

Merlin grinned, amused. "Mm…well, he may appear less assertive because the Great Pendragon just showed up unannounced at his doorstep." He motioned toward the people buzzing around the fire. "This village is a fragile one. It was a small settlement to start, but then the refugees from Llyonesse came to settle here. Most of them women and children, with very few men, and none of them warriors. Marcus was one of the refugees, and likely the strongest leader amongst them, even though he is old."

"I am sure Celyddon does much to keep them protected. I know Thul. He does well to pay attention to the needs of his people."

Merlin nodded in agreement. As he raised his mug for another draught, he caught movement behind Arthur. He lifted his head. A gangly boy appeared out of the darkness wearing the brown robe of a filidh. He was not tall, but the light stubble on his chin and above his lip confirmed he was nearly a man.

Merlin and Arthur stood to greet him, but the boy's eyes remained pointed at the ground. "My king," the lad said, bowing, "and Lord Emrys." Slowly, he lifted his face, peering first at Merlin. His round brown eyes were youthful and innocent, and yet there was something baleful hidden behind them.

A rush of uncertainty chilled Merlin's spine. A sudden thought, like an awen, struck Merlin's mind. He saw the black crow of warning, and the resonance of its caw echoed into his thoughts.

Merlin took a wary step back to observe him better.

"You must be Gethin," Arthur said, inviting him closer. "We are here to see your master."

Merlin narrowed his eyes at the boy. He concentrated and reached with his mind to see if he could detect anything.

"My master," Gethin mumbled, almost as if he were afraid speaking would reveal a secret, "has gone to listen to the Triple God in the forest. He said he felt a pulling to go." He shot an uneasy side-glance toward Merlin. "The evil of these days is stirring."

Merlin breathed out, sharpening the steel of his magic. The stirring in the pit of his stomach urged him to be vigilant. "Why do you not go with your master to learn and hear as he does?"

"He desires to be alone, Lord Emrys." The boy's eyes whipped back to the ground.

Merlin pressed his brows together. He wasn't sure what the deception was, but it was there. *Could the boy just be nervous?*

"When will he return?" Arthur asked, eyeing Merlin. His look confirmed to Merlin that he, too, felt the lad's behavior was strange. "Could you fetch him for us? We have come with some urgency to speak with him."

Gethin bowed, then responded, "I would do so, my king, but it is very dark, and I am unsure where he has gone."

Now that seems a lie. A filidh shadows his olham and is aware of where his master goes to meditate.

This filidh was either being dishonest or unfaithful.

Why?

"We will wait until morning when he returns." Merlin leaned his tall stature over the youth. "But our errand cannot be delayed further. I know Marcus well. He would want to know that we have come. He will not be happy you chose to wait until morning."

Gethin's timid eyes blinked up at him. "I know well you are right, Lord Emrys. H-he would not want me to delay." The youth gulped a nervous swallow, then glanced over his shoulder as if afraid someone would overhear them.

Merlin peered behind the boy into the dark void between the trees. No one was there. The boy turned back around. Panic radiated in his eyes.

"I could go with you to find him this evening," Merlin suggested to the boy. "My sight is keen."

"N-n-n-NO!" Gethin stuttered with unexpected urgency, holding up his hands and taking a step back. "I assure you; I would point you in the wrong direction. Th-the moment he returns, I will send him to you."

Merlin lifted his chest. None of this was sitting well with him.

"Boy," Arthur questioned, "what is it you are not telling us? Is there something we should know?"

Gethin fidgeted with his robe. Merlin bored his eyes into the boy.

An abrupt shout from Tomos broke the tension. "Your beds have been prepared, my sires. Would you like me to take you to your rest?"

Merlin glanced behind at Tomos, and when he turned back, Gethin was gone—disappearing into the shadows.

"Yes," Arthur responded to Tomos. "It appears we are waiting for Marcus until morning. Please show us the way."

Merlin glared into the darkness, unsure what the warning in his heart meant. But he knew he would need to pay attention and not let his guard down for even a second. Especially not within the serene comfort of this peaceful village. He could not afford to be lulled into a false sense of security.

"That boy acted strange," Arthur whispered to Merlin, following behind Tomos who stumbled through the dark ahead of them between two huts.

Merlin nodded, then quietly said, "That boy was not being entirely truthful. He could have retrieved his master, but was choosing not to."

"Why would he—"

"Here you are, sires." Tomos pushed open a door, and the yellow light of a fire beckoned them inside and out of the dark. "There are two beds, just there." He walked to one and patted it. "One on each side of the fire to keep you warm."

"This is wonderful, Tomos." Merlin reached to give him an affirming pat on the arm.

"I am here wishing I could offer more kingly hospitalities, but there is clean water over here." He lumbered over to where a large bowl sat on a table. Tomos nodded his head with an awkward smile.

The room quieted, and Arthur shifted his footing.

"Oh…shush…please excuse me." Tomos patted his chest as though he were looking for something he had lost. "I have overstayed my welcome." He headed toward the door, mumbling to himself, then said, "There is s'more kindling just outside the door to keep the fire stoked. Anyway, have a pleasant rest. I will not bother you further. You just let me know if you need anythin'." With a nod, he opened the door to leave and had just stepped over the threshold when Arthur called to him.

"Tomos!"

Tomos peeked back in.

"It is my honor to be here in your village. Thank you for the soft wool and fire. We will sleep very comfortably."

"Oh." Tomos's grin broadened and his cheek flushed bright red. "I…I thank you." Again, he gave a timid nod and slipped out, shutting the door behind him.

"Now that fellow," Arthur said, "has no guile."

Merlin chuckled, then plopped down onto the straw and wool. "Yes—at least him, I do not have to look out for."

"Now that we are alone, tell me more about that young filidh."

"There really is not much to say, except we *need* to be on our guard. I could feel warning rising in me at every glance and word he spoke. And yet…it was almost like something inside him was"—Merlin squinted at the fire—"*calling* for help."

"I could not tell if he was lying, or afraid," Arthur said. "His eyes kept searching the trees. Do we need to worry for him? Marcus?"

"I do not know. All I can tell you is that I am not waiting here until morning. I will only delay until things silence around us, and the village has gone to their beds. Then, I will go find Marcus myself."

"How will you know where to find him?"

"I do not think he has gone far. I have been here before and I think I might know where he is. It may be a little difficult to find my way in the dark, but once I am far enough away, I will light a torch. That should be enough to guide me to him." Merlin laughed. "Here I wish I had one of Elanor's electric torches from the future."

The curves of Arthur's mouth dropped at Merlin's mention of her name.

Merlin sighed and shook his head. He was not in the mood to deal with Arthur's broodiness. He lay back onto his bed and put his arms under his head. "We are already in the midst of it, Arthur. Keep one hand on the hilt of your sword throughout the night."

"I am not worried over that runt, but it may be wise to keep watch."

'I'll take the watch until I leave."

The village had gone still, and Arthur breathed heavily in his sleep. Merlin quietly sat up. The dull orange pulse from the fire's embers highlighted Arthur's features. He lay on his back, gripping Caledfwlch on his chest. Merlin stretched and stood.

"Going to go find Marcus?" Arthur mumbled.

"Glad to know you are sleeping with one eye open."

"Cannot allow myself to be murdered in the night. At least I have gotten some shuteye. Now that you are leaving, I will sit awake." Arthur rolled to sit up, hanging his legs over the edge of his bed, and leaned his elbows on his knees. "I do not truly expect any danger though. Do you?"

"No," Merlin said, reaching for the door handle. "Still, it is wise to be ready. Something is amiss. Hopefully, I am wrong."

Arthur cupped his head into his hands and sighed.

"I should not be gone long. If he is not where I think he is, then I will come back, and we will wait until morning and hope all is as it should be."

Arthur made no reply, so Merlin nodded and slipped out the door. Against the side of the hut was a pile of prepared torches. Merlin grabbed hold of one and swept his eyes across the sleeping village. Everything was still. The chilly wind blowing through the trees was the only sound.

Carefully, he crept around the back of the little homes, and then out toward the west end of the village. That was where Marcus's hut was located, and Merlin would check there first. It was hard to see, so once he left the final house behind, he blew on the torch. It sparked aflame. The warm golden light illuminated his surroundings.

He reached Marcus's hut on the outskirts and cautiously moved toward it. Gethin would likely be around somewhere. As he drew closer, he discovered a pile of leaves gathered in front of Marcus's door step. The torchlight revealed it was Gethin huddled on the ground, wrapped in his cloak.

Merlin halted. He did not want to approach any closer and risk waking the lad.

Likely Marcus had not come back. Gethin was here to catch him the minute he returned. Still, Merlin gazed at the hut to be sure. There was no smell of wood smoke, nor any light emanating through the slats. No one had been home; Merlin was fairly certain.

He looked at the boy sleeping in a heap and wondered if he shouldn't wake him and drag him along. That way he could keep a close eye on him. But he thought better of the idea and soundlessly turned toward the dense trees.

The last time he had come to this village, Marcus had taken him to a secluded place where they could be alone—away from prying eyes. It was a small opening in the forest that he had made his own, just deep enough that even an adventurous child was not likely to find it.

Merlin remembered hiking down a small ravine between two high ridges. Finding it in the dark would be difficult but manageable. Over Merlin's many years he had become an experienced navigator—though venturing in the dark would still be a challenge. But Merlin had another trick up his sleeve. He could possibly find Marcus through his awen. If Marcus were listening, he might reach back. Like a light trail, two druids could call to one another; however, both had to be reaching. Merlin was hopeful that, since Marcus had come to the forest specifically to listen, this might work if he lost his way.

He looked up to locate the moon for direction, but the boughs of the trees obscured what little he could see of the black and clouded sky. Sighing, he moved in the direction he thought was right. Maneuvering through the trees, he pressed on, questioning his own choice. If he was going to use his awen, he would wait until he reached the ravine to be within closer range.

"I should be nearing it soon," he mumbled, reaching the top of a ridge. He held his torch closer to the ground and moved slowly, knowing the ravine was near and hoping not to fall over its edge.

Finally, there it was. A black edge where the torchlight stopped illuminating the ground. He knew where to go from here, and he followed it to the right. Feeling more confident, he moved more swiftly and used the tree branches as handholds to keep away from the ledge. The rift leveled out, and he found himself solidly at the bottom. Swinging his torch above him, he saw the ravine rise high on both sides of him. Marcus would not be far on the other side of this gully.

He knew the way from here but decided to try his awen anyway—in case Marcus had wandered somewhere else close by.

Merlin dropped to his knees, closed his eyes, and reached out with his magic.

"Marcus galw allan ataf. Rwy'n chwilio amdanoch chi." He repeated the druidic words and pushed his search through the air, hoping it would carry to Marcus. Then he focused, waiting for a picture of Marcus's whereabouts to materialize in his mind. "Rwy'n chwilio amdanoch chi."

Echoes thrummed on the wind, reverberating like many voices calling at once. He tried to focus, hoping one of them was Marcus, but then…the dark speech of the old religion growled through the voices. The black mumblings intensified, drowning out all the others.

Worry hovered like a shadow in Merlin's head.

Using my magic may have been unwise.

Fear clamped around his throat, and his breath sharpened. His presence had been exposed like a beacon to those he did not want to find him.

Alarmed, he stood, shaking off the magic. He had learned a long time ago that just because a magic could be useful, did not mean it should be used. He gritted his teeth, glancing around, feeling a fool for being so impetuous.

He had no idea the danger he might have invited upon himself, yet the fact that the dark presence was so easy to find, meant that—whoever it was—was already uncomfortably near. Staying alert, he listened for any unwelcoming sound or rustle. The abrupt whooping of an owl startled him.

"*Fool.*" He scolded himself. "I should have known that others would be intentionally listening."

"*Fear will only draw them closer,*" a faint whisper spoke inside his mind. "*They are out there, but you are not the prey. Remember who you are. They are the ones that have something to fear.*"

Alone in the dark, Merlin wrestled. He was never quick to fear, but the darkness he had invited made him feel small.

"*They are coming for you. They have heard you—but they cannot have you.*"

Merlin closed his eyes and breathed a heavy sigh. He slowed his heart and calmed his mind. Then, with clenched fists, he kindled his magic. A golden hue flashed over his vision, his eyes lighting through the darkness.

Any darkness coming to beset me will be ill-prepared for the power I would wield against it.

He stood tall. The forest croaked and creaked louder and louder. Spectral swirls emanated from his fingertips.

A branch snapped behind him.

Merlin reeled, turning with his hands raised.

A voice cried out, "It is only me, Merlin!"

Merlin gasped, "Marcus!"

THE CALL OF THE UNICORN

Merlin quietly pushed the hut door open, revealing Arthur asleep, hunched over his sword. As he closed the door, it creaked, startling Arthur awake. He grappled with his sword, nearly dropping it.

"Merlin!" He rubbed his hands over his eyes. "Did you find him?"

"Yes. He was where I thought he would be." Exhausted, Merlin grumpily tossed himself onto his bed.

"Why is he not with you?"

Merlin did not reply but draped his arm over his face.

"Merlin?"

He sighed. "Marcus has gone back to his home for the night. He will speak with us come morning."

"Why do you seem so irked?"

Merlin lowered his hand to his chest, staring up at the thatch and clenching his teeth.

"Merlin."

He turned to Arthur, then paused, reluctant to say. "In the woods, I discovered more than just Marcus."

Arthur's eyes turned serious, and he leaned forward. "Tell me."

"I discerned fell voices in the wind. They are close…and—" Merlin shook his head. "They know, at least, that I am here." Merlin pounded his bed with his fists and sat up. "I am worried our presence here has put this village in the way of danger."

Arthur squeezed his sword's hilt. "Osian?"

Merlin nodded, pressing his lips into a tight line. "Or his demons. Though we should not be surprised at this. His evil permeates these lands, making them sick."

Arthur stood, rubbing his forehead. "What does Marcus say?"

"He said that he sensed the fallen spirits even before we arrived here. That is why he was seeking the Triple God."

"Has he heard anything from Him? Any wisdom?"

"We mostly spoke about Gethin."

"What did he say?"

"Marcus was surprised at our leeriness. He said he has been a very honoring and contrite filidh. He was, however, surprised that Gethin had told us he did not know where he was, and further confused at his refusal to fetch him upon our arrival. He said that the boy knows where he is at all times, and was specifically told where he would be."

Merlin grunted. "I was right that he was lying."

"Does Marcus know why?"

"Marcus thought maybe he was nervous. Two of Prydain's lords questioning him might have made him forget his mind." Merlin shook his head. "Marcus did not believe there was anything suspicious to worry about. 'Unheard of,' he said."

"What do you think?"

Merlin shrugged. "The boy was sleeping at his master's doorstep when I went out to check Marcus's hut—as he should have been. I almost made the gremlin come with me. I think Marcus is probably right—he knows the boy. Anyway," Merlin yawned, rolling back onto his bed. "I am determined to get some sleep, and hope that by morning all my suspicions will be put to rest."

Arthur grunted in agreement. "You get some rest. I will stay up and keep watch."

Merlin closed his eyes, knowing full well that sleep would not come to him. Not with what he had heard in the forest. He hated the dark voices, and abhorred that Osian's evil had infected the lands, destroying the peace that had been hard fought for. He was killing innocent people and blackening the land with the soot of his fires.

If only I could find him.

The thought of the people of this village, who had already had one home destroyed, potentially having to face the threat of another attack from Osian, sickened him. He thought long into the night until the morning sun rose.

Elanor woke from a dream, gasping for breath.

"What is it?" Adhan asked. She had fallen asleep in a chair next to the hearth's fire.

Elanor peered down at her daughter, who slept curled into her side, relieved she was safe. Her heart thudded in her chest, and she slowly exhaled, catching her breath from the fright. The sight of Gwendolen comforted her. Elanor feathered her fingers around a strand of her child's hair that curled her round cheek, observing her sweet rosy lips.

Sweat moistened her brow, and she exhaled another long breath, reminding herself the dream was over.

"Elanor?" Adhan's voice beckoned.

Elanor glanced back up at Adhan. Her mind raced to understand what she had just dreamt. She lifted her hand to her head.

Adhan came quickly beside her and whispered, "Did you have a dream?"

Elanor nodded. "I…I do not think it was just a dream." She gulped, searching through the details of what she had seen. The more she sobered, the more alarmed she became. "Mother…I think they are in trouble."

"Who is in trouble?"

"Merlin! A-Arthur!" Frantic, Elanor jumped from the bed and snatched up her clothes. "I have to find them. Grwyrthrhodd—he is warning me. He knows where to find them."

"Elanor, you are scaring me. Are you sure it was not just a dream?"

Elanor paused, doubt and uncertainty warring within her. "I have only ever had a dream like this once before. When the dragon called to me. If I had not gone to Gwyliwr that night, she and I both would be dead." She threw a white under-dress over her head, hesitated, and then cast it away. "I will need to wear something different." She dashed across the room, grabbed a pair of Merlin's breeches from his trunk, and held them up. She shook her head and stepped into them. "I cannot risk that this is just a dream. If I do—they might die."

"What will you do?"

"I do not know. Only I know I must go. And *now.*"

Adhan watched her struggle with getting breeches to stay on. "Wait. They are too big. Let me help."

Elanor smiled, relieved she was coming to her aid. Adhan grabbed one of Elanor's sashes and wrapped it through the top holes of the breeches. Then, taking one of Merlin's shirts and leather vest, she threw them over Elanor's head, tightening them the best she could with a belt. Merlin's vest hung halfway down Elanor's thighs, but by the time Adhan had finished, she looked ready to ride.

Elanor quickly laced her boots up over the breeches, then tied her hair up with a leather strap. She halted, glancing across the room at her short sword. She moved hesitantly toward it, then slid her fingers around the hilt, feeling the cold leather against her skin.

She lifted it up and swept her eyes across the blade.

What am I thinking?

She knew Arthur didn't believe in her, and she had never been tested in any real hand-to-hand combat. But then she remembered Arthur's words: *"Don't cast away your identity as easily as you did that sword. Let them see you. If you do not believe it, then the enemy does not have to believe it either."*

Why would Arthur encourage her in such a way, and then only see her weakness—refusing to believe she was capable of more? To him, she was helpless.

Adhan gripped her shoulders and said, "My daughter—all of us have to come to a place where we decide to be what other people *think* we are, or become who we *know* we are called to be."

"But…what if this is not what I am called to be? What if I am only fooling myself?"

"Who is the one that gave you that dream? Do your dreams not come from the Great God?"

Elanor looked down at the sword and turned it in her hands. She was never entirely sure where her dreams came from, but they had never failed to guide her.

"None of us are capable of anything entirely alone," Adhan encouraged. "The weight of what you are destined to become does not rest with you alone. That is why there were two stars…and also, Arthur."

Elanor stiffened at the mention of his name. "I should at least take the sword as a protection."

"Of course, you should."

Adhan fastened a sheath to her belt, and in one swift motion, Elanor slid the sword inside.

"Now go, quickly. I will take care of Gwendolen."

Elanor nodded, then gently kissed Gwendolen, careful not to wake her. Adrenaline heated her veins as she rushed from the room and down the hall toward Gwynevere's chamber. Elanor hoped with all her being that Gwynevere would understand—that she wouldn't hold her back.

Elanor was determined. Her dream was alive—tangible. If she didn't do something, then Arthur and Merlin would die.

She burst through the door of Gwynevere's chambers. She was already awake, and wrapping herself in a robe when Elanor entered.

"What is it?" she asked, startled. Then she looked over Elanor's attire and grimaced. "What are you wearing?"

"That is not important." Elanor shook her head, glancing at the ground. "I have to go. I had a dream. Grwyrthrhodd…." Elanor swallowed down the tension chafing her dry mouth. "Arthur and Merlin are in danger."

Gwynevere dropped her hands to her side. Her eyes, radiating worry, searched Elanor's face.

"Please, I have to go—*now*."

Gwynevere called, "Cathah!" Her servant stumbled in. "Make all haste. Go as swiftly as you can. Summon the lords Peredur and Bedwyr to my chambers. *Immediately*. Tell them they are to prepare to ride." The wide-eyed servant bowed. "*GO NOW!*"

The servant raced from the room. Gwynevere exhaled, looking over at Elanor. She paused for less than a second, set her jaw, then turned to hurriedly dress.

"What are you doing?" Elanor asked.

"I am going with you," Gwynevere said, not even glancing up as she pulled strange-looking leather straps and a rustic short sword from her trunk. She whipped her hair into a knot before pulling on a white flowing shirt and leather breeches. She strapped the thick leather around her chest and abdomen, then took smaller strips and wrapped them around her palms and wrists.

She snapped her sword into her sheath just as Bedwyr and Peredur entered the chamber. They stared in bafflement at the two women clothed like men.

"One of you will stand guard to protect the citadel," Gwynevere commanded them. "The other will be coming with us. There is no time to explain. We must go now. Merlin and Arthur are in danger."

Elanor was amazed and affirmed by Gwynevere's belief in her. She never questioned her—not even once.

"I will go with you," Bedwyr volunteered.

Peredur added, "Should I have more men at the ready to ride with you?"

"Immediately," Gwynevere confirmed, throwing on her cloak. "They must be equipped and ready to ride."

Peredur did not hesitate but left the room to fulfill her command.

Bedwyr approached Elanor. "Should you not stay here—"

Gwynevere cut him off. "We are on an errand that has everything to do with her. And you *will not* question her as so many others have in recent days."

Bedwyr's cheeks flushed. "I only wish to protect her, my queen."

"As we all do, but there is more behind Elanor's gifts. Have we forgotten that now Arthur has returned? Has her value suddenly diminished because we got our king back? She still has purpose in these dark days, and to hide her away to preserve her life would be a mistake."

Tears welled in Elanor's eyes; she turned her head to hide them.

"All our lives are at stake," Gwynevere said, "as long as Osian continues to ravage our lands. This citadel, this Palisade, is only an illusion of safety. And we are fools to forget it."

Bedwyr lifted his eyes to Elanor. "Do we ride to the forests of Celyddon?"

"Yes," Elanor said. "But first, we must go to meet the unicorn."

MARCUS & MEAD

In the gray of the morning, Merlin and Arthur rose to find Marcus already awake, stoking a fire in front of his hut. His thin, white hair blew over hunched shoulders in the morning air. The village food had been kind to Marcus's belly, filling in what used to be a frail frame, making him appear stouter.

The fire was a welcome comfort against the cool, damp air. Gethin was splitting firewood around the side. His axe came down and the wood pieces tumbled to the ground. He shot Merlin a timid glance, before picking up another log and continuing with his work.

Marcus greeted them, bowing his head toward the king with solemnity. The wrinkles around his kind blue eyes deepened as he smiled. "Great Pendragon, I have dreamed of this day. The wish of your return was always on the edge of my mind."

"It is much nicer seeing you in the light of day, my friend," Merlin said, taking Marcus's arms, and squeezing them tight.

The old man patted Merlin's side. "Last night, the forest teemed with evil. Both our minds were distracted. The air is clearer in this morning light. I had not the chance to tell you how my heart leapt when word came that our lost princess had been found. And what more," Marcus said, lifting his hand to Arthur, "the king had returned. The witch spoke true that Arthur would be awakened. A miracle we all were hesitant to believe, and yet"—Marcus's eyes sparkled and his voice lifted with esteem—"the king stands before me."

Arthur bowed his head with a gentle smile. "It is my honor to meet you, Marcus. I have heard tell of your words of prophecy, which is why we have come to speak with you."

"Yes, yes, my king. Of course. Merlin told me as much last night. Please, sit." Marcus offered them a seat around the fire. "You wish to hear the prophecy of the two stars?"

"Not quite." Arthur nodded for Merlin to begin.

Merlin leaned in. "Arthur wonders if there might be more to the prophecy. More that you have not shared that could reveal some light on our hidden enemy. Maybe even further prophecy you have received from the Great God. You sought him last night. Did you hear from Him?" Without waiting for a reply, Merlin shook his head. "I have been seeking for answers, and I have heard only fragmented pieces that have kept our next move a mystery."

Marcus sat back, lifting his brows, and the lines on his forehead deepened. "I am sorry to disappoint you, my king, but I have not heard anything that I think would help. What I do know is what you already know. Our enemy is strengthening. The land has become ill with symptoms that are crying louder and louder as the days continue to darken." He peered up at the sky, and his eyes grew distant. "It feels to me the return of the Great Pendragon has set certain plans in motion. The enemy is active—the shadow of his hand is moving toward the north."

Marcus leaned forward, placing his hand across his mouth and chin. He squeezed his eyes, considering his next words, then said, "Darkness is pressing down upon us, but that is because the prophecy of the king's return has come to pass, and the enemy is afraid. Merlin and Elanor's presence was already a threat." He held up three fingers and locked eyes with Arthur. "But now, there are *the three*. And it is the three that are prophesied to destroy the darkness. Not the one, or even the two. All the pieces are now in play." Marcus lifted his chin to Merlin. "Where is Elanor? I should have loved to see her healing light."

Merlin smirked at a frowning Arthur, who then grumbled, "It was not safe for her to come."

Marcus slapped his knee and chortled. "Safe?"

Arthur glared at the old druid, clearly annoyed.

"Forgive me, my king," Marcus quickly repented, with widening eyes. "I did not mean to be so familiar."

Arthur nodded, and a humble smile returned to the old druid's face.

Merlin chuckled lightly. "It is true, Marcus. It is not safe for her to come; though you should know that she requested to come. She longs to see you also."

"That does this old man's heart good to hear." Marcus sniffed with delight, but then his grin faded, and his face went gray. "Arthur, you are my king. I honor you. So, please hear this warning in the highest respect of your sovereignty. The lady Elanor will *never* be safe. Nor shall you, Gwynevere, or Merlin be, as long as Osian is alive. All that you are is a threat to the old religion. Osian is after *you*. He is after her. His aim is fully aligned with no other purpose but to kill you all."

The mood sobered and the conversation silenced. Their eyes stared morosely into the fire.

After a long moment, Marcus puffed through his lips and smacked his gums. "My boy!" He shouted over to Gethin. "Bring us some bread and dried meats. My stomach growls."

Gethin dropped his axe and ran to the hut to fetch some food.

"He is a good boy, I promise you. You have no need to worry about him. I know he appeared off to you last night, but it may have been his nerves in the presence of the king. I think we all get a little nervous in the shadow of your sovereignty."

The old druid stood, and then bent strenuously over to grab another log for the fire. "I will tell you," he said, placing the log, "that I have had an awen. I do not understand it, or how it pertains to this hour, but I will share it in case it helps. Maybe Emrys will have the power to interpret what I cannot." He slumped back down to a seat. "I saw an acorn that had been singed by fire. It fell into a pile of ashes, and then through time and rain, it was buried. Out from the ground came a green shoot of life—beautiful, new, and tender. However, the feet of armies came charging over it and stamped it out.

"To my delight, even as it had been trampled, more shoots sprouted. The one small, burnt acorn, had become many. The seed, a new life that could not be stopped. Soon, shoots grew stronger and taller. They entwined and became one oak, so large, its roots stretched out across the land. I do not know its meaning, but it gives my spirit hope."

Gethin arrived with the food. While they ate, satisfying their bellies, Merlin mused over Marcus's awen. The vision felt hopeful, but he could not discern its meaning. Were they the acorn? And if so, would they have to be buried before there could be life? The thought unsettled him.

"Arthur is right, though," Merlin said, gnawing on a piece of meat. "There has to be something…*something* more to prepare us against our enemy and reveal him in some way. This vision you have had is hopeful, but still gives us little to go on. The kings arrive in Prydain soon, and we are about to declare war without *any* direction."

Gethin returned, this time with three cups. Merlin took the first cup and raised it to thank him. Something almost suspicious flashed in Gethin's eyes. Merlin swirled the liquid in his cup and waited for Gethin to leave before sniffing it.

Marcus began, "There *was* something I wanted to talk to you about. Do you remember that farm boy—" Marcus paused to take a sip from his cup.

Something was off. Alarm flared in Merlin's chest. His skin tingled, and the hairs on the back of his neck and arms rose. He snapped his gaze up at Marcus.

"—you know? The boy that attacked Elanor when we first met? He had a twisted knife. You remember the one." Marcus nodded to Merlin, then continued, "I have wondered about that ever…ever since…ever-ev—" Marcus's face turned sour, and his cup fell from his hands.

Then Arthur hit the ground next to Merlin's feet. Merlin threw his cup to the ground.

Poison!

Merlin jumped to his feet. He clenched his fists and looked toward the hut where he thought Gethin had gone. A loud *crack* stole his attention. Before he could turn, what felt like a large stone hit him upside the head. He collapsed to the ground.

Crack, crack, crack.

It was the same bizarre sound he'd heard when Elanor materialized into his chambers when they first met. Blood pooled over his eyes, but quickly, with the aid of adrenaline, he labored to his feet.

A voice shouted, "Quick! Do not let him get up."

Whack!

A sharp blow struck Merlin behind his knees. His legs buckled, and as he fell, his gaze locked onto Gethin, who stood above him tight-fisting a long stick. The filidh's eyes bulged. He hoisted the stick high, poised for another vicious strike. With a primal snarl, Merlin launched at Gethin, tackling him to the ground. He unleashed a guttural roar, slamming Gethin's head against the hard earth. The little weasel yelped, struggling to wiggle free from Merlin's grip.

"Get him!" someone shouted.

Before Merlin knew it, several men swarmed him.

"Do not let him use his magic."

Merlin thrashed. Enraged, he twisted his head right as a blur of yellow cloaked men seized his arms. One man forced something into his mouth. The bitter liquid splashed onto his tongue, and he spat it into his assailant's face. The man wailed, thrusting his hand over his eyes.

"Cael ei ddiarddel!" Merlin shouted. A force shot out from him, hurling the men off him.

The world slowed. Merlin panted, gazing around. Hooded men appeared throughout the village. Screams reverberated into his ears from villagers scattering in panic. The smell of fire irritated his nostrils. Merlin struggled to get his bearings, to focus on the enemies surrounding him. His head swam, and the world blurred more and more.

"No!" he cried.

The poison.

Whatever they had forced into his mouth, he must have swallowed some.

He stumbled, and fear pounded his gut. Arthur and Marcus lay on the ground, motionless. They drank the poison? Were they dead?

"Aaahhh!" Merlin thundered at the hooded men who darted his way. He wouldn't let them take him without a fight. He lunged forward, then crashed in a heap. The world blurred into a muffled, numb dream. His sight dimmed. He felt arms lifting him up and tilting his head back. Desperation clawed at him, urging his limbs to move, to fight back, but they hung unresponsive, heavy as stone.

More bitter liquid poured down his throat.

"Not too much…" he heard someone say. "It will kill him."

"Give it all to him," a more grizzled voice replied. "I will take him to the master dead. Neither of their lives will be spared."

Dread seeped into Merlin's spirit. His belly ached. The poison leaked into his stomach. He thought of Elanor and Gwendolen. Maybe he could find the will to fight. Maybe he could find the magic. But then his world faded.

Elanor led the charge upon Brynn's back—the beloved horse that Bedwyr had given her. She had seen in the dream the same open field between the two forests of Caer Lial, where she and Merlin had met the dragon. Within the dream, the pure white enaid charged toward her over the hill at the southern edge of the field.

She imagined how foolish she would feel if they arrived and the unicorn wasn't there. It was one thing to lead Merlin on a flagrant chase because of a dream—it was an entirely other thing to lead Gwynevere, Bedwyr, and a small band of Cymbrogi in faith that what she dreamt was real. What would they think of her if she were wrong? The little clout she might have held would be destroyed.

She knew why Bedwyr had challenged her before they left. Her magic saw in his eyes the pain he had experienced watching her die the last time they set out—rending his heart. She didn't want to face his disappointment if her dream had been a false alarm.

No…no. It was not just a dream.

She knew it, but still the anxiety pressed against her chest. They were almost there. The speed of their horses thundered over the lush terrain. Elanor glanced back over her shoulder and captured Gwynevere's eye.

Mother.

Gwynevere always supported her, and yet, Elanor wrestled with accepting her as mother. She had never really had one. Adhan, Merlin's mother, had filled that position for her more than anyone else ever had. While Gwynevere…she was a peer. A friend. A loving confidante. Though, Elanor saw in Gwynevere's eyes that she never struggled. Never once. From the moment they met, Elanor was known to her. She feared letting Gwynevere down.

These thoughts pounded through her head, until finally they arrived. Elanor pulled on her reins to slow her horse, leading the others behind her to do the same. The wind's gentle howl blew across the empty field—with no Grwyrthrhodd in sight.

Elanor gulped a knot of fear, forcing it down so she would appear brave. She dismounted, feeling the heat from the eyes behind her. Merlin had a way of pulling magic out of her, but this time, she would have to do it alone.

I can do it, she told herself. Butterflies flitted through her stomach. Determined, she walked forward, distancing herself from those waiting behind her.

It was not just a dream. Grwyrthrhodd called to me. He will come.

She brushed her cloak behind her and stared insecurely down at her clothes.

Who am I pretending to be? I am no warrior.

She squeezed her eyes shut, working to silence her doubt. If she was going to call the unicorn, she needed to be calm, confident, and of a level mind.

Remember him. Remember Grwyrthrhodd. Remember what his magic feels like. He has already called you. Connect with his spirit.

The enaid, the dragon, Merlin—they all felt like *the song*. The song of the New Kingdom.

She whispered, "Teyrnas yr haul…Teyrnus yr haul."

She imagined it—The Kingdom of the Sun. It wasn't a place. It was something more. The more she beckoned, the more it stirred inside her, as though belonging to her. Its sound inviting her deeper into the promise. It was golden, bright, and without shadow. The more the idea of it grew, the more its warmth ignited within her.

"Teyrnas yr haul…" Emboldened, she lifted her voice higher. "Kingdom of the sun…you must come. Fill these days with light and remove the shadows' hold." Then she commanded, "Grwyrthrhodd! It is time to come. I know you beckoned me. I have come at your call."

A burst of blue pulsed out of Elanor, sending a wave over the hills and trees. The wind increased like a sudden tempest; its swirling gusts danced wildly around her.

A whispering voice echoed back through the wind, "Teyrnas yr haul." And then everything stilled.

In the silence, Elanor waited with bated breath.

The cry came first. The echoing whinny of the unicorn. Elanor breathed a sigh of relief. A trickle of gladness radiated through her cheeks, bringing tears to her eyes. Those behind her audibly gasped. Over the hill, he appeared, just as Elanor had dreamt—a white specter floating down the hill toward them. The horses nervously stamped.

The unicorn strode nearer, aided by a swift, supernatural wind. Elanor's heart lifted with excitement. She felt validated, even to herself, that she had done what was right. The Great God had met her, delivering what she had dreamt. Now, she hoped Merlin and Arthur could be saved.

Elanor turned toward Bedwyr and Gwynevere. Bedwyr had dismounted and stood with his mouth gaping. Gwynevere smiled as if she, too, were affirmed by her belief in Elanor. She turned back and Grwyrthrhodd approached her with a slowing canter. She lifted her hand to greet him. He neighed, shaking his head. She brushed her fingers over the soft velvet on the bridge of his nose.

"I've missed you," she said into his neck. "Though, I know you have been with me."

The unicorn neighed, and the warmth of his breath puffed down her neck. For a moment, his presence was enough. The world stood still. Her palms caressed his cheeks.

His voice, familiar to her now, whispered inside her mind. Elanor listened intently to his careful instructions; his plans made her heart race. Most of it came in pictures, like an awen playing inside her thoughts. Her eyes shot open. A sheen of blue light passed over her vision, and she said, "I am ready."

The enaid knelt beside her, inviting her onto his back. She curled her fingers into his silken mane, and he lifted her up. His stature rose far above the height of the other horses, his neck narrower and longer. Elanor gripped tight with her thighs, and he trotted over to the waiting riders. His traipse was light, and she found it unexpectedly easy to hold on.

The unicorn halted before the others, and Elanor instructed, "You must follow close behind. This enaid's magic will carry us on a quickened pace. Do not deviate from the wake that will stream behind him, and do not fear it. We are going to the forests of Celyddon. There, a village is under attack. Be prepared to fight." She looked to Bedwyr. "You and I will not stop at the village. We will continue on to find Merlin and the king."

Bedwyr lifted his head as if shaking off the wonder. He tightened his jaw, gripped hold of his reins, and pulled himself back up onto his horse. The others, including Gwynevere, aligned themselves behind, while Grwyrthrhodd positioned himself at the lead. Brynn followed in line, almost as though she instinctively knew to follow.

They all leaned forward, and then they were off—across forest and plains like a wave of the sea easily flowing over the sand. They bounded over hills as though they were flat lands, riding on a cloud that carried them forth—thundering toward Celyddon.

THE HOODED EXECUTIONER

rthur groaned, struggling to open his eyes. His eyelids were heavy, and his body felt numb. He tried to pull his hands to his face, but they hung tied above his head; his wrists ached at each pull.

Wake up!

Urgency tugged at the fringes of his mind as though he were in a nightmare. His breaths muffled in his ears.

Wake up!

His lids cracked open, but the world was unclear—a blended mesh of brown and yellow. His eyes shut again, and he started slipping back out of consciousness. He grunted, toiling against wakefulness. In an effort to make his eyes obey, he scrunched his face. Slowly, they opened. This time, the blur focused.

Forest…I am still in the forest.

Above him, the treetops swayed, and the yellow leaves rattled like dry bones. His legs were stretched out in front of him, and rough bark dug into his back. Out of the corner of his eye, he saw a lump.

A body!

There, lifeless and unbound, was Merlin. He lay on his side with his back toward Arthur.

"M-M-Mer…" Arthur couldn't quite get his mouth to speak. The present danger quickened his breathing. He tried again, "Mer-Merlin."

No response.

Arthur narrowed his eyes to see better but his mind was too muddled. Was Merlin's side still rising and falling with breath? The fact that Merlin wasn't tied did not bode well.

Please do not be dead.

Arthur yanked on the ropes fettering his wrists above him. The bindings tore into his skin, tightening with each pull.

"Is the king awakening?" a grizzled voice asked.

Arthur snapped his head toward the sound. Not far to his left crouched a man in a yellow hood.

"W-Wha…." Arthur swallowed, forcing out his words. "What is happening here? Who are you? What have you done to Merlin?"

"Oh…" The man stood, towering over Arthur, and donned a triumphant smile. "You mean the great Emrys? He is dead. We killed him. The druid who could not be beaten was easily dealt with. And soon also shall you be."

A piercing pain struck Arthur's heart. He twisted in his bonds, staring at Merlin's body. His friend. His brother—crumpled over, limp and lifeless. Arthur darted his eyes over his surroundings, grasping for anything that could help free him.

"Get him on his knees," the man commanded.

Two other hoods surged toward Arthur.

Arthur's legs lashed out instinctively. He strained, vying to put up a fight, but his limbs betrayed him. The remnants of the treacherous poison the enemy had given him still coursed through his veins, leeching away at his strength.

"Struggle if you must." The man laughed with condescension. "We are not fools. We know the strength of the Great Pendragon. We would not risk hand-to-hand combat with you. Neither did we risk it with Merlin. Black henbane can lay low the strongest of men. We gave a little too much to your mighty druid, and now he is dead. We were unwilling to risk his magic. But you…I will kill you while you are awake, and still unable to fight." He slithered closer. "I want you to watch your own head roll to the ground before I deliver it to Osian on a pike."

Arthur glared at the devil whose face remained shadowed under his hood. Only a scarred chin, with thin lips exposing yellowed teeth, was visible.

One man gripped Arthur's arms, while another sawed through the rope that tied him to the tree. Once free, they wrangled his hands, binding them behind his back. They pulled the rope tight, jamming the bones of his wrists together, and forced him onto his knees.

Arthur resisted their hold, but in the drunkenness of the henbane, he only succeeded in launching himself face down into the dirt. They seized him again and shoved his cheek to the ground.

"You can fight, but you have already lost. Even if we had not given you poison, you would not be able to defeat me without Merlin to help you." The man knelt next to Arthur's head. The other two grunts drove his ear into the dirt. "You can do *nothing,*" the villain yelled, and dripples of saliva sprayed Arthur's face. "The Lord Osian gives me magic. My power could put you down, but why waste it, when I have a sword."

"Your dark magic is weakness!" Arthur spat, thrashing with all his might to not let this be his end. The devil rose to his feet, and the ringing sound of a sword being unsheathed gripped Arthur's chest.

"You just returned from the dead." The man tsked. "Does it not sting knowing how quickly we were able to defeat you? The hope you brought your people will *break* them. It would have been better if you had stayed dead."

Arthur swallowed, hating how helpless he felt. His mind scrambled for a solution, but he could think of nothing to stop them. He winced in bitter defeat. He felt stupid—ignorant for having so easily fallen into their trap; clearly, he underestimated his enemy. Where was his strength? Or his ability to hold back the tides of evil and decimate his enemy? Had he truly lost it all on the fields of Camlan?

What was the point of returning?

Hopelessness pressed in like a fog. He closed his eyes, awaiting the sword to slice through his flesh. He held his breath. The forsaken wind of a sword whipped past his face.

It has happened. I am dead.

The world silenced, and he waited for it to fade. Instead, screams erupted from the men who pressed him down.

Arthur gasped. *I am still alive.*

The men's grip slackened, and Arthur snapped his eyes open, beholding a chaotic scene. A piercing white light bolted toward them through the trees.

All at once, an invisible force flung him through the air, slamming his back into a tree. The hooded men were also hurled into the air. Merlin's body rolled from the forceful blast, whipping him onto his back. In that split second, Arthur saw his face. He gasped at his unnatural pale-blue skin.

No... His heart sank in defeat—loss stinging his soul.

In his doomed moment, the advancing light stopped, hovering before Arthur. He blinked against its blinding brightness. It wasn't a horse...no, it was something else. Its sleek legs were unnaturally long. Its form more like a giant stag—one shining antler piercing the middle of its head. On its back sat a dark-haired rider with her sword drawn. She leapt from the creature, and one of the hooded men rose to face her. Her eyes beamed blue as she stood amidst the white light emanating from the creature.

In that instant, Arthur recognized her.

"Elanor?" he uttered, just as a hand grabbed hold of him. Startled, Arthur turned. "Bedwyr!"

"Yes, brother! Let us set you free." In haste, Bedwyr leaned Arthur forward and cut through his bonds.

The villain lunged toward Elanor, arcing his sword high over his head.

Arthur's heart plummeted to his gut. He leapt from the ground—stars dizzied his eyes. His vision cleared just as Elanor swung her sword, slicing through the fiend's arm. Blood dripped from the blade, and the man wretched, screaming as his arm dropped to the ground, lobbed off at the elbow.

Elanor's face went pale. She stared at the blade in her hand, then at the bloody limb on the ground. Horrified, she dropped her sword.

The hooded assailant fell onto his back, crying out in pain and coddling what was left of his arm into his chest. Arthur stumbled over and picked up the man's sword that lay next to his freshly dismembered hand. He blinked away the dark spots threatening to take his consciousness, then charged the wounded man like an angry bull. The villain tried to scoot away with his good arm, but Arthur caught him. He kicked the man and jammed his boot against his foe's neck. He pressed down with his full weight, pointing the tip of his sword at the man's throat.

The villain wretched and his eyes widened in terror. Behind Arthur, the fury of clanging swords ceased. Bedwyr had dispatched the other two hoods, nailing them to the ground.

Arthur leaned over the struggling worm beneath his foot, ready to end his life—when suddenly—he thought better of it. Here was their chance to learn more about their enemy. One of Osian's footmen…alive to answer questions.

Arthur lifted his foot from his enemy's neck, then slammed his fist into the man's jaw, knocking him unconscious.

Breathless, and still lightheaded from the henbane, Arthur peered over at Elanor. She was holding Merlin in her arms. The fear of loss seized him, and he collapsed next to them on the ground.

Elanor sat trembling; her eyes wide.

"Is"—Arthur breathed—"is he dead?"

Her shaking fingers caressed Merlin's chin, and then worked their way down his neck, feeling for a pulse. Elanor gasped. A tear dripped down her cheek. "His heart…th-there is a heartbeat, but it is weak."

Arthur dropped his head and sighed. "They poisoned him. Henbane." His chin tightened as he stared into Merlin's gray face. "They have given me some as well—I am still feeling the effects."

"Poison." Another tear streamed down her nose. She looked up with pleading eyes at the tall white creature that stood motionless, like a ghostly tower, above her. "Please, Grwyrthrhodd," she cried, "you must help him. I c-cannot lose him. His life is hanging by a thread."

Could this creature do something?

The beast bobbed its head at Elanor and lightly whinnied. Elanor nodded in reply, as though it had said something she understood.

"Help me," Elanor called to Bedwyr, who quickly scrambled over. "Support his back. Help me sit him up." She shot a worried glance back at the beast. "I am not sure I can do it. I do not know if I have the power."

Arthur felt her doubt. Aiming to encourage her, he said, "I do not know what this creature has said, but you can help him, Elanor. You healed me. Remember?"

Elanor did not lift her eyes to acknowledge him, making Arthur's heart twist tighter inside his chest. He turned, hoping the creature would aid them further, but the white beast had vanished.

Elanor dropped her head onto Merlin's chest and wept.

"Is it gone?" Arthur groaned.

"No," Elanor sniffed. "He is not gone. Only from our sight." She lifted her head, inhaling a long breath. She closed her eyes, then told Bedwyr, "Keep him upright."

Bedwyr gave a confirming nod.

Elanor pressed her palm onto Merlin's stomach. To Arthur, each second felt like an eternity. He hoped with all that was within him that Merlin would take a full breath.

Elanor mumbled words into his chest, and then, Arthur felt it—a surge of power. A virtue of magic flowed through Elanor into Merlin. Arthur leaned forward, anticipating a sign of healing.

*Come on…*he wanted to say out loud, but kept it contained.

Elanor sighed, opening her eyes. She searched Merlin's face, her expression that of one struggling to keep faith.

"Wake up," she whispered. "Please."

Arthur saw her hope faltering. So was his.

Even Bedwyr dropped his head, despairing. Elanor had done all she could with her healing magic—there was nothing more to be done. Her face grew more distressed with each second Merlin remained unchanged. She gripped his tunic and shook him, demanding through her teeth, "Merlin!"

Merlin's eyes shifted underneath his lids and his eyelashes flickered. Arthur exhaled his held breath.

"Hold him up," Elanor quickly reminded Bedwyr.

Bedwyr shifted him further upright. Merlin's eyes rolled open. His brows raised, and he released a painful moan.

"Merlin…" Elanor said, caressing his cheek.

Arthur stretched his hand toward Merlin's shoulder. Relief flooded his heart seeing Merlin's amber eyes weakly connect with Elanor's. But then, Arthur's head started spinning again. He clutched his forehead and squeezed his eyes shut, waiting for the dizziness to subside.

Merlin groaned beside him and slumped forward. Through the haze, Arthur watched Elanor scrutinize Merlin with the intensity of one searching for a diamond in a chest full of pearls.

"Y-you will be alright," Elanor eagerly encouraged him. "You have been poisoned."

Merlin's face contorted, and with an angry resonance in his voice, he grumbled, "I know—I…"

Merlin's eyes bulged. He pushed Elanor out of the way and wretched. Bedwyr held him. Violently, he spewed poison onto the ground. He leaned back to catch his breath, just as another wave of heaving reeled him forward. With each hurl, the color returned more and more to his face, and the dread churning Arthur's stomach slowly lessened with it.

At long last, with watering eyes, Merlin collapsed onto his back. Bedwyr pulled him away from the vomit and leaned him up against a tree. The whites of his eyes were red, his lips pallid. Gasping for breath, he covered his eyes with a shaky hand.

Elanor's fingers reached for him, and as soon as her hand grazed his, Merlin pulled her into an embrace.

Elanor murmured, "Oh, my God—Merlin! I thought I had lost you."

"I," Arthur began, "I thought you were dead."

Merlin turned his eyes to him. "I thought I was too, my brother." He gazed around the forest, breathing heavily. His gaze settled on the three hooded men on the ground. His face scrunched as though confounded, then he lifted Elanor from his chest. "What are you doing here?"

Elanor gave a tearful smile. "It was Grwyrthrhodd. He brought me here."

"Hah!" Merlin's complexion warmed with a weak but amazed grin. "Tell me ever—" his face soured, and he gripped his stomach.

Bedwyr stood to retrieve a waterskin from his horse. "Here," he said, returning and handing it to Merlin. "This should help. Some bread would do you some good too, but unfortunately"–he shrugged—"I have none. Elanor allowed no time to prepare. We came to you in urgent haste."

"This was far too close." Arthur leaned forward, placing his elbows on his knees. "I was nearly beheaded. You—you were dead." He glared at the hooded man he had spared. "That one is still alive. We will need to bind him."

"Bind him?" Bedwyr huffed. "Why should we keep the fiend alive?"

"Information. Now we finally have someone who can tell us what we need to know about Osian." Arthur paused, then faced Merlin. "And we may need to do more than just bind him. He is a sorcerer—that is what he claimed before he tried to cut off my head."

Merlin took a breathless mouthful of water, swished it through his mouth, and spat it onto the ground. He wiped his mouth with his arm, then took a slower sip. His face twisted, swallowing it down. Shaking his head, he said, "I cannot take any more right now. Here." He offered the water to Arthur. "It appears you may need some as well. You are looking a bit green."

Arthur gladly took it, then snarled at the unconscious devil. "Scum."

Bedwyr nodded in agreement. "If we want him alive, we can't let him keep bleeding like that, or he will soon be dead."

Merlin squinted at the obvious injury. "Ah, yes. I see he is missing part of his arm."

"Elanor did that," Arthur replied without turning his head.

Merlin grinned. "Really?" He stroked Elanor's face. "And look at you. Are those *my* clothes?"

An abashed smile bloomed on Elanor's face. Merlin pressed his hand against her cheek. "I did not have much time to think about what I was doing. I just knew I needed to be ready to ride."

Merlin's eyes softened. "You are just as you should be."

Arthur shook his head. He still felt miffed.

Of course. She will feel justified now that she saved the day.

Though, pinging the back of his conscience was a sense that he had underestimated her.

"We may have taken you for granted," Merlin said, carefully sitting up. "Without you and Bedwyr, Arthur and I would be dead."

Elanor dropped her head, then lifted a timid glance at Arthur. "I—I was terrified.

Not only of losing you. Both of you." She paused, biting her lip. "But terrified to face an enemy I knew I was not strong enough to fight. I dropped my sword." She lowered her gaze and whispered, "I knew I would drop my sword."

Arthur wanted to reach for her, encourage her that she had done well, but he resisted. She had been lucky. Or had she? There was a force that came with her he had not considered.

"It is not only Elanor and I that have come," Bedwyr said, staring down at the wounded villain. "Gwynevere and a company of Cymbrogi have ridden with us."

Arthur sat a little taller. "They have? Gwynevere also?"

"They are defending the village." Then Bedwyr said in a marveled tone, "We saw the great white enaid. We rode with him on the wings of the wind."

"The Great God fights for us." Merlin smiled, looking enlivened.

Arthur rose to his feet. "How far are we from the village?"

"Not far, but we only have the one horse." Bedwyr said, "We can get there on foot easily enough, once you are recovered." He kicked at the man on the ground. "But we have to deal with this one first."

Arthur joined Bedwyr. "Then let us deal with this viper."

8

THE FACE OF TREACHERY

Merlin spelled their captured sorcerer into a deep sleep, then they cauterized and bound what remained of his arm. If he survived the journey home, they would hopefully have information, or at least something substantial to go on. This villain was the closest they had ever come to the source, proving their journey to Celyddon was a benefit after all.

They tossed their prisoner over the back of Bedwyr's horse. Merlin rode in front, loathing his proximity with the fiend. He was still too weak to walk with the rest of the group. The effects of the poison addled his head and weakened his legs. The nausea writhed inside his stomach, making him more sensitive to the wet ash that hung in the air. Smoke floated through the trees like a fog the nearer they came to the village.

They moved with caution. Bedwyr scouted just ahead of them, his sword drawn, ready if they should need to fight. Merlin gritted his teeth, preparing himself for the potential carnage. Hopefully the village had beaten their attackers with the help of the Cymbrogi.

They finally arrived close enough to hear shouts echoing through the trees, but it was not terrorized screams or yells of battle. Instead, they heard rushed orders to douse what was left of the flames.

The trees parted, and both the Cymbrogi of Caer Lial and the archers of Celyddon worked together, dragging hooded corpses into a heap to be burned. Others raced with water buckets to douse flames from burning thatch. Merlin's eager eyes danced across the village, counting the innocent casualties resulting from the attack. Not many could be seen, and thankfully, it appeared that many of the huts and structures had been saved.

Merlin smiled, watching Arthur exhale with relief.

"Ho!" Bedwyr hollered, raising his hand to hail the villagers.

Tomos's lumbering frame appeared from around a hut with black soot covering his cheeks and clothes. After him came Gwynevere and the captain of the Celyddon guard.

Seeing Arthur, Gwynevere gasped and threw herself into his chest, wrapping her arms around his waist. "You are safe. If we had not come at Elanor's warning"—she shook her head—"I hate to think."

Arthur dropped his cheek against her head, his eyes drawing over to Elanor. "We would not be alive if Elanor and Bedwyr had not shown when they did." He pointed at Merlin. "Merlin was all but dead."

Merlin grunted, nodding toward the queen.

"Still unwell, I see," Gwynevere replied, her eyebrows pinched together with concern. "Marcus will be glad to see you."

"He is alive, then?" Merlin asked, hopeful.

"Yes! He did not get much of the poison."

Tomos gave a grim look. "I am sorry, sires. I saw them wicked men appear and attack you. I came after to try and stop them." He curled his burly hand into a fist. "I knocked many of them down on my way to ya', but they disappeared with you in their arms. *Pfffttt!* Into thin air you went." He raised his thumb over his shoulder. "But I got the young one with my club. He did not disappear. He is still alive, over there. But he is dyin'."

Arthur gave Tomos a firm pat on the back. "There is nothing to forgive, Tomos. You have done well to defend your village."

"They had fire, sire." He humbly bowed. "B-But once the main one left with you and Merlin, our archers were quick to defend us. And then, the queen and her men arrived. It was over before too much damage had been done."

Arthur's brow creased. "Were many among you killed?"

"They were a few, yes." Tomos lowered his head, and his eyes reddened. "Some wounded we are still tending to. Mostly it was the men who fought back. Though, there were some women 'n children who got caught in the wake."

"I am so sorry, Tomos." Arthur lifted his chin, his eyes awash. "I am so sorry if I brought this death upon you by coming here. I promise you I will do *all* that is within my power to destroy this evil."

"That you must, my sire—that you must. Though, I assure you—it weren't your presence that brought the evil. It was already here." Tomos lifted his chest and jutted out his chin. "We may not be warriors in this village, but we were prepared to fight."

"Ah, there it is," Arthur said with a sober gleam in his eye. "The proud shoulders of a Cymbrogi."

Tomos stood taller, his cheeks reddening from Arthur's praise.

"Yes, Tomos. I am with you. Along with all Prydain. We will spare *not* one breath in waiting for these devils to spring again."

Merlin moaned leaning over the saddle, then carefully slid down from the horse. Bedwyr and Elanor reached to support him.

A shout came. "Bring him here. I have some medicines that will help him—and Arthur."

Merlin lifted his heavy eyes to see Marcus waving from his hut. He chuckled. "How is that old man doing so well? I mean…." Merlin motioned to his slouched and sick frame leaning against Bedwyr's.

"Tough as a boot." Arthur laughed.

"Or he just has medicine." Elanor chimed. "Medicine, you need. Come on."

Merlin laughed with a sickly cringe. "Yes, and I could definitely use some, or I fear I may be of no use at all."

Elanor and Bedwyr supported Merlin, and with Arthur following alongside them, they led him to Marcus.

Marcus hobbled toward them. "Oh, my Great God, I am so grateful you are alive." He shot a contrite glance at Arthur. "Please forgive my naivety, my king. I should have seen the treachery in my filidh. All of this could have been avoided." Then he faced Merlin. "I feel so foolish."

"Stop, Marcus," Merlin groaned. "I understand it is hard to see evil in those you are meant to trust."

Arthur made no reply, but his miffed gaze revealed he was still ruffled by the deception and not in a forgiving mood.

"There is something I must show you both. It is exactly what I was about to tell you before all this evil started. But first." He reached for Elanor. "My dear," he cooed, hugging her close. "To see you alive—I am lost for words. And I hear it is *you* that has saved us."

Merlin smirked at Arthur as they continued toward the hut.

Arthur rolled his eyes, shifting his shoulders with irritation.

Merlin asked Marcus, "What is it you have to show us?"

"N-Not yet. You must have medicine. Set him to rest over there." Through the entrance, Marcus pointed to a cot. Elanor and Bedwyr guided Merlin in and laid him down.

Merlin sighed, relieved to be on his back. "Ack—this poison is awful."

Marcus smirked, lifting a concerned brow. "Henbane can be used as a sleeping draft if very distilled. What they gave you"--Marcus shook his head—"it is a miracle you live."

Marcus quickly mixed up two cups from a pot he already had boiling over a flame. "Here." He handed one cup to Merlin, and the other to Arthur. "This will help with the stomach and clear your heads."

Merlin sat up to drink it. The steam hit his nose with a pungent smell of mushroom. He blew on it before taking a sip. A bitter, earthy taste rolled over his tongue, making him gag.

"All of it now," Marcus encouraged, lifting the bottom of Merlin's cup toward his mouth.

Merlin held his breath and quickly guzzled the rest. He wretched against it, but swallowed it down anyway, then collapsed back onto the cot and rested his head.

"It should be quick. You will feel better."

"Whoa!" Arthur said, straightening. "I am feeling the dross lift already."

"Yes." Marcus nodded. "The root I gave you nullifies the poison. I know all about henbane, as it was my supply that Gethin got into."

Arthur grumbled, "Tomos said that Gethin is still alive."

"Yes." Marcus turned his solemn face toward Arthur. "He is what I want you to see. I have discovered something. I think it is important. It will explain why I believed Gethin was innocent, and why that young farm boy attacked Elanor in the woods those few years back. There is more to this than treachery."

Merlin sat up. "Take us to him."

"Are you feeling recovered?"

"Not quite." He slowly rose to his feet. "But I will soon enough. This does not sound like it can wait."

They approached the wheezing boy lying on the forest floor, his head bloodied from being struck. The broken tip of an arrow was lodged in his gut. He stared painfully up at the tree boughs and didn't look their way when they approached. Once Merlin stood over him, the boy's remorseful eyes shifted.

Gethin swallowed, and tears welled in his eyes. "Oh, L-Lord Merlin. Please," he gasped. "Please forgive me. I saw myself do it. I tried to stop. For…f-for days, I tried."

Merlin peered up at Marcus, confused. The druid nodded at Merlin, encouraging him to continue with his questioning. Arthur loomed back and listened.

Merlin knelt closer to the boy. "What do you mean?"

"I—I tried to stop. I did not want to hurt you, or betray my master." Gethin's breathing became more strained; his eyes stared aimless through the trees. "I saw the men days ago—in the forest. They did something to me—got into my head." One tear dropped from his eye, and he turned back to Merlin. "It hurt to think. My mind got lost. Wicked thoughts cloaked my own. I d-did not understand. I—" His panting increased. "I could hear *her* in my head."

"Hear who?"

"She—she has the loveliest voice." Gethin shut his eyes and smiled, as though remembering the sound. "Like silken ribbons or chimes on the wind. I could not keep myself from listening. She told me to do things. I watched through my own eyes, like a prisoner gagged and tied. I could not stop myself from doing things I knew I should not do."

"Do you know who she is?"

"No…no. Only that I obeyed her every word. She made me feel important. She made me feel"—Gethin paused—"like she needed me."

"Was it she who told you to use the poison?"

The boy's sad eyes stared at Merlin without reply, then he said, "I wanted to honor my people. I had been so jubilant knowing the king had returned."

Merlin sighed. He saw only truth in the boy's eyes and compassion for him welled in his heart. "Can you still hear her?"

"No," he sobbed. "She has left me."

Merlin stood and said to Marcus, "Why has he been left here on the ground to die like this?"

"We feared moving him would kill him. His injury is too severe. I examined him. His neck might be broken."

Merlin shook his head. "Can he not be saved?"

Marcus's chin trembled, and he shook his head.

Merlin wrestled with whether or not he could bring Elanor to save the boy, but as he watched Gethin struggle with breath, he doubted there would be enough time.

"Please," the boy sputtered. "Please for-forgive me."

Before Merlin could reply, Arthur stepped forward so the boy could see him and said, "This evil is relentless. Osian stole from *all* of us this day. You are no less its victim." He knelt beside Gethin. "Be at peace that your king has forgiven you."

The boy's lips quivered at Arthur's words; his face reddened, and deep solace poured out through his tears.

Arthur touched the boy's head. "He should be moved to be more comfortable."

Marcus nodded.

"Wait," Merlin interceded. "Elanor might be able to heal him. It is worth it to at least try."

Merlin was about to hurry away when Marcus sullenly stated, "It is too late." Merlin stopped and returned to the boy. "There is no longer a need. He is gone."

Tears were still wet on Gethin's face. His placid, glassy eyes stared up at the sky. His breathing had stilled and his lips parted.

Merlin stared at the boy, and the longer he did, the more he imagined grinding Osian into dust. His mind raced, remembering the young farm boy who tried to attack Elanor. If Osian was able to twist minds like this, how could they know who to trust? The youngest and most innocent were being used against them.

If this was something the enemy was doing—deluding minds—then how would they know who had been corrupted? There had to be something similar between this Gethin and the farm boy that had made them vulnerable.

Osian's Talisman.

The cursed pendant with a power over minds. A milky white stone beneath a bronze crescent moon. It was rumored to have come from the eastern lands. Osian's father was its keeper. His job as druid was to hide it away from evil hands. Osian had wanted it so badly, craving its power. After Osian's father died, his mother kept it hidden. She saw that her son hungered for it. Osian was still a boy when he discovered where it was hidden. He stole it after murdering his own mother.

Merlin always regretted that he hadn't gotten to it first. That he hadn't destroyed it before Osian's lusting hands got ahold of it. The boy, Osian, ran away with the talisman and was never heard of again. At least, not until his darkness started ravaging Prydain.

Merlin's stare pierced the ground as he mused.

I know of Osian, but who is this voice Gethin spoke of? This woman?

Twice now she had been revealed. In Elanor's dreams, and now in the mind of this poor lost boy who seemed only to be in the wrong place at the wrong time. This voice he knew was the more dangerous part of Osian's evil.

Merlin flashed a warning look at Arthur. This was all too familiar. He knew someone once whose words could manipulate the strongest of men, and seduce any weak enough to listen. Dare he say her name out loud? He remembered how her twisted designs manipulated Arthur's mightiest warriors: Llenllaewg's life was stolen, and the life and innocence of Gwalahad nearly compromised.

She...he seethed inside his mind...*is dead.*

FAMILIAR DEVILS

They rode out from Celyddon back toward the caer. Elanor stared warily at the prisoner just ahead of her. He lay unconscious over a saddle, his one arm flopping with the horse's gallop. His hood hung over his head, and she wondered what face might lurk underneath. She dared not look. Seeing the villain's face would make him more real, and she did not want that. The more removed he was from her the better.

Osian's hoods had a way of inflicting fear in her. Just the passing thought of them made her tense up. Their yellow hoods and faces epitomized pain and terror. Twice she had been trapped by these violent and merciless snakes. Both times nearly killed her. In truth, they had scarred her more than her nightmares—even more than the thought of Osian himself. Osian was still immaterial, just a shadow. Whereas these, his footmen, were real. They had inflicted cuts to her skin at the edge of a knife, and death at the tip of their arrows.

She closed her eyes, trying not to think of *his* eyes. The glare of the one who poisoned and beat her. The memory of the light glinting off the tip of his knife before he pressed it to her throat quickened her heart. She remembered his hot stinking breath and grizzled voice. She never forgot how close he knelt to her face, revealing the craters in his cheeks and the sweat on his upper lip. She cringed just recalling it.

Her stomach churned at her anxious thoughts. She gripped the blue pendant that rested on her chest. The feel of it in her palm always brought her comfort. There was a piece of Merlin in it, even if imagined, that consoled her.

She glanced to her side. Merlin peered over at her, and she forced a smile, not wishing him to worry for her. She lowered her hand away from her necklace and swallowed down her distress.

Maybe, if I cannot see the hood, I will feel better.

Elanor clicked her tongue, kicking Brynn's haunches and galloped ahead. She pushed past the villain that riled her nerves. Now that he was out of her sight, she sighed in relief. The sweet brisk air blew across her face, calming her mind. The change of scenery helped. She wanted nothing more than to avoid the site of the vile hood until they arrived back home. They didn't have far to go.

A rider pulled alongside her in her peripheral.

Merlin has come, she hoped.

But when she turned, she found Arthur. She jerked her gaze away and stared ahead, pretending she hadn't seen him.

Not now.

She did not want to speak to him. She had already made a fool of herself the last time she tried. The shame and embarrassment of what happened still clung to her.

What must he think of me?

She lifted her chest, putting on a guise of confidence. Arthur continued to ride alongside for what felt like an eternity. Elanor ignored his presence. She was too afraid to look in his direction or acknowledge him. The thought of speaking to him heated her face. She wouldn't know what to say. Perhaps if he were to speak first? But he remained silent.

Arthur snapped his reins, shouting, "Yah," and charged away.

Elanor exhaled. Her taut shoulders relaxed as she watched Arthur ride ahead. At last, the arduous moment had passed; however, mingled within her relief swirled unsettled disappointment.

Was he going to speak to me, but then changed his mind?

Elanor hadn't helped the situation by refusing to look his way. She turned again to Merlin; his eyes told her he had seen the agonizing moment. She grunted, feeling the sting of the events, well aware it had been her mistake that created the tension in the first place. She regretted it with every fiber of her being.

I should have never spoken to him like that. I should have just kept my mouth shut.

She stared ahead at Arthur's back and pursed her lips.

*Arthur was right about me. Grwyrthrhodd saved the day. Without the unicorn...*she sighed...*I would not have been able to do anything.*

Now, she doubted herself more than ever. The hooded prisoner reminded her of her own inadequacy. She was deficient. When put to the test, she failed. After cutting off that devil's hand, she panicked and dropped her sword. The same way she had every time she practiced.

Would she have been able to defend herself if the hood had charged again? What if Arthur and Bedwyr had not been there? She was powerless. Defenseless. Useless.

She relished the memory of how safe her loft used to be. But that was now gone forever. Her solitary world of not being important to anyone was predictable and secure. Maybe all this time, David's wife Helen had been right. How could she be the daughter of the most renown king and queen of all British history, and yet—

"That is right." A voice spoke inside her head. *"You belong nowhere. You are nothing. You are better at being a shadow!"*

Chapter Nine

The stinging words pierced her, and Elanor gasped. She recognized the sound of that voice. She had conquered that liar before.

I will not listen.

Steeling her resolve, she forced herself to remember who she was. With all her self-pity, she had let that voice back in.

No!

Her heart reignited with grit. She recalled the circle of stones, and the warriors surrounding her that day she struck the wraeth down within her dream.

I will not forget who I am. Arthur may not see it. I am struggling to see it. But I refuse to agree with the voice of a devil. I will not hide myself away. I am not a shadow.

The thud of hooves drew near, and Elanor turned to see Merlin approaching. Relief washed over her. She needed him.

Merlin gathered up beside her. She pulled the reins and slowed her horse's gallop to a walk.

"What is it?" he asked.

She pressed the edges of her mouth together and lifted her chin. "I-I am…I was wrong to have spoken to the king the way I did before you left. Had things turned out different—those might have been the last words I spoke to him."

"Mmm." Merlin smiled. "You know, Arthur is not proud of himself either."

"No, he was right. I had no business coming with you. I just did not like being told so."

"Really?" Merlin huffed. "You say this after rescuing us from certain death?"

"I did not save you—Grwyrthrhodd did. If it had been left up to me alone, I would have been killed along with the rest of you."

Merlin reached for her hand and lifted it to his mouth, giving it a gentle kiss. "Elanor, it was you who obeyed the call to come to our aid. You did not hesitate. None of us are likely to face this enemy alone and come out alive. Were you strengthened by the enaid? *Yes.* But it was through your obedience that the Cymbrogi charged and a village was saved."

"I barely fended off *that man.*" The mention of the hooded prisoner reignited her anxiousness, and she glanced over her shoulder at him.

"Well…none of us gain experience in battle without having ever been in one. And none of us are asking you to be a swordmaster. Only that you gain skill enough to defend yourself. One day you will see the warrior within you. One that does not have to match the strength of others. You are only required to match the strength that you were meant to. I have seen it. It rises in flames above my own at times. You must trust, Elanor."

With a sting of pain in her chest, she admitted, "I am still *so* afraid. Those hoods—they frighten me."

"I was frightened," Merlin confessed. "I was not quick enough to break free, and they poured that *poison*—" His face turned bitter. "All I could think was that I had lost you and Gwendolen. My life was leaving me, and I could not stop it. With all my strength and power as druid *and* warrior—in that moment—it did nothing to save me. I have seldom ever come closer to death. The last time I was faced with my own mortality, the venom of that demon snake twisted through my veins. Your courage saved me then too." He squeezed her hand. "And it was not the unicorn that healed me. It was you. Your treasure…your gift."

"That was also Grwyrthrhodd. It was the gift he gave me that saved you."

"A gift that was meant for you." He shook his head. "Listen, the Great God has given me my gifts, and tells me how to use them. Does that mean I have not played a part? We have a choice whether to say yes, and to make something of the gifts we have been given. Without that choice—that *brave* choice," he said, leaning in close, "the gift's power and authority can never be released."

Elanor dropped her chin, mulling over his words, then lifted her head. "I needed to hear that."

Merlin smiled. "I will *never* let your light go out."

Elanor tilted her head toward Arthur. "Should I apologize to him?"

"Perhaps you should. And *perhaps*," he said with a sigh, "there is more the both of you must do."

"He does not want me as a daughter."

"And there, my soul, is the more you must do. You believe you know his mind, but you do not. And because of that, you have wounded him. You have assumed too little of him. Do you remember how hard it was for me to wrap my mind around the fact that you were Arthur's daughter after that *witch* declared it for all to hear? It made me doubt everything. I struggled not to fall into a pit of my own depraved selfishness." He flashed his eyes toward Arthur. "It made me question *everything.*

"I saw him in your eyes." He paused, fumbling for words, then said, "Forgive me. It was more than my mind could handle, and it took me far too long to remember that it was *not* wrong for me to love you. When the gwyllgi attacked, it slapped me back into reason."

Elanor's mouth gently gaped. She understood. She also had been completely disconcerted when the revelation of being a Pendragon first came.

What must it have been like for Arthur? She had never really considered the weight of the rubble Arthur had to sift through when he woke, discovering he had a daughter and a kingdom to save.

Realizing her own selfishness, she muttered, "I have been only thinking about myself."

"Maybe so, but also have the grace to remember what you have been through. I know how suffocating and small it feels inside of grief."

"I am still responsible for myself."

Merlin added without hesitation, "As is Arthur."

THE KINGS OF PRYDAIN

High-backed chairs in the Palisade had been placed in a circle in preparation for the arrival of Prydain's minor kings. Arthur walked around them, brushing his fingers on the backs of the ornamental, dark wooden seats, etched with whorls and leaves. Between each chair, the tiled floor detailed feats of Arthur's mighty men—depictions of Prydain's history and past, with himself, The Great Bear, at the center of the circle. When he became king, the kings no longer journeyed to Lindonium for a council outside their realms. His rulership changed all that. Each council member understood they were equals seated within the circle of the High King Pendragon.

Many years had passed since the kings were united in one place. Arthur's stomach swirled with angst. Today was the day the council would begin. The kings would be arriving in turn, and Arthur hoped to convince them that the time had come for them to arise, and once again, unite with him as their king.

Arthur didn't know what to expect from the lesser kings. He had been dead. Now alive, what would their reaction be?

Light footsteps shuffled behind him, and Arthur turned to see Gwynevere approaching. She lifted her soft eyes. Her gaze quieted his anxious thoughts.

"I...I have failed these men." Arthur's shoulders drooped along with his despondent eyes. "You they honored in my stead."

Gwynevere said, "And they will honor you now."

Arthur pulled his fingers across his cape of red and gold colors. Doubt of the kings' fealty pressed on him.

Gwynevere reached her delicate fingers to straighten the folds around his shoulder. "Arthur, all of Prydain has been given back the breath that was stolen at your death. By an impossible miracle, we have *all* been given a second chance. This will not have been missed by the kings." She gave a gentle smile and ran her fingertips over his cheek. "These men are your brothers and allies. Save for Lugh and Croighcat. That has never changed. The defiant kings played at giving you sovereignty, but it was never given willingly. You know that. They never esteemed me their queen either, and had Merlin not returned, they may have tried to take it from me.

"While you slept, Thul and Bram kept their distance. Cormach sailed away with no intention of coming back." Her eyes drifted. Arthur saw pain flicker in them and dark memories shadow her countenance. "Cormach returned from Eire only after word came that Merlin still lived. If it were not for Merlin, the kings would have all been lost. There would have no longer been a high ruler of these lands. All would have faded. The people felt it. The land was in great despair.

"The kingdom started coming back to life, not because of me, but because of the druid that first brought them their king. It gave them hope that maybe Prydain could be as it was before—and it was true. The kingdom awoke with Merlin's arrival. Then, they hoped all the more when Elanor appeared in our world. Now, they arise— *alive* once more because their king lives." She shook her head. "You are an indomitable symbol. The people know that because *you live*, Osian is a conquerable threat.

"These kings...*your* Cymry brothers, will not make you pay for the past." She glanced at the unopened doors. "They did not make Merlin pay for his sins, even though he *willingly* chose to abandon us. I almost did not want to forgive him, but"— tears formed in her eyes—"even I could not resist the hope that came with him."

Arthur breathed a frustrated sigh. "I am just as guilty as Merlin. I chose to chase that *blasted*"—he clenched his jaw—"Holy Cup of promise. I abandoned you, and Prydain, for many long seasons. As king, I should have been here. That is what started the cascading storm that broke this kingdom. *My* mistake. *My* failure."

"Those choices only define us if we remain in the shadow of them," Gwynevere encouraged, cupping her hands over his beard. "What you do next will be what creates a fuller portrait of you."

Arthur gazed into her loving eyes. Then he took her hands and folded them into his own. Pulling her closer, he pressed his lips to hers, savoring her warmth. Part of him feared he might wake inside a tomb without her. Who was he without her? Her strength and beauty pulled him through like a torrid gale in the sails of a ship. How could he have ever left her behind for so long, allowing Mordred to rob everything from him?

"I am so sorry." Arthur's cheeks flushed, and his eyes moistened. "Please, forgive me for leaving you."

Gwynevere leaned her forehead against his and whispered, "I would never waste a moment in unforgiveness toward you. Not now that I have you back. Your death drove away any resentment I could have held."

They lingered in the embrace until Arthur said, "I want Elanor to come to the council."

Gwynevere lifted her head in surprise. "Really?"

"I do not know what it is she wants from me, but...I have considered...and I realize that I cannot continue with her the way I have. She is impetuous...but I realize now that my forcefulness has been the cause of some of that." He implored Gwynevere with his eyes. "I can at least acknowledge her as my own, even if she will not receive me in return. I must be true to myself regardless of her choices. She can despise me. Her resistance will no longer have bearing on my actions toward her."

"She does not despise you."

"I have offended her at the very least."

"Yes," Gwynevere chuffed. "That you have done. But I think that will heal. It is only a matter of time and patience. She is…so much like her father. Determined and at times, willful, but she is not impetuous. You have brought out something new in her. It rings of a familiar pride." She glanced at him sideways with a knowing grin. "Elanor is afraid, and so are you. It has not brought out the best in either of you. She feels the pressure to be the king's daughter, whereas before *you*—before me—she had been an orphan."

Arthur nodded, working to accept Gwynevere's words. It reminded him how it was for him as a boy; hidden behind Merlin's hand all those years, until, all at once, the kingship was thrust upon him.

The memory of that moment, the condescending stares from the kings and chieftains, infiltrated his mind as he stared down at Caledfwlch's hilt, bringing it all back.

Merlin forced Arthur to stand before Aurelius's sword. The blade taunted him from the stone. He felt like an impostor even touching it. But Merlin urged him forward with a look. Arthur wrapped his fingers around the hilt. Then he gave a tug and freed it from the stone.

Arthur knew in an instant, with the gleaming sword clutched in his hand, everything had changed.

The ringing metal declared him king. He did not feel ready, but there was no going back.

Gasps rose from the onlookers. Arthur stared wide-eyed at the silver blade. His instinct was to plunge it back in, and hope that the whole event could be forgotten.

Some of the chieftains roared with anger, slinging accusations against Merlin, declaring it had all been trickery.

Merlin shouted back at them, "I am kingmaker in these lands, and as long as the old law of the druids prevails, I will continue to be the one to call forth the rightful king."

This proclamation was met with jeers, rejecting Merlin's justification of the old ways.

Arthur felt like a fraud, clutching the hilt of the sword. It didn't feel like it belonged to him. Only moments ago, he had thought himself an orphan with no claim to anything.

Maybe the kings are right. How could it be that I am the son of Aurelius?

Here Merlin declared Arthur the one true king and heir, all because he delivered a sword from a lifeless stone. The shock raced through his mind. The kings' disputes echoed deep into the recesses of his identity. He was only in his seventeenth year, and far too inexperienced to be considered a king.

Do I even want to be king?

He always believed there was something important he was meant to be. Doted on his whole life by the highest of all druids. So, was this it? Was this the thing of importance?

"He will have to prove himself!" King Lot of Orcades protested above the din of voices.

"Yes," Merlin interjected, silencing the debate. "He *will* prove himself. So that you all may see and have no doubt."

Prove myself?

Arthur's heart pounded as he glanced agape at Merlin, who he felt had just betrayed him.

How can I prove myself when I do not believe it myself?

He felt small and insignificant—set up for a trial he was not prepared for.

Merlin announced to them all, "He will become Prydain's High Battle Chieftain, as Uther was when Aurelius was king. He will deliver us all from the Saecsans that plague our lands."

What?

Arthur's jaw slackened even further at Merlin's impossible announcement. He had become a skilled warrior, rising above his peers, but this—

King Croighcat of the Western Coast attested, "Not even Uther could do that, and he was the best of us."

Merlin lifted Arthur's hand with the sword still nestled in his palm. The tip pointed to the heavens. "You will send your men and resources to back him. When you see how he has leveled our enemies to dust, you will throw your weapons before him, press your cheek to his feet, and declare him your king."

Arthur's world spun as he stared at the faces before him. Some looked back at him with hope. Others grinned with the surety of his destruction.

What has Merlin done to me?

Clang!

The reverberation of a sword hitting the ground shook Arthur out of his panicked reverie. He peered at the sword that now lay at his feet, and then suddenly, Bedwyr's voice rose above the clamor.

"I will follow you, my High Battle Chieftain, and honor you as my king until it is declared by us all." Bedwyr knelt before him with a smile of support and faith.

Then another sword struck the ground, and this time it was Cai who professed, "I, too, will give my fealty. You are my High Battle Chieftain, and my king."

King Ector jubilantly shouted in praise, clapping his hands with hope brimming from his round cheeks.

Croighcat rolled his eyes and growled, "*Children.*"

However, the sight of Arthur's friends in league with him unlocked a glimmer of something deep within him, something new and profound. Maybe they saw what he could not. Maybe they had seen a quality that had remained hidden until now.

Bedwyr rose and clapped Arthur's shoulder. "I will follow you anywhere, my brother."

The memory faded, and the Palisade doors groaned open, snapping Arthur back to the present.

A manservant entered, bowing. "My King—three kings have arrived. They are being refreshed in the Great Hall while I come to you." The servant straightened, lifting his arm to his chest, a jubilant smile on his face. "King Thul of Celyddon has arrived with his son Thanul, also the southern King Cormach of Dyved, and then the young King Bram of Caer Edyn has come with three of his Cymbrogi."

Arthur sighed, girding himself up. "Prepare the welcome cup and have it brought here. Once the kings have refreshed themselves, bring them here to the council. Let Peredur and Bedwyr know that the time has come."

The servant bowed, quickly disappearing behind the doors as they shut.

Gwynevere bobbed with anxious excitement. "It begins." She turned to leave, then peered back. "I shall return with our daughter on my arm."

Elanor swallowed, squeezing Gwynevere's arm a little harder. Together they descended the stairs to the Palisade's main hall. She felt encouraged that Arthur had requested her presence at the council, though they had not spoken a single word since the event in the forest, leaving nothing resolved between them.

Her heart fluttered when she noticed Merlin and Arthur jovially bantering with Bedwyr and Peredur; anticipation brimmed in their voices.

Elanor was also eager for the kings' arrival. She adored both Thul and Bram, and had heard such wonderful adulations of Cormach. The devious pair of kings, Croighcat and Lugh, further piqued her curiosity. She wondered if they would come.

Merlin had told her earlier that he was doubtful Lugh would come. He explained, "What I witnessed in Llyonesse was a deranged man who cares for *nothing*. Though, if Lugh knows what is good for him, he will not risk the possible consequences of declining the High King's summons. With Arthur returned, he would be a fool to take that chance."

This was a different council then Elanor had ever been to. In past councils, she had been more an observer, but that was not how Arthur held his meetings. Everyone within the circle was granted the privilege to speak. Was that Arthur's expectation of her? She would keep her mouth shut unless called upon. What could she have to say of any value amongst kings?

A nervous sweat moistened her neck the closer they drew to the gathering. Arthur peered their way, and she instantly sought the floor, not ready to meet his gaze. His expectations—she would see them in his eyes and was sure she had already fallen short.

Sometimes she wished her magic didn't make it so easy for her to see within others' minds. It was too tempting to look. Every time she did, she saw things she wished she hadn't. Her gift only allowed her to see in part, never discerning the whole picture. Then it became hard not to fill in the gaps with her own insecurities.

She dared a glance up and saw Merlin's eyes beaming at her with pleasure; immediately comforted, she grinned back at him.

"Now…you will sit here," Gwynevere said, guiding her to her place. "I will be at the king's left hand, with you beside me. Merlin will be at his right, with Bedwyr, and then Peredur."

Elanor frowned at the large ring of chairs. "Why are there so many seats? Surely, there are only the few kings to fill them."

"Many will remain empty. In this way, we honor the men who occupied them in past times. Gwalahad, Bors, Ector and Cai. Then also, Gwain and Llenllaewg." Gwynevere's eyes flickered with sadness at the mention of Llenllaewg. Elanor had never heard his name before.

"Who was Llenllaewg?"

"He—" Gwynevere started, then stopped. "Perhaps, I will tell you of him another day."

Elanor nodded, resisting the lure to look deeper into Gwynevere's eyes for answers.

Bedwyr approached her with his hand extended. She lifted her hand, and he caressed it with a gentle kiss.

"A pivotal day, the king's council." Bedwyr subtly grinned.

"Not really sure what I am doing at one," Elanor admitted.

"Ai, my lady—you must know you belong. No one here would ever doubt as you do. None of us have forgotten the queen's gift." He pointed to the torc around her neck.

Oh yes.

She had forgotten what the silver ring around her neck symbolized to the Cymry people. She looked at Gwynevere's torc, and then to Merlin's. Bedwyr and Peredur bore them also. She was part of this club of nobility but had struggled to see herself as one among them.

She ventured a glance at Arthur's. His golden torc was broad and golden. It twisted like a golden rope, with the mouths of two dragons meeting at the center of his throat.

The rattling of the Palisade doors silenced the voices in the hall. They croaked open, revealing three kings. Thul entered in his usual Cymry regalia. A war commander at the ready, his shoulders wrapped in the gold and blue colors of Celyddon. His white-yellow beard, woven into three gold-beaded braids, rested on his dotted leather breastplate.

Bram, the youngest of the kings, followed with his umber eyes sparkling and vigilant. He had not changed since Elanor had last seen him. Still, he was the Cymbrogi soldier who had become king. Elanor esteemed him ever higher for his humility to remain as he always had. At his waist, alongside his sword, was the ornate, golden dagger that Arthur had given him as part of the spoils of victory. It stood out from all the gray and brown that outfitted his attire. His only colors were in his cape of burnt orange and green.

Then Elanor's eyes settled on the new king.

This must be Cormach.

He was tall and broad shouldered, donning a neatly trimmed copper beard, which highlighted his proud green eyes. His fiery hair was just long enough to brush the shoulders of his neatly tailored cape. The leather wrapping his chest and arms shone like new.

Cormach's countenance shifted the instant he saw Arthur. Disbelieving tears filled his bottom lids. He bowed to his knee, folding his head into his arms. In an act of mourning, he pulled his cape of deep red and blue onto the floor in front of him. Cormach's shoulders shook with surging sobs. The other kings followed his example and lowered to their knees.

"My king," Cormach groaned, "I left these lands thinking you were dead. I left Dyved vulnerable. Forgive me."

Thul, particularly misty-eyed, murmured through a broken, grisled voice, "Great Pendragon, I scarcely believed the word of your return to be true, but to see you with my own eyes…I—how can this be? The rumors of your estrangement or captivity are untrue. I saw you buried. Your lifeless, pallid frame was carried into the tomb at the Hill of the Kings. Your cairn and stone erected where I stood."

Cormach looked up from the floor, his cheeks flushed from his tears.

"Please excuse our doubt, my king," came Bram's humble response. He lifted his head and peered at Arthur, revealing a red scar from his chin down his throat. Elanor had never noticed it before. "Some have wondered whether we are being deceived."

Arthur raised his hands, waving assuredly. He bit his bottom lip and slowly approached them.

The kings marveled in astonishment as Arthur knelt before them.

"I…" Arthur paused, then grabbed Cormach's cape of colors from the floor and pressed them back against Cormach's chest. "Do not mourn, my brother. Not for me."

Arthur's actions softened Cormach's brow and lifted the corners of his mouth.

"I have much to explain…I assure you, this is not a trick, nor have I been deliberately estranging myself from my kingdom." He turned to Thul. "I had died, or at least that is what the cursed enchantment led us all to believe."

Awestruck, Thul whispered, "Enchantment?"

"There is much to reveal, but I must wait. I want all the kings to be present when

I tell the tale. But know it would be better for most to assume the rumors true. It would be too much for my people to know the truth. But you are my fellow kings, and should know all that has transpired to bring me here. Merlin and"—he inhaled sharply—"and Elanor will confirm it all to be true."

Elanor sat up straighter in her seat, hid her jittery fingers in the folds of her dress, and then nodded to the kings.

"It is all true," Merlin said, approaching Cormach, and lifting him from the floor. "I am happy to see you, my friend." He shook Cormach by his shoulders with a sober smile. "The land has been broken without you, but time…is about to be redeemed."

Cormach smiled, firmly grasping Merlin's arms.

"We are, all of us, together once more," Merlin said.

Arthur stood, wiping fallen tears from his cheeks, then glanced down at Bram and offered his hand. Bram rose like a warrior affirmed by his commander.

Honor gleamed in Bram's eyes, reminding Elanor of the day she first saw him— when he stood before the queen and her court, humbly offering her his most prized possession as a symbol of fealty. Elanor had listened, enraptured, as he told the story of Arthur giving him the jeweled dagger as a spoil of war. When Gwynevere returned it to Bram, he had grasped it tightly as if reclaiming a lost treasure.

"I remember you," Arthur said with sadness in his eyes. "Your kin, Ector and Cai, would be proud. You have honored them by becoming Caer Edyn's king. I welcome you into the fold."

Bram gave a quick nod, then pounded his fist to his chest and bowed.

Thul burst into laughter, as if the revelation of Arthur's return had just hit him. He unabashedly leapt at Arthur, wrapping his arms around him and lifting his feet off the floor. "The king lives!" His shout caused everyone else to join in his celebrative laughter. The sound of their joy was like thirsty men, drinking long draughts of deliverance.

"Bring the welcome cup!" Arthur commanded.

A servant swiftly complied, and the cup passed from hand to hand, all drinking in merriment. The years of grief dissolved from their countenances with each sip of the golden brew. Elanor breathed in the joyous reunion, watching everyone's spirits soar, unburdened at last.

11

THE DUPLICITOUS PAIR

"When will we begin?" Thul asked, looking up from the cup and wiping the froth from his beard. "Do not tell me we are delaying to wait for those other two braggarts that call themselves kings."

Arthur nodded, then motioned to their seats. "They are part of this fellowship. We must at least give them a chance to represent their lands. We must also discuss matters that affect all of Prydain—which includes them."

Thul smirked, shaking his head with disdain. "Croighcat does not consider himself belonging to Prydain. He believes he governs lands untouched by the rest of us. Whereas Lugh has lost his mind."

Arthur narrowed his eyes. "Then it would be wise of them to come to this council and prove themselves otherwise."

"Ai! Ai!" the council echoed in agreement.

The servant returned before the king and bowed.

"Yes?" Arthur inquired.

The servant leaned in close and whispered in Arthur's ear.

Croighcat!

Arthur closed his eyes and sighed. Though the kings of the Southlands needed to be part of the council, he loathed dealing with them.

"Bring him in," Arthur announced, glaring at the doors.

The servant ran to open them.

Daylight shone through, revealing the silhouette of the tall, gangly figure. Arthur leaned forward, knowing how contentious this king could be. He gripped the arms of his chair and clenched his jaw.

Croighcat entered slowly, the pointed metal on the tips of his boots tapping the floor at each step. The gaunt king wore a solid purple cape—no Cymry colors adorned his shoulders.

The lack of honor. But of course I expected nothing less.

Arthur scowled at Croighcat's haughty, wrinkled face. His short, white hair was feathered back to a point over his shining bald scalp. The king's steely gray eyes loomed large above his high cheekbones, pointed nose, and thin pursed lips. Never had Arthur known of another man, in all of Prydain, so proud to reject their Cymry ways. His austere demeanor was more like a roman ruler than a king of Prydain.

Croighcat stood with one hand on his hip, and the other lifted as though balancing a goblet. He wore iron plates of armor instead of leather across his chest, arms, and shins.

Arthur cleared his throat, rose, and commanded, "The cup."

Quickly, the servant placed it into the waiting hands of the southern king.

"Croighcat…" Arthur began. "You are welcome. I am glad to see you have come." Arthur swallowed down his dishonest comment.

Croighcat curled his lip at the bowl, then, rolling his eyes, he snatched it from the servant's hands. He leered over at the servant who stood waiting, then took a sip, scrunching his nose as though the ale were repugnant. He thrust the cup back into the servant's hands, and then delicately dabbed his mouth free of the liquid.

He cleared his throat, lifted his upper lip to reveal a row of crooked teeth, and said, "Am I to believe that we are not just being fooled?" His eyelids narrowed into slits as he glared at Arthur. "I am wise enough not to refuse my presence at this council, but I want proof that we are not being *lied* to."

Arthur held back his disgust and retorted, "Still the same as you have always been."

Croighcat leaned forward with accusation in his irreverent stare. "What would you know of it, *deluder?*"

Arthur barely shifted in his chair at Croighcat's brazen dishonor. With steel in his voice, he replied, "I am the one who slew your son, Cenwael, after he betrayed me to the Saecsans. You swore me your fealty so I would not do the same to you."

Croighcat's eyes widened at the pronouncement. "Bah," he spat. "Suppose it is you. I will need more to go on than that."

Arthur sighed. "I will be happy to explain, and then you can decide if I am false."

Croighcat folded his arms, thumping his spindly fingers one at a time over his forearms. He slithered to a seat next to Bram, then turned a sly smile toward Elanor. "It is amazing the *liars* that have slipped through in your absence, Arthur."

Croighcat's accusing eyes cemented on Elanor. Her cheeks flushed pink, and her eyes widened.

How dare he accuse her.

Arthur's anger flared, and he bolted to his feet. "Careful, Croighcat. You know very little of what you speak. Wisdom would be to keep your mouth *shut* before I rob you of your tongue."

With a dismal sneer, Croighcat leaned back into his chair, pressing his lips into a pout.

Thul, who seemed to be enjoying the fiery escapades, chimed in, "To be sure, Croighcat, you accuse so many of us of being liars, when you and Lugh have been the deceivers, in league for years. Pretentiously, you bow to the throne of the Pendragon, while working to usurp it."

"That is old dribble," Croighcat retorted. "My domain has flourished. And that weasel, Lugh, has been nothing but a thorn in my heel. If it were up to me, I would destroy him myself." His eyes flashed, and he clutched his fingers into a boney fist.

"This is strange news," Cormach said. His bright green eyes leered toward the king of the southwestern coast. "You and Lugh have always been at each other's confidence. My domain is in the Southlands too, do not forget. I have had my eyes and ears to the ground concerning you."

"You know *nothing*," Croighcat snapped. "Your eyes and ears have all but lately been as absent as Merlin's and Arthur's. You could *not know* how my dealings have changed with Lugh."

"Please," Arthur grumbled, "enlighten us."

Croighcat let out a long condescending sigh. "My kingdom thrives on the routes of trade ships. I have always relied on Lindonium's eastern ships, in cooperation with my own, for our gold and iron. I like the fine things these trades supply me with." He shot a scowl at Cormach, then hissed, "Lugh's wily and barbaric manner has disrupted my gains. I put up with it when it benefited me, but now it infects my lands with *poison*. My warriors have been battling with Llyonesse, but we have gotten nowhere. That was until everything went silent from the *insipid king*."

"How did Lugh affect your trades?" Arthur pressed.

"Well…his dealings with devils started to infect my posts. Many of my warriors have gone missing, and five of my ships were stolen."

Arthur raised his eyebrow. "Lugh did this?"

Croighcat growled darkly, "Yes. I am unafraid to charge him. He is part of it." He glanced across the circle. "I may not have always been the most trustworthy, but I would never do dealings with the *dark ones*. They are ruinous. My coin is far too important to throw away on the likes of destructive foes."

"Dark ones? Who do you mean?" Arthur asked.

"Yes, dark ones. The sorcerer's hooded fiends. Defiled scratchings appear on the posts of my trade markers. We remove them, but then I find more cursing my routes."

Arthur looked to Merlin. "Dark marks?"

Merlin rubbed his fingers over his lips. "These marks have appeared in places and on objects associated with the enemy."

"Tell me wh—" Arthur halted, seeing his servant once again returned at the doorway. His face was tentative and agitated. "It appears as though our final guest has arrived."

Gasps erupted from the council. The question of whether King Lugh would come had been answered.

Elanor sat up, keen. She had always wondered what this disreputable king looked like. She glanced over at Merlin, who fixated on the doors. The servant pulled the doors open, and in limped the disheveled king.

He appeared just how Elanor thought he would—unkempt with stringy black hair. Lugh wore no colors at all but was wrapped in a cloak of gray fur, bound in front by a silver chain, making him appear every inch a wolf. He had none of the traditional pieces the rest wore.

Lugh slunk forward with an arrogant smile as though relieving everyone with his presence. "My king, Arthur…h-h-how happy I am to see you are alive and well."

Elanor took notice of a nervous twitch on Lugh's sweating lip.

"I am aware of my tardiness, and I ask your forgiveness." He bowed, then grinned back up with his greasy teeth.

"What has happened to you?" Croighcat said, eyeing Lugh with unmasked disgust. "Have you forgotten how to bathe?"

Lugh's eyes narrowed, but the smile remained eerily plastered to his face. Arthur did not rise, nor did he offer him a cup, but opened his hand to direct Lugh to one of the empty seats.

"Thank you, Lord Pendragon," he almost sang.

All watched while the king made his way over to a seat further away from Croighcat, but leaving a space between himself and Cormach. Cormach lifted his hand to his nose, shooting the bedraggled king an offended glare.

Arthur stood to address them, rubbing his hand down his chest and straightening his stance. "Now that you are all here, I will explain everything, and answer your questions. Though, we also must discuss Osian"—Arthur peered at Lugh, who shuffled in his seat at the mention of the sorcerer's name—"and what I have planned. We are at war…and a war that must look different than any other we have ever waged. But wage we must, for our lands will not be further *desecrated*."

The kings mumbled in unison—their fierce eyes lighting at the mention of war.

"But first, I will have Merlin explain." Arthur exhaled, motioned toward Merlin, and sat back down.

Merlin began, "There were two stars that lit the sky. Out of the phenomenon came a prophecy that there would come a *great three* that would destroy the darkness, and establish the Kingdom of the Sun: The Pendragon and the two stars. The two stars were named Emrys and Gwenddydd. Emrys is my name, and the other is Elanor's."

"She is the queen's kin?" Bram asked, his eagerness like that of a battle-ready soldier.

Merlin peered at Elanor, then continued, "It is true she is of the queen's blood."

Elanor had never considered how Gwynevere's concocted story, giving explanation of her, had actually turned out to be true.

"But many of the druids of the New Way believed this prophecy to have failed at the death of Arthur, because the original prophecy included him as part of the three.

"Though, Elanor's coming to Prydain sparked hope that the prophecy of the two stars might still endure. Despite the death of the king, the Great God's promise may not have failed. However, there was more." Merlin paused. "There came another prophecy. One discerned by the druids of the old religion. We captured one of Osian's witches in a plan to murder Elanor. As she writhed in my hands"—Merlin cringed, clearly remembering it—"she confessed that she must stop the prophecy of *the three* from coming to pass. For you see, the dark druids had also seen the two stars that passed through the sky. Their prophecy revealed that the two stars would break *the curse* and resurrect the Great Pendragon, destroying the old ways."

Thul had been stroking his long beard, but then his aged face slackened, and he dropped his hand. "A curse?"

Merlin nodded. "The enemy did not want us discovering the curse, nor that we had the power to break it."

"What was the curse?" Bram fired first.

"When did this happen?"

"But he was dead?"

Merlin lifted his hands to still the voices. "Not dead…but poisoned."

Gasps erupted from all but Lugh, who leaned back in his chair, twisting his lips.

"Mordred tipped his blade with a poison laced in dark sorcery." Merlin growled as he said it. "Once it infiltrated Arthur's blood, it made him sleep as though dead. We, too, wondered at the truth of the witch's confessions. It was far too *incredible* to be believed. But we also could not leave to chance that it was true and ignored it."

Elanor noticed how decidedly Merlin diverged from the details of the magic of time, and of her being a Pendragon.

They wouldn't understand. The explanation would be too inconceivable.

"When Elanor went missing—" Merlin dropped his head.

"How was she found? What happened to her?" Thul wanted to know.

Cormach's ginger brows pressed together, and he growled, "Was it Osian?"

Merlin glanced at Arthur, who nodded for him to continue. "I will only tell you that it was when I found her, that we were able to discover how to wake Arthur. The witch had spoken true. The king was only spelled into a deep slumber. A curse that we broke at great cost."

Her father David walking toward the cyhyraeth flashed in Elanor's mind, quickening her breath. She tried to force the trauma from her mind. She remembered Merlin holding her back, and her flailing arms reaching for David. "No! Father!" The echoes of her own cry reverberated through her soul.

A mumbling voice snapped Elanor out of her thoughts.

"She is the *witch* that has deceived you all." All eyes turned to Lugh, whose shaking finger pointed at Elanor. "She should have died. An arrow pierced through her chest, and yet she lives. *Sorcery!*" he spat. "She is the *curse*. She is the *blue temptress* that has twisted Merlin's mind, and creates this illusion of Arthur before you."

Arthur and Gwynevere both rose at the accusation.

"Look." Lugh jumped from his seat, as though the king and queen's reaction was evidence of her evil. "This *she-demon* has bewitched herself to the highest place beside the queen, making all who lay eyes on her—*love her.*"

Elanor stared in horror at all the eyes glancing her way. She wanted to defend herself, but shock stole her words.

"SIT DOWN, YOU WORM!" Arthur's voice boomed, breaking off the vile spell Lugh's words were attempting to spin. Lugh stumbled back into his chair, raising his arms above his head as though Arthur was about to strike him.

The wary eyes of the kings remained fixed on Elanor. They doubted her innocence. Gwynevere returned to her seat and grasped Elanor's hand, but nothing calmed her. She frantically searched for a way out. The ground felt like it was crumbling beneath her.

Merlin stepped toward Lugh and snapped, "I know who you are, Lugh. I came to your kingdom and saw how you have abused your people." He shifted toward the kings. "He lets his lands and peoples burn, and does not lift a finger to help them. He calls it all lies, when evidence of their murder is presented. Llyonesse sits empty and void of life. Its people hide behind the slats of their homes. I have seen it with my own eyes. Thul knows. His forest became home to refugees who fled the Southlands. Their southern village was burnt, and they sought Lugh's help. He turned them away. Women and children journeyed to the north for help, starving and weak."

"Lies!" Lugh crowed, like a coward still hiding beneath his arms.

"Do not listen to this *craven*. Every single one of you knows his drought of integrity. To take his word will only make you a fool." Merlin shifted his gaze to Croighcat. "Even you cannot deny it. You yourself have separated yourself because of his madness."

"*Madness?*" Lugh protested. "How dare you attack me with more falsehood."

The council was becoming a boiling pot—the tension pressing down on Elanor. *I must do something to stop Lugh's lies.*

Suddenly, something occurred to her. Just as she had done with the witch, she could do now. All would see. They would know Lugh was a spurious liar if she made him confess. Slowly, she rose from her chair. All eyes watched.

She locked eyes with Lugh.

He lifted his chin at her as if he had the upper hand. Her magic kindled, and she hated what she saw in him. His insanity swirled like a devouring plague. Through her magic, she spoke in a low, echoing vibrato, "Tell us the truth, King Lugh, Lord of Llyonesse."

Lugh sucked in his breath. "The *witch*—she uses her power."

"You will tell us the *truth*," her ethereal voice commanded.

"Y-y-yes. I w-will tell you the truth. I…" He paused, panting like a frightened dog in the corner. "I came here as a servant of Lord Osian. He is the one who will be ruler of these lands, after he has drenched them in blood and fire. Th-there is not hope for any of you. His power is greater than you know. He…he will raise the demons of the earth to devour you. I care nothing for your hope and light. It-it is *disgusting*. This mighty Pendragon never deserved the throne. Merlin manipulated you to fall at his feet." Glancing up from underneath his eyelids, he declared, "It should have *never* been. The New Way will be shut out *FOREVER!*"

"Cymbrogi!" Arthur yelled, and quickly the guards, who were just outside, sprinted in. "Seize him." Arthur pointed at Lugh, and the guards leapt upon him.

They seized Lugh's arms. He bellowed like a screeching owl.

"Take him to the cells in the guardhouse."

Bedwyr aided in dragging Lugh back, while the fallen king kicked and screamed. The kings stood aghast, watching him tussle.

"You have no right to do this, *Pendragon!*" Lugh yelled the name of the high king like it was an insult. They pulled him from the council, and his heels scraped upon the floor.

His voice diminished as Bedwyr shut the doors behind them. He returned to the council of kings, who were now up on their feet, boisterously hurling questions one after the other like a throng of barking dogs.

Amidst the chaos, Merlin grabbed Elanor's arm and hissed between his teeth, "You should not have done that."

Elanor stared up at him, bewildered. Why was he angry?

Have I done something wrong?

Quickly, she glanced at the faces within the circle. Were they also offended?

"She has magic?" one of the kings questioned.

Elanor searched for who had said it, then shifted her gaze to Arthur and mouthed, "I am so sorry." She sank back into her seat, realizing she had made another damning mistake.

Arthur pressed his lips together, his eyes brimming with compassion toward her. He quickly adjusted his attention back to the council.

"My brothers!" The conversations settled, and the kings gave Arthur their attention. "You see me as I am before you. You touched my hands and looked in my eyes. If you think I am an illusion, if you think I am *false*, then I will not stop you from doing what you must. You chose to make me king after I led you in victory over the Saecsans, and it will be *you* who shall choose whether I am to be your king now. I have never forced you to receive my kingship, and I never will. As hard as some of this may be to swallow, it is the utmost truth. I place my High Kingship into your hands once again. I will not take what has not been given."

First Thul, then Bram and Cormach after him, unsheathed their swords and laid them on the tiled floor.

"I am in no doubt," King Thul declared, "you are my king. Though, I do not know what to make of this—that young woman beside you is Merlin's wife. She and Merlin have only ever done what is just and right. Merlin is our High Druid, and has been our ally throughout the ages. He is no deceiver—he is my friend. I do not believe Lugh. His words have always been steeped in lies."

With hesitation, Croighcat joined his sword with the others. "I believe you are Arthur. Reluctantly, I have followed you, but my old age has taught me I prefer my wealth over the lordship of Prydain; there is no better High King."

Arthur breathed a sigh of relief, then said, "If this be so, that you take me as your king, then I have one more impossible thing to set before you." He grasped Elanor's hand and pulled her to his side. "Look at her. Discern her features and then peer at my own. Once you have done so, rest your eyes upon the queen. See how their mouths and frames are the same. You say they are sisters, but this is not the truth. Elanor is not her cousin or of the queen's people."

The kings scrunched their faces, leaning in, clearly confused by what Arthur was aiming to reveal. Then it happened. A gasp. It was, surprisingly, Croighcat who caught it first.

"My king," he said. "Are we to believe that your *daughter* is a sorceress?"

"Daughter?" came a surprised reply from Cormach. He raked his fingers through his red hair.

Their eyes widened, glancing at Elanor. Heat spread up her neck and into her cheeks. Thul gawked in unbelief as he rose from his seat. She witnessed the switch in his eyes, the veil lifting where he clearly saw her for who she was.

"How can this be?" Thul asked, aghast.

Merlin stepped forward. "It is the truth. Elanor is Pendragon. And she does have magic. Magic like mine that honors the Great God and follows the path of the New Way. She is not a *witch*, nor does she use dark magic." His eyes met Elanor's with a sting of warning.

Dark magic?

No one had ever accused her of dark magic before. Peredur had his suspicions at the beginning, but not since then. What had she done?

"How she has come to us as she is," Merlin continued, "would be hard to explain."

"She is my daughter," Arthur said with finality, squeezing her hand more tightly.

The fact that he said *"daughter"* made Elanor flush, and a tear dared to leak from the corners of her eyes.

"She is Pendragon. Much strange magic has been involved in bringing her here, and myself back from death, giving us this second chance to rule over our enemies." Arthur nodded to Gwynevere, who proudly smiled in return. "This magic has not come from the old ways or dark religions. This magic is of the Great God, whose purposes have always been before us. His hand is upon us. Elanor carries the promise of the Kingdom of the Sun. The song is within her, within Merlin, and is also within me. We are the promise foretold in the prophecy, destined to end the darkness threatening to destroy Prydain. And it is because of this promise that I refuse to delay my command to crush Osian before he can inflict any further death and destruction on our lands."

The council sat in awestruck silence, each member clearly grappling with the fullness of this revelation.

Then, like a faithful warrior, Bram boldly stood, raising his fist to his chest. "What is the plan, my king?"

All heads turned and gaped at Arthur with bated breath.

Arthur took a seat and leaned his arms onto his thighs. "We have captured one of Osian's hooded mongrels. He is imprisoned in the guardhouse. Now that it is a certainty Lugh has also betrayed us, we have him as a source. Before we can storm the enemy, we must know more. I plan to squeeze what I can from these men, pressing them down until we get what we need. We must know where to find Osian, and any hidden designs the enemy may have for us. Since he hides, he has not been easy to defeat. But he cannot remain hidden, now that the true king of these lands has returned."

THE WRONG KIND OF MAGIC

Elanor panned the faces in the council, watching as Arthur's announcement was met with grunts and nods of agreement.

"Osian has already been allowed too much reach," Thul added bitterly. The lines between his eyes deepened. "Too much destruction. A village within my own lands was recently attacked by his assassins."

"What?" Cormach's brow lifted.

Merlin nodded. "Arthur and I were there. That is where we captured one of Osian's hoods."

"We cannot underestimate them." Arthur fingers were pressed white against the armrests of his chair. "Merlin and I were almost lost if it were not for—" He halted, shifting his gaze to Elanor. "If it were not for Elanor's action."

Again, all eyes lit on Elanor. She squeezed the folds of her dress. The attention, an uncomfortable pressure, turned her stomach.

Arthur leaned back in his seat with a taut brow. But then the tension melted away as if he'd jogged an idea loose, and he sat up. "Your magic." He pointed to Elanor with a gleam of hope in his eyes. "You could make our prisoners speak. You could use the same truth telling magic to get what we need from them."

"No!" Merlin stood, swiping his hand as if brushing Elanor away. "She does not understand this magic. This is not magic used by druids of the New Way. She has used this magic in *error*. This…this is why Croighcat and the others were confused by it. Think, Arthur."

Elanor sank further into her chair. She didn't know she had used a *wrong* kind of magic. Her mind raced. How could she have known? What had made it wrong?

Gwynevere's fingers reached for Elanor's sleeve—her eyes peeled on Arthur.

Arthur appeared undaunted. "But she has *you* to guide her. This would be to our aid."

"It is too dangerous. Just because it is accessible and easy does not mean we use it. It ought not be messed with." Merlin's voice growled with warning. "*Dark magic* has a cost."

Arthur panned his eyes around the circle. "Let the other kings tell us what they think."

Merlin bit back, "This cannot be up for debate."

"Are you telling me," Arthur countered, "that you have *never* used old magic when helping us against our enemies? Never in the past have you dabbled with what you did not fully understand?"

"I have, but that does not mean I *should* have. There were times it was a mistake."

Croighcat scoffed, "Was it *truly* a mistake, Merlin? Truly? I recall our armies having the upper hand because of your power."

"You are *not* a druid, Croighcat. You cannot be the judge. I have changed. My ways are not the same as they used to be."

Croighcat lifted his brow. "Are you saying that you regret using your magic to fool our enemy? What about when you blinded the Saecsan invaders from seeing or hearing us, enabling us to sabotage their camps. What was the cost of your magic then? Did it not save many lives? Weren't those lives worth the magic?"

Merlin grunted in frustration. "I hardly think you would know the difference between magic that is *just*, versus magic that steals."

"What is the difference, then?" Cormach asked.

Merlin narrowed his eyes. With an irritated drawl, he said, "Magic that controls, manipulates, or distorts is untrustworthy. Good magic gives life, hope, and reveals truth. It is not guided by our own desires, but by that of the Great God's. In that way, it cannot be self-serving. That is the guide post."

The longer their debate persisted, the more uncomfortable Elanor felt. If what Merlin said was true, then she had unknowingly done the wrong kind of magic when she made the witch confess.

Why didn't he tell me then that it was dark magic?

She had done it reflexively. She just reacted. There had been no forethought. She had never even known she could do that sort of magic, until it happened. It never occurred to her to use that form of magic again until now. She hated how Merlin was making her feel, revealing her mistake so firmly in front of the kings. The urge to run from the council hounded her thoughts. She tried to pull her hand back, but Gwynevere held it tight. Her fiery eyes locked on Elanor; they burned with eagerness to defend her.

"I-I did not know," Elanor whispered for only Gwynevere to hear, yet it stole everyone's attention. She swallowed and said it again a little louder, "I did not know I had used a wrong magic."

"It was innocently done," Merlin said with a forced smile.

"What was the cost of her using the magic just now, Merlin?" Croighcat pressed again. "Has anything but good come from it? The enemy was revealed. It has hurt no one."

"I do not disagree," Thul grumbled in his throaty voice. He shook his head, his bearded chin clutched in his hand.

Elanor, feeling a little vindicated from their response, looked at Merlin and spouted, "You used the shade magic. Is that not old magic?"

Merlin gave an exasperated sigh. His eyes flared with condescension that made her insides boil.

"What was the cost of *your* lapse of magic?" she snapped.

"What is the shade?" Thul inquired, turning to Arthur as though he might know.

"I—" Merlin paused. He looked stunned by Elanor's charged rebuttal. "I have experience in these sorts of magical practices. Years of wisdom. This magic is not to be messed with by those who are *unpracticed*."

Resentment smoldered in Elanor's chest like a slow-burning ember. She wanted to lash out but knew better than to put herself on display like she had with Arthur. Quietly, she clutched the arms of her chair and took a slow deep breath.

Croighcat smirked, appearing to enjoy the pressure his questions placed on the council, and more particularly, Merlin. He asked, "Are you saying you do no *trust* your wife?"

"I am saying," Merlin snarled, glaring at Croighcat, "that it is not to be messed with."

"Merlin," Arthur said, "I think this may be a moment where both your wisdom, and Elanor's gift, may be required. Could you not guide her? She was quite capable in the forest in using her magic."

Again, Arthur's acknowledgement lifted Elanor's spirit. He had hardly said one word to her—she never knew what he thought about what she had done. A desire to prove herself roused.

Arthur went on, "Why can we not trust that this could work in our favor? We have had little to no answers of Osian, and now we have this chance to gain as much knowledge as we need before sending our Cymbrogi to battle."

"Listen," Merlin countered, taking a deep breath. "When I used the shade, it was never against a dark sorcerer. When old magic meets dark magic, it invites the unexpected. The dark is only expelled by the light of a spiritual flame, not more darkness."

"Elanor has no edge of darkness in her," Gwynevere said in defense, to Elanor's relieved surprise. "She is ever only a purveyor of light."

Merlin's shoulders drooped. "Of course, she is—" He kept his eyes from meeting Elanor's questioning gaze.

She felt hardness and fear emanating from him. It was as if, without warning, Merlin had lost his belief in her, while Arthur had gained it. How had the tables turned so abruptly?

"What say you?" Arthur turned to the other kings.

"I say," said Thul carefully, "that we are in times where difficult decisions must be made. Let us all go down and see the traitors. Merlin, you can protect her. Elanor *must* do this."

Merlin hissed, "*Must?*"

Then Cormach responded, "I, too, believe it is worth it to try."

Merlin gritted his teeth and dropped his head.

"It is hard to know what is right," Bram said thoughtfully, his jaw muscles twitching. "We have something we *can* do. It seems unwise to not use it to our advantage."

Even Gwynevere nodded to Arthur in agreement.

But Peredur shook his head and grumbled, "We should listen to Merlin."

Merlin lifted his head.

"Rarely has Merlin's warning gone without warrant. To use this magic would be"—he pulled his mouth tight—"a risk not worth taking. It could open doors to the enemy. The very same it did when the witch Morgan trapped us within the forest. Remember how she confused our minds because we sought her with magic? She found us first, and it cost us many Cymbrogi lives; her *demon men* ripped them apart." Peredur snarled through his teeth, "Is this not the very same trial?"

"The undead…" Bedwyr gasped, leaning forward—the memories brimming in his eyes. "We could not kill them. She used the *Chalice of Life.*"

Peredur nodded with a stark glare of warning. "Yes. The very antithesis of the Holy Cup. It was the healing of the Holy Cup in Gwalahad's hands that saved us, breaking her spell. The Great God's spirit within it saved us—*not* magic."

Arthur turned. "Elanor? What is it you think should be done?"

Elanor's throat tightened. She felt unprepared to respond. What could she do? She was being placed between two solid rocks. Her choice was to disappoint her husband, or Arthur—who she felt was finally seeing her, even if only a little. She knew better than to disregard Merlin's counsel, but was he always right?

What if Arthur is right this time? What if Merlin is just afraid?

She glanced up at Merlin in earnest and asked, "What is the bad you fear will happen?"

His worried eyes met hers. "Just as Peredur has said. We do not want to invite the enemy." Frustration was evident in his voice, yet there was more behind his eyes; they begged her to heed him.

She was not eager to do what Arthur had asked. In truth, she was afraid to face Osian's man. Merlin had taught her that fear hindered magic. Fear opened doors that should not be opened.

But what if I am the only solution? What if this is exactly the role I am meant to play in all this? Maybe without me, they will never be able to discover the enemy.

Elanor forced herself to look at Arthur. He wanted her to do it. He believed this was the right thing to do. With trepidation, she said, "I believe Merlin is right. It is very risky—"

Merlin sighed audibly, his hands loosening at his sides.

"…but…"

His hands tightened again.

"…I do believe this may be a necessary danger. What if this is the key that gives us the upper hand? No more villages burned, or innocents murdered. Haldin's village," she pleaded to Merlin to understand, "the enemy was allowed to use it as his playground. Dunnoc manipulated them, and set a trap for us. Osian's men killed every single one of them, hanging them from their own stable rafters." She clenched her teeth against her rising emotions. "Merlin, I will *not* defy you. But even you have considered the older magic in times past."

"That does not justify—"

"I know." Elanor nodded. "I know."

Merlin lifted his chest, staring down at her.

With quiet solemnity, she asked, "Can you not do this magic? The same magic I have done? You have the wisdom to navigate it, as you understand the old ways."

Merlin shook his head. "There is much powerful natural magic within me, and I have gained other abilities trained as a druid, but I do not know this magic. This magic—like the shade—is used to manipulate. This power is *usually* only gained through many seasons of training, or evil rituals. Somehow this gift has come to you as a natural ability. I cannot explain it."

"If it comes to me naturally"—she peered at him in confusion—"then why is it wrong?"

Merlin's eyes softened. "It may not always be wrong, Elanor. But to use it against the enemy, who is *evil*, is not a good place to practice such power."

"I do not understand." Elanor shook her head. "If I had never used this magic, then we would never have known that Arthur was still alive. Would he *even* be here as he is now?"

"This is true." Merlin sighed, conceding. "But I warn you—both times you used this magic in ignorance. This time it would be different."

"Trust me to try," she gently urged.

Merlin flashed a cautious look at Arthur. "You have not heeded my advice in the past. What did it bring you?"

Arthur winced at Merlin's words. He opened his mouth as if to defend himself, then stopped, appearing to think better of it. He worked his strong jaw, musing over his next words. "I do not believe this to be the same."

Merlin took a long-suffering breath. "I will be there to protect my wife. I *will*. This should not happen without my presence. But I have warned you. That is all I can do." He shot a disappointed glance toward Elanor, then, pulling his hands back into fists, stormed from the council.

13

THE TRAGEDY OF RANOK

Merlin sat brooding in the solace of his chamber; his face shadowed in the dimming light. The hot throb of what had happened pulsed against his temples. He couldn't stand another minute of the council's reckless and hasty decisions. None of them could possibly understand what they were dealing with, and it infuriated him that Elanor was being placed at the center of it.

He massaged his forehead as resentment burned in his stomach.

Why could they not just listen?

He inhaled a sharp breath through his teeth. Peredur at least had seen his wisdom, but it appeared his words fell empty—only caught by Bedwyr. Not enough clout to steer the kings' opinions.

Arthur had always been far too eager to act. Though, most often, he did heed Merlin's warnings. Many times, when Merlin hesitated with doubt, it was Arthur's brazen boldness that won the day. But this...this just didn't sit well. If he were the one to wield the dangerous magic, then he would not be so ambivalent. However, this was Elanor being asked to use a dangerous magic, not him. A sharp pain raced through his heart at the thought of her in harm's way—*again*. He whispered, "She does not know how dangerous this could be for her. Her purity, her mind, even her life." He cringed thinking of it. He recalled some of the fatal mistakes he had made—others had made. "I should have said something all those years ago."

The first time Elanor had used the *truth telling* magic, it completely bewildered him. He could have counseled her then that the magic was dangerous, but the overwhelming revelation that she was Pendragon left him stunned. He never brought it up again, and she never used the magic a second time until this day.

He thought the first unusual occurrence was possibly brought on by the Greater Spirit. Many moments throughout his life, unexplainable magic had happened in times of need. Magic like when Elanor was saved from the gwyllgi's attack—she was translated to the safety of another room. He had not done that magic. At least he didn't think so. Something, or someone else had intervened.

And that was exactly what bothered him now. Elanor was growing more confident in her magic. Without guidance, right and wrong magic was easy to confuse. *Motivation is the key.* Her use of this magic during the council was *not* divine intervention. It was intentional.

"I should have guided her better," he admonished himself. Of course, he had mentored her magic, but he took for granted her innateness for purity. When he was young, he also had to be guided by his ollamh to understand the lines drawn in magic. No one could walk that line without erring.

Maybe I am overreacting. Maybe Elanor needs to do this.

But still, he could not shake the caution in his spirit telling him otherwise.

The door creaked open, and Elanor timidly stepped into the room. Her forlorn eyes drew to meet his. Her confused and questioning countenance was hard to resist. He turned his face away, biting his lip and strengthening his resolve. She approached and knelt before him, gingerly trickling her warm fingers over his knees. He avoided her gaze, but her lavender scent doused the hot coals of his temper.

Closing his eyes, he murmured, "Why do you—" His heart pinched, choking his words. "Why do you not heed my warnings?"

She turned his chin, and he opened his eyes. Her blue irises searched his face; the edges of her supple mouth turned downward. "I feel," she started, glancing dolefully down at her lap, "so confused. I did not know I had done something wrong. I…" She twisted her lips. "I did not mean to create another problem. I just reacted." A large tear slid down her cheek, and her mouth tightened. "Why did you have to be so scathing toward me in front of the kings? You…you treated me like—"

Scathing?

Her words sobered him, stinging his pride. Merlin rubbed his hand over his mouth. It had all escalated so quickly. The council reignited his old anxieties. His anger swelled at the unexpected use of old magic, along with the division roused by Lugh and Croighcat. His instinct to crush the deceit, as though demons were on the prowl, rose above everything else. She had gotten in the middle of his furor. He didn't mean to wound her.

Merlin sighed. "I am—so sorry, Elanor. I forgot myself." It stung him, realizing he had unintentionally shamed her. Her eyes stared up at his awash with an edge of anger. He could no longer resist her and pulled her into his arms.

Oh, how I love her, he thought, pressing her into his chest. That was the hardest part. So many times he had been unable to shield her from the darkness, or keep her safe from the ache of death. Witnessing her hurt was a pain that had nearly driven him mad. He could not just willingly open his hand and allow her to recklessly jump into the fire. Who was he without her? She was his balance in all things. She was his other, filling the empty hole of his life. Her presence, a constant reminder of that.

"I did not mean to shame you," he finally said, shaking his head. "Forgive me for hurling my fear at you. The times we are facing require hard choices." He worked his jaw, wrestling with a surge of regret. "I should have guided you better in this way of magic, but instead, I left you to discover it for yourself."

Elanor joined him on the cushioned bench by the hearth and rested her head on his shoulder. "You know I do not desire magic that is dangerous."

Merlin could hear the hurt in her voice.

"I want to do what is right. Sometimes it is hard to know what that is."

"I know." He dropped his head, and she folded her soft, delicate fingers into his. He swallowed, running his thumbs over her silken skin. "Are you firm in your decision to do what Arthur asks?"

She shook her head.

His shoulders relaxed. "We must be more careful now, more than we have ever been. I know Arthur has decided what he thinks is best. He wants to save his people and is not fully considering the cost of a magic he does not understand."

"He was so adamant about me *not* going to Celyddon, but now seems unconcerned of the current risk."

"Arthur is not unconcerned. He just does not fully grasp this danger. He saw what you did in the forest, and what you did to Lugh. He now sees your power, and within the safety of the Palisade, he thinks we are protected. He would be there. I would be there. And…" Merlin sighed, hating to say it, "he might be right."

"What evil could happen?"

"That hooded villain—"

Elanor winced and pulled her hands into her lap.

Merlin noticed her anxiety peak. "This is what concerns me," he said, motioning toward her. "You would be facing more than just a man. He confessed to Arthur that he has sorcery. It would be different using magic against him than when you forced Lugh to tell the truth. This villain could fight back in ways you cannot even imagine."

"I am afraid of him…the hooded man." She picked nervously at her nails. "He reminds me of the men that hurt me."

Merlin eased his hands around her waist. "These are the men we must face. Whether it be now, or another time. You *do* need to understand that you wield a power they do not possess. The light within you could crush them, if used wisely. That is why Osian hides. He will not risk my power. Even *you* took on that witch and she could do nothing to oppose you. Your power far outweighed hers. We cannot be afraid of these evil ones—but we also cannot use their own power against them. Not all power is useful. We want to reveal, expose, and disarm. Battling with the tools of darkness could ensnare us. And I *do not* want you hurt. It has worked for you without consequence in the past, but we cannot rely on that experience. The curse in Haldin's village was not broken because I understood the dark magic; it was broken because I knew light dispels darkness."

"Why would I have dark magic?"

"You do not." Guilt pricked his heart; he felt terrible he had made her feel that way. "You have power you must learn to use with wisdom. You cannot let it use you.

I—" He paused, remembering the last time he used magic irresponsibly. "I made your friend Demetri speak in babbled tongues."

"You what?" Elanor lifted her head, flashing him a small, curious grin.

Merlin chuckled. "He deserved it. He would not shut his mouth, so I messed with his words. To no ill effect." He shrugged with a smirk. "It would have worn off shortly and hopefully left Demetri a bit more humbled. But…that kind of magic could be harmful if used for the wrong ends, or on the wrong person. I just"—worry needled his brow—"I believe this will be dangerous, and…I fear other circumstances. Like the ones Peredur wisely reminded us of. We need to keep the doors shut to the enemy, not open them wide."

"I understand."

"We must face these demons, Elanor. You and I—we were meant to face Osian. Neither Arthur or I can hide you away from that. Though, I *wish* I could. You were given your gifts for a reason. But please understand, just because you have a gift, does not mean you can use it whenever or however you choose."

Bam! Bam! Bam!

Their heads snapped up at the fist pounding on their door.

What is the urgency? Merlin thought, approaching the door. He opened it, discovering Bedwyr breathless on the other side.

"What is all the haste?"

"I am sorry, Merlin, but you need to come quickly."

"What is it?"

"Ranok of the Southlands has come with his son Halok, and the news is not good."

"Ranok?" Merlin asked, perplexed, trepidation rising within him. "He is so aged. I am amazed he made the distance to the caer."

Merlin remembered the last time he saw the old one-eyed chieftain and his small Cymry village. Ranok and his son were from an older time. A tribe that had refused the changes brought by the Romans. Merlin and Elanor had visited their village on the way to visit his mother in Dyved just after they were married. He remembered Halok's wife. She was a burly woman that never offered a smile, though, underneath it all hid the warmth of Cymry hospitality.

Elanor rushed to Merlin's side.

"You are more right than you know," Bedwyr confirmed. "The kings were still in council when he came. They are with Halok now; however, Ranok has been rushed to the healers. He was badly wounded. I fear he is dying."

Merlin gasped. Instant grief squeezed his heart. "This cannot be."

"Halok is prepared to tell us what has happened. The council waits for you and the lady to return."

"Right," Merlin said. He grabbed Elanor's hand, and together, they quickly followed Bedwyr down the hall. Dread plagued his thoughts over what had happened to Ranok and his caer.

Was it the hoods again? Have they burned another village?

They raced down the stairs as though gliding over wet stones. Arriving at the council, Merlin searched the somber faces. He found Halok hunched down in a lump before Arthur; his hands covered his tattoo-dotted face. His round nose and cheeks flushed red between his fingers. Tears streamed down his beard; his breath pulsed heavily between sobs.

"Halok!" Merlin said, bursting toward him. He knelt and placed a hand on Halok's shoulder. Elanor followed in beside him.

"Ah," Halok sniffed, peering up from his palms. His wet eyes squeezed a few more tears free. "Emrys Wyllt and the Lady Bluebird. How much my father would be blessed to see you."

"How is he?"

"I fear he will quickly meet the mother goddess."

Arthur moved to speak, his voice heavy with honor. "It has been many years since I have seen the great strength of the old Cymry world burn within the brightness of Ranok's eyes."

Halok spoke through a sobbing groan, "It will soon be no longer, my king. My father is almost gone, and our people left captive and slaughtered."

Merlin narrowed his eyes at Halok. He hated to ask, but they needed to know. "Was it Osian's hooded devils?"

"There were no hoods. No." Halok's sad gaze lifted to the king. "It was a nightmare far worse."

Croighcat leaned forward, intrigue flickering in his eyes.

"I would know," Cormach injected, "what has inflicted the lands so near my own. Is Dyved in peril?"

"M-My," Halok started, his voice choked, "my son, Haleth. The devil got inside him. He is not himself. And it was not just my Haleth, but many other of our younger Cymbrogi. They"—he swallowed—"have demons in their eyes and on their tongue."

Alarmed, Merlin glanced at Arthur. The reminder of Gethin dying in Celyddon floated through his mind.

"Something got to them…ya' see? It filled them with rage." Halok ground his teeth and clenched his fist to his chest. "Haleth no longer recognizes his kin. His mother"—he sobbed against his words—"she got in his way. She thought she could reason with him. He…h-he killed her. My woman was murdered by my own son, right before my eyes. O-o-oh!" Halok wept into his hands, shaking his head in deep sorrow. "Haleth declared himself the new chieftain of our caer, and that all who rebelled would be killed. We resisted…too stubborn to let this evil rise. But we…we are mostly old men, and the young ones dominated."

Halok peered up, and his eyes were pools reflecting the horror he had witnessed. "He killed so many. He threatened his own grandfather to yield the caer to him, and when he did not, he ran him through with his spear—leaving just enough life in him to watch Haleth burn down his hall. In the chaos of the flames, many of us scattered, running for our lives. I grabbed up my father and thought of nothing else but coming here." He dropped his head and whispered, "We had heard the Great Pendragon had returned."

The kings sat somber-faced, with many of their eyes tearful. Evil was sickening their lands.

"Please," Halok begged, "is there nothing to be done to save my son?"

Croighcat cleared his throat. "This greatly concerns me. As many of my own men have gone missing, and my trade posts compromised. I knew it was some sort of evil and I blamed Lugh for it. He allowed it—somehow," he seethed. "Evil fills minds, and they forfeit themselves."

"Arthur and I have seen this in Celyddon," Merlin confessed.

"On my lands?" Thul asked, his eyes wide with shock. "I knew of Osian's attack, but not about any minds being corrupted."

Arthur turned to Halok. "When did this begin? How did the evil get inside them?"

Merlin squeezed his eyes shut. He knew what source was being used to confuse minds. The cursed talisman flashed in his mind, and he balled his hands into fists.

Halok shook his head in despair. "It happened suddenly. Haleth leads our Cymbrogi out along the perimeter of the caer to scan for danger. My strong, kind son led them with honor, and protected us. You saw him," he said to Merlin. "He was a good boy. Strong, with a good heart."

Merlin nodded with compassion. He remembered the lad helping them to the caer, his innocent eyes smiling toward him and Elanor when they departed.

Halok, seeing Merlin's confirmation, continued, "Without a warning, a dark shadow hovered over them. More and more, as the days passed, the younger Cymbrogi became withdrawn—not themselves. One day they returned from the fields, and they were ours *no longer*."

Croighcat pummeled his fist into the arm of his chair and snapped, "What is there to be done, High King?"

Elanor walked to the center, wide-eyed, and shaking like a leaf. Everyone's attention turned to her as she said, "W-We do what we have to." She faced Merlin, her expression apologetic. "We make Lugh, and the hooded prisoner, tell us the truth."

Merlin inhaled a sharp breath, then dropped his head into his hand.

"It must be done," Elanor continued. "We cannot allow more destruction, not when there is something we can do…something *I* can do."

Arthur stood, proudly gazing at Elanor. The others grunted in agreement.

"Tomorrow, we will go down to the guardhouse. Elanor," Arthur said with gentle assurance, "I will be there with you. My sword drawn."

Merlin reached for her hand, his head still hanging in defeat. He wanted to hide her away, tell them all he refused to let her. Instead, he said, "I will also be there with you." Elanor took his hand, and he lifted his head, whispering a warning. "We do not know what may happen, and maybe nothing sordid will occur, but in case, I will be there to guide and protect you as I always have. I promise."

LAST BREATH OF THE OLD WORLD

That evening, Merlin accompanied Halok to his father's bedside in a quiet hollow chamber where Cilaen had attended him. Ranok lay wheezing in a feverish sweat. His white, cottony beard hovered above his chest. His chin quivered. The wound seeped red through the linen wrapping his abdomen. Merlin reached out his hand and gingerly rested it upon the old chieftain's arm.

"Oh," Ranok croaked. His raspy voice was stretched thin. "Who has come?" He blinked his one tiny eye, the other eye still covered in a patch.

"It is me, Father," Halok quickly answered, "and...and the Lord Emrys."

"Ai?" Ranok gasped. "Oh...I am beyond blessed that I should be with you now, ancient one—now that my end has come." He rolled his head, squinting his eye. "Oh, this blasted eye. I cannot see you."

Merlin leaned closer. "How about now, old friend?"

"Ah...ah, yes. That is a little better." Ranok lifted his wrinkled hand and lightly patted Merlin's cheek. "My father's lands are truly gone. Nothing now remains of the old peoples. We are no more. I—" A tear trickled down his temple. "I fought hard to keep the old traditions. I wanted to bring back what was lost. But ai...I must let it all go now." He turned to his son and sputtered, "I am so sorry this is all I have left to give you. I am so sorry your woman has died."

Halok sobbed, dropping his head into the fold of his arms.

"She really did make the finest ale...and...her hands held us all so tightly."

Sniffs and groans garbled up from underneath Halok's round arms. "Y-y-you have"—he gasped —"given me a life of honor. I am...I am a son well-loved, Father."

"Yes...yes." The old man squeezed his one eye shut, then took a long-stuttered breath.

Merlin could not stem his own tears. His heart sat heavy in his chest. The tragedy of Ranok and Halok's caer was more than just a loss of people and land. It was the loss of a world that was now almost entirely gone. The Cymry tribes of the past were dying away. Were there enough peoples hidden away—maybe in the Northlands—to redeem this collapse? He had not seen the remnants for many long years. The Romans really had done irreparable damage. Prydain had been forever changed.

It made Merlin reflect on the loss of his own people. His mother's folk. The Fair Folk of the Fisher King, and his daughter of the lake. Would he ever see any of them again? Had they also all gone?

Merlin sighed. "We reach for those things that were once beautiful. We contend to keep them alive, yet it all fades in the end. But for the hope." Halok glanced up from his arm, and Ranok opened his eye to Merlin. "The Kingdom of the Sun contains it all, and it will *never* fade."

"Where is the Kingdom of the Sun?" Halok sniffed.

"I am unsure." Merlin shook his head. "But I feel it. It calls me. The Great God holds it, I believe. I know he is offering it, somehow—to all of us. It has all the promises in its hands, and it calls us back to what is right—to what is whole. It cannot be stolen away or broken, like it is here and now."

"I want to go to this place…the Kingdom of the Sun," Ranok said, the longing brimming within his glassy eye. "Will it be within the arms of the mother goddess?"

Merlin shook his head. "All I know is, it is *now* closer to your reach than it is to mine."

Halok's eyes shone from the small light of the candle's flame beside him, burnishing his tears. "How is it in reach?"

"I have almost touched it," Merlin continued. "I have seen it within the Crystal Cave, and I have seen it within the eyes of the monks that came from Eire so long ago. They brought it here with them, and left a piece of it to grow. The Man in Blue held it within his eyes."

"Who is this Man in Blue?" Ranok whispered.

"I believe he holds the power to make the heart of our lands new, and restore the broken, stolen things." Merlin did not understand what he was saying. It just, sort of, flowed out from him like sweet wine. The more he spoke, the more he could feel his spirit light with hope. The awen expanded into a vision that soon enveloped him. He started to sing:

Sweet…Are the healing days, when pain will find no way.
The earth will sing, for the Sun has made it day.

The mourning in his voice created an atmosphere…tangible…and light…

Sweet…As it will be proclaimed the new days of the Sun.
Its rays will rise high, setting thrones upon kings' holds,
The New Way coming, and the land set in gold.

Merlin paused to take a deep breath. The quiet murmurs of Halok's sobs soon became sighs of courage and hope. Then, as Merlin began again, his bardic lyrics burst into resounding reassurance, hitting the three of them like sunbeams through dark rafters that had hidden the light...

Oh, Kingdom of the Sun, renew our land with grace.
Oh, Kingdom of the Sun, the warmth of its bounty upon our face.
Blood will stop dripping, as the oil of gladness is tipping.
The sword no longer killing, but its emblems triumphing.
A new day rising, with the old moons setting.
Sweet...days of the Sun are coming.

Those final words of the song echoed into a vision where Merlin found himself standing next to Ranok upon a green hill; a robust and radiant smile lifted his cheeks to the lines of his eyes. Both his eyes appeared bright and shining. No patch or scar lay across his once missing eye. His fluffy hair wafted in the wind, and he laughed as though no tear or sorrow had ever come, or ever been.

Ranok faced Merlin, his smile brimming with joy. "I understand now. I understand the Kingdom of the Sun." He closed his eyes and drew in a deep, refreshing breath. "It calls me into its bosom."

Merlin stood in awe, the enigma not being revealed to him like it was to Ranok. Then a light broke over the top of the hill, and Ranok peered over at it. As if it called him away, he subtly tilted his head to Merlin, then walked toward the edge of the beautiful rising sunlit hill.

Merlin felt the light on his skin, reminding him of warm honey. It encompassed the scene, until the vision melted away. When Merlin opened his eyes, Ranok's one eye lay shut, and his breathing had ceased. Now forever sleeping, he had left them behind.

Merlin tenderly grasped the back of Halok's head, gripping his hair in his fingers. "Brother, the Kingdom of the Sun has taken your father, and it remains to us to fight and save your son."

The morning sun rose sullen, hidden behind the clouds. Elanor wished she, too, could hide away from her looming task. She tossed and turned all night, dreading the dawn.

Merlin had returned late into the night with red, swollen eyes. Ranok had died, leaving a bitter taste in their mouths. At times, she had seen Merlin cupping his head in his palms, and at others, pacing the room mumbling under his breath.

But now that morning had come, her dread increased tenfold. The memories of what the hooded man had done to her in the forest gripped her chest. His growling voice made her heart pump faster.

She would have to face a man that reminded her how weak and powerless she had been. Traumatic memories surged, suffocating her, bringing up what it felt like to be bound and unable to escape her enemy's grasp. She fought against the fear, recalling what Merlin had said—that it was the tormentors who ignited the power within her to call the unicorn. She had discovered her strength despite them.

He was right, but the price she paid—her blood pouring onto the damp leaves— was not something she wanted to face again. Yes, she was stronger now. The trials she faced had changed her. She wouldn't know just how much courage and strength she had gained without being tested. Today was that test. Though, chipping away at her courage was Merlin's warning.

I have to do this, she said to herself, scooping her legs over the side of the bed.

Merlin lay asleep on the bench by the fire's dying embers, one arm draped over his head. His brown wavy hair lay tussled underneath. His other hand rested on his chest.

She trusted Merlin's admonition of the risk, but she could not ignore that she had a chance to do something. Faced with Halok's pain, she refused to turn her back.

Even if there is backlash, it will be worth what we might gain. The truth. The unveiling of Osian. He cannot be allowed to hide any longer. He must be found and made to face his retribution.

She whispered, "I just hope I do not freeze. Or"—she shrank back against her own failures—"drop my sword."

She'd seen disappointment in Merlin's eyes when she made that final decision, but she also knew he understood. He knew she wasn't making a flippant choice, and she did not believe Arthur's pressure to do it was an unjust or unwise move. It was a calculated risk. And deep down, she hoped it would make him find her worthy.

Worthy of what? His love? His affection? Probably.

Merlin opened his eyes and stared dejectedly at Elanor from his crumpled position. She wrapped her arms tightly around herself, holding the waves of her fears inside.

Merlin slowly sat up. "Ah…" he moaned, rolling his shoulders with an audible *pop.* He rubbed the back of his neck, scrunching his face while he stretched. His shoulders relaxed, and he exhaled, staring forward—as if lost in the abyss of everything.

Elanor moved toward him with hesitant steps. She didn't want to see the despondency in his eyes.

As though he guessed her fear, he reached for her hand without peering at her. "I told you I would be with you, Elanor."

Elanor nodded warily, biting on the inside of her cheek. The heavy melancholy pressed on her tears.

"If it helps at all…I do not resist this. The warning is still there. I *do* think we are inviting danger. It already presses on the walls of this Palisade, and I am not sure we could hold it back whether or not we use this magic." He finally faced her. Concern knitted his brow. "But you must *not* continue when it goes wrong."

"When?" came her faint reply.

"Yes," he reiterated with a serious tone. "*When.* The caution I feel is not just my own apprehension. I can feel the evil begging us to do this. It lingers in the corner waiting." He shook his head. "But after Ranok...I agree, we must do something. There is nothing more presented for us to do."

He pulled Elanor toward him, taking both of her hands. "Sometimes the right thing to do is to draw our swords and charge into battle against the enemy. The choice has been removed to keep Osian at bay." His brow creased. "I can only do what I can to protect you. The time has come. We are at war. You are part of this, Elanor. I love...I love you so much."

The lines of his forehead drew even tighter. He squeezed her hands, pulling her closer. His breath brushed across her forehead. "It is unnatural to willingly place you in harm's way. But...I must learn to trust in something more. I had to do it in the future time when that darkness tried to steal you away, and I must do it again." He lifted her hands and pressed them to his warm, soft lips.

Elanor's chin trembled. "I could *never* lose you."

"That is exactly my trouble." He chuckled soberly, drawing a loose piece of her hair behind her ear. His slender, gentle fingers made her lean in, closing the small space between them. "I have lost you—more than once—and it wrecked me." Then he said more severely, "Yet here we are, and in truth, I am not the man I once was— the man that runs from grief. I have learned because of you that I can be stronger. I choose to be. I must, if we are to see Osian done away with. Draw your sword, Elanor, and *do not* allow the enemy to strike it from your hand. Not this time."

Her pulse raced and she stepped back, glancing at her hands, splaying them out in front of her. She turned them over, observing her small wrists.

Merlin wrapped his fingers around them. "Your skill with the sword has grown, but right now, a physical sword is not what you are fighting with. You are much stronger in magic. In that, you are not as delicate." He flashed her a smile, and his flaxen eyes drew her toward his lips. The strength of his arms, his chest, made her feel secure—strong. "You have healed a dragon taller than twenty men. Now as you wield your magic, do not just wield it with strength alone, but also with wisdom and cunning. Think first, act second. Do not let fear dictate a response. Pay attention, and choose to be one step ahead of your enemy."

Elanor breathed deeply, lifting her shoulders.

"You made a difficult choice. I know you did not settle on this lightly, or without thought."

She clenched his collar and drew his lips to hers. Pressing into him, she relished the feel of his hands slipping around her waist, finding their way between the laces at her back. Her fingers moved up to sift through his hair. She lingered in his embrace, not wanting this moment to pass. Not wanting to think of what came next. All the dread disappeared into his warmth. She kissed him, feeling grateful he was near. And would remain near, girding her spirit and resolve.

"We should get ready." He sighed, pulling himself away from her. He kissed her one more time, and with reluctance in his eyes, he let his arms fall to his sides. "They will be gathering soon."

Oh, the taste of him made her feel bitter when he pulled away—resenting the task at hand. Emotions quelled up in her throat. She sighed, turning toward the chest that held her clothes. Soon, Samara would come to knot her hair into braids—the thought of them made her think of the somber preparation before a battle.

I hope Merlin's warnings are exaggerated. I wish I knew what I was watching for. What evil I am to have wisdom against.

Her brows pressed together, and she laced on her dress, pulling the bodice tight. The ashy blue dress was embroidered with green. The sash at her hip, a darker shade of blue, hung gently. Her pendant pressed between her dress and chest, so she pulled it out to hang in front. She squeezed it into her fingers and whispered, "Nowhere to hide."

THROUGH THE EYES OF THE ENEMY

Elanor had never been to the guardhouse. In fact, until yesterday, she hadn't even known a dungeon-like prison existed within the Palisade. Once the kings had gathered, Peredur led the council around the circling walls to the entrance. She followed with Merlin just in front of her. The flat stones that built the Palisade—one stone atop the other—stretched the walls higher and higher the further they descended downhill. Elanor peered up at the lofty edges of the terrace that jutted out from the top of the edifice, unfamiliar from so far below.

They arrived at a dip in the earth, with a rustic, jagged staircase leading down, and leveling out to a wooden door supported with three iron beams. The beams connected to a black iron latch above a ring door handle. Butterflies swarmed in her stomach at the sight of it, and she grabbed hold of Merlin's hand. He gave her a reassuring nod.

What lay behind that door? Was it a cavernous dungeon—dark, dank, and moldy?

Peredur pulled a ring of keys from his belt and moved toward the lock. The black keys were more like short, twisted firebrands than a typically forged key. He unlocked the solid door to the sound of a loud *thunk*. It opened with a yawning croak, and Peredur led the way, disappearing into the dark.

Thick, damp air, heavy with the smell of wet dirt, hit Elanor full in the face. She cringed as she caught her breath. Once inside, Bedwyr tasked several men with lighting and handing out torches. Then they descended a narrow staircase into blackness. Wet stones on the walls shimmered against the torchlight.

Ahead, the echoing creak of a door unlocking reached her ears, though she could not see it. When they at last reached it, she discovered the door was made of iron bars. The stairs widened, and then slowly, flickering yellow light brightened until her feet touched the level floor. She breathed in relief. The cramped tunnel made her feel squished. After their last underground escapade, barely escaping the collapsing tomb they rescued Arthur from, this did nothing to ease her agitated nerves.

They arrived in a round room lined with torchlight, where four Cymbrogi guards jolted up from their chairs at a table near the center. Wooden doors covered four chambers behind them. Each door had small windows covered in latched iron shutters.

The guards bowed, gazing anxiously at Arthur and the group of high lords entering behind him.

"Be at peace, men," Arthur commanded. "We have come to see the prisoners. Are they still bound?"

"Y-Yes, my king," one of the guards timidly answered. "They are chained to the wall inside their cells. The *one* remains gagged and blindfolded."

"Why is this so?" Croighcat inquired.

Arthur lifted a brow and answered, "The hood has claimed to have sorcery. I wanted to keep him incapable from doing harm in secret."

"Right." Bram nodded tensely, his eyes darting back and forth across the cell doors. His fingers tapped the hilt of his dagger.

Arthur turned to the guard. "Has anyone been in or out of this chamber?"

"Not since the lesser king was imprisoned here yesterday at midday."

Arthur nodded for Peredur and Bedwyr to enter first. Peredur moved to unlock the first cell, then he and Bedwyr went in, leaving the kings to wait.

Elanor swallowed, watching them disappear into the darkness. Slowly, the chamber glowed with lit torches. Bedwyr emerged first, his eyes narrow.

When Peredur returned, he jerked his chin toward Arthur. "The prisoner has managed to free himself from his gag."

Arthur approached the cell and leaned in. He turned, peering at Elanor. Concern brimmed in his eyes, but he quickly glanced away, nodding to Peredur. "Now Lugh."

Peredur unlocked the door. Again, he and Bedwyr went in and lit the torches.

"Ah!" A disgusted holler resounded from inside the cell.

Elanor jumped into Merlin's chest, her fingers gripping his tunic. A heinous, garbled laugh echoed from inside the hood's cell. Elanor sucked in a sharp breath.

Arthur balled his hands into fists and strode into Lugh's cell. "Agh!" he moaned, sounding repulsed.

Peredur raced into the hood's cell next door. A loud slam silenced the miserable rise of the villain's laughter.

Merlin edged forward and looked into the hood's cell. Elanor resisted his pull to go along with him but followed behind him anyway. The hood lay on the floor, licking blood from his lips. Apparently, his laughter brought Peredur's fist to his mouth. His eyes remained covered, but his gag lay crumpled on the floor.

Merlin then turned toward Lugh's cell. Elanor was glad to move away from the hood. She peered through the second cell door, and when her eyes settled on Lugh, she gasped in horror. He lay on his back with the chain from his own shackles wrapped tight around his neck. His face was blue and his tongue swollen.

"He's dead," came Thul's voice.

Again, the hood's cackles echoed from next door.

Arthur's head snapped toward the other cell. His lips curled, exposing his clenched teeth. Rage lit his eyes, and he blazed over to the hood's cell.

"You did this," Arthur accused, bursting into the chamber.

Merlin and Elanor arrived to see Arthur gripping the prisoner by his tunic, yanking him across the floor; his chains clanged as Arthur pounded him into the wall.

The man responded in a slithering, graveled tone, "How could *I* have done it?"

His voice sent shivers skittering up Elanor's spin. She shot a frightful glance at Merlin.

"What is it?" Merlin whispered.

She wanted to run. She wanted to cry. She remained locked within the safety of Merlin's gaze, avoiding a closer glimpse of the prisoner, afraid his face might reveal the truth.

That voice.

She could never forget it. She had heard it in her nightmares for years.

"Stand him up," Arthur commanded, clutching the hilt of his sword at his hip.

Bedwyr and Peredur lifted the villain to his feet, then pressed him against the wall. The chains pulled taut on his one wrist, the other arm a stump bound to his chest in blood-stained linens.

"Did you kill him?" Arthur questioned through gritted teeth.

"I could not allow that weak fool to blabber." The villain chuckled with a vile lilt. Peredur shoved his elbow into the man's throat, making the crude monster sputter. "He"—the prisoner coughed—"has outlived his usefulness."

The muscles in Arthur's jaw rippled. "How?"

"With my *words*." The prisoner's voice echoed eerily, trailing throughout the cell.

Elanor fought against shoving her fingers into her ears.

His words have power. Just like—

She stopped for a moment, then her eyes widened. She remembered when he used that voice to curse her when she lay dying on the forest floor. Her pulse raced. She grew lightheaded, and the world spun around her. This was the same devil who had squeezed her neck and poured poison down her throat.

Merlin gripped her shoulder, but she couldn't feel it. Her vision blurred, and the blood drained from her face. Quickly, Merlin pulled her from the cell. "What has happened? Elanor—" He patted her cheek to revive her.

Inside Elanor's mind flashed the trauma of the forest. His face…his teeth…his oily cratered cheeks. This was worse than she could have ever feared. She not only had to face a man who had dark magic, but she would be facing the very man who had haunted her for years.

She gripped Merlin's forearms to steady herself and forced out breathy words. "It's…it's him."

"Him?"

She crammed her eyes shut, fighting to hold it all together. "He is the one."

Merlin's brow crimped as though struggling to understand.

Elanor intentionally slowed her breath, breathing in and out. Her lips tingled, and she thought she might black out. Doubling over, she clutched her knees.

I have to be stronger than this.

She warred against her panic. Catching her breath, she leaned toward Merlin. "He is the one…from the oak forest," she said, her voice quavering. "Th-the very one who forced the poison into my mouth. Cut me. *Strangled me.*" Just saying it out loud made her knees buckle.

Merlin caught her elbows before she could fall and pulled her into his chest. Fire burned in his eyes, and he snapped his head back toward the cell.

He growled, "I will *kill* him." He held her closer, shutting his eyes.

Amidst her panic, Elanor sensed Merlin wrestling to control his rage. He kept inching closer to the cell, his fingers pressing into her back.

He groaned, shaking his head. "We are *not* doing this. We are leaving. *Now!*" He pulled her toward the stairs.

At first, Elanor was relieved.

Yes, let us leave this awful place.

She wanted to melt into the solace that she wouldn't have to do it after all. Obligation absolved. There was nothing she could do. There was no way she could face *that man*. But then, something pinged within her subconscious. Like a low humming of a song, a presence strengthened her. Reason slowly leaked through her fear, and she resisted Merlin's leading.

She tugged against Merlin, and he pulled harder.

"No…Merlin. *Stop!*"

He halted, turning his wild, narrow eyes at her. The dull light of the torches barely lit his face within the dark stairwell. The flickering shadows revealed the fierceness of his stare and the clench of his jaw.

"You said"—she panted for breath—"to think first, then react." She dug her fingers into her hair and squeezed her eyes shut. Her chest still pumped from sheer horror.

Merlin twisted his lips. "There is now *even more* at risk."

Elanor couldn't agree more, and yet, peering back over her shoulder toward the cell, she felt like a coward for fleeing. This could be their best chance. The knot of regret already formed in her chest, knowing that if she did not do what *only* she could—with so many lives already affected, and potentially many more—she could never live with herself.

"H-h-has he not already done his worst to me?" she whispered.

Merlin's shoulders slumped, and his furrowed brow deepened. "I do not understand."

"I cannot feel good about abandoning this opportunity. I would forever regret what I could have done to help Prydain—to help Arthur."

"It does not all hinge on *you!*" Merlin said with a severe edge.

"Does it not? Who else can do what I can?" she pressed. "I do not even know if

I can do this, but it almost seems worse to walk away." She caressed his face, drawing his gaze so he could not look away. "Now that I know the worst that could happen—and I survived—I am stronger. Like you said."

She spoke, trying to convince herself, but the temptation to run away still pulled on her. "*Please*, you have to help me be strong."

Merlin bit into his lip, then mumbled, "That was not the worst that could have happened."

Elanor watched him wrestle with his own reason and will to protect her. Slowly, his eyes shifted to meet hers. She wrapped her fingers around his hands. She gave a tremulous nod, and then led him back down the stairs. As they entered the main chamber, two guards shuffled past them, carrying the strangled corpse of King Lugh from his cell. The horrific sight jolted Elanor, and she backed up into Merlin. Her anxiety swirled through her gut, telling her to run.

What am I doing?

She questioned her resolve, even as she forced herself toward the cell.

Do not think. Just move forward. Do what you must. Do not allow him to knock the sword from your hand.

Letting go of Merlin, she clenched her hands into fists and pressed them into her stomach to stop the anxious flutters.

"Let me go in first," Merlin said, stepping in front of her.

Elanor sighed with relief, grateful to let him go ahead. Her body shivered, and she forced out a deep breath, hoping to calm her unsettled nerves. She shut her eyes and tried to think of something else—anything else. But even the peaceful images of Gwendolen's sweet face, or Merlin's affirming smile, were replaced by an ominous yellow hood.

If I can just get past this—maybe the hooded villains will never make me feel this way again. Yes, she nodded, gulping hard. The idea of her finding freedom from that fear gave her an unexpected burst of courage. She opened her eyes and Merlin stood before her, offering his hand.

Elanor walked into the cell, feeling like she was outside her body, having left the rest of herself protected on the other side of the cell door. She glanced first at the kings, who stood strangely quiet against the side wall. Bedwyr drew beside her, taking a protective stance. Merlin led her from the front. She kept her eyes on the floor, hoping it would somehow keep her safe, but it held no comfort. It was empty and cold. Tense breaths filled the air as the monster, chained to the wall, groaned. The chains rattled, daring her to look up.

She lifted her head. Arthur stood threateningly near the fiend. His hand twitched as if itching to pull his sword. Peredur's broad silver blade was already unsheathed and pressed against the scoundrel's throat. The once hooded wrecker puffed from his knees, underneath his newly gagged and muzzled mouth—his eyes still blindfolded.

The expectation of her first move saturated the cell.

She relaxed her tense shoulders and pressed her quivering lips together. Silent and steady, the cell grew stale with hate. Elanor lifted her chin, begging the magic within her to kindle. In all her anxiety, she sought the assurance of her power.

"T-Take—" Fear choked her words, and her voice squeaked high in the silence. Blood rushed to her cheeks.

You can do this.

She closed her eyes and drew another long breath, then started again. "Take off his gag."

Upon hearing her voice, the prisoner snapped his head in her direction. She jumped, then sensed the heat from Merlin's body just behind her.

Do not be afraid of him, she commanded herself, refocusing her energy into her magic.

Peredur cautiously untied the gag and let the cloth fall to the floor. Then, with a disgusted frown, he pulled the wadded cloth out of the prisoner's mouth.

Elanor's eyes lit with blue light. "What is your name?" Her voice reverberated with an ethereal, dualistic tone.

The man grinned eerily but made no response.

She tried again. "Who are you? What is your name?"

He cringed, straining against her magic, then forced an intimidating smile. "I will tell you my name…*girl*…but not because you *willed* me to. I am Malik. And you…*blue witch*…can have no power over my tongue."

His challenge should have daunted her, but to her surprise, it fueled her. She pressed again with more energy. "You *will* tell us the truth." Her words resonated with such force that those within the cell covered their ears.

Malik bent forward, moaning against her power. "I…I crushed you once," he threatened, "like a fragile bird in my fist. I will do it again. You are nothing but a *whelp* that needs to be broken."

Arthur's sword rang as he unsheathed it in response to Malik's vile words. Merlin whipped out his hand—*snap*—his magic forced the wretch hard against the wall.

"AAaaahhh!" Malik cried with groans of pain.

"Tell us what we want to know," Elanor demanded, her voice echoing off the cell walls. "Tell us where Osian hides."

A sinister laugh gurgled from Malik's throat.

Elanor knew what she needed to do but feared peering into his hateful eyes. The same eyes that floated above her own when he cursed her, then left her for dead.

But if I look, I can take what is inside them.

She always knew she had the power to delve deeper into the soul of the eye, but always chose not to. Her ability to gaze beyond, into what was not offered, was an unrightful intrusion. Merlin had told her from the very beginning that her unwillingness to be tempted was what made her different from the dark ones. She *refused* to take what was not rightfully hers. She never wanted to invade others so uncaringly.

However, we are already breaking the rules, aren't we?

"Remove his blindfold," she told Peredur.

Peredur's eyes snapped to Arthur's, then to Merlin's.

"No," Merlin cautioned.

She turned to him. "Trust me."

He sighed and, with hesitance, nodded to Peredur.

As Peredur picked the knot, the eager villain tossed his head free of the blindfold and shot a malicious grin at Elanor. His brown eyes gleamed. His hateful stare made Elanor take a step back. She gulped against every alarm bell ringing inside her head— telling her to flee. Get away. Find a safe place.

Within her mind, her fear spoke.

"You stood against him once and you lost. Nothing has changed. You are no match for him."

No. She pressed against the voice of doubt. *I will use wisdom. I will not react in fear.*

As she dared hold his gaze, her mind was assaulted with what felt like the gnashing, barking teeth of the gwyllgi. She struggled to center her thoughts. But the bitter memory of Malik's grip around her throat paralyzed her lungs. It stole her breath, making her feel like she was suffocating.

Out of the tiniest corner of her thoughts, a glimmer of light slowly pulsed.

The song. The song.

The tune blew by her ears like a soft breeze. She meekly hummed it to herself, fighting off the stifling alarm. Then she flicked her eyes at Malik, the azure light blazing fiercer over her vision. She charged toward him. His gaze met her challenge and did not look away.

She screamed into his mind, *"Where is Osian?"*

Malik lifted higher onto his knees, staring at her unafraid.

She pressed deeper, and the haunts she was searching for slowly unveiled. "A forest," she said out loud to everyone. "On the eastern edge of Llyonesse. What is its name?" She searched his mind. "Goll. The forest of Goll."

Arthur glanced at Merlin, his face tight with alarm, as if knowing the place.

"There are men, Cymry traitors and men of the eastern lands, hidden inside. More sails…Ships are sailing to Llyonesse." She stumbled, feeling the brevity, then swallowed and pressed again. "But that is not where Osian hides. Where is Osian?" she growled.

Malik cried out in pain, and a drip of blood trickled from his nose. She was hurting him. A mixture of remorse and satisfying revenge welled up within her at his cry. It felt good to have power over the one who had beat and scarred her. She gritted her teeth and leaned closer. "Where is Osian?"

"You'll ne-never find him," Malik whimpered, his face twitching with renewed strength.

All at once, Elanor felt herself falling into a dreamlike awen inside Malik's mind. Removed from the safety of Merlin's arms, everything darkened.

Her feet soon touched down on level ground. Candle flames flickered to life. She peered around, discovering she was inside a cave. The musty, stifled air, mingled in smoky sage, wafted into her nose.

She heard his breathing first. Was it Malik? A tinge of fear prickled the hairs on her neck. She spun, then went stock-still. Within a shroud of shadow, the whites of dark piercing eyes stared out at her.

Could he see her? Who was it? His eyes flickered, changing from human to the yellow irises of a bird of prey. He leaned forward. The crescent moon talisman dangled forward from his neck.

Osian.

He rose from his chair; spiky fur wrapped his neck from the top of his cloak. His dark hair was tied back in a knot at the nape of his neck. A sharp nose cast a shadow over his firm chin. He drew closer, and her heart seized. Cold pinpricks of fear cascaded down her limbs. He was tall. So much taller than she had imagined—and strong. She had thought him the gangly, hopeless child Merlin had described, hiding behind his hooded men. But now, she shrank with the realization that he was an ominous figure exuding strength.

He stalked toward her, and she was ready to flee when she noticed his eyes peered past her.

Maybe he does not see me, she hoped.

She tried to move from his path, but an invisible force riveted her in place. Whatever this strange nightmare was inside Malik's mind, she no longer held the control she did a moment ago.

He was inches from her. She closed her eyes and gasped. To her relieved astonishment, he passed through her like a ghost. She turned and saw him pull objects from a table. But then, from the back of his head, a swirling mist formed. Elanor squinted, watching the violet hue shape into tendrils of long hair surrounding a pale, hollow-eyed feminine face. It stared at her, and an eerie, whispering wind echoed words throughout the cave's chamber.

The words.

Elanor begged her ears to understand the breathy vowels.

"I…sss…ooo…" Then again. *"I…sss…you."* The mist wisped into the figure of a woman, separating itself from Osian's back. It floated toward Elanor, gazing right into her eyes. Now she heard them, clear as a bell, buzzing into her ears like a malicious drum. "I…SEE…YOU!"

Terror gripped Elanor. Osian spun around to face her. His voice, combined with the ghost's, declared, "I…SEE…YOU!"

Elanor screamed a soundless scream. In desperation, she reached for a way to escape. The spirit dove toward her, enveloping her in its whorls, and growled, "Now I have you."

Elanor mouthed words without sound, *Who are you?*

The voice radiated hot inside Elanor's mind. "MORGAN!"

16

A GHOST FROM THE PAST

Merlin watched Malik crumple under the pressure of Elanor's magic. The hood shook violently, his eyes bloodshot with strain. Merlin leaned forward, eager to jump in if needed. Arthur and Peredur stood ready, while Bedwyr edged closer. Blood gushed from Malik's nose and dripped from his chin. Elanor remained solid, keeping him locked in her magic.

Something shifted. Merlin sensed a sinister magic permeating the cell. Like shadowy fingers, it reached across the four corners like a cold frost. Merlin turned at the sound of the kings murmuring. Their eyes darted like cornered prey. All of them fingered their weapons, as if prickled by the growing invisible menace. Croighcat lifted one brow. Both fear and curiosity played across his face.

Elanor whimpered.

Merlin spun back around. Malik had risen to his feet and now towered above Elanor. His eyes were hollow; something new strengthened him. His teeth clenched together, and a devious smile curled the corners of his mouth. The glare in his eyes was bone-chillingly familiar. Alarm shot through Merlin's body. Elanor was no longer in control. This was what Merlin had feared. A darker presence had infiltrated their midst.

Merlin shot Arthur a foreboding glance. Arthur tightened his grip, wrenching the leather on his sword's hilt. Bedwyr peered at Merlin through the corner of his eye as though anxiously awaiting the command.

"Elanor?" Merlin carefully beckoned.

Silence was her eerie reply, until her shoulders shot back, straightening her back. Her hands clenched into fists against her sides; her arms extended and locked.

Malik's growling voice unfurled into an echoing roll of dark speech. "Rwy'n… gweld…chi."

A foul poison, like tar, flooded the atmosphere. Merlin snapped his eyes to Arthur, and before he could even blink, Arthur's blade had flown. *Shing.* Malik's eyes widened, then his head fell from his shoulders and thudded onto the floor.

The shadow retreated, and Elanor's knees buckled. Bedwyr dropped his sword and captured her before she toppled, cradling her to the floor.

Merlin knelt beside her. "Elanor?" He touched her face.

She inhaled, then wrenched up like one waking from a nightmare. Her eyes locked with the severed head on the floor. She shrieked, throwing herself against Merlin; her fingers dug into his chest, gripping the fabric of his tunic. Merlin gritted his teeth, swallowing down the venom. He hated seeing her like this. His every instinct had begged him not to put her in this situation.

Bedwyr unclamped his cape and flung it over the head and body. The pooling blood seeped into the fabric, plastering it to the floor.

Elanor panted, searching the cell with wild fear. "I am—I am alright." She gave Merlin a reassuring glance, but the distress in her eyes was unmistakable; her chest still pumped. "I just need a moment," she said, running her trembling hands over her face.

Merlin reached for her, eager to offer comfort, but she shrugged him away.

Her body stiffened, and she raised her voice. "I am alright, Merlin!"

Elanor closed her eyes and placed her hand on her chest. Her pale skin was moist with sweat.

Merlin's heart thumped like a drum, his adrenaline still boiling beneath his skin. *What had she seen?* he wondered, watching her cheeks shudder as she bit her bottom lip.

Arthur moved toward her. Merlin raised his hand to stop him. Her eyes opened and narrowed at the blood leaking out from beneath Bedwyr's cape.

With a careful tone, Merlin said, "He is dead, Elanor."

She huffed out through her nose, and her shoulders relaxed. Color flooded back into her neck and cheeks. Her face shifted. Boldness replaced the fear. She pulled herself up from the floor, setting her shoulders back like a queen before the wide-eyed kings. Merlin rose beside her and softly touched the end of her cold fingertips, hoping she was ready this time. Without looking at him, she snatched his hand into a solid hold.

"What did you see?" he asked Elanor.

She faced him. Fright still dilated her eyes, though she appeared quite composed. "I saw him," she whispered. "I saw Osian. His eyes." She shook her head. "They *change*."

Merlin narrowed his gaze. "He is the shapeshifter—the falcon."

"Ye—" Elanor stopped short. She turned back toward the kings, and more loudly, she said, "Osian is in a cave. A large cavernous one, and…he is *not* alone."

Merlin lifted his chest, anticipating her next words. He was prepared for this. He already had his suspicions, but still could not perceive how.

"It is *Morgan!*" Her body started trembling all over again.

A resounding gasp lit the room before murmurings flowed from the kings' lips.

"How is that possible?" Thul interjected. His glare shadowed his aged eyes.

Bedwyr cried, "But she is dead."

Peredur's teeth clenched. "*Impossible!* I was there. I witnessed Gwalahad's spear pierce her heart and pin her to the ground."

"She…She is *not* alive." Elanor shook her head, her expression turning grave. "She is a spirit—she is inside Osian. I heard her. I saw her."

"How can this be?" Arthur growled. He lifted his hand toward Merlin for an explanation. "Is this not only a dream, or a vision?"

"It was *not a dream!*" Elanor shot back with a vexed tone. "I was inside Malik's mind, but then, I was translated somewhere else. I was inside the cave with them. I could smell its *rot*. Morgan, sh-she—" Elanor stopped and peered at Merlin. Her cheeks quivered. "She saw me."

Merlin glared at Arthur. "You know the cave. It is the very same. Within the Forest of Goll. This is her old stomping grounds. Her wicked fingerprints have been on everything since the beginning."

Arthur's face sobered. "It is as though history is repeating itself."

Merlin hated to confirm it. This was the worst kind of trick, and it awakened his deep-rooted enmity. Morgan was a fire they had already stomped out. All the freedom that came with her death felt instantly snatched away. "Osian's fallen evil has conjured her. Somehow, she possesses him."

"No wonder he hides," Bedwyr muttered. "Morgan was the same—always afraid to show herself—sending others out to do her witchcraft. This is the very same."

Every expression in the cell soured. The kings seemed appalled by the vile suspicion that Morgan could be behind all this pain.

With a bitter growl, Thul spat, "All the years she swallowed down her serpentine throat. The pain it took us all to destroy her. And now"—his jaw rolled with indignation—"to learn she has not been destroyed after all. It makes it all seem like *worthless* sacrifice."

"No." Arthur shook his head, hope alight in his blue eyes. "It was *not* worthless. She is *not* living. She is but a wraeth—a ghost. Be thankful," he said, acknowledging the other three kings, "that you have not had dealings with her like the rest of us."

Croighcat lifted his sharp chin. "It does not appear we will have the luxury of not *dealing* with her this time."

"We now have a direction," Merlin said. "We know where Osian hides, and that there are dark plans developing within Goll. Osian cannot evade me now, and so neither can Morgan."

At Merlin's words, Elanor peered up at him; distressed lines creased her forehead. Merlin saw in her countenance that there was more she needed to tell him.

Arthur sighed. "We are leaving this cell with two of the enemy slain, and with understanding we did not have before." He dropped his head and rubbed his beard in consideration. After a moment of silence, he started again. "Thul, your sons have served both Caer Lial and Celyddon with honor. Your younger son shall return to you as your battle chieftain. He is now able and ready for the task. Whereas, your elder now must be ready for more responsibility." Arthur moved toward the kings. "We must reclaim Llyonesse. We cannot allow the southern corner of Prydain to be lost. Your eldest, along with a number of men from each of our flanks, will follow your son Thangul, and gird him up as the new steward of Llyonesse."

Thul's mouth widened, and he bowed. "Thank you for honoring my sons, my king."

"I will go with Thangul, along with a small army of my own men to establish the citadel, and secure his leadership. Any of you that will follow me are welcome. But your need will soon come for war. Whether or not you come with me now is up to you, but I will be raising the call. My hope is to not meet the enemy on their lands. The Forest of Goll has been treacherous in the past. I will not risk the lives of Cymbrogi by blazing into that godforsaken forest without great cause. I have *needlessly* lost many inside its tangled webs before."

"The cave Elanor spoke about," Cormach asked, placing his hand in the center of his polished breastplate, "is it within Goll—within the Southlands?"

Merlin nodded. "If it is the one we suspect, it is within a craggy ravine at the forest's center."

"We will raise up scouts," Arthur continued. "Men from each of our kingdoms will survey the forest perimeter and coast. If there are ships landing on Prydain's shore, we will know about them." He tilted his head, and a dark edge governed his countenance. "We have dealt with invaders on our shores before. They will soon discover my iron fist."

"I will ride with you," Thul declared with pride.

"As will I," said Bram. Eagerness dripped from his brow, as though, finally, the call to action had come.

"And I," came Cormach. "On the way, I will summon my armies to meet us."

"Galen?" Merlin smiled.

"Yes—my chieftain will come."

Croighcat lifted his chin with smugness. "I will not join you to Llyonesse. I have business and trades to attend to. But," he said, "I will not hesitate to answer the call when the time comes. My warriors will be made ready."

"It may come sooner than you think, Croighcat," Arthur said with suspicion in his glare.

"Do not worry, my king." Croighcat swished his hand with a conjured smile. "I will send my scouts and supporting Cymbrogi to Llyonesse."

Arthur narrowed his eyes at Croighcat, then shook his head. "Let us leave this stinking cell. We will reconvene to solidify the stratagem at council. For now," he said, his stare alighting on Elanor, "we need to rest and wash the taste of this vileness from our mouths."

"What is it? What else do I need to know?" Merlin asked with tenderness, escorting Elanor into their chamber. Adhan was inside watching their child, who lay asleep on the bed. She stood to her feet when they entered and approached them with a smile. But she halted upon seeing Elanor's face. The corners of her mouth turned down.

"It is alright," Merlin whispered to her, then looked to Elanor. "We are alright."

Adhan cupped her hand to Elanor's cheek. Her eyes radiated concern.

Elanor forced a smile. "I just need to rest."

Adhan nodded. She squeezed Elanor's shoulders, then stole silently out of the room, carefully shutting the door behind her.

Elanor felt Merlin's eyes on her. Her head still swam. She floated past him, directing her steps toward the napping child in their bed. She wanted nothing else but to curl up beside her, and caress the warmth of her little body. Her perfect round cheeks were already beginning to thin. The ache of lost time while she had been away nagged at her heart.

What she saw down in that cell would rob more time. Time that was meant to be spent loving her daughter. She stroked her finger down Gwendolen's nose and across her fine silken hair. "She is so beautiful," Elanor whispered with sorrow heating her face.

Merlin drew near and wrapped his arm over her shoulder, caressing her.

"Tell me I can leave the nightmares behind, and just stay here with her." She squeezed her eyes tight. Wet tears sprang free, and her chin trembled. The monsters she had just faced still bared their hideous teeth inside her head.

Merlin kissed her temple. "I want that with all my heart."

Elanor turned into his chest with a long sigh.

"Please," he said, his voice low. "Tell me what you saw."

Elanor pressed her lips together, wishing she could forget. She knew the enemy now had a grip they did not have before. She had opened the door, just as Merlin warned. The demons had not only seen her—something had happened that filled her with dread.

"Elanor?"

"Morgan, she—" Elanor did not want to say it, for fear saying it aloud would make it true. Her tearful eyes peered up at him. "She saw me. Her eyes—they *owned* me." Regret sank in, and she shook her head. "Osian saw me."

Merlin leaned in, a desire to understand gleaming in his eyes. She didn't want to tell Merlin what more Morgan had said, but his eyes told her he already knew.

"Caer Lial has always been protected," he said. "Almost like the hand of the Great God has covered us, and kept us safe. Though pain has entered, there still has always remained an invisible armor. I have never had to fear for you within the Palisade walls—except for when the gwyllgi was unleashed upon us." His face soured at the memory. "But even then, Osian would never have dared walk these halls for fear of meeting me." He fingered the pendant that hung from her neck. "This is my own way of protecting you."

"What do you mean?"

He dismissed the question, as if his mind was plagued with other worries. "I do not know what all this means, but I felt it in the cell when you were losing your grip.

Even now—" He turned an untrusting eye toward their door. "There are uninvited ears."

"What must I do?" Elanor instinctively turned back to Gwendolen and wrapped her arms around her sleeping child, feeling the need to protect her.

"We do battle. But not just one with swords and spears. An invisible one."

The sound of their voices disturbed Gwendolen. Her little body squirmed, and small moans escaped her. Elanor wanted to wake her up. Her brightness, a joyful distraction.

Merlin gripped her hand, pulling her up from the bedside. He nodded for them to sit by the hearth so Gwendolen could sleep.

Elanor settled on a cushioned chair; Merlin sat across from her on the bench. Her eyes drew back to the child wrapped in blankets. Her brow crimped as the ghostly face of Morgan appeared again inside her mind. Fear tightened her throat, but she swallowed it back down.

"Who is Morgan?" she asked. "I mean…who is she *really*? I have heard mention of her. I know that Mordred was her son, but who is *she*? In stories I was told as a child, she was Arthur's half-sister, hungry to take the throne she believed rightfully hers."

Merlin huffed. "Arthur's sister? No." He shook his head. "She has no relation to you or Arthur. She is closer to my kin than his."

"Your kin?"

"Well, not directly. She is of my mother's race. A Fair Folk. I do not know exactly when it happened that she turned toward darkness, but what I do know is that she hated the race of men for flourishing, while her people diminished. She thought humans a lower race of beings. While human kings and kingdoms rose, she turned to witchcraft. The power akin to her from being of the elder race made her a powerful witch.

"It became her favorite device to trick and manipulate kings. But when I helped shield Aurelius, and then Uther from her, she became especially enraged against me. My power inhibited her from tearing them down. But when Arthur became king, her hatred boiled even more. Arthur and I became her target. She tried to kill me on multiple occasions, and once left me for dead, buried within a cave."

"Buried?"

"Gwain's brother, Geraint, was there." Merlin shook his head, and his eyes grew distant. "He saved me."

"Geraint?" She gazed at him in marvelment. There was still so much she didn't know about his past. The thought of it all made her want to know more.

"I will tell you of him another time. Great man. King's man." He smiled, then shook his head. "Morgan believes she should rule over men. That she should be Queen, and the lesser men enslaved. She will connive and deceive to reach her aims. Her twisted words are her most powerful tool. She has the ability to make the best of us lose our reason and falter…and it is this power that I think is amplifying the power of Osian's talisman."

Elanor rose and walked over to the window. Her insides wrestled with the disturbing image of Morgan's phantom face. Even now she felt Morgan's fingers resting on her shoulders, pulling her toward darkness. But the bright sun glistening on the green treetops made her want to believe all could be right with the world. That it had all just been the illusion of a bad dream. But it wasn't. The nightmare was becoming more real with each passing day.

Elanor asked, "What is in the Forest of Goll?"

17

THE CONSEQUENCES OF MAGIC

erlin stared into the hearth's fire, the flames casting shadows that danced like specters of the past. He hated to begin the tale. As with the battle on the fields at Camlan, it bore the bitter taste of failure, ending in a hollow victory.

"So many wrong choices," he murmured.

A vision of a tree dripping with blood flashed in his mind, stealing his breath. A ghostly reminder of those wrong choices. He leaned back, and he lifted his gaze to Elanor's entreating stare. So many secrets he wished were left buried. But indeed, he needed to reveal it. The time had come.

With a reluctant sigh, he started, "It all began with the Holy Cup."

The midday sunlight created a shadow on Elanor's pinched brow. "The grail?"

Merlin frowned, then continued, "The Fisher King—he was its keeper. It had been given to him to steward by the Arimathean after he died. It was a cup that had traveled with him from the east to Prydain. It was a simple cup that a god-man drank from in display of his kingdom." Merlin stopped, musing for a moment. The thought of *the song* played through his mind. The idea of the kingdom and this god-man stirred him.

"Merlin?" Elanor asked, calling him back from his reverie.

"Arthur lay ill from sickness—a fever was taking him. We had not seen the Fisher King since that day on the silver lake years before. But he had heard of Arthur's dire illness and traveled with his daughter to Caer Lial. Like spirits from another age, they came, delivering a sip of water from the Holy Cup to the king." Merlin paused, remembering their ageless glow, just like his mother's.

"The cup was simple. Wooden. Carved with runes from the eastern world. But when I looked upon it, something in my spirit leapt. Life itself dripped from its rim. When Arthur drank, his pallid skin grew flush. He drew larger, fuller breaths. His eyes opened brighter and bluer. I rushed to inspect the swollen lump below the pit of his arm. The infection was gone.

"Arthur sat up renewed. He asked the Fisher King if this was the cup he had spoken about that day by the lake. The king nodded that it was. I remember seeing such heavy remorse in the old king's eyes. I felt the weight of it too, though, at the time, I did not understand. I knew by his stare that he had hoped this day would never have come. Almost like he knew that healing Arthur with the cup's water would make him hunger for it.

"From the moment Arthur was healed, he believed the cup was a gift to him from the Great God himself. He wanted it, and asked the Fisher King for it—saying it should become a symbol of Prydain's kingdom.

"The Fisher King looked so sad." Merlin slumped his shoulders. "He said to Arthur, 'I have been the guardian of the cup these long years; it is time for me to let it fade.'

"Those words—I remember how they pierced me." Merlin shook his head. "The Fisher King gave the cup to Arthur. To this day, I am unsure he should have. He gave it up so easily. I saw the heartache in his eyes when he handed it over, as though he knew what would come because of it. Though, it also seemed he knew he must.

"However, he gave this warning: 'The kingdom you seek, nor its healing, is within the cup. There is more to be known and there must be patience to understand.'

"I saw Arthur's eyes gleam. He held the cup like a greedy king with a hoard of gold. I had never seen that look in his eyes before, and learned to loathe it long after. Little did we know the trial it would bring. One that would soon be at our doorstep.

"These days—these times—are still in echo of what began then. Everything had been so good, so right, until Arthur lost his heart to the cup.

"Arthur did not heed the Fisher King's warning, nor would he after when I reminded him. We never saw the Fisher King again, and the cup itself only remained but a short while. Arthur established a stone shrine, an edifice to hold the cup. It sits empty—just there." Merlin pointed out the window to the right.

"In the apple Orchard?" Elanor asked. With haste, she peered out the window. Recognition dawned on her face. "I have seen it. The old moss-covered mausoleum. It always appeared so empty and lifeless—a relic I thought I should never ask about. So, I never did."

"It had fewer trees surrounding it then, and a broader pathway that led to it. Arthur had his best men watching it both day and night." Merlin sighed, not wanting to begin the next part of the story.

He joined Elanor by the window, remembering the night the cup was stolen. The gray, round top of the shrine poked above the orchard branches. His face heated. The memory flickered to life as though it were yesterday. Llenllaewg had been in charge of the Cymbrogi guarding the Holy Cup—when something occurred. Still to this day, no one fully knew what happened. No one remained alive to truly tell it.

Merlin remembered the morning's vivid sunlight reflecting off the blood staining the grass. The domed shrine loomed ominously, like a harbinger of death, as he and several guards raced toward the alarmed calls emanating from the orchard. Six guards lay dead on the ground in front of the shrine—one still gasping for breath. Merlin's eyes searched inside the portico, settling on the pedestal at the shrine's center. It was empty.

The Holy Cup was gone.

"Where is Llenllaewg?" a guard shouted.

Merlin ran his fingers through his hair. His mind raced. Was Llenllaewg dead? Surely not. He was almost unbeatable. A giant among men.

Gwalahad arrived breathless beside Merlin, his eyes bitter.

"Have they found Llenllaewg?" Merlin asked, hoping Gwalahad was not about to announce he had found his body.

"Gwynevere is gone. Some report she and Llenllaewg departed together— betraying us."

Merlin shook his head. "That does not make any sense." His stomach turned, and his mind raced to put pieces together. None of it lined up.

The dying guard wheezed, capturing Merlin's attention. *He would have seen what happened.* Several guards and a healer were attending to him.

Merlin rushed over and knelt beside him. "Give me a moment to speak to him," he said to those preparing to take him.

"Lord Merlin, he—"

Merlin held up his hand with a stern glare, then leaned over the dying guard. His eyes fluttered, and his lips and jaw were slack. *He is so young.* Merlin twisted his mouth, hating that death had come to the Palisade like this.

"Please," Merlin begged the guard, lightly tapping his cheek. "Please. I must know what happened."

Llenllaewg did not betray us. I refuse to believe it.

The young guard's eyes slowly opened. A pained moan escaped his lips.

Merlin hated to press him, but he was the only one left who had seen anything. "I need to know what you—"

"Llenllaewg," the guard groaned through a strained breath. "He—he took it."

"No," Merlin hissed through gritted teeth. "No, try to remember. Llenllaewg was guarding the cup; he must have been defending it."

The guard's eyes widened. "He attacked us." His body tensed, and then a last breath seeped through his lips. His eyes glazed over.

Merlin closed his eyes. The young Cymbrogi's life was gone.

"Merlin?" Gwalahad's voice beckoned from behind him.

Merlin didn't turn around. He knew the *Holy Cup* should never have come here. It was like a curse blighting Arthur's mind—tainting the Palisade.

"Merlin!"

Merlin spun, facing Gwalahad with an acrid glare.

"Many think Gwynevere and Llenllaewg formed a tryst."

Merlin growled, "Is that what you believe?"

Gwalahad's gaze dipped to the ground, his brown locks falling over his dark eyes. "No," he finally said.

"Has Arthur been told?"

Gwalahad nodded. "Bors has already gone to him."

"Then why isn't Arthur here?" Merlin bit more aggressively than he meant to. "Men need to be sent after Llenllaewg. Gwynevere—she could be in danger."

"I will gather some men."

"Yes." Merlin nodded. "I will go to Arthur. Be ready."

Merlin wasted no time running through the Great Hall and the courtyard. When he opened the door to the Palisade, he expected to see Arthur ordering his men, but he found only Bors standing alone on the tiled floor. His wide, dazed eyes stared at the floor.

"What are you doing?" Merlin yelled.

"I—" Bors fumbled, tugging at his red and gold cape as if he were contemplating tearing it off in an act of mourning. "Llenllaewg, he—"

"That is *enough*," Merlin snapped, setting his jaw. He grabbed Bors by the collar, pulling him close to his face. "All is not as it seems. I am sure of it. Pull yourself together."

"We have been betrayed."

"Yes." Merlin nodded, resisting the urge to slap Bors across his square jaw. "We have been betrayed, but not by Llenllaewg. Something more has happened, and it is your duty to find out what."

"But, Arthur—he will not—"

Merlin's heart sank, suddenly realizing Arthur had bought the lie.

Merlin cursed, letting go of Bors. "We cannot delay. I will seek the king for what will come next. For now, meet Gwalahad in the yard. He is gathering men ready to ride." Merlin started toward the stairs, then halted. Bors hadn't moved. "Go!"

Bors snapped out of his stupor and jogged from the Palisade.

Exasperated, Merlin rushed up the stairs and down the corridor toward Arthur's chamber. He barged through the door and found Arthur crumpled on the floor. He held his head in his hands, his fingers sifting through handfuls of his blond hair.

"Arthur!" Merlin shouted, racing over to him. "What are you doing?"

Arthur lowered his hands, his mouth agape, and glanced up with hollow eyes.

"What is this?" Merlin asked.

"She—she has left me. Gwynevere. Llenllaewg. She has gone with him. T-Taken the cup."

"Arthur!" Merlin's shout rang in the hall, jolting the king. "None of this has been confirmed. Something else has caused this. We need men to go after them and discover the truth."

Arthur just stared at him as though none of Merlin's words penetrated his ears.

"She has *not* left you. Llenllaewg would *never* betray you."

Arthur retreated back into his hands. His spirit lay shattered on the floor somewhere; his heart broken. Merlin wanted to shake him, hit him, force him to stop believing the lie. He needed to be king. He needed to take action. But Merlin could see there was nothing he could do to pull him out of his despondency. At least, not right now.

"Bah," Merlin huffed, storming from the room. "I will send your men. I will *not* sit and wallow, and neither will they." Disappointment welled in his chest. Where was the dauntless king he had raised? He had never seen Arthur like this, yet even Merlin struggled to believe it was not true—that Llenllaewg had not betrayed them. The little evidence they had pointed at the ultimate breach of trust.

Who could have gotten through the gates? Who could have gotten past Llenllaewg?

"Unless I see it with my eyes," Merlin said, rushing down the hall, "I will *not* believe it."

"It took us a few days," the Cymbrogi rider said, catching his breath as he stood in the Great Hall before Merlin and Arthur, both anxious for news of the search. Four days had passed since Gwynevere and Llenllaewg went missing, and Merlin's faith that they would be found was waning.

"Gwalahad followed Llenllaewg's trail, until we found slain bodies," the rider reported, his cheeks flushed "Bors and Peredur read the ground. There was some sort of clash. Pieces of Gwynevere's garments and also Llenllaewg's brooch were found amongst the remains."

Vindication, mingled with horror, rushed through Merlin. The rider stepped forward and placed the brooch and red sash into Arthur's palm.

Arthur's jaw rippled as he squeezed the items into his fist. He still appeared not fully convinced.

"There is more," the rider went on. "A day further on their trail, we found Llenllaewg."

Arthur's eyes snapped up from the garment. "You found him?"

"He was wounded. Stabbed through his shoulder with a spear. Gwynevere was not with him. Llenllaewg tried to stop Morgan but failed."

Morgan. Merlin's stomach dropped to his feet.

"Llenllaewg said—" The rider hesitated, staring at the ground. "He said that the Cymry guarding the Holy Cup that night had been bewitched and attacked *him*. He defended the cup, though he said it was already gone. No one had taken it—or, at least, he saw no one."

"Why did Gwynevere go with him?" Arthur demanded, his gaze growing fiercer.

"Llenllaewg said he heard whinnying horses by the stables. He ran and discovered Gwynevere draped over a horse, with Morguese, the rider, galloping away from the Palisade."

"Wait…Morguese?" Arthur growled.

"She has been the one to betray us?" Merlin asked, his mind racing to put it all together. "That is how they got through the gate—she was already here. Within the Palisade walls."

"Yes," the rider said, nodding. "Morgan joined Morguese on the trail with a small army of men."

Merlin bit his lip. He glanced at Arthur, whose eyes flamed with sudden regret. Merlin resisted the urge to call him a *fool*, thinking better of it.

The rider stared at the ground, chewing the inside of his bottom lip. "Morguese—sh-she is Morgan's daughter."

Merlin and Arthur gasped in unison. Bitter bile welled in Merlin's throat. He realized he had not seen Morguese since it happened. Why had he not noticed Morguese was missing? No one else had either. He had his suspicions of her. He had watched her loft around the Palisade with seductive eyes. She even managed to get to him.

Merlin shook his head with shame. Her alluring voice made him want to offer her the world, keeping his mind from perceiving her intent. He cringed at the thought of her red lips and sultry voice. He snapped spitefully, "She is *just* like her mother. Her words—*poison*."

The rider then said, "Llenllaewg wasted no time pursuing Morguese to rescue Gwynevere."

Arthur winced, gritting his teeth.

"Of course, he did," Merlin said, hating that even *he* had doubted Llenllaewg as the days wore on. Llenllaewg and Gwynevere had been inseparable—tied—like a brother and sister. He was Gwynevere's singular guard since long before she ever met Arthur. Their relationship had always flared Arthur's jealousy, so it was not hard for him to believe in Llenllaewg's infidelity.

In truth, Llenllaewg was the *best of them all*. He had not been deceived by Morguese's wiles, and was the only one sacrificing himself to rescue Gwynevere now.

"Llenllaewg fought against Morgan and her men," the rider continued, "but they ended up capturing him. They could not keep *him* bound, my King." The Cymry lifted his chest. A look of honor hung in his eyes. "Not Llenllaewg. He fought to get free just before they entered Goll. He killed many more of them, but unfortunately, Llenllaewg faltered—struck through his shoulder. Morguese slipped through his fingers, with Gwynevere still in her grasp."

"Great God. Gwynevere." Arthur's eyes welled. "Where is Llenllaewg? Is he with the healers?"

The rider shook his head. "Bors did his best to patch Llenllaewg's wound, and then Gwalahad ordered we take him back with us and report to you. Gwalahad stayed. He went into the forest with Bors and Peredur. Once we were loaded for our return, Llenllaewg was gone. We think he might have gone into the forest."

18

THE FOREST OF GOLL

Merlin stepped away from the window and settled himself into a nearby chair. "The Forest of Goll," he said to Elanor, rubbing his forehead. "If only we had known what we would meet on the other side of that boundary of trees."

The space between Elanor's brows tightened. She slipped over and sat back on the edge of the chair, her eyes curious.

"If we had delayed any further—" Merlin shook his head, hating to think what might have happened. "Morgan, along with her daughter Morguese, had taken Gwynevere deep into Goll. Arthur had come to his senses and now we stood before the forest, with an army of Cymbrogi ready to save her." Merlin sat back, his eyes drifting. This was the part that really pained him. This was the part that rang with familiar evil.

His thoughts wandered back to that day they stood before the wicked forest, and the memory took hold.

Arthur's gaze was steely, but Merlin saw the scars of regret etched behind his eyes. The forest would only deepen those scars. Arthur had not been quite the same since thinking he was betrayed, and it worsened when he realized he let Gwynevere be kidnapped and he had done nothing.

The army left their horses behind and quietly filtered into the trees. Their feet slithered through the brush; their weapons held at the ready. Merlin led just ahead of Arthur, using the keenness of his magic to discern what lay in front of them. Cia's wild red hair brushed his broad shoulders as the warrior hunted the ground to Merlin's left. Bedwyr on his right scanned through the trees.

"It is only Morgan and her few remaining warriors, right?" Bedwyr whispered to Merlin.

Merlin shook his head, looking back at Arthur so he could hear. "Morgan always has a trick up her sleeve."

"We have been lured into a forest. It is a trap," Arthur whispered back.

"Morguese has deceived us. Morgan has been behind it all. We can assume witchcraft will be at play."

"Foul witch," Cai cursed.

Merlin tsked. "I am discerning nothing. We have been searching for hours and the sky is darkening. This does not bode well for us."

"What do you suggest?" Arthur asked.

"We must know what we are walking into. I could make a druid's fire. It would enable me to stretch my sight to find our enemy—to see through her tricks." Merlin shuffled through his satchel and retrieved a leather pouch of ash. A twinge in the pit of his stomach made him suddenly reconsider. The magic of the old religion was untrustworthy.

Arthur rested his hand atop Merlin's shoulder. "Would it work? The more we delay, the more I worry we are too late. Gwynevere, she—" His eyes reddened, but then he sniffed his emotions back.

Merlin pushed aside his apprehension. "Yes. It would work."

Arthur whistled, calling the Cymbrogi to stop and make camp.

Merlin quickly cleared a space for the fire. The canopy of trees made him feel closed in and trapped. Shaking it off, he pointed to where Cai could lay the wood.

"Dark magic?"

Elanor's voice called Merlin back from the past.

"I used a seeing magic. Different from the kind you used, but still it was a magic of the old religion. I set a fire, placing inside it the ancient ash of the druids. Then I conjured out of the flames spirits of sight to find where Morgan and Morguese had taken Gwynevere. Because I invited enaid that were not of light, I gained the power to see, but I also unlocked the ability for the dark ones to know where we were.

"I discovered Gwynevere's location within the fire—a camp at the center of the forest. There were more warriors—*traitors*—ready to defend than we had expected with Morgan leading them through her witchcraft. Within her hand she held a cup, but it was not the Holy Cup. This one was ornate, golden, and delicately lined with ruby gems. This, we later discovered, was called *The Chalice of Life*. We did not know then what magic it held, but soon we saw how it robbed those who drank from it from their very soul. It made them alive with an immortal death, impossible to kill."

Elanor scrunched her face in disbelief. "How can that be real?"

"Dark magic like this *is possible*, though costly to the conjurer. The witch's life is attached to the curse. No man with hope for life would ever bind themselves to such sorcery."

Merlin shuddered, recalling it. "I did not understand then what I know now. The forest had already been set with demons, but because I *meddled* in magic, Morgan knew exactly how to target us, and quickly. From the moment my fire went out, her fallen voice echoed through the air. The men started screaming—they were seeing things that were not there. Some even lost the ability to recognize friend from foe. They attacked one another, thinking the other a monster. Our ranks scattered. Men lost their minds and ran wildly into the depths of the forest. With quick fury, I released another magic to shield Arthur, and those closest to us. Bedwyr and Cia being amongst them.

"I thought it had worked, but it only served to keep us from altogether losing our minds. I do not know how long we wandered the wilds, but in truth, we lost ourselves. We circled the same bit of forest over and over, trapped in an inescapable loop. We lost several men in the night. Dark creatures snatched them one at a time. Our numbers dwindled, until finally, exhausted, we came to an opening in the forest. A meadow with a tree at its center."

Merlin swallowed hard. Still, the horror of what he saw that day haunted him. The nightmare blazed like an inferno in his mind. And again, he found himself lost in the memory:

Following Arthur's lead, Merlin rushed into the meadow. Arthur drew his blade, his eyes vigilant. The tree in the middle of the meadow drew their focus. It was the white forms Merlin noticed first. Their contrast against the green foliage seemed wrong. His heart started beating up into his ears, his footfalls matching each dreadful thump. A red tar-like substance dripped from the leaves. Merlin raced closer, hoping his eyes were betraying him. But then he saw them. A horrified wail gushed from Arthur's throat. The scene shot cold prickles through Merlin's body.

Bodies—torn, broken, and lifeless—hung from the branches.

It was Gwalahad's glazed eyes that Merlin saw first. The deep brown color was gone, leaving them blue and milky. Merlin's body stiffened. Shock froze his steps. He forced himself to look at the rest of the tree. Bors, Peredur, and Llenllaewg were strewn like meat for vultures.

Merlin took a horrified step back. A tear fell from his eye. Screams of dread erupted from the men, striking a chord of hopelessness. The sound wrenched the muscles in Merlin's chest, but it jerked him out of his panic.

Merlin's eyes connected with Arthur's. His teeth flashed white and his eyes blazed with strength. There was his king, awakening from his slumber. Merlin ran toward him, ready for their next move, when a flash exploded white around him. His body flung through the air, and he hit the ground. He anticipated a stab of pain but felt nothing. Heard nothing. Merlin sat up and saw the Cymbrogi scattered on the ground. The tree was split in half and on fire. Burnt flesh wafted through the air.

Lightning.

Arthur pulled himself up, and Merlin shouted to him, "Witchcraft!" But he couldn't hear the sound of his own voice. Even as the words left his lips, the clouded sky turned scarlet and rain started to fall.

Arthur stood heaving. The rain sluicing over his face looked like blood. Merlin lifted his own hand in front of his eyes. His palms streamed with rouge.

This cannot be real. This is sorcery.

Merlin clenched his jaw and leapt from the ground. He pulled his sword free from his sheath. His magic jetted down his arms in golden swirls. "This isn't real," he shouted to Arthur, running to his side.

"No!" Arthur confirmed.

The other men labored to their feet. Arthur shouted orders for them to gather. Merlin peered over his shoulder, and emerging from the trees were shadows shaped like men. The cursed warriors Merlin had seen in the druid's fire lumbered toward them with spears lifted high.

Cia was the first to meet an enemy warrior. The ground had turned into a crimson sludge. When Cia's sword met the spear of the first devil, the enemy slipped backward into the mud. Cia raised his sword and thrust it into his foe's chest. He pulled his sword free and stood back, ready to take aim at the next attacker. But the stabbed enemy rose from the ground, and lifted his spear once again. Cia's jaw dropped.

Merlin didn't hesitate. He screamed, releasing a blast of his power, blowing a dozen or more adversaries to the ground.

The battle commenced. Steel hitting steel. Blood and mud flinging through the air, covering them like war paint. Merlin fought with his sword, splicing through the enemy that rose again and again. His magic forced them back, twisting their bodies through the air, but it only held them back for brief moments of reprieve.

The battle waged on, and he grew weary. They all were, but they couldn't stop— he couldn't stop, or else they would die. Time disappeared into a hell the armies of Prydain could never defeat.

"Then," Merlin said to Elanor, his eyes filling with tears, remembering the moment the horror ended. "The sky broke with light and the rain disappeared. The warriors stopped, and I heard this shrill scream. Morgan stood with Morguese at the edge of the forest. I saw her clenching her fists, baring her teeth like a savage. She grabbed hold of Morguese's wrist and stormed into the center of the field. I still remember the look of terror on Morguese's face. Her blonde hair floating behind as she stumbled behind her mother. Morgan had one hand extended in front of her, reciting words of dark speech. She stopped to face us. I was preparing to defend."

Merlin glanced up at Elanor. Her mouth gaped with anticipation. "What happened?"

"It was Llenllaewg who appeared when the light broke. I remember feeling confused. We had seen him dead upon the tree, but now he silently snuck onto the field with his sword in his hand. He launched from behind Morguese. She screamed, but it was cut short. Llenllaewg's sword sliced through her back.

"Morgan screeched, hurtling Llenllaewg through the air with a burst of her magic. When I turned, I saw that the tree behind us was no longer filled with the bodies of our brothers. Lightning had never singed its branches. It had all been an illusion. The earth below my feet was dry; there had never even been any rain.

"Through the trees appeared Gwalahad." Merlin smiled, remembering the triumph of seeing his face. "Gwalahad knew he had Morgan the moment he stepped onto the field. Behind him marched Peredur and Bors. All three of their faces beamed with the light of the otherworld. With one hand Gwalahad held the Holy Cup, in the other he clenched a spear."

"He had taken the cup?"

"No." Merlin shook his head. "But he did find it. Or rather, I think it may have found him. Either way, he had it, and the sight of it made Morgan writhe. I remember how he marched toward her with a vengeful stride. Her hand pulling on strands of her black hair. The closer he came, the more the undead warriors bled. Their bodies no longer enchanted with false life, they all began to die, falling one by one. Morguese had been the link—her death broke the curse of the chalice.

"Gwalahad gripped his spear and lifted it high. Morgan turned heel to run, but Gwalahad had already sent the spear to flight. It sailed through the air toward its target, piercing through Morgan's back. Its speed ran her through to the ground, sticking in the turf like a pike. She hung there dead—on display for all to see."

Merlin chuckled only to keep his rising emotions at bay. "I saw Gwynevere kneeling at the edge of the meadow. Her bonds were cut and she wept. Llenllaewg was laying in her arms." Merlin shuddered. "His wound took him. Every last bit of his life had been spent freeing Gwynevere.

"Arthur fell to his knees beside him, begging his forgiveness. I remember how he squeezed Llenllaewg's tunic as if it would pull him back to life." Merlin paused for a moment. The memory still felt so raw. Llenllaewg was not buried in The Hill of the Kings like the rest of them. He had been laid to rest next to the shrine that had held the Holy Cup. Merlin glanced back toward the window. It was a shame Elanor was only learning about him now. He deserved to be better remembered.

"Arthur did not let go of Gwynevere for a very long time after that," Merlin said, then sat quietly, pondering.

Osian hiding in the Forest of Goll confirmed Merlin's suspicions about Morgan's involvement, and now with Elanor having invoked the old magic, he sensed a trap. They had doomed themselves, unleashing a malevolent force that now loomed at their doorstep.

Elanor asked, "What happened to the Holy Cup? Did Gwalahad not still have it?"

"Mm," Merlin moaned. "It disappeared."

"It was just gone?"

"Arthur never gave up the search for it after that day. I believed the cup to be immaterial. It was never a thing that could be owned or physically grasped."

"The Chalice of Life?"

"Also gone."

Elanor nodded, clearly taking it all in. "And what of the cave I saw? You seemed to know it."

"Yes…the cave we discovered later. Leaving the forest was still no easy task. A residual enchantment of evil remained in Goll—still does to this day. We stumbled our way through and found a crevasse. Inside, we discovered the cave, which held all kinds of witchery. We destroyed it with fire, leaving it forsaken."

"Why had they taken Gwynevere?" Elanor paused, frowning. "Was it Morguese who took the cup?"

"The whole aim of Morgan's plan was to lure Arthur into Goll to be destroyed. But the cup is a mystery. We do not know if the enemy tried to take it and lost it, or if it chose to no longer remain. Gwynevere's memories of the ordeal are not clear—she only remembers glimpses. Morgan enchanted her to keep her from fighting against them. All I know is, the cup is not something that can be owned, and Morgan was frightened when she saw in it in Gwalahad's grip."

THE ENEMY'S MOVE

"We have her," Osian said, twisting toward the apparition lurking behind him. "She has let us into her mind." He leered forward with a devilish smile.

The wraeth pulsed. There was no form to its purple-amaranthine glow—only a voice. "I hold her, though she does not know it. Her mind is a tangle of loss and insecurity. This is the sort of mind that does well when I want to *break it*. I knew she would overreach with her *immature* magic. Merlin might have prepared her better, but I see his own fear has kept him from it."

The ghost's light burst and fizzled away. Inside Osian's mind, he heard her say, *"She is afraid of me."*

"We should take her *now*."

At his words, Morgan released a stinging jolt. Osian reeled backward with pain radiating in his head and shooting down through his spine. He pressed his fingers into his skull, falling forward into a crouch.

"Your lack of patience is tiresome. You spend power you do not have, just like you did when you tried to have Arthur's body destroyed in the tombs at the Hill of the Kings. Pointless. Reckless."

The pain stopped, and Osian gasped for air, licking the saliva from his lips. "I thought I could kill his cursed corpse. That way, he would never be awakened. I did not know," he growled, "that there would be a powerful white wraeth guarding the door. It *killed* my druids. So, I cursed it with your cyhyraeth."

"Wasteful! As a result, my cyhyraeth has been freed from my power."

The pain struck Osian again. He curled back into himself, clenching his teeth. The agonizing pang surged up and down like a current of lightning.

"None of it accomplished anything, and only resulted in draining your power—leaving you weak for far too long. Too many times your impatience has cost you. I waited years, training my children to manipulate kings. This is what gains you power. That is when they offer you keys without having to even fight for it."

"What is it you would have me do?" he eked out. Sweat streamed down his temple.

"Arthur is coming. He seeks to stop us and take back his lands. We will meet him."
"We?"

"NOT YOU AND I," Morgan's voice screamed, knocking Osian onto his knees.

The magic stabbed through his skin like needles. Osian howled. "I cannot think straight…not while you punish me."

Morgan's power relented. Osian gasped, eyes squeezed shut, and wiped the sweat from his forehead. Biting his lip, he forced his nerves to relax. Sometimes he wondered why he ever let Morgan in. But then—he remembered that day. The day he discovered the *chalice*. Its bowl stained with dried blood.

He was still so young when he stumbled into the Forest of Goll. He had been all alone since fleeing Caer Lial. The yelps and gurgles of his mother still haunted him.

Her wide eyes becoming bloodshot. His hand strangling her.

Osian cringed at the memory. He was never going to allow Merlin the chance to take the talisman from him. The white stone and moon pendant was all he ever wanted. Merlin would have taken the magic it held away from him and destroyed it. He resented that his mother knew where it was hidden and refused to tell him. She deserved to die. She betrayed him by telling Merlin where to find it.

Osian got to it first. He killed his mother and then fled from the only place he had ever called home. But he had the talisman. He remembered the excitement, the fear, mixing with the rising bile in his stomach. He refused to be weak like his father—afraid to use the magic of the talisman. The power he had dreamt of was finally at his fingertips. He was thrilled at the thought of all he could do to those who had teased him for being different. Tall. Lumbering.

As he stumbled into Goll, he saw a glow through a tangle of ivy. Its golden glint captured his eye. He pulled the treasure from the weeds and wiped his thumb across the bowl, revealing a golden chalice lined with rubies. It held unusual power. He felt it immediately—just like with the talisman. It heated his palms and pulsed with eerie, dull vibrations. It chilled his spine and turned his stomach. Over time, he learned to love the feeling that came with the tainted magic.

Drawn deeper into Goll's forest, he found the cave. Within the blackened debris, he heard her. She beckoned to him through what had remained. He was no longer alone.

Osian came back to himself and snarled at Morgan, "You would have me send Dunnoc with the Southlanders." He grinned, understanding the impact of her plan. "The weak young ones will bring our enemy the most pain."

"We will weaken them before they ever meet Dunnoc. I will cause despair, making them demoralized prey— easily taken." An echoing laughter ricocheted off the cave walls, intensifying as it reverberated. *"I will break Arthur's heart and crush Merlin's soul, then we will strike the land and destroy those who have stolen what belonged to my people."*

"I have news!" Merlin hollered, capering over to Elanor and Adhan, who were watching Gwendolen stumble through the yard in front of the orchard. Even as he spoke, the child's giggle tickled his ears. The three-year-old dashed into her mother's arms with a cry of joy. Elanor lifted her into the air with a spin. Gwendolen's dark curls tumbled over her cheeks, her small teeth showing beneath her wide, enthralled smile.

Elanor turned, a delicate smile on her face, but then, her lips parted with a frown. Merlin saw the flash of her magic capturing the seriousness behind his eye.

"All has been decided," Merlin said. "We are marching out in a fortnight. I go with them."

The light in Elanor's eyes dwindled. Gwendolen burst away from her to tumble through the grass, and Elanor said, "I know it does not make sense for you to stay. Arthur needs you with him."

There was more he needed to tell her, but he hesitated, glancing away so she could not use her magic to discover it for herself. He and Arthur had come to a decision.

"What is it?" she pressed, walking toward him; her fingers folded over his arm.

He didn't want to tell her his decision was because of what he saw behind her eyes. A shadow prowled inside them ever since she used her magic against Malik. Merlin watched her try to convince herself it wasn't there. It made him want to keep her close.

"Elanor," Merlin said with a careful tone, "you are being outfitted to come with us."

Elanor's neck and cheeks flushed.

Adhan floated to Elanor's side. Her ethereal stature was like a tower of protective armor as she wrapped her arm around Elanor's shoulders. Her brows tightened, and she asked, "Should not Elanor stay? She should be here, protecting her child."

"Yes—I understand. But this time Arthur is right."

Adhan stared at him. Her silvery-blue eyes scanned his, analyzing his motives and making Merlin feel small. His mother always knew when there was more. She asked, "Arthur, who would not let her go to Celyddon, wants her to come now?"

"Things have changed," he said, hardening his voice. "Arthur has begun to see Elanor as I do. She has a part to play in all of this. One that cannot be ignored, and I would rather be beside her, protecting her, than leave her behind. This venture is a mission to restore the lands of Llyonesse, not one for battle."

"There could be resistance," Adhan argued.

"There is danger now, no matter where we are. Here or otherwise."

Elanor sighed, her exhale like a forlorn stream.

Merlin turned toward her—despondency deadened the brightness of her blue eyes.

"What about what *I* think?" Elanor asked quietly, her stare distanced beyond the trees. She didn't appear angry, but conflicted.

Merlin knew the trapped feeling. The pattering sound of Gwendolen's feet grabbed his attention. Her innocent smile pierced him, sinking his heart with bitter remorse. He did not want to leave his child. He knew Elanor did not want to either. Not again. Not right now.

Elanor turned to him. There was an edge to her voice as she said, "Both you and Arthur go on as though I am not even here, making decisions for me."

Merlin drooped his head, biting his lip, but held her gaze. He saw the struggle within her eyes. "It was not meant to—"

"I am not a Cymbrogi that sits at the ready, waiting for orders. Why could you not have me part of the conversation that involved my life—my time?" She folded her arms, opened her mouth to argue further, but then appeared to think better of it and fell silent. Her face slackened and her shoulders relaxed. "I accept it anyway."

She faced away, watching Gwendolen hop from one stone to another. A smile twitched the corner of her mouth when Gwendolen landed without stumbling. She clapped her hands with triumph.

"Arthur—" Merlin paused, pressing his lips into a tight line. "It was my decision that committed you. I fear leaving you here would be to our—*your* detriment."

Elanor's brow softened. "I would probably have the same complaint had I been left behind. I just—I do not want *any of it*. I just want this," she said, pointing to her daughter, who, at that moment, spun and playfully fell to the ground. Elanor's eyes narrowed. "Yet, it is there. In the pit of my soul. A desire to see this *thing* done. I am still learning to accept that I have a part in this. You and Arthur are not wrong."

THE BEAR

Clang!

"Elanor!" Bedwyr shouted. "It is not how hard you strike. You will burn out your arms. It is in your form. Follow through, like this." He lifted his sword and swung with perfect grace. His whole body moved along with the motion of his sword. He snatched her wrist before she had a chance to try his action. "You put too much of your hope in the strength of this"—he shook her hand—"to hold your sword."

"This," he said, drawing a line down his arm and torso, "all works together. Your wrist strengthened by the whole." He swatted her side with the back of his hand, making her squeak.

Merlin burst into laughter. Elanor shot him a glare, then grumbled, turning back to face Bedwyr.

Before they had set out for the Southlands, Arthur had a leather breastplate made for her that formed to her chest, along with leather bracers. They had been journeying now for four days, and she may have looked a little more the part of a warrior; however, it didn't make her perform any better. Every evening, when they stopped to camp, Bedwyr and Merlin took turns honing her swordcraft. The same way they had done for the past few years. Only now their instruction had intensified.

"Again," Bedwyr commanded with a half-cocked grin.

She gripped her blade and positioned her feet. Her side still stung from Bedwyr's slap, reminding her to pull up and tighten her stance. Now that she wore breeches instead of a skirt, this seemed to also give Bedwyr permission to smack the inside of her thighs to reposition.

"Ow!" she griped, grimacing.

"That's it." Bedwyr smiled, delight brightening his eyes. "Take that energy and channel it into your fight. It is what is in your head that makes you weak, not your body."

"RAH!" she yelled, launching toward him. Her frustration made her wish she could smash him.

Bedwyr spun like an elegant deer, leaping around her charge. He shifted his feet and whacked her across her derriere with the flat of his sword.

"Ow," she yelped, rubbing off the sting.

"You give me too much warning before you move. You are like a loaded sling. Relax. Breathe. Study my stance. You are the predator; I am the prey. This is the dance."

The loose hairs from her braid stuck to the sweat on her brow. She grunted, exasperated. She felt like the Cymbrogi were getting an eyeful. They watched with obvious pleasure, made evident by their handshakes and exchanges—either betting on her success or failure. She had become their entertainment each evening. She rolled her eyes. Neither Merlin nor Bedwyr seemed inclined to tell them to leave. Her skill had grown, but against these seasoned warriors, it made her wonder why she even tried.

"Come on…Let us go again."

"Right." She sucked air in through her nose and out through her mouth. Her shoulders and body tightened as she lifted her sword. She took in another long inhale, allowing the tenseness to dissolve. It felt refreshing not to hold the hilt so tight, feeling the wind cool against her skin. She steadied her feet, then lifted her chest.

"Yes." Bedwyr grinned, locking eyes with her. "Now I can see it. Your sword is not separate from your arm. You are strong enough now not to be wearied by its weight. Flow with it." He took a focused step forward. "Keep your eye on my movement. Predict my steps and match them."

She stepped forward, and Bedwyr's sword sliced through the air toward her. *Shing!* She met his attack. With elegance, she glided to the side, digging her sword under his, blocking it.

Bedwyr beamed with pride, then launched again. His sword lunged toward her. Elanor pivoted and slammed her blade against his, knocking the tip of his sword into the ground.

He sprang back. "Well done, Elanor!"

Merlin stood and clapped. He hollered between his hands, "Keep Going! This is where it matters! Do not back down!"

She couldn't believe it. She had blocked two of his attacks. But her excitement disrupted her focus.

Bang!

Bedwyr's sword struck, sending a painful quake through her arms. She wasn't prepared. Elanor held onto the hilt, but she fumbled backward. She had gone from offensive to defensive in one breath. She tried to regain—*Clang! Clang!* His sword hit twice more. She gripped the hilt with both hands just to resist his power.

Bedwyr sprang around her flank. Before her eye could catch him, he swept her feet with his sword, knocking her onto her back. She hit the ground hard, the impact driving the wind from her lungs. She tried to breathe, but the air was trapped. Closing her eyes, she waited for the spasm to pass.

She finally caught her breath with a long, gasping inhale. Black spots dotted her vision, and she rubbed her forehead. The whoops and hollers from the men registered in her ears—apparently pleased with the spectacle. She grimaced and looked up to find Merlin offering his hand. His charming smile made her want to both slap him and kiss him. She smacked her hand into his, and he lifted her like she was a feather.

She huffed with frustration, "I am glad I have been the source of everyone's amusement." She peered at the dispersing Cymbrogi. They were wandering back to their tents—finally minding their own business. She glared at Bedwyr who was happily sheathing his sword.

Merlin elbowed her with a wink. "I do not think you understand how well you have just done."

Bedwyr exhaled, catching his breath. "Yes, you actually gave me a challenge just then."

"But I still failed."

Merlin leaned in close, meeting her gaze. "Elanor, Bedwyr is one of the best swordsmen I have *ever* known. Most men do not stand a chance against him."

Bedwyr remarked, "Truly. That was unexpected." He rubbed his forearm across his sweaty forehead. "I have not been taking it easy on you. I know how important it is for you to learn. You got some strikes in there."

Merlin kissed the top of her head. "You have likely impressed the men."

Elanor looked back where the men had been, and suddenly, she wished Arthur had been there to see it. "I felt it," she said, a little excited. "The flow."

"I saw it in your eyes," Bedwyr said, nodding. "You can always see when your opponent is properly engaged. I also saw when you lost it, and fear came back in. Now we must have you practice holding on to that confidence."

"Oi! Oi!" came hushed shouts from several of the men.

The three of them turned toward the sound. Cymbrogi were clamoring together as they gazed over the edge of the gorge they camped alongside.

Bedwyr protectively grabbed hold of Elanor's arm, pulling her while he rushed to the ledge. He settled her behind one of the boulders that lined the rift before peering over. His tense expression loosened with a cocked grin. He put his finger to his lips for her to stay quiet, then motioned for her to look.

Elanor smiled, and with curious excitement, she peered over the frigid boulder. Far below, she saw the large brown animal everyone was gawking at. It slowly lumbered up the hill.

"What is that?" she whispered.

"Look closely."

Elanor squinted at the umber fur as the creature steadily moved closer. It grew larger, and soon she heard its grunting, snuffling noises until its frame was finally clear.

It couldn't be.

"It is a bear," Elanor said. She couldn't believe her eyes. In awe, she watched it rummage the ground ever closer.

"But…" she said in a quandary, "there are no bears in England."

"England?" Bedwyr scrunched his face in confusion.

Merlin chuckled. He had joined them on Elanor's left side. "She means Prydain. And next time," he said to Bedwyr, "I can be responsible for my own wife."

Bedwyr lifted his hands. "Instinct." He winked.

"I have only ever seen one other bear in Prydain before." Merlin stared down at the animal with a wondrous look on his face. "It was the day Arthur was born."

"Yes," Bedwyr said. "The old prophecy about the *Great Bear* coming to pass."

Merlin gave him a confirming nod. "It is very rare to see one of these animals. It almost makes me wonder." He glanced up, spying something that captured him more than the bear.

Elanor tracked his line of sight and discovered Arthur standing high above the crouching warriors at the top of the ledge, looking down upon the animal.

"This is an omen."

"An omen?" Elanor's brows tightened.

"It has to be," Merlin said, flicking his eyes between Arthur and the bear.

The bear suddenly halted. It lifted its head, seeing the men above. In an instant it shot up, revealing its intimidating, giant height. Its head was wide and its shoulders the breadth of two men. The bear's chest rippled. It sniffed the air. Its wide claws hung slack at its sides. The wind parted its light brown fur, revealing patches of darker fur beneath. All the while, Arthur and the bear remained locked.

With bated breath, all hung quiet and still. The whistling, chill wind offered the only sound. The bear stood steady. Arthur stared as if deciding to draw his sword, or—no. There was something else in his eyes.

Merlin noticed it too. He slowly stood. His lips moved soundlessly, uttering druidic words against the silence.

As they waited, the setting sun dipped between both sides of the gorge. The yellow lines of sunlight faded into orange, leaving behind the blue and purple hues of evening.

The time between times, Elanor thought. *The time when the space between worlds is thin.*

The bear lowered to the ground, breaking the trance. A grunting moan bellowed from its muzzle, and it scampered back down the hill, disappearing into a group of trees. It was then that everyone released their held breath. No one could deny what they had seen was unusual. A sign.

Merlin climbed atop a rock, towering over the men, and drew every eye to his attention. He pointed to Arthur, and a strange magic fell upon him, changing the appearance of his face. His dark hair blew sideways. Strands streamed across his face, his eyes narrow and hard.

Elanor had seen this change only a few times before, when he went from the man she knew, to that of an ancient druid. One that appeared to see across time.

The wind rippled through his white tunic. He was mesmerizing. Elanor couldn't take her eyes away from him. He lifted his hands and prophesied, *"Saif y Pendragon, arth fawr yn frenin pob Prydain.* The Great Bear Pendragon stands king of all Prydain." Then to the Cymbrogi, he said, *"Ni phalla ei deyrnasoedd i'r tywyllwch, ond erys yn gyflawn o fewn dwylo'r duw mawr."* He turned his face toward the winds and open gorge before him, his voice supernaturally amplified. "His realms will not falter to the darkness, but will remain fully within the hands of the Great God."

The wind ceased at his proclamation, and an eerie hush fell. Eastern clouds rumbled with distant flashes, heralding the imminent rain.

GHOST IN THE DARK

hat night, Elanor lay next to Merlin on their mat, nuzzling her face into his chest. She felt unsettled. The sighting of the bear had brought hope, lifting everyone's spirits and strengthening the men's resolve. So much so, she could still hear their excited murmurings around the campfires just outside the rustling flaps of her canvas tent. The wind was picking up. The rain would soon be upon them. She pressed in a little tighter to Merlin.

She wished the event had made her feel expectant like it had the men. Merlin had also been in a dark mood since the bear; his brow furrowed in strained thought. Elanor knew why. She felt it too. Something stirred in the unseen realms. The promise of cataclysm was in the air. The bear omen declared to all who watched from the otherworld that Arthur had taken back his power.

The clouds outside pulsed with anger, adding to Elanor's unease. Now bordering the Southlands, the danger was closer than ever.

Elanor closed her eyes, hoping to sleep before the oncoming storm—eager for the light of morning. Merlin had fallen asleep, but he jerked anxiously as though troubled with dreams. She rolled away from him; his tension agitated her.

With a deep exhale, she stared at the door flap. The tent's tassels swayed, almost as if they were vibrating to the voices outside. She listened to the consoling sound of the men's conversation. Her eyelids grew heavy, the irresistible pull of sleep tugging at her consciousness.

The voices silenced.

Elanor opened her eyes and shot straight up. She stared over at the dark crack between the flaps. It felt darker, colder. Her heartbeat increased, and she turned to Merlin. He had rolled over onto his side and now slept deeply.

She whispered to herself, "Did I fall asleep?"

She rubbed her forehead, then got up to investigate. *Everyone has just gone to bed.* Within reach was her sword. It leaned against the tent post. She grabbed it, hoping the action would frighten away the shadow in the pit of her stomach.

It is nothing.

She stared at the sharp edge of her blade, squeezing the hilt tight in her palm. With a long-drawn breath, she moved toward the door flap, feeling a bit silly for her anxiousness. She lifted it back and peeked out.

Sparks of red and yellow glowed from the embers of dying fires. She saw very little in the darkness; the stormy clouds covered the light of the moon. Rain threatened to fall at any moment. The sky rumbled and lightning lit the ground, revealing a quiet camp.

The dull golden light from the small lantern hanging inside her tent called her back, its flicker a comfort from the eerie darkness outside. Lowering the flap, she placed her sword beside her mat and sidled next to Merlin. He was warm. Secure.

Nothing is amiss. Everyone is sleeping. She nodded, assuring herself, then curled up and closed her eyes. *I fell asleep—that is all.*

Rain started tapping on the tent, making her pull the wool up a little tighter around her shoulder. It bothered her knowing the rainfall was putting out what little remained of the fires' embers. She scrunched her eyes shut and tried to ignore the unsettled feeling knotting her insides.

A sudden, loud crack of lightning boomed, and Elanor jumped.

"It is only a little thunder," Merlin muttered, rolling over to drape his arm around her.

She clung to his words, wanting to believe them, and grabbed hold of his arm, pulling it against her chest. A tingle of apprehension danced along her nerves, prickling her skin. It wasn't the darkness or the distant thunder. There was something else. A shadow had been with her since the day she used her magic in that cell. And now, that same fear crept like gangly fingers along her scalp. She turned in toward Merlin, wishing she could disappear inside his embrace.

The words of Morgan floated through her mind: *"I…see…you."*

Merlin jolted up, eyes wide with alarm.

"What is it?" Elanor quavered, grabbing her sword again.

"Stay here." He roused to his feet, throwing on his tunic.

"No. Wait. Do not leave me." Fear slithered into her throat. "Tell me what you heard?"

"I did not hear—" He shook his head. His eyes rounded with concern at the door. "An awen flashed before me. I saw—"

"What?" Elanor gulped, working to calm herself. She did not want to be abandoned. Not now.

"I saw the falcon—Osian. He is here."

Panic pulled her to her feet. She reached for him, clinging to the edge of his sleeve. "Do not leave me here alone. Please, Merlin."

"You are safe. Stay here," he insisted, grabbing hold of her arms and staring into her eyes. He studied her face, waiting for confirmation she understood.

She nodded and Merlin released her. He strode for the door flap but stopped short, turning back to her. "Do not let your guard down." Then, with a flash of amber sparking in his eyes, he said, "I have him. If he reveals himself—I will destroy him." He burst from the tent, the canvas door flapping closed behind him.

"Osian," Elanor whispered. The tent felt ominous and empty without Merlin there to protect her. The warmth of his hands lingered on her arms, amplifying his absence. She rubbed her arms, working to control her trembling.

Has the devil truly come?

She snapped herself out of her frozen stare, then raced to put on her boots.

What kind of evil is Osian capable of? How powerful is he? she wondered, quickly lacing her final boot at the knee. She grabbed up her breastplate, and with shaking fingers, fumbled to buckle it over her flowing white nightgown.

Do I really just stay here and wait? Her breath hitched. She was vulnerable—alone. *Surely, being alone was not the safest scenario? Maybe Arthur—would it not be safer to go to him?*

Her shoulders tightened and fear locked her jaw. She took a breath, recalling the lesson she learned earlier from Bedwyr. She released her tension and stood a bit taller, then dared herself to run to Arthur's tent. She listened intently for movement outside. Her eyes fixed on the door. Any moment she expected the sounds of a clash. But nothing came—only the pattering of rain, making her grow more anxious.

She focused, kindling her magic—like Merlin had done. Maybe if she coupled her magic with her sword, she would stand more than just a chance. She took a step toward the door, lifted the canvas, and spied outside. Immediately, she cowered back and returned into the safety of the tent.

Merlin said to stay here.

"Do not be afraid," she whispered to herself. She leaned forward and peered across the blackness. Another flash and rumble highlighted the falling raindrops. No sign of Merlin, or anyone.

She took a few solid steps onto the muted grass. Rain dropped cold and soulless on her face. She held her sword ready, moving forward with cautious steps, searching the darkness.

Where is everyone? Are they all still sleeping in their tents? Has Merlin not woken anyone?

Maybe he hadn't. Maybe his whole goal was to search before raising an alarm. She squinted, orienting to the dark, and crept through the camp. White tents were gray in the darkness.

The trees are just over there. Arthur's tent is at the center of the camp. I can get to him.

Her eyes adjusted, and she saw the faint outline of his tent just ahead.

She took a step toward it when a large dark shadow rushed past her. Shivers crawled up her spine.

Adrenaline pressed her to run, but she stood still, unable to move. Behind her, a horrifying huff, coupled with a whining, guttural growl pierced the silence. She twisted around and froze. A black mound stood just a few paces away, and it was moving closer. The mound grew larger—taller. Its panting created a picture in Elanor's mind of a terrible monster. Carefully, she backed away.

The sky flashed, revealing the silhouette of two round ears, amidst a furry frame. It was the bear, towering like a titan above her. A growl rumbled from its chest through heavy, hollow breaths. Its head, illuminated against the lighting, loomed large, its paws the size of her torso. She stutter-stepped backward, resisting the urge to run, lifting her sword. Her weapon was immeasurably small compared to its mammoth size.

But then, the animal tilted its head. The action momentarily quelled Elanor's terror and piqued her curiosity. It appeared unthreatening. It cooed with a tender, tremulous growl. The change in its stance bewildered her, and she dared to believe that maybe it meant her no harm. She stared into its small black eyes, surprised to discern intention inside.

It means to protect me.

She gasped. This creature was more than a bear; it was an enaid. She lowered her sword, and—

"Elanor!"

She snapped to the sound of Bedwyr's voice. The bear grumbled, collapsing back down on all fours. When Elanor turned back around, it was gone.

Bedwyr rushed to her side.

"Did you see it?" she asked.

He puffed, catching his breath. "What are you doing out here?"

"Did you *see* the bear?"

"Bear?"

"Yes. It was just here. It stood as though it were—"

Bedwyr gave her a flummoxed stare. Rain dripped from his hair.

"He was just here, and then scampered away when you called to me."

"Elanor," he said sharply, looking for the bear with doubtful eyes. Seeing nothing, he shook his head. "You should not be out here. Merlin just warned me of the danger. I was on my wa—"

"I thought I would be safer with Arthur than stuck alone, awaiting disaster."

Bedwyr nodded. "That is why Merlin sent me to get you. Come on." He gripped her arm and pulled her along. "I will take you where you will be safer."

They scrambled over the turf. The rain pelted harder.

Boom!

A peal of thunder tore across the clouds. Out of the sky, large wings fluttered over Bedwyr. He stumbled, letting go of Elanor and falling onto his back. The flurry of feathers passed by them, spreading wider. Bedwyr sprang to his feet and drew his sword. The large, russet wings broadened, morphing into pallid flesh before furling to the ground.

The demon took shape. Morbid bones crackled and moans emanated from its mouth. Clenched fingers uncurled, snapping into joints—connected to pale, naked arms. His face revealed devilish yellow eyes underneath a tilted feathered brow. He blinked and his eyes changed, appearing black in the darkness. A sharp nose, emulating a beak, shrank and pointed downward as a jaw jutted out underneath.

"Be ready. *Your sword*, Elanor!" Bedwyr commanded, jerking her arm up to hold her blade ready. The wet glint of Bedwyr's cheeks shined, and his eyes fiercely glared at the demonic transformation. He stepped in front of Elanor, his arms spread wide as if to hide her.

The villain stood fully man, his white bare chest glowing in the darkness. His arms extended outward, with his fingers curving like talons. The sight of him stole Elanor's breath. Feigning strength, she held her blade, hoping Bedwyr's boldness would give her courage.

Osian took a large ominous breath, rotating his reformed jaw with a *pop*, setting it into place. His dark voice growled to Bedwyr, "Do not stand in my way. It will only cost you your life."

Bedwyr took a bold step toward him. "I *will* stand in your way, *jackal.*"

Osian lifted his arm—a few more falcon feathers fell away—and pointed to Elanor. "I have come for her."

Elanor shrank. Somehow, she knew this was why he had come.

"You shall *not* have her," Bedwyr yelled. The deluge swallowed the power of his voice. He positioned himself for a fight.

Where is Merlin?

Elanor searched in desperation. He was meant to protect her. That was why she came with him instead of staying behind.

Why did he leave me?

Osian grinned, pulling out a wide sword that narrowed at the hilt. It looked like a hammer, with steel that gleamed with unnatural light. Black leather strings dangled from the bottom of the hilt.

"It is enchanted!" Elanor shouted, flicking rain from her eyes. But Bedwyr had already moved toward Osian, unshaken by his display.

Osian shrugged off his black cape. It dropped to the ground like a pile of wet feathers. Then he lunged for Bedwyr. Their swords clashed with a supernatural ringing, matching the lightning in the sky above. The dizzying sound quaked her bones, and she stumbled to a knee. But Bedwyr, standing fearlessly, swung through again, striking Osian hard a second time. Bedwyr was grace itself against the clunky threats of his enemy's defense. Osian's sword was heavy and slowed his movement.

Bedwyr arched his back as Osian's sword came within hair's reach of his side. Then, with a swift juke, Bedwyr spun and crashed his elbow into Osian's jaw.

Osian stumbled back, and his eyes narrowed. Blood, mixed with rain, streamed from his lip. He spat on the ground, then sprang forward, challenging Bedwyr again. He arched his sword over his head and swung it down like a club. Bedwyr easily swept past him. The weight of Osian's blade pulled him toward the ground, leaving his naked back vulnerable. Bedwyr lunged, slicing Osian's upper back, cutting into his unprotected skin.

Osian whirled and Bedwyr swung again, cleaving a blood trail across his chest. The wounds weren't deep, but Elanor hoped they would be enough to—

Osian screamed through his bared teeth, "Digon ohonoch!" The reverberations of his dark speech hit Bedwyr like a punch to the jaw.

Blood sprayed from Bedwyr's mouth. Then, as if lifted by magical strings, an invisible force yanked him up into the air before flinging him to the ground at Elanor's feet. The smattering sound of his body hitting the ground paralyzed her to the bone.

"Bedwyr!" she cried, overcome with dread.

Bedwyr lay motionless. His mouth hung open; blood reddened his lips. The sight of him buckled her knees. She snapped her eyes to meet Osian's. If he had outdone Bedwyr, what chance did she have?

"Enough!" Osian yelled, wrath boiling in his eyes.

She needed to escape. Her eyes searched for Merlin…Arthur…anyone who could help her. In the dark, she saw no one. Only rain. She looked down at Bedwyr. "Please wake up." Panic clamped its fingers around her throat. "*WAKE UP!*" she shrieked.

Bedwyr lay there like a stone. Rain pooled in his eyes. The piercing fear that he was dead stabbed her heart, and she fully grasped that she was alone. No one was there to help her. She wanted to run, and almost did, but then, to her surprise, she remained.

"No!" she shouted to Osian, who seemed to enjoy watching her tremble with fear. She couldn't let this happen. She wouldn't. His taunting pleasure sparked something within her. Determination pressed down the suffocating alarm, and she lifted her sword. She swallowed hard and set her chin.

Osian stood smiling. Rain poured down his pointed chin in a never-ending stream.

"I am not your *prey*," she growled between her teeth. She ignited the flame of her magic within her gut and curled her fingers tight around her sword's hilt.

Osian craned his neck. "Ahh, the *blue witch* wants to fight."

She steeled herself when Osian stepped toward her. His face contorted with pride as though he had already won. His sword extended outward.

That was when she saw what Bedwyr had trained her to see. Osian lurched back, ready to strike. His lack of experience gave him away. She knew what his first move would be.

He swung at her, and Elanor spun to the side, pressing her advantage. She drove her sword forward with a quick thrust, colliding with Osian's blade. A buzzing vibration radiated up her sword through her arms. Osian's sword bit with an electric pulse, forcing her to jump back. Before Osian could lift his sword again, Elanor countered and swung toward his face. He flailed back, almost losing his footing.

Her magic amplified her strength and the keenness of her sight. She did not allow her enemy time to rally. She dove in again, delivering a slice across his sword arm. He slapped his free hand over the wound. Blood drained through his fingers.

Osian's lips snarled, exposing his teeth. His eyes flamed. "You little *witch*." He reeled back like a viper about to strike. He screamed, thrusting his sword like a spear toward Elanor's chest. She maneuvered her sword around his blade, and Osian's hilt tore from his hands. His weapon whirled into the air and twanged as it struck the ground.

The strike against Osian's sword sent burning pain through Elanor's arms, stealing her breath. She shook her head and forced herself to breathe.

I can't lose focus.

She stepped forward and swung for his neck. As her sword arced, she imagined his head falling from his body, knowing what it would mean. The only thing tying Morgan to this world—destroyed while his head crashed to the ground.

She cried out. Her sword flew.

But then, her arm was caught midair—suspended and frozen. Osian's fingers twisted, holding her blade at bay with his magic. The ridges on his brow deepened with concentration. "Clearly," he groaned with strain. "I have underestimated you. The first one I should not have dared to battle, but you—I thought I would toy with by letting you try."

He snapped his head to the side. His magic ripped her sword from her hand, launching it into the ground hilt up. Stunned, she stared at her blade—now too far away for her to deal the final blow. The hot rage in Osian's eyes tore away her confidence, making her feel like a fool. She pulled against Osian's magic to free herself, but her struggle only bolstered his resolve.

He drew closer, his eyes empty of human empathy. Angry, warm tears streamed down Elanor's face, mixing with the rain. She tried to muster her magic—anything to keep him from touching her.

Her magic. The light. Where was it?

"You let us in," he growled.

Elanor noticed the white stone of Osian's talisman glow against his bleeding chest.

"I have been amplifying your fear, draining you of your strength. It is too bad, really," he said, mocking her with false compassion, "you fight so hard, and for *nothing*."

Elanor closed her eyes. She didn't want to look at him. She could feel the heat from his body nearing ever closer. Could he really rob her of her strength and deny her power? She clenched her jaw.

No, she thought, rallying what little power she had left. Searching, she found it. Her magic. It was there. Her eyes snapped open. The magic blazed to life. And then—

A force, like a rock hitting her in the gut, shot her through the air and onto her back. She gasped, coughing, trying to recapture her breath.

"Elanor!"

She darted her eyes to the far-off silhouette; Merlin sprinted toward her through the darkness.

Osian knelt over her and wrapped his fingers around her throat, whipping her up from the ground as though she were nothing but a doll. Elanor's feet dangled above the wet grass. She tried to call out for Merlin, but Osian's grip was a vise, cutting off her ability to scream. The feeling of his fingers around her throat conjured images of being strangled by Malik. Helpless.

Elanor kicked, desperate to free herself, but to no avail. She dug her fingernails into his arm. Osian glared at her with a mad spark in his eyes. Curling his lip, he pulled Elanor's face to his, their noses almost touching. His insidious, hot breath wafted across her face. Elanor saw within Osian's obsidian pupils her own reflection struggling to breathe. Indeed, she should have run, but now it was too late.

22

THE LIES OF THE TALISMAN

Merlin hurtled across the camp. The moment he'd sensed Osian's presence, he rushed back to Elanor. In horror, he watched Osian lift Elanor off the ground, his hand clutching her throat.

"No! Elanor!" He extended his hand, the magic to knock Osian off his feet on the tip of his tongue. But before he could invoke the spell, Osian disappeared with Elanor in his grasp.

"NO!" Merlin shouted, skidding to a halt. All air left his lungs in an instant. *No.* She couldn't be gone. Not again. His mind raced, flooding with unimaginable horrors.

The sky rumbled—the lighting subduing and the rain lessening. His panicked breath whirled out in white wisps. He gripped his wet curls in handfuls, then clutched his chest, trapping the terror seizing his insides.

A silver glint in the darkness captured his eye. A sword had been stabbed into the earth. Hot tears flooded his vision. It was Elanor's sword. He swallowed down a painful lump and approached it. With bitterness twisting his lips, he ripped the sword from the soil. His heart pounded in his ears. He wanted to tear into Osian—flay him alive. If he were still here, nothing would hold Merlin back from killing him. But he was gone. Beyond his reach.

Rage spilled out of him, and he clenched his fists, wishing he held Osian by the neck.

His head felt like lead, but he lifted his heavy brow and saw another sword. Osian's blade lay on the ground. Black and evil. He drew closer to it. Through his magic, he felt the pinch of dark witchery embedded within it.

"Not again." He cringed, then kicked the blade away, refusing to touch it. Anguish surged through him, shattering his control. He crumpled to the ground, hanging his head between his knees. The world spun. It was a bad dream. He begged himself to wake.

"Elanor," he whispered, hoping she would appear. He placed his palms on the wet grass, hoping it would center him. He couldn't lose it. Not right now. *Elanor…* he needed to do something.

The sound of coughing caught his attention. He lifted his head, discovering a body sprawled on the ground.

"Great God! Bedwyr!" He had not seen him in the darkness. Merlin scrambled to his feet. He raced, slipping through the muddy grass to reach Bedwyr. "Brother." Impatient, Merlin patted Bedwyr's cheek. Desperation pinged inside his chest, disrupting his focus. Merlin summoned his magic. It felt weak in his terror, but he pressed into it regardless. He placed his hand on Bedwyr's chest. "Iachau, Bedwyr."

Bedwyr cried out, then spat a mouthful of blood onto the ground.

"What happened? Are you hurt?" Merlin searched Bedwyr's chest and sides for evidence of injury.

"Elanor," Bedwyr moaned through gritted teeth. He tried to move as though gearing back up to fight, but his face contorted with pain.

"She's gone!" Merlin shook his head, fighting to keep himself together. "Lay back. Let me help you."

Bedwyr's lips thinned and his eyes reddened. "Gone? Dead?" He lifted his head, quickly glanced around as though desperate to see where she lay.

Merlin struggled to answer. "Not—dead. He-he took her."

Bedwyr sank his head against the ground, gasping. "No—no. I tried to fight him—to keep her safe. I—" He rubbed his hand over his face. "I would have had him. Osian was not skilled. He struck me." He tried to sit up, grimacing in obvious pain. He groaned, "Sorcery."

Waves of fury rose within Merlin, heating his face. His whole body shook. Every breath was a hot gust from his lips. If he had been there, Osian would not have held the advantage.

Despondent, Bedwyr muttered, "I am—so sorry."

Bedwyr's apology gutted Merlin. His words came out stifled. "How…hurt… are you?"

With a cry of pain, Bedwyr labored onto his knees. He panted for a moment, clutching his chest. His face was flushed red. "I feel as though I have been struck by lightning—but there is no time. We need to go after her." He rolled his neck and wiped the blood from his mouth. He peered up at Merlin and went rigid. "Your eyes burn, brother."

Merlin curled his lips. "I hoped Osian would be destroyed this night."

Bedwyr sat back, his chin taut. A tear rolled from his eye. "Arthur *must* be told." Bedwyr slowly dug his feet under him and made to stand.

Merlin thrust his hand into Bedwyr's chest, stopping him. "You are hurt. Only I can break Osian's dark witchery. I can get her back. If I do not—" Merlin cut off, glaring into the distance. He moved to his feet; his fists squeezed white at his sides. "I am going after her."

"This night?"

"I will not waste one second. Every moment I delay—" He squeezed his eyes shut at the thoughts rushing into his head. Torture. Death. All this was possible, and likely. "The night is almost done. The morning light will be shortly breaking."

"Do you know where he has taken her?"

"His cave," Merlin guessed, but felt confident that was the place—hidden within the folds of the cursed forest.

"Brother," Bedwyr warned, "it could be a trap. You could be playing into Osian's hands."

Merlin turned to Bedwyr, ferocity rushing through his blood. "Do you *think* I fear his traps? It is those within the forest who should be afraid. If he harms her—he will pay with more than his blood."

"I am coming with you."

"No, *brother*. There is an evil air to the wind. It has not lifted with the rain. Arthur will need you."

"*Elanor* needs me—us." Bedwyr was quick to change his words, then hung his head, shaking it subtly. He started again, "It is too risky going into that forest alone. I cannot stand the thought of her trapped in there with *him*."

Bedwyr's words got under Merlin's skin. He pressed his arms against his sides, resisting the violent urge to send his fist into Bedwyr's jaw. "SHE IS MY WIFE… NOT YOURS!"

Bedwyr rose to his feet, his mouth agape with surprise. He stepped toward Merlin, lifting his chest. "I meant to protect her. It is my job to—"

Merlin grabbed Bedwyr by his collar and yanked him close to his face. "*You*," he growled, "consider yourself closer to her than you ought."

Bedwyr ripped Merlin's hand away and shoved him back. With his fist at the ready, he snapped, "Your anger has stolen your head…*brother*. You ought to stop before you do something you will regret."

Merlin squared his shoulders. He couldn't see Bedwyr. In the darkness, all he saw was someone who stood between him and his love. Someone who had failed to protect her.

"I *do* love her. But not in the way you *accuse* me of." Bedwyr's voice held a sober, reasoning tone. "She is my family. As are you and Arthur. Brother…I am *not* your enemy. You know me better than this. And right now…she needs our help."

Merlin did not budge. He glared underneath his brows, his mind a confused jumble of fury.

How could I have let this happen—AGAIN?

Who was he really angry at? Who was it that had left her alone?

Regret forced its way into Merlin's madness. He shook his head, refocusing his furor on Bedwyr. Magic lit on his palms. Golden furls of light extended down his fingers.

Bedwyr retreated, lowering his hands in a placating gesture. "Fine. Take your rage out on me. I will not stop you."

Bedwyr's words snapped Merlin from his rage. He loosened his arms at his sides, but still he wanted to wreak havoc on something—anything. His anger, eclipsed with sadness, pushed him against the edge of his own rationale.

It is my fault. I left her. Bedwyr fought for her.

He knew he couldn't take his rage out on Bedwyr, but he also knew he could not let it go. Not right now. He was too tightly wound, ready to spring, and not in a reasonable mood.

"I go *alone.*" Merlin turned and walked away, leaving Bedwyr to stand forsaken in the damp pre-dawn. Already the sky was lightening with hues of blue.

He stormed toward his horse, refusing to glance back. He couldn't. His torment made him want to burn down a forest. If he stayed any longer, he would do something he regretted, and Bedwyr might pay that price. He could not think straight until he was on the trail to find Elanor.

Low voices hissed inside Elanor's head. Slowly, as she neared consciousness, she realized the voices were not inside her mind, or part of a dream. They were real, and they were close.

The more aware she became, the more dread stirred in the pit of her stomach, making her heart quicken. Last she knew, Osian had her by the throat. She hoped she was waking to find it had all been a bad dream.

Eyes still closed, she tried to pull her arms in for comfort but met resistance. The subtle jangle of chains hit her ears. Cold iron wrapped around her wrists. She was still locked inside the nightmare. Emotions swam inside her chest. She lay on a frigid damp floor, her back against a rugged stone wall. Her wrists were in chains, loosely hanging above her.

She opened her eyes and turned toward a subtle light flickering from around a corner; its faint glow illuminated her surroundings.

She could still hear the voices. She knew them.

Osian and Morgan.

She did not know if they were inside the room with her, or just nearby. She was afraid to peer around the chamber—they might discover her awake.

She now knew without a doubt where she was. Osian's cave. She recognized the familiar smell from Malik's mind. Quiet and careful, she tried to sit up, but found her feet also bound at the ankles, keeping her in an awkward reclined position. She shut her eyes, hoping her conversing enemies didn't hear her movement.

"Why did you use your magic?" The woman's voice floated like it was coming from every corner of the cave.

"I had no choice. I did not expect the warrior to be there. When I approached her, I thought she was alone, and then…she proved stronger than I anticipated."

"It *cost* you. Now you are weakened. Injured. That makes *me* weak."

"I can quickly recover from this," Osian snapped. "It is not the shapeshifting and transference that weakens me. These abilities have already been paid for." He went silent for a moment, and Elanor's stomach turned at what had been done to gain those gifts. "It was the defending spells that emptied my power."

"You were unwise," Morgan scolded. "You should have been less hasty."

Elanor noticed for the first time just how silky Morgan's voice was. Even with her harsh words, she found herself allured—wanting to hear her speak more. Her voice, like a mother's, calling a child into her arms.

"Merlin's eyes were after me," he defended. "I could not risk him finding me first. And I do not have the natural abilities that both she and Merlin possess. Neither did you when you were alive. I had to think quick. If I had left—"

"*Ssshh!*" Morgan hushed. Her echo bounced over toward Elanor, and she squeezed her eyes tighter. "The little *imp* is only pretending to be asleep."

Elanor's nerves heated her face. She held perfectly still, holding her breath. The room brightened with flickering light. She felt Osian nearing, his presence large and foreboding above her. There was no escape. Soon, she would meet his eyes and she would have to be brave.

He knelt close; his boots' leather creaked. "Open your eyes, *girl!*"

There was nothing she could do but obey. She timidly blinked her eyes open. His face stooped close to hers. She jolted, leaning away.

Osian smiled, appearing satisfied by her reaction.

What would he do to her now that she was in his clutches? She looked at the talisman hanging from his neck—the wound on his chest left open and untreated. She wished she could rip the cursed stone from him and destroy it.

She met his gaze, and he snatched her cheeks between his fingers, forcing her to stay locked on his hardened, empty eyes. They were black in the dully lit chamber. His young features made her pity him. Pity the loss of all the promise he had wasted in evil.

"He is coming for you." Osian sneered. "But he will not find what he hopes for. Only a broken shell." He squeezed her face harder.

Tears formed in her eyes and coasted down her cheeks. She tried to avoid his cruel stare but could not refrain. She saw the rage and pleasure he felt in hurting others, and it made her shrink back. Morgan flickered through his irises—a violet mist of oppressive power. Elanor wished he would let go so she could turn away.

"We will destroy every hope—every dream. Nothing will remain of *your* New Way. The old religion—" Osian suddenly stopped; his attention diverted to her blue pendant.

Elanor trembled as his eyes sparkled with the blue of her stone. Merlin's gift. A promise of safety. It emboldened her. In an instant, she did not feel so alone.

"Take it from her," she heard the disembodied voice command.

No.

Osian wrapped his fist around it, then tore it from her neck. He held it up, dangling it over the edges of his fingers.

His taunt wrenched Elanor's heart. "Give it back," she cried, angry tears brimming in the corners of her eyes.

Osian gave her a satisfied, devilish sneer, then peered back at the necklace. He knew he held something she valued, and relished the control.

His dark countenance shifted, and he leaned in close. "I told you. Your ways will be destroyed. This pendant contains magic. Merlin's magic." Osian stared into the pendant. He leered, exposing his teeth. *"Doesn't it?"* he yelled.

Startled, Elanor yelped.

"Well, be not worried. I will stop Merlin's heart from beating, and his power will be no more. This pendant will become nothing but an empty stone."

Courage rose within her chest, and she jerked her chin toward him. "Who are you compared to Merlin? *You* cannot destroy him. That is why you hide. You know you cannot win." The more she spoke, the more impassioned her words became. "It has already been written. Your death was declared. The Great God backs the might of the winds, and you are but a small *little beast*, easily crushed. Go crawl back on your belly, where you—" Her words were cut short.

His fist smashed into her face, pounding her head against the jagged stone behind her.

Disorienting pain blurred her vision. Warm blood trickled from the back of her scalp down her neck. Black spots blotted her eyes, and she struggled to remain conscious. Osian's slithery voice seeped into her ears and into her mind.

"Where is your god now? Does he come to save you? You have easily played into our hands." His last words were a foggy droll. "You…have only *ever*…had false hope."

Her heaving breath echoed inside a swirling world. Osian's eyes blazed through it all with a tantalizing hatred. They gleamed, releasing a pulse that made her feel like she was being held over a ledge. She frantically struggled to find secure ground. But then, Osian let go, happy to let her fall.

Terrified, she descended into an abyss.

When her eyes burst open, she jolted, expecting demons ready to pull her deeper into darkness. Instead, she discovered she was in the Palisade, in her very own room. Light streamed in through the open window. Cool wind refreshed the chamber with the sweet scent of apple blossoms. Relief washed over her, and she turned toward the hearth. Merlin was there, leaning against the mantle.

Was it just a dream?

Elanor gasped, capturing her breath. She'd had intense nightmares before. *But it felt so real.*

"Merlin?" she called, relieved to see him—desiring his comfort.

He didn't move at her words. Maybe he hadn't heard her.

"Merlin?" she beckoned again, swinging her legs over the side of the bed, clutching her chest to calm her racing heart. She moved toward him. "I had a terrifying dream. Osian—he had captured me."

Still no response. Merlin remained unmoved. He stood like stone—rigid and without breath. She stopped. Her stomach swirled, and a slow fear crept up to her cheeks. Surely, she was imagining things. It was the nightmare. It had put her on edge. She shook her head and continued to approach.

She reached for his shoulder; an unsettled brooding emanated from him. She pulled back, but then gently brushed his arms. His muscles were taut, and his fingers were squeezed white against the mantle.

Merlin is safe, she told herself, and careened her head to see his face. He stood, stoically staring into the fire, his jaw rippling with tension.

He slowly turned to face her. His sallow eyes lacked brightness, and they gazed at her as though she had done something unforgivable. Her heart beat faster, and she jerked her hand away. She suddenly felt like she was touching a snake.

"Merlin? Is everything—"

He launched at her, and she screamed in sudden fright. With an angry snarl, he seized her wrists and cast her to the floor. Confusion and fear strangled her throat. She ached from the force of the fall and stared horrified up at Merlin. His face was like malevolent steel. She clamped her hand over her mouth, inhaling the shock-filled dread consuming her world.

"Why?" was all she eked out from between her fingers.

Merlin seethed, "*You* are the cause of all this mess."

"What?"

"I wish you had *never* come. I wish I had left you to your future world."

"Stop it, Merlin. Why are you saying this?"

He took an intimidating step forward that made Elanor yelp and scoot backward. Scorn dripped from his eyes—eyes that looked at her as though she were someone else. She saw inside them. He wanted to hurt her. His boiling rage would stop at nothing.

"What have I done?" she cried, panic tightening her chest.

"Your magic is all that made you special, and now I...I do not want it. Nobody does. You should go."

The tears unleashed; she could no longer hold them in. His eyes. His face. All that she ever loved and trusted rejected her. "This does *not* make sense," she said, pulling herself up from the floor. "This is not real. *You* are not real." She took a bold step toward him.

He flung his hand and threw her with his magic. She smashed against the wall behind her. Her head rang from the impact. She held her breath against the searing pain in her ribs. This certainly felt real.

His face twisted as he came closer, holding her against the wall with his fingers splayed. The pain of his unseen magic radiated through her body. His golden hollow eyes flared. There was no love...no kindness.

She swallowed hard, forcing herself to speak. "What of my father and my mother? They would want me." Tears leaked at her words. "Gw-Gwendolen is *my* child. I will not leave her."

"What is this you say? You have no father or mother. You have no daughter."

Now she knew this was a lie. This was not Merlin. This had to be Osian.

But something about the forcefulness of Merlin words pushed against her reason, making her believe it was true. Lies trickled like tar through her mind—one right after the other.

Of course. I have been deluding myself. How could it have been true that I was loved by Merlin?

He drew closer—like a monster threatening to devour her. She held her breath, blinking her eyes, expecting him to strike.

How do I wake up? Wake up…Wake up!

She gasped for air, as if coming up from nearly drowning.

Merlin's hand snatched her arm. Everything in her wanted to cower, but instead, she turned her tearful eyes at him and shouted, "YOU ARE NOT REAL!"

It all happened so fast. He yanked her down from the wall, and before she knew it, he was dragging her across the floor. His strong grip was like a talon's, impossible for her to break away from, but she fought anyway. Amidst her thrashing, she managed to slip an arm free, but his hand flew like a cudgel, knocking her sideways.

She reeled, trying to recover from Merlin's blow. Her body ached, but deep inside, her heart was shattering. Merlin grappled her forearm with frightful force. He was so powerful—so strong. Coupled with his magic, he was terrifying—indomitable.

"LET ME GO!" She beat him with her free fist, but to no avail. It was as though her strikes were non-existent.

He approached the window and shoved it open.

"NO!" she screamed, terrified, resisting him with all her might. Her death was coming fast and there was nothing she could do to stop it.

In a dizzying blur, he hurled her over the side, his fingers squeezing around her arm, the only thing keeping her from plummeting to the ground far below.

The cold air seared her cheeks, just like Merlin's gaze—two golden sunbeams set on scorching her soul. The haunting wind howled as if calling for her doom.

"Merlin," she whispered in desperation. "Please…this is not real. This is not you. I know it cannot be you." This was the worst thing she could ever possibly imagine. Her love—a monster with no mercy.

"Please," she cried, one last time peering into his soulless countenance. Then— he let go.

There was a *flash,* and then she found herself trembling on the floor of the cold, dark cave.

Oh, my Great God! She gasped. Now that it was over, she began to weep. Still, Merlin's reproachful glances played through her mind. For him to look at her that way, to want to hurt her—it all felt so real. She just wanted to forget.

"Ssshhh! Ssshh!" the ghostly voice of Morgan echoed. Elanor wished she could press her hands over her ears, but they were held fast in chains. *"There, there—do not cry."* The voice was so smooth, so tempting to listen to. *"We have only showed you what is. Already, Merlin's heart is changing toward you. You have become too much of a burden to him, though he would not say it."*

"That is not t-true," Elanor said through her tears. "You are a *liar.*"

"My words are all you can hear in this place. My words speak truth. He will be done with you. He is tired of you. You were never strong enough. So weak."

The word *weak* made Elanor cringe. That was the one thing she always feared would make them all cast her out. It was like the dark secret she always kept hidden. She feared her weakness would lessen her value. She felt it keenly in the future time, when her magic felt drained from her. What if she had no magic? Would she still have worth to any of them? Arthur only started to see her after what she had done in the forest.

"Always, you need helping. Always, the inconvenience. Even Arthur wishes he did not have you. But—" Morgan paused, then said with tenderness, *"You have value to me, Gwenddydd. I would not cast you away. If you let me in, I will show you the power to never be weak again."*

Tempting. Could I really feel powerful? Could Morgan set me free?

Elanor shook her head. *No.* She might not have been able to plug her ears, but she refused to listen. There was power on Morgan's foul words; Elanor could feel it pushing on the cracks in her heart. So, in defense, she started chanting in a low whispering hum. She sang ever so gently verses from the Kingdom of the Sun.

"Oh, Kingdom of the Sun, renew our land with grace."

She couldn't muster the strength to sing loudly. Her emotions were still too raw, but in rapid succession, she repeated the words over and over to fill her ears with something other than the toxic words.

"The blood will stop dripping, as the oil of gladness is tipping."

Like a prayer, she repeated it. When finally, exhausted, she stopped. The chamber fell silent. She sighed in relief. No more deceiving words pressed down on her. Her head and body ached. She was cold, and there was nothing to cover her. She tried to rest. Maybe she could sleep and it would help her forget the nightmare.

Slam! Crash!

Raised voices echoed from around the corner. Men were fighting.

Is it Merlin? She hoped. *He has come.*

All the lies immediately melted away. All the things she knew to be true made her heart leap. She knew Merlin would come for her. He loved her. If he had found her, he would take his retribution against the vile deceivers.

Footsteps hastened down the tunnel toward her.

"In here!" she called, anticipating the moment someone would appear to save her.

A dark silhouette burst around the corner. The torch in his hand blinded her unadjusted eyes. He approached, and Elanor blinked, trying to capture the light so she could see. Finally, she saw him.

"Merlin," she gasped with joy. "I prayed you would find me." All she could think about was throwing her arms around his neck. She shook her wrists, indicating the chains, eager to be set free. "Help me free. The chains, they—"

She stopped; the figure in front of her remained still. She squinted in confusion. "Merlin?" The hope in her heart disintegrated. Something was wrong. Another trick.

He bent down, hovering close to her face, and snarled, "I am not here to save you. I do not want you."

"No-o-o-o," Elanor groaned with a sob lodging in her throat.

"I have come only so that you might know I chose to leave you here—alone. With Osian dead, I no longer have need of you."

He stood, and she hung her head. Wrenching sobs tore from her mouth, her tears wetting the ground. Wordless, he turned and walked away.

"No…no…no," Elanor cried, her entire body trembling. "That was not Merlin. It was not Merlin."

Methodically, through her keening, she started chanting *the song*.

23

THE SOUTHLANDERS

Arthur glared across the ravine, searching for a spark of hope in the amber, after-rain sunrise that bathed the ground. The Cymbrogi were busy breaking camp, preparing for their continued march for the Southlands, though now with the bitter burden of what they had lost during the night.

Peredur approached Arthur. "We have gathered."

Arthur hung his head with no response. Elanor had been taken. His stomach churned. The danger she was in gnawed at his thoughts. He bit his lip, angry Merlin had left them to go after her. Though, in truth, Arthur would have done the same.

Peredur called again, "Arthur?"

He sighed, steadied his stance, and faced Peredur.

"The kings and chieftains have gathered and are awaiting you." Peredur started walking away but halted when Arthur did not follow.

Arthur tried to ignore the deepening lines on Peredur's forehead—it drove in the nail that twisted Arthur's stomach.

Peredur's lips pressed into a line, and he gave Arthur an understanding nod. "I also hate this. We should be out there with Merlin. The thought of Elanor captured by that *vile snake*…I hope she still—"

"What?" Arthur snapped, daring Peredur to say it.

Peredur set his jaw and shook his head. "I could not."

Arthur lifted his chin to squelch the wrathful emotions lapping at his throat. "This is my fault…my fault for bringing her."

Peredur stared at the ground, his lack of response all but declaring his assent.

"I see you agree."

Arthur turned away. The knot tightened in his throat. He hated this. The worry. The fear. He had felt this before—the hoping without hope that the worst had not been born. Always the regret surged over a different choice that could've been made.

He knew through experience, that even with great faith, sometimes the worst still occurred. But now, no matter how much he hated it, the trial had come. He couldn't turn back or prevent it. Forward was his only choice. And forward he would go. At least he knew Merlin would do all he could to save his…Arthur swallowed and squeezed his eyes shut…his daughter.

He clenched his fists, his feet still cemented to the ground. There was nothing he could do to stall the moment any longer. With a begrudged sigh, he broke his vigil and approached the chieftains and kings who awaited his orders. Peredur followed in his wake. Arthur's feet were heavy like lead, but he pushed himself forward anyway.

The Cymry leaders stood in a cluster, their listless mood apparent, like men who had marched days through mire.

Arthur took a deep breath and stepped into their midst. The group widened to make room. He searched their eyes, knowing they did not want to hear what he had to say any more than he wanted to say it.

Bedwyr stared ahead with a fire burning in his eyes. Arthur understood. He knew how Bedwyr felt. His fury was so raw when he crashed into Arthur's tent only an hour earlier. The news pounded into Arthur's chest like a battering ram. He had been sitting at the edge of his cot, awakened by the sound of the lightning, not knowing some of the clashing outside had not been the storm, but the enemy.

"Elanor's been taken…" Bedwyr yelled, bursting in through his tent. He dripped with rain and his shoulders moved with heavy breath. He stepped toward Arthur with a limp, his hand cupping his side.

Arthur jumped to his feet, his jaw slack, noticing the bloodstain on Bedwyr's chin.

"…and Merlin has gone. Left to go after her."

Arthur's head spun. Shock stung his limbs. He tried to wrap his mind around what Bedwyr was telling him. "Taken? By who?"

"Osian!"

Anger and confusion battled for Arthur's attention. His words fell from his mouth in a jumble. "He—Osian—he was here? How—"

"Merlin was preparing to raise the alarm, but too late."

"Why did no one wake me?" Arthur no longer felt confused. Only angry. How could this have all happened just beneath his nose?

"I was on watch with several others when I saw Merlin—he told me to wait and keep Elanor safe. He had suspicions Osian was about but was unsure. He did not want to raise the alarm until he was certain. I ran to secure Elanor, but as I found her, Osian was already there. I fought to save her—" his voice cracked. "After Merlin left, I checked on the guards. They had all been struck down."

"Enough." Arthur waved his hand, his mind reeling. He stumbled back a few steps, struggling to take it all in. He gritted his teeth and pressed his eyes closed.

Merlin should have woken me. He sat back down on his cot. The weight of what had happened suffocated him. *Would it have changed anything if he had? Would I have been able to keep Elanor safe?*

He rubbed his hands over his eyes. "Wake the men."

"What will you do?"

Chapter Twenty-Three

"You will know shortly—go!"

Bedwyr lumbered from the tent, leaving Arthur alone. His breath sat shallow in his chest. The thought of Gwynevere's reaction was like a vise squeezing his heart.

And now, just an hour later, standing before the kings, the same vise wrenched, making his temples pulse. He hated to tell them. The turmoil within him struggled with the decision between his own blood, and what needed to be done for Prydain. He could not pull the kings and their men off track to pursue a rescue. Not into the Forest of Goll. The loss of men would be too costly.

Arthur cleared the lump of emotion in his throat and addressed the kings "You may all know by now what has transpired this night." He paused, feeling the heaviness of their stares, grasping for him to give them hope. "El…the young Pendragon was stolen during the night by our enemy—*Osian.*"

A woeful grumble rolled through the gathered Cymry lords.

"How?" one asked.

Another said, "I heard nothing but the storm."

"When?"

"Where was Merlin?"

At this question, Bedwyr's mouth twisted like he had eaten something bitter.

Arthur shook his head, then waved his hand to quiet them. "The details are not important. Only, you should know that Merlin has gone after her. I have chosen to trust the task of rescue to him. Goll is a trap, and I will not make the decision to spill Cymry blood within the wickedness of that forest."

His mind wandered into dark memories of the forest. The thought of Elanor trapped just as Gwynevere had been years ago—*Gwynevere only lived because she was bait. But Elanor, she is…* A surge of fear caught in his throat. *Osian would not keep her alive.*

Arthur was grateful when Thul's voice called him back to the present.

"But Osian is within Goll," Thul protested, his eyes peering beneath his white-blond, bushy brows. "He is the enemy we aim to kill. He is the one who holds the princess. We could save her and our lands."

Arthur swallowed, pursing his lips with a subtle nod. "I have thought of this. I would like nothing more than to save her, and run my sword through the stomach of that *serpent.* But"—he stared hard at each of them—"in the forest, we would be at a disadvantage. We would be in the den of our enemy.

"May I remind you all that Osian busies himself raising an army. And he wields sorcery that we have *no way* of preparing ourselves against. Not without Merlin. There are still too many unknowns, and we are not currently gathered in our full strength for a battle with him. Our scouts have yet to report back to us their findings. We need the Southlands fortified in our favor. This is our task." He softened his gaze, then said, "Merlin is powerful and stands the best chance of overcoming the witchery of Goll to find Elanor." He lifted his chest and pulled back his shoulders. "We must strengthen our arms so we can dash our enemies like the refuse they are."

Merlin rode hard through the remainder of the night and into morning light. Every part of him was rigid with trepidation. He had to keep telling himself to breathe. She could already be dead. He hated to think it. Osian had already proven he could be merciless and swift. Merlin's heart pressed up into his throat like a stranglehold, making him feel like Elanor was already lost. The tiniest bit of hope remained that the enemy had kept her alive. He would search for her until he found her—dead or breathing.

Thinking of the condition he might find her in sent a shudder skittering through him. He tried to shake off the crippling fear that clawed at his insides.

"I will not give up," he said to himself, spurring his horse into a more quickened pace. The cold morning mist hovered over the ground when he finally arrived. He had not seen the twisted trees of Goll since they survived it the last time. He slowed his gallop to a trot and stared up at the shadowy treetops. A large group of swifts burst from their hidden perches. Their flapping wings, a humming flutter, brought no comfort.

Narrowing his eyes, he stared through the wall of trunks and boughs. An old mix of oak, chestnut, and elm wound together, blocking out the light. This forest might have once been beautiful—green with life and wonder—but now its dark history left it dead, dank, and untrustworthy.

Merlin pulled his horse's reins and halted. He lingered a moment. The horse's anxious hooves shuffled. "I know, boy," Merlin said, patting his steed's neck, "I know." He threw his leg over the saddle, dismounted, and swept his eyes over the shadowed spaces. His instincts tingled, the old magic tempting him to cast a spell to protect himself.

No. Merlin shook his head. He could not put his trust in what was easy. There was a magic he was created for that required something more.

"Great God," he muttered into the stagnant air, lifting his eyes to the skyline above the forest. "Will I find you in there? Do you even go into dark forsaken places like this?" He tsked to the silence. "Please let her still be alive. Keep her safe from harm."

He waited for a response, and his eyes warmed with tears. When nothing came, he sniffed and wiped his sleeve across his eyes. He cleared his throat and rubbed the velvet of his horse's nose. "I cannot take you with me, good fellow. Though you would have been a great comfort to me in there." He loathed to let his horse go. But this was no place for a man, let alone a horse that would be of no help once inside the dense trails.

He glanced over his shoulder, hoping Bedwyr would forgive him. The bitter taste of their last exchange lingered as he pulled his pack and supplies from the saddle.

"Yah!" He smacked his horse's haunch. "Go find home!"

The horse reared, then dashed away. Merlin watched the mahogany form gradually disappear into the cold mist. With reluctance, he wrapped his cloak snug around his neck, trapping in what little warmth was left. He tightened his pack, then stepped into the forest.

The heavy droll of the Cymbrogi behind Arthur set him on edge. The whinnying huffs of the horses matched their stomping strides, creating a cadence. Though he tried, his mind refused to stop worrying about Elanor and Merlin.

The enemy has only lit the flames of their own pyre. If Elanor is dead—

His face heated at the thought. He shook his head.

Merlin will find her, he assured himself.

They neared Llyonesse and would reach the citadel by nightfall. Arthur had no idea what they would discover there, but he felt ready for whatever resistance they might meet. As they rounded the top of a hill, a forward scout came riding up, hailing them.

"Halt," Arthur shouted, lifting his fist to stop the march. Thul, Cormach, Bram and even the chieftain Halok, gathered close beside him to await the rider.

This is not good.

The rider's anxious, rounded eyes told Arthur that something was off. He gripped the reins of his horse and lifted his shoulders back, ready for bad news.

"My king," the scout hollered, breathless, pulling his horse to a whinnying stop.

"Speak," Arthur demanded.

"A small army of foot soldiers await us at the bottom of that hill." He pointed where the land disappeared at an incline.

"There are no riders?"

"There is but one rider who commands them."

Thul interjected, "It cannot be their plan to attack. If they were to face us on foot, we would crush them. They are even further disadvantaged as we hold the high ground."

Arthur turned to the scout. "How many men?"

"There are only a few hundred. We outnumber them greatly."

"What sort of men are these? Do they mean to join us? Are they Cymry?"

"They appear to be"—the scout paused, then said carefully—"Cymry, but I do not believe they are here to stand with us. Their rider bears a standard strung with black horse hair—a deer skull at its top. His clothing is that of a druid." He shook his head. "The men do not appear experienced warriors, though some do wear Cymbrogi colors. But—" The scout glanced at Arthur, seeming reluctant to continue.

"*Cymbrogi*, tell me," Arthur commanded. "What more?"

"There are ones wearing the cursed yellow hoods, my king. A hundred or more."

Arthur's heart sank. *Sorcery?* It was very possible. But certainly Osian's men.

"These are the enemy," growled Halok. His eyes flared above the tattooed dots beneath his eyes.

"This bodes of a trap," Cormach warned, eyeing Arthur.

Thul cleared his throat, rubbing his fingers over his yellow-bearded chin with a solemn stare. "These are sorcerers, my king. These hoods show no mercy. They trap and ensnare. They hide and attack their foes unaware. This is foul."

Arthur was silent for a moment, considering what move to make. "Their aim cannot be to meet us in battle with such a small number. There is trickery." He directed his attention to the scout. "Is there anything else you have not told us?"

"No, my king."

"Thank you." He waved his hand, dismissing him. "Cormach—Halok! These are your lands. Do you know this hill? What are we to expect over that ridge?"

Halok pointed. "There is another shallower hill behind this one. A small valley at the bottom, with an outlet to the left, more hills to the right." His gruff voice matched the wildness of the old world staining his countenance. "They have positioned themselves very unwisely if they plan to attack us."

"However," Peredur countered, "it is also a perfect lure. If we go down there— there remains only one exit." His hands clutched at his hilt. The itch of battle flashed in his eyes.

"We will not be lured. Let us see if the druid will speak to us." Arthur paused. "However, if there should be sorcery, without Merlin"—he grimaced, shaking his head—"we could be in great danger. I *did* expect we could encounter this, but I did not expect to meet it without Merlin or—Elanor."

Even now, he felt the trap tightening like a noose around his throat. But that could not hold him back. He was never one to be daunted by a threat. And this day would be no different.

He inhaled a sharp breath, then commanded, "We will approach the ledge, and you will all follow my lead. We will not attack—and we will *not* be lured down. Not until I know more. My gut instinct tells me that engagement is inevitable, regardless of the outcome. I believe this enemy expects a hasty charge from us, since we could swiftly crush them. This we will *not* do. This is where they are wrong. I did not defeat the Saecsans because I was boundless or hasty."

He clicked his tongue, facing his horse toward his Cymbrogi. A signal he was ready. "Peredur, tell your commanders to prepare the warriors."

Peredur nodded, then burst off to the task.

"Take up your arms!" Arthur called. A chorus of stomping feet and clanging metal rose. The commanders shouted orders and lines quickly formed.

Arthur stared dauntless at the kings and chieftains before him. "Follow me, and be wary. Look at every edge and corner. Miss *nothing*. We will *not* be trapped or defeated this day."

Arthur turned his horse about-face, and Bedwyr gathered beside him, his eyes still doleful. Arthur knew Bedwyr. After last night's loss, he was eager for a fight. "We have the upper hand," Arthur told him. "Always the bringers of truth see more than those who are deceivers. Always their eye is set on their deception. The noble have the opportunity to see through the guise. We can all be confident in knowing that, in this, we are not cornered."

Bedwyr pulled his spear out of his saddle and held it parallel to his horse's flank. He rolled the shaft in his hand.

Arthur stared at the edge, and then lifted his hand to raise the standards. Great poles rose with flags emblazoned with a red dragon. When the wind blew, they unfurled for all to see, and an unspoken confidence lifted the Cymbrogi. Their once dead Pendragon's banner flew over their heads. Now alive, his symbol stood as a formidable sign to any enemy who dared stand against them.

Arthur moved forward, leading the army to the hill's precipice. He steeled himself for war, yet secretly doubt forced its way into his heart. The last time a moment like this presented itself, he had the full strength of his mighty men. Back then, he confidently pounded toward the enemy without fear. But he never imagined so many of his men would be slain, with only two left remaining. The battle frenzy of Cia and Llenllaewg had always been his tip of the spear. Their combined might was like two giants stomping flat large armies. Where were they now? Lost by his negligence. Both times, the result of his unrelenting need for that *blasted* Holy Cup, blurring his reason. He gritted his teeth, stuffing down each jolt of uncertainty.

He eyed Bedwyr on his right, who, along with Peredur, was the last spark of the solidarity Arthur once had. The eyes of his mighty men used to dare death to come; the lack left him feeling the void. Did he still have what it took if it came to a clash? Had the sting of loss stolen his might?

He rolled his shoulders back and set his chin. *It helps nothing for me to think like this. The time has come to be prepared.* He leaned forward, coming within view of the ledge. *I will die fighting to protect this land. Loss or no loss.*

The hill was not steep, but long, and led all the way down to an oval-shaped field. There, like a small gathering of abandoned castaways, there stood not an army, but a mix of ragtag men. In front sat a hunched, thin man on his brown horse, holding a druidic pole. He wore all black, with a roughly rounded iron helm. He did not look like a warrior. He was too slight and held no weapons. Behind him stood Cymry traitors. Few had the look of experienced fighters. Most appeared only farmers or adolescent boys. But further back were lines of Osian's hoods.

"What is this?" Arthur asked aloud.

Bedwyr also stared agape, as though trying to make sense of the enemy's battle array.

The man on horseback trotted closer until he reached the base of the hill. He peered up, saying nothing at first, but grinned, as though happy to see them.

"Hail, Arthur! King of all Prydain." His voice was sharp and high in tone.

Arthur shouted down to him, "Who are you? What have you come for?"

The man bowed his head, then removed his helm. Dark sweaty hair stuck close to his scalp, revealing his pallid complexion and large round eyes.

Bedwyr gasped.

The man shouted, "My name is Dunnoc, my lord."

Bedwyr worked his jaw, then angrily whispered, "He is a *traitor*. He is a spy for Osian, and is the one responsible for the deaths of the people in the eastern village near Caer Lial."

Arthur's eyes flared, then he called down, "I have been told you are a traitor and a murderer, Dunnoc. You are in league with our enemy. What is to keep me from executing you here and now?"

"Yes, yes," Dunnoc confirmed, a weak smile still on his lips. "Though you might hold off and hear what I have come for. I have not come to fight you; as you see, we are too few against your greatness. But I *have* come to show you something. I think you will like it." He lifted his hand and called some men forward.

Dunnoc's men advanced, and Arthur shouted, "Stop!"

They halted, and Dunnoc leered up at him. The first gleam of devilish intention lurked in his eyes. He pursed his lips. "Why do you stay my men—Arthur, *king* of the Britons?" His tone mocked Arthur's title as though his kingship were a farce.

"Your actions are full of wickedness. I know who you are, and I know what you have done. Your master is a deceiver. I trust *nothing* you wish to show me."

"Hm," Dunnoc sniveled. "It will be revealed whether or not you are willing to look. Though, for your sake, I would not turn your back. All lessons must be learned, and this lesson will help you to understand."

Arthur raised his arm and bows snapped at the ready. The enemy darted their eyes left and right, shifting in their stances. Arthur seethed, "I always work to extend mercy, but *do not mistake*—I will not leave a single one of you alive that aims to harm my men or these lands."

Dunnoc tested Arthur's threat and twitched his fingers for his men to continue forward. "Oh, Pendragon, if you thought a single one of us stands here without understanding, that our lives are forfeit, then you are a fool!" Dunnoc leaned forward as if he were challenging Arthur to strike him down. "Would you kill these men?" he asked, presenting three young Cymbrogi soldiers, each with a hooded man looming behind them.

Arthur sucked in his breath. They stood in their colors, alongside Osian's wretches. "These men are traitors."

"Are they though?" Dunnoc shook his head, then said, "I think you know better by now that these men have very little control of their choices to betray you."

Fear and dread surged through Arthur's chest. Even as the three Cymbrogi started to lift their helms, he remembered Gethin of Celyddon—the innocent whose mind had been taken.

Their disheveled hair dropped from underneath their helms. Their faces were revealed, and a dreaded cry rose from Arthur's ranks, sending a cold rush through his blood.

"Ha-a-leth! My boy!" Halok leapt from his horse and bolted for his son. Cormach quickly intervened and snatched Halok's cloak. But the pull from Halok's charge ripped Cormach from his horse, and he crashed to the ground. Still, he held fast and yanked Halok back.

The father's cry curled Dunnoc's lips into a satisfied grin, then he snapped his gaze back to Arthur.

"What is this?" Arthur demanded.

"It is a gift." Dunnoc flung his hand down.

In one horrific blink, the hoods pulled knives across each of the three men's throats. Haleth's face contorted. He dropped his spear and gripped his throat. Blood gushed between his fingers. Terror rounded his eyes. In that one small second, his mind became his own, and he collapsed onto his knees with a gurgled gasp.

Another blood-curdling cry rose from Halok, releasing waves of fiery sorrow across the field. His hands reached for his son. More men joined Cormach, pulling Halok back and tackling him to the ground. The cries tore open fresh wounds of despair.

Arthur struggled to resist. It took every bit of control he possessed to prevent his rage from pouring forth and blinding his judgment.

Bedwyr lifted his spear, a focused fury blazing in his eyes.

Halok howled from amongst the men who fought to hold him down. His only son lay sputtering through his last breaths. "Let me go!" Halok wailed. "I will not let my son die alone."

This was the trap. This was the enemy's aim. To wound. Arthur ground his teeth together, feeling the pressure of his warriors begging him to action. He refused to let the rest of the victimized Cymbrogi, who stood with the enemy, be murdered.

Dunnoc and his hoods will meet their end.

Arthur nodded to Bedwyr, and quick as a flash, he released his spear. It sped through the air, leaving Dunnoc no time to respond before it pierced halfway through his chest. Dunnoc teetered to the side and thudded to the ground.

As if on cue, the hooded men pulled their swords and attacked the Cymbrogi in front of them.

Arthur brandished his sword and raised a shout. "Cymbrogi! Capture the traitors! Kill Osian's hoods."

The Cymbrogi charged the field. Their horses' gallop was a thunderstorm the enemy stood no chance against. The clash of drawn swords rang and spears flew, but the enemy offered little challenge to Arthur's seasoned warriors.

All too quickly, the ease of their battle baffled Arthur. Hooded men fell, struck by arrows and spears, while others ran from the battle. Arthur's sword had not even met one foe before the realization hit him.

None of these men are experienced warriors—not even the hoods. They are all pawns.

He shut his eyes with shame, comprehending his mistake.

"Halt! Halt!" he shouted. The clanging of metal continued. "Halt...halt!"

Bedwyr's eyes widened. The terrible realization had also struck him.

Bedwyr jumped from his horse, shouting into the fray, "Stop!" He ran to the body of a slain enemy, and using the tip of his sword, he flipped the hood away from its wearer's face. The man was old and frail, hardly fit for fighting. He was likely from a village in the Southlands that had been infiltrated by Osian's evil.

"Halt!" Arthur hollered in anguish.

Still bodies dropped. Commanders scattering the field shouted the order to stop. Too slowly the battle ceased.

Those left of the enemy's ranks fled in terror.

"Go after them," Arthur commanded. "Capture them—*do not* kill them."

Arthur watched his soldiers chase after the stragglers, and then, gasping, he dropped his head into his palms. After all he had done to keep from falling into the enemy's trap—he had failed.

Rising above the settling din was a keening wail from Halok, who cradled his deceased son within his arms. His roar lit like a beacon of anguish, twisting the dagger in Arthur's gut.

Arthur glanced at Bedwyr, whose mouth hung in utter shock. With a mournful lull, Arthur squeezed from his throat, "How?"

Bedwyr shook his head. "We did not see through their tricks. The deceivers saw us more fully than we saw them."

PART TWO

THE WOLF OF DESPAIR

Merlin trudged through the perilous forest. Every crunching step rang like an alarm bell to lurking demons. He scanned the horizon for the ravine where the cave lay, but it was still out of sight. The sky darkened, snuffing out what little light squeezed through the tightly woven branches above. He dreaded spending a night restless in these woods. Worry gnawed at his thoughts. Every hour he wasted getting to Elanor was another hour she faced danger.

Images of her lying dead and alone haunted his mind. He tried to block out the visions, but nothing else could occupy his thoughts. Just her.

When night fell, he lit a fire, unafraid of the light it emitted. He mumbled a threat, "I dare any dark thing to try and hinder me." He twiddled a piece of kindling between his fingers, then snapped it, casting both pieces into the fire.

How did I let this happen?

Elanor's closeness to him was the safest place she could've been.

Why did I go out there and leave her alone?

He knew why. It was his pride. He saw the threat of Osian's presence as an advantageous moment. He was going to kill him and end the days of his wickedness. So consumed with his own power to destroy Osian, he didn't even stop to consider Elanor's vulnerability.

I thought I would find him first.

"Gah!" he shouted, dropping his head into his hands. He rocked back, regret chewing on his insides like a starved rat. Why could he never seem to protect the ones he loved most? His mind raced, remembering his first love, Ganieda. Her red hair glistening in the sunlight when she danced. Her innocent smile and sweet laughter. Everything that was beautiful—destroyed. Gone.

He gulped, struggling to suppress the torrent of pain that threatened to break free.

Always they were there at his weakest moments: grievous memories, reminding him how he failed to keep the ones he loved safe. All that he had cherished, violently ravaged—stolen. He remembered the tears dripping from his face onto Elanor's when she lay dying in his arms, pierced by the enemy's arrow. By the miracle of the dragon's magic, she lived; without it, she would have surely died.

That this should happen again tore open a deep wound that had been slowly healing ever since Elanor came into his life. The beauty of love had come again. Even Arthur had returned from the dead, rekindling the hope that existed before Merlin's collapse in Avalon. But now—in this distressed moment—it felt like nothing.

A guttural whisper floated to his ears, *"You never truly left this place."*

Merlin snapped his head up toward the sound. A low shadowy figure skulked through the trees. Umber light blazed over his vision as he awaited the threat.

"Do not be afraid, Emrys. You know me. Do you not remember?"

The scampering gray demon darted back across the trees. Merlin narrowed his eyes.

"Years we spent together in the forest. I consoled you. I—your friend."

"You are not my friend," Merlin replied. "You are a *thing* of darkness." He steadily rose to his feet with hands extended, ready to fight.

The breathy sound of hungry panting circled him. The shadow raced back and forth behind the tree line like a predator scoping out its prey. Finally, it stopped and stared at him through the shadows.

Merlin leaned forward, his hands flaring with magical whorls.

A growl rumbled in his ears, and then out of the darkness emerged a large wolf. Its flaxen eyes glowed. Its high shoulder blades rolled with each step. Its fur bristled like ashen spikes on its back that faded into a shadowy black hide.

"Do not come any closer."

The wolf leered in challenge, but then slowly curled its haunches to the ground. It stared at Merlin through the flames.

"Look closer," it begged with eerie breathiness. "You have not forgotten me, or else you would have forgotten all your pain and grief."

Merlin glared at the wolf. "Grief?" He narrowed his eyes on the yellow of the wolf's; they were familiar, like a reflection in a mirror. Merlin leapt back in horror.

"Yes." The wolf seemed to grin, exposing long white fangs. "Now you see it. Now you remember me." It licked its teeth. "I am *your* despair. I am *your* grief. Never have we been fully separate, nor will we *ever* be."

Merlin's knees buckled, and he dropped to his seat. All at once, the emotions of loss strangled him like a tightening cord. The cataclysmic pictures of death played in his mind, stealing his full attention.

But a weak spark of hope made him fight. "N-No. No. This is the forest. It lies to me."

The wolf snorted a condescending snuffle. "You know better. You can blame the forest. But this forest only amplifies the truth. Deep down you know *you* are my owner."

Chapter Twenty-Four

"I-I do know," Merlin conceded with a reluctant nod.

"Remember when you ran and cast yourself away?"

Merlin's eyes searched the ground, as though he could discover his memories amongst the dried, crackling leaves. "I could not be king after I let Ganieda die. I did not want to see their faces. Too heavy was my sorrow. My life ruined. It had been my fault for not being there—so I ran away. I wanted to die. I hoped to never return."

He closed his eyes, remembering the site of Ganieda's mangled body. He wished he had never seen her like that. Her pale skin against the scarlet ribbons of blood. The image still scalded his mind.

He was too young to be king. King Murrian's heir was Cormach, the current Cormach's father, but he was still a boy and abdicated to Merlin—Murrian's adopted son. His mother Adhan was Murrian's wife.

Merlin was only in his seventeenth year when King Murrian died in a battle with the Saecsans. Ganieda was just fifteen when he asked her to be his bride. He had not been king even a full year before the Saecsans returned and devoured all his happiness on the day of his wedding. He had been hunting. A tradition for the groom. Missing while the enemy shattered everything. Just like he was missing when Osian stole Elanor away. That was when he ran away—forsaken—dead to the world.

"But did you ever return?" The gray shadowed wolf crept closer.

"Yes—I did. Years later."

"Did you?"

Merlin felt the sweltering breath of the creature brush his ear. "I returned, and rose Aurelius to the high throne of Prydain—and then Arthur after him."

"Did that really happen, or was it only dreams of hope tricking your mind? Did you not end up in the same place of despair, alone on the island of Avalon, waiting to die?"

"Yes—but then Elanor came. A reason to come out from hiding…l-l-like before."

"And then?"

"She died." Hot pain speared his chest, and Merlin sucked in a sharp breath.

The wolf's voice echoed even deeper, and he asked again, "And then?"

"She was given back to me, by some miracle."

"A trick of hope. For she is dead, and never was."

No.

"Arthur was only a dream that betrayed you. You have only ever been here with me. You never left. Look!" The creature's eyes flashed with fire. "Look at your hands."

Merlin lifted his hands against the flickering orange firelight. They were boney, and the skin was thin, veiny, and wrinkled. He touched his face and felt a great, long beard hanging from his chin. He clutched a handful of the slate-white hair.

"What is this?" Merlin gasped, and the sound of his voice was aged and strained.

"It is the illusion lifting. This is where you have lived many, many long years since Ganieda's death. I have fed you. I have kept you. You chose me, and closed out the world of light. Your delusions of hope have told you stories in your dreams. You imagined life in a better world. But always they came back to me—*despair, loss, grief*. I will never leave you. Grief is a scar that can *never* be removed."

When Merlin lifted his eyes, the Forest of Goll no longer remained. Instead, he sat numbly upon a frigid rock within a small grotto. He remembered it now. That was where he lived—up a hill, away from the eyes of others. The old druidic staff he had made lay at his feet. He was an old mystic and hermit, ready to damn all who should find him. Beside him was his wolf. He stroked its head, and the wolf leaned against his leg.

Merlin felt better now. Like a dream that fluttered away upon waking, all the pain—and the memories with it—disappeared.

"My only friend," Merlin mumbled, patting the wolf.

Now the wolf sat silent like an animal with no powers of speech. Merlin knew this was the truth. The rest had all been lies. His life ended long ago on the devastated fields of battle against the Saecsans. That was where he had left his heart.

He stood, emotionless, remembering he had left some herbs to boil on the fire. He bent to stir them and told the wolf, "I had a dream I was young again."

The wolf yawned, then stretched to its feet.

Merlin coughed. "You hungry?"

He shuffled across the room, his staff clicking on the stone floor, to where drying meats hung on a string. He yanked a piece down.

"Here." He cast it to the floor and the wolf gobbled it up. "I am trying to remember the dream," he said, scratching his head. "I think there were kings and wars. Always wars. And—and a beautiful woman with blue eyes." With a moan, he shook his head. "Pointless!"

Arthur's army captured twenty of Osian's Cymry puppets. These were all that remained alive after they attacked.

Peredur had told him, "Dunnoc would have had them all slaughtered anyway—his gift was an execution."

That sentiment brought Arthur little consolation, feeling certain he could have prevented the loss.

If only I perceived what the enemy had devised.

But how could he have known? The thought was distressing—like an arrow lodged between two ribs. The long, defeated faces of the Cymbrogi confirmed his woe.

The message was clear. Osian cared little for life. He extended no mercy, which made Arthur dread even more the thought of Elanor within his clutches. Despite it all, he could not delay.

The next morning, the Cymbrogi rallied to Llyonesse with the prisoners in tow. Arthur hated tying the captives and pulling them along on foot, but he couldn't let them go. Their minds were not free of Osian's grip, and they could not be trusted. Either they would run back to Osian's armies, or potentially do themselves harm trying to attack. Arthur's one hope remained: that, in the end, these could be redeemed and their minds set free from the poison.

Halok stayed behind to bury his son, along with a few others. Arthur seethed, thinking about the devastation the enemy had inflicted upon Halok's kin. His entire caer likely gone. His father, wife, and son killed, and with them, the innocent, beautiful echo of the Cymry past.

Such great loss.

The gates of Llyonesse came into view. A stone fortress surrounded an ominous and lonely gray tower with four pointed spires jutting into the bleak sky. Arthur glared at the walled city. An unsettled feeling churned his gut, and he shifted in his saddle. No Cymbrogi guarded the walls or ramparts. The gates hung wide open for anyone to enter unheeded, and yet the citadel seemed hollow within, like the soul of a ghost.

A chill wind blew at his back. The cold season of Imbolc was coming soon. This had to be done with, and soon.

Arthur and the Cymry lords, along with Thul's two sons, went inside. The armies remained just outside the citadel and set up camp. No flags or standards festooned Llyonesse's walls, declaring no one a lord of the caer.

When they entered through the vacant gates, the few working town-folk and trade-smiths froze. One woman dropped an armload of cloth and darted into her house. An iron forger set his hammer down and walked out from under his awning, staring open-mouthed. Many others joined him, all peering in stunned silence as if wraeths were passing through.

"They seem starved," Bedwyr grumbled.

Arthur's gaze swept over the villagers' gaunt cheeks and deep-set eyes. Rage boiled his blood, igniting a fierce blaze of empathy within him.

Peredur caught Arthur's eye. His jaw rippled and bitterness twisted his lips.

"Where are all the city's Cymbrogi?" Thul asked, his grizzled voice like shattering glass in the dismal quiet.

Arthur had no answers for him. His hands trembled, and he clenched them into fists around his reins. Lugh's treatment of his people was jarring. The desire to stop and aid them gnawed at Arthur's chest. But first, he had business to do.

He led the company on toward the tower where King Lugh had ruled, and most likely remained his queen.

Bedwyr pointed. "What are those?" Thick iron posts lined both sides of the lane in front of the tower where several wrought-iron trappings hung. "Are...are those cages?"

Arthur's eyes widened, taking in the hellish cages. The closer they approached, the more he regretted the scene. What remained of arms and legs dangled outside the flat, rusted bars. The wind blew the offensive stench of death into his nostrils.

"Agh!" A chorus of abhorred groans resounded from the company. Many flung their arms over their noses.

Arthur refused to react but gripped the reins of his horse even tighter, pressing the blood out of his fingers.

"Look at them," Thul murmured. "Their colors. They were Cymbrogi."

"That is where they are, then?" Peredur pulled on his horse's reins. He dismounted and stormed over to the cages. With indignation in his voice, he growled, "These men *will not* be left to rot."

"Surely, this cannot be all of them," Bram said—horror edged his voice. "There had to be more warriors in Llyonesse to prevent this from happening." The warrior-turned-king bore a grim face like he'd been gut-punched. These were likely men he had fought with.

Peredur walked past the first group of cages, looking at each one with his fists squeezed at his sides. He spat onto the ground with unmasked vehemence, then stared back up toward the decomposing skulls and rotting bones. Others appeared more freshly dead, trapped in cages with their own refuse.

Peredur snapped his head toward Arthur. Tears welled in Peredur's eyes; his mouth twisted with clear contempt. Arthur felt it too. These warriors fought for Prydain, and now they hung like forsaken carcasses, starved and tortured to death.

Peredur approached a second group of cages. He paused before one where the prisoner's forehead rested on the bars. His sunken eyes lay shut and his mouth was a pendulous black hole. Peredur yelled to Arthur, "I can see his brooch. This was the battle chieftain!"

The caged Cymbrogi's eyes shot open, and he sprang to life. "A-a-h!" He flung his hands out like a drowning man begging to be saved.

Startled, Peredur jumped. He drew his sword and stumbled backward.

"O-o-h, my Great God!" the prisoner cried in a scratchy wail. His eyes raced back and forth over them. "Have I died?" He gasped, his mouth hanging open in disbelief. "My eyes…see…the king!"

A few more of the cages rattled with a waking remnant.

"They are alive," Bedwyr declared, jumping from his horse to join Peredur, who was still standing awestruck.

Arthur rode over to the first man's cage. The height of his horse brought him eye to eye with him. "You are not dead." Arthur searched the prisoner's pronounced cheekbones and sunken eyes for recognition. He would have known the chieftain. "I have come to take back these lands."

"Ooh!" the man moaned, his eyes filling with tears. "I am one of your faithful warriors—battle chieftain of Llyonesse. That is why I hang here condemned. I would not betray Prydain to follow the evil wiles of my mad king."

"King Lugh is dead." Arthur spat out his name like it was poison.

The chieftain cried out, and keening sobs fell from his cracked mouth. Hope shimmered in his eyes, deepening the lines on his streaked face. "Can this really be true? We are free?"

Arthur's eyes misted with tears. "For-forgive me that I allowed Lugh to rot these lands. *No longer.*" He shook his head, still wrestling with the atrocities before him. With a heavy sigh, he grasped the man's thin, dirty fingers gripping the bars. "What is your name, chieftain?"

The man sat up and pulled back his shoulders. "I am Elian, my king. I have fought with you in many battles."

Arthur caught his breath. "Elian?" An unbidden tear fell free from his eye. He knew him. "I remember you, commander." Anger amassed like a darkening storm cloud within his chest. This loyal chieftain had been starved until he became the unrecognizable form before him.

"I will fight for you again, once I am freed"—Elian shook the bars fiercely—"of this *god-forsaken* cage."

"Where would we find the keys to free you?" Bedwyr called to him.

Elian's face turned grim, and he pointed to the tower. "The keeper is within that tower. The queen has not been merciful in her husband's absence."

Arthur entered the stale tower hall. Musty air tainted the light beaming through the tall lofty windows. Two wooden doors leading to the throne room sat closed. He glared at the doors, then kicked them open. They slammed wide, echoing through the empty hall. A lone woman leapt up from the floor, her face white with fright. She squeaked and ran toward a back passage.

"After her," Arthur ordered.

Bedwyr charged like a bull, followed by Thul's son Thanul. His ginger hair whipped behind him, and his long legs crossed the room in quick strides. They both disappeared down the shadowed corridor. Within moments, a frightened scream resounded and the men re-emerged, dragging out a frail-looking woman. They set her in a crumpled heap before Arthur's feet. Her eyes rounded and her body trembled.

"Who are you?" Arthur demanded.

"P-Please, my lord, I am but the lady's handmaid." The thin woman panted like a small mouse cornered by a predator. Her eyes scanned the high lords, and her fingers pulled at the sleeves of her torn, gray dress. A white kerchief wrapped her limp, chestnut hair.

This is just another starved victim.

Arthur swallowed his frustration and asked with gentle firmness, "Where is your mistress?"

"She...sh-she—" she gulped, afraid to speak.

A red and blue blur bursting across the back passageway caught Arthur's eye. Bedwyr had seen it too, and he rushed after it. Bram and Thanul gathered by the passageway, ready to help.

A screech, followed by forceful breaths and scuffling feet, emanated from around the corner. And then Bedwyr appeared, holding a feisty red-headed woman by the back of her cobalt dress. She flailed against Bedwyr, and her tight hair fell loose from her struggle. A ring of keys jingled at her hip, and swift as a viper, Bedwyr ripped them from her belt.

"Those are mine!" she snapped. "You have no right to do this. Let me go!" She hissed and scratched, thrusting her hands like claws at Bedwyr, but she could not reach him. His one hand kept her firmly at bay. She looked like a cat pulled from a tree by the nape of its neck.

Arthur had reached his limit. After all he had seen, he could no longer contain his fury. "I HAVE ALL THE RIGHT!" he boomed.

The queen of Llyonesse shut her thin lips and scuffled back, bumping into Bedwyr's chest. Bedwyr jerked back with a disgusted glare, then thrust her forward to face Arthur.

"What have you been doing to *my people?*" Arthur demanded, seething

Her large brown eyes appeared odd on her slender, pointed face. Her small, narrow nose accentuated the wrinkles edging her mouth, and the lines under her eyelash-less eyes. She reminded Arthur of a rat dressed in finery.

With timid defiance, she dared to say, "These are King Lugh's pe—"

"They are *my* people, and your husband no longer rules here. He is *dead.*"

She dropped to the floor and shrieked, "You *killed* him!" The chamber rang with her writhing howls.

"Silence her," Arthur commanded, resisting the urge to fling his hand across her face. Bedwyr jerked her up by her arms and onto her feet. She panted, her face now flushed, staring daggers at Arthur. "I did not *kill* your husband." He paused, feeling his tolerance slipping. "One of your own evil cohorts killed him. A hooded man named Malik strangled him in his own chains."

She yelped as though the news bit her. Her reaction seemed a farce. No real grief appeared in her eyes.

"Why have you sentenced my Cymbrogi to death in those"—he clenched his teeth, hating to say it—"those cages?"

She huffed and pursed her lips. Her eyes shifted away, refusing to speak.

"ANSWER!"

She jumped and clutched her chest. "Th-they are braggards. Men who *refuse* to serve their masters."

Arthur moved closer and she recoiled. He leaned over her, flames igniting inside his gut. "And who is the *master* they are being commanded to follow?"

She dropped her head. The tolerance for her words had run out.

Arthur pointed a threatening finger at her. "Answer me carefully, woman. Your life is on trial. Where are the rest of the Cymbrogi of Llyonesse?"

Her eyes peeled up slowly, a wicked flicker of satisfaction floated within them. "WHERE ARE MY MEN!"

She screamed, shaking, then snapped to say, "They have…they betray you, my lord. They now serve the armies of Lord Osian."

Arthur scoffed at the mention of Osian as a lord. "Clap her into one of those *iron cages* for a while," he ordered. He turned away from her, despising all that she represented. But his fury still boiled over, unsatiated. He spun back around and growled, "Without food or water."

"No—*stop*," she pleaded. They dragged her from the chamber, and she struggled against them, her feet skimming the floor. "They will come for you. They will break down the warriors you have left, and rob you of your lands. Wait and see. You are finished. *Finished!*" She continued her threats until her voice disappeared around the corner.

Arthur drew a steadying breath, then rubbed the anger from his face. "Thanul," he called, glancing over at the lone wooden throne seated at the back of the hall. Thanul arrived beside him. "Your first actions as steward will be to order your men to empty those cages and bury those wasted to death. And then, those abominations—those torture devices—" His body shook, and he pointed in the direction of the cages outside. "*Destroy* them."

"What of the Llyonesse queen?"

"Leave her caged for a while. I have yet to decide what to do with her, but I want her to watch Lugh's evil dismantled." He put his hand on Thanul's shoulder and gave a stern stare. His lips curled as he spoke. "Execution awaits those that murdered my people and desecrated these lands. Are you prepared to steward these lands?"

Thanul bowed. When his eyes lifted, Arthur could see the same vengeful flames burning within them. In a low grim tone of solidarity, he growled, "Yes, my king."

THE SILVER STREAM

"When did I get so old?" Merlin asked the wolf. "It feels as though life has disappeared here inside my lonely corner." The wolf blinked at him, quietly panting next to the fire. Merlin sighed, slapping his knees. "I wonder if there are any songs I could sing. Seems I have forgotten so many. As a boy, my ollamh taught me many songs. It all had a purpose then—being a bard."

The wolf dropped his head sleepily, and Merlin continued, "I remember the monks of Eire came with new stories—new songs—" His voice fell away into thought.

A sudden gust of wind, powerful enough to make Merlin cover his head, blew into the small alcove. The wolf swiftly stood alert, eyeing Merlin with a bowed head. When the wind ceased, Merlin lowered his hands. His rowan staff had blown over onto the ground. He picked it up and blinked his old eyes, staring at the gnarl on top. "Just how long have I been here?"

He glanced over at the wolf. "No need to be alarmed, Wolf. It was only wind."

The wolf lay back down with a suspicious glint in his yellow eyes.

Merlin stared at his one free hand. Something felt wrong. He balled his fingers into a fist. *What is it? Is there something more I am supposed to know?*

He stood and walked to the edge of the grotto's entrance. Gazing below, through the oak branches to the forest floor, he noticed a steady flowing stream. It glistened like a silver thread in a sea of brown and amber leaves. A light breeze blew across the crackling foliage, and he thought he heard something—almost like a song. Merlin squeezed his eyes shut, straining to hear it. Even its faint sound pulled on his deepest longings. He sighed, exasperated, not quite able to capture it.

"Do you hear it, Wolf?"

The swarthy predator made no move in response.

"Songs are meant to be sung." Merlin stroked his long beard, whispering, "Stories are meant to be told. Where have all mine gone? I-I can almost hear them. They hover about, just out of my"—he stared down at the stream—"reach."

The wolf growled inside his mind, *"You traded your song for grief."*

"Oh, yes." Merlin nodded with a somber air. "That is the way it was. I tried to let the grief go, but it filled every part of me. Every face betrays me when I try to remember them. The Great God hates me, or else he would not have robbed me so completely." Merlin raised his fist. "I owe this God nothing."

His confession stirred his anger, and tears gathered in his heavy eyes. Bitterness swelled within him as he glared at the stream below, as though it had been the one to offer him hope, betraying him. With a heated tsk, he stole back to his rock, slumped down, and leaned against his staff.

"You have always been here, remember? All else are lies, false hopes, that the Great God throws to torture you."

"Have I lost myself to madness?" Merlin swallowed hard, his mind fighting to tell him something else. "Have I really been here, all these years, lost to the world since Ganieda died? I was just a young man. Now I am old." He felt his years wasted, drained away.

Frustrated, his anger flared up again, and he stood. As he did, a memory flashed in his mind. He remembered his fingers clutching the tunic of a young monk, and casting him to the ground.

The monk's voice echoed into his spirit, *"When you let yourself awaken, you will no longer feel this way. Though, it will be hard to open your eyes. The strength is still in you; it only seems lost because you stopped moving forward."*

Merlin remembered the monk's face. His mouth widened and his eyes grew larger. He murmured, "Avalon. Rian. That was his name." Merlin's eyes met the wolf's ominous gaze.

I have been here before, but this is not where I stayed.

He laced his fingers over his forehead, considering the past. It was hard to think with wave after wave of despair bashing his subconscious, hindering his clarity.

Is this wolf really my friend? Is this den truly my home?

He lifted his head. "I am thirsty." He walked away from the dark recesses of the alcove. The wolf shifted. Merlin felt its eyes watching him as he climbed down the jagged boulders that created a descending stairway. Once on the bottom, he peered up. The wolf stared in warning over the ledge. Merlin pursed his lips and continued toward the stream. He didn't know what he was doing, only that the trickling water ahead had called his name. There was something hidden that he needed to find.

In haste, he shuffled toward the stream; his tattered robes swished across the leaves. He couldn't stop. The wolf was coming for him—he knew it. The scrape of its claws upon the rocks overhead scratched at his senses.

Finally arriving, Merlin knelt with anxious breaths before the clear water. It gurgled gently over its stony bed. The sight of it awakened his thirst, and eagerly, he leaned closer to drink. Just as he went to scoop his hand into the pristine water, he froze. The wolf threatened Merlin's next move with a hot growl behind his neck.

The water was right in front of him. He could feel the bottom of his white beard dangling in the current. He closed his eyes.

Either I return with the wolf to the safety of my den, or I drink and die.

Merlin knew the wolf would never let him go. Though, in this moment, the idea of death was tantalizing. Freedom from the weary world might be worth a sip from the stream. Decided, he dared the wolf to attack and delved his fingers into the icy spring. Any second now he expected the sensation of fangs stabbing into his neck.

There was a sudden flash of light and the wolf fell silent. Merlin held his eyes closed. Had his death come? The rushing waters swirled around his finger, and his hand settled around something that did not feel like a stone. Slowly, he opened his eyes and, lifting his hand from the stream, discovered he held a wooden cup with a wide-mouthed bowl atop a delicate stem.

Sparkling liquid beads dripped from its overflowing brim. He lifted the cup higher. The water ran down his arm. In awe, he gasped, "The Holy Cup!"

He marveled, noticing a figure standing on the other side of the small stream. He was an old balding man, with a long white beard like Merlin's. He had a mysterious glow that emanated from his muted blue robe and tunic.

The man knelt before Merlin, mirroring his posture and gently cradling the cup beneath Merlin's fingers.

"Are you thirsty, Merlin?" the man asked.

"I am very thirsty," Merlin blurted, his trembling mouth turned downward. A tear broke free from his eye. He didn't know why, but he felt like he had been dying of thirst and was finally being offered a drink. His curiosity deepened. The kindness in the man's eyes baffled Merlin.

"Do you think the contents of this cup will quench your thirst?"

Merlin gazed at the cup, observing the ornate markings of eastern script carved deep into the polished vessel's sides. "Am I being tested?" The light from the man shone down upon Merlin's grief, heating his entire body.

"This is not the day for testing, my son. Right now, you are being offered the restoring sip of this cool water. But this water"—the man slid his hand over Merlin's wrist—"will only take your thirst away for the moment. There is another water that will take away your thirst forever."

"How would I discover such a wonderful drink?"

"You must surrender everything to me."

Merlin dropped his head and wept. The wolf had taken his life when he surrendered to his pain, but this offer seemed different somehow. The cup started spilling at the tilt of his hand. "Who are you? I know your voice."

"You know me, Merlin. You have asked me many times my name. But *I Am* more than the names men call me. I have revealed myself to you many times, and always I have been there to help and to heal. But you resist knowing me fully—"

Merlin slumped, and the cup spilled over even more.

The man said in a low voice, "You are still angry with me."

"You killed my love." Merlin peered up, sniffing in his tears.

The man's eyes lit upon Merlin with compassion as he lifted him by his elbows to stand, guiding his feet into the stream. The cool water rushed over Merlin's toes, and a strange calm brought quietness to his angst.

"Merlin," the man continued, "your grief is a deep wound. I touched it with joy once, but the pain still takes you away from me."

"The grief pounds like a drum, making me want to die. It never leaves me."

"It will never leave you."

Merlin sighed. "Then where is there hope? Why not let the wolf consume me? With him, I am numb, and there is no time or memories."

"No, Merlin. It is but a shade that traps you inside grief like a cage. There is no freedom there. Only death."

"Then how do I break free if the grief will never leave? Am I doomed to the pain picking away at me like vultures on a corpse?"

"The grief can only be exchanged. My life for yours. In this surrender, the grief and loss will remain, but my life will live beside your grief, soothing and healing it, like this water that now flows over your feet. It will never run out. It will never run dry."

"I do not understand."

"You do not have to. You just have to choose."

When the man spoke, Merlin could not help but feel completely held. His every word nourished like water, quenching a fire that had scorched pieces of his soul. If he never had to be alone—maybe he never was.

He looked up at the man, thirsty once more, and gasped through his tears. "I do know you."

"You have been lied to long enough, Merlin. If you are thirsty, then drink. It is not the contents of the cup, but the agreement as you swallow that will bring you— my life."

With a trembling hand, the old version of Merlin pulled the cup to his wrinkled lips. When he drank, the wolf howled—the mourning sound thinned and slowly disappeared into the air.

All at once, Merlin was awake, sitting before the cold coals of a long dead fire. The same place he had been before the wolf had appeared. He looked at his hands and, turning them over, saw no wrinkles. A wave of relief rose in his chest as he touched his chin and found a short trim beard.

I am young again.

Across from him stood the same man with him at the stream, but he also was no longer old. He was the man Merlin had seen so many times before.

Merlin exclaimed, "Man in blue!"

"*I Am*," he replied simply, with a gentle smile.

Merlin clutched his heart and closed his eyes. He felt changed. A transaction had taken place. He did not have the forsaken feeling in his heart anymore, and the anger was gone. Merlin swiftly rose and approached the Man in Blue. He halted before him and stared into his wondrous eyes. His face had always been with him, but now for the first time, he understood who he was.

"Y-You are real?" Merlin stuttered, his thoughts reeling.

The Man in Blue tenderly cupped the sides of Merlin's head, then pulled him to his shoulder. Merlin sighed, leaning into a fuller embrace. The relief of a child held by a father rushed over him. Rarely had he known that feeling in his life. The Man in Blue gripped the sides of his head, and more of the grief fell away. "Who was the wolf, my lord?"

"He was the part of you that did not belong. The malignant part, where your pain festered. Now he is gone, and because of that, this forest can no longer take anything from you."

"Thank you," Merlin said through misty eyes. "I never believed I would be free of it."

"You must be free if you are to conquer these enemies of *the kingdom*. If they can ensnare you with pain, lies, and un-truths, then you will not have the authority to stop them."

"Elanor," Merlin said, slapped back into awareness.

"Yes—she needs you, Merlin. You have been caught up here for many days. I pressed against the darkness a long while before you were willing to hear me."

"I am sorry it took me so long."

"I would have pressed no matter how long it took."

Merlin smiled. The truth of his words made Merlin feel a value he had only felt in the arms of his own mother. He shook his head and jumped to action.

"I must go!" With haste, he grabbed his pack.

The Man in Blue pointed, and without words, he commanded the trees to part. They groaned, and their leaves rattled and fell. The trees settled, revealing a wide-open trail. It was as though the unhindered path had always been there, just shrouded in illusion. Dumbfounded, Merlin looked back at the Man in Blue, but he was gone.

26

THE WATERS OF LIFE

Elanor lay listening to the hollow drips leaking through the darkness. Her whole body felt rigid. She ached, shivering with cold. Her head hung against her wrists, chafed by the biting iron chains. The discomfort amplified the night-marish illusions that endlessly assaulted her. She had no way of knowing how many days had passed—it was always dark.

She lost her grip on reality. As far as she knew, the cave was just another illusion. Any good thoughts were dashed the moment she had them, which made her fearful to even try.

Even her father David's death replayed over and over; except this time, she was the one who called the cyhyraeth to kill him. The guilt ate at her soul, making her wish for death. Arthur and Gwynevere had cast her out, stripping her of all she could have been. She was left ashamed and orphaned. But the worst visions were of Merlin. She learned to fear his face. He had become a worse demon than the hoods or even Osian, and he haunted her relentlessly in the dark.

She tried to hang on. Her only relief came when she mustered the strength to mumble the words of *the song*. But even then, Merlin was there to shove his hand over her mouth to silence her. She fought against him, forcing out a wordless hum. She would shake her head free, and persistently sing, with tears streaming down her cheeks. If she just kept singing, a dim flickering light always came. She reached for it as hard as she could.

"Just keep singing," she would tell herself, hoping the light would not diminish.

"Grwyrthrhodd! Man in Blue, please—help me," she would beg.

Small echoes seemed to call back, *"Keep fighting."*

Her stomach groaned for food and her parched lips cracked, begging for water. She feared calling out for sustenance, because if it came, it was in the hands of someone who hurt her.

She strained against the raw ache in her stomach when an abrupt, growling voice above her spoke. "We are leaving."

Fearful it was Merlin, she closed her eyes and turned her head away.

"Either he will find you, or you will die," Osian said. "The time has come for us to move from hiding. This place is no longer secret, and work needs to be done."

Elanor struggled to understand, unsure who was speaking. She dove into her chants with the hope that nothing worse would come—no hand would strike her.

Osian's cackles echoed through the chamber, then dwindled away. Elanor was once more alone. Her heart thudded in her chest. She swallowed into her swollen, dry throat. She winced into her arms, refusing to open her eyes, and faded into a tormented sleep. Inside a hazy dream, she ran, screaming from a shadow that chased her.

"Elanor!" a voice beckoned, piercing through the nightmare.

Was it real? Or just a taunt luring her to her doom? Frightened, she kept running.

Then solid hands shook her. "Elanor!"

The distressing dream blurred with another gentle shake.

"Elanor!"

Barely conscious, she felt her arms loosened and lowered to the ground. Her arms radiated with an odd sensation of throbbing tingles. The blood flowed back into her fingertips, making her moan. Someone jostled her feet before the chains rattled to the floor. Her eyes felt glued shut. She worked to pry them open.

Who's there? she wondered, fearful of what pain she might endure. Her mind was steeped in mire, and she struggled with consciousness, unsure she wanted to fully wake.

A soft, reassuring hand cupped her face and stroked her arm, triggering the expectation of pain. Her blood pulsed at the touch, and her eyes jerked open. Within the darkness, a shadow moved above her. She yelped, covering her head. She scooted back, anticipating abuse, and rubbed her now free hands over her scabbed wrists.

"Do not be frightened. You are safe. Osian is gone."

She recoiled even further at the sound of his voice. Tears flooded her eyes. "Get *away* from me."

The shadow reached for her, and she screamed, petrified.

"Do not *hurt me. Please*"—she clenched her teeth through tears—"just leave me alone."

He reached again. This time, she shrieked, throwing herself into a ball and covering her head.

"Elanor," the voice said through anxious breaths. "It is me. Merlin."

She felt him nearing and curled tighter, wishing she could disappear into the cracks between the rocks.

"You are safe. No one will harm you."

It is a trick! The Merlin she saw in this place never meant her well. He was so strong, and she could never get free from him once he had her.

How I wish he were not a trick, she thought woefully. *He never really comes. He never really helps.*

She stammered through frightened tears, "S-Sweet…are the healing days, when pain will find no way." She panted through each phrase. "The earth will sing, for the Sun has made it day. Sweet…as it will be proclaimed the new days of the Sun."

Her body quivered. "PLEASE. PLEASE. Leave me be." Her sob caught in her chest, dreading the oncoming torture.

Merlin stood back, aghast, his body trembling with shock. His eyes hovered over his wife. She quivered like a small animal unsure of where to run. Black sooty dirt splotched her skin, and her hair was caked with dried blood. His gaze fell upon the stark gray bruising and lacerations encircling her wrists, a visceral tableau that unraveled him from within, stirring a tempest of emotions too powerful to contain. His heart crashed to the cave floor, guilt and rage coiling within him like two tangling serpents. His hands tingled at his sides, wishing, *longing* only to hold her in his arms and never let go. But he could not.

By some cruel trick, she was convinced he was her enemy. She stammered through the lyrics of *the song*, as though she had gone mad. His heart broke seeing her in this weak, fractured state.

She peered up at him through her fingers. Bright blue eyes, the only thing that still resembled her, glowed through the darkness. Wide horrified eyes revealed her weariness. Her cheek bones protruded from lack of food, and her clothes sagged.

Tears fell unrestrained from Merlin's eyes. He almost could not keep looking. The sight of her so battered…put lumps in his throat.

Her gaze captured Merlin's tears, and slowly she lifted her head and dropped her hands. She was curious, but mistrust still hovered in her eyes. Merlin backed away, giving her distance. His action wrenched his heart. She thought he was a monster.

What an evil design. This stings worse than grief.

He pressed his lips together, his breath shallow as he listened to her mumble lines of *the song*. He dared to gently sing along with her. "—its emblems triumphing. A new day rising, with the old moons setting. Sweet…days of the Sun are coming."

She stopped and gasped, lifting her hand to her mouth. "Merlin?" she breathed.

"Yes, my soul. It is me." He scooted nearer, sniffing back his tears. "You are safe now. I promise."

A hopeful spark appeared in her eyes, and her face softened. Her countenance called to him, and he reached his hand toward her.

Her eyes flared with fear. She inhaled a sharp breath and let out a terrified scream. Her eyes flashed blue, and she flung her hands out in defense, hurling Merlin across the chamber. He crashed against the hard wall before collapsing to the ground. His head throbbed. Anger and sadness collided within his chest. He lifted his hand to his head and stared wide-eyed at Elanor.

Gasping, she coiled her body, as if preparing to lash out a second time.

A sob choked him, but he held it in. He whispered to himself, "I do not know what to do." He looked away from Elanor and stared at the floor. The dark corners of the cave held no answers. It was an evil, empty shell with no warmth. Part of him was tempted to just drag her out of there—even if she struggled. But the other part of him knew that would be a mistake.

He squeezed his eyes shut and clenched his jaw. When he opened his eyes, he gently shook his head, then waved a consoling hand. "Do not worry. Y-You can rest." He needed to clear his head and figure out what to do. Right now, he was too emotionally charged and falling apart. He turned to leave.

"Please—d-do not leave me. I do not know if you are real. But, please," she bemoaned in desperate breaths. "Help me."

Hearing his wife beg for help squelched his sobs. He spun around, tears splashing from his eyes. He crept closer to her once again. She shut her eyes tight, as though bracing for a blow.

"I-I will not hurt you." He opened his palms to show he meant her no harm and knelt beside her.

She opened her eyes and glanced at his hands, then shut them again, holding herself tight.

"I am going to take you from this place." Merlin reached his shaking hand toward her and lightly brushed her cheek before lacing his fingers through her knotted hair.

Elanor winced, squeezing out tears. But then, she leaned her cheek against his hand.

"There," he said with a tearful exhale. "I love you—I would *never* harm you."

She whispered through her parted fingers, "I want to believe you."

Merlin ground his teeth, his gut twisting with the thought of what dark thing Osian had done to her. What had he shown her that would make her so afraid? Within the darkness of her mind, what manipulative lie was contrived against him? Vengefulness heated his veins. He loathed the enemy for convincing Elanor that he would *ever* hurt her.

"Let me carry you from this dark place."

She studied his face, giving him a quick but hesitant nod. He scooped her up into his arms, lifting her slowly. She gripped at his shirt and tucked her head into his chest.

"It is alright," he said, swallowing down another sob. He felt every shiver quake through her frail body.

"I will keep you safe," he soothed. Emotion choked the rest of his words. He rounded the corner, anxious to flee the filth of the cave. Beams of light fought through the darkness around the next bend.

Maybe in the light of the sun, the blanket of deception will fall from her mind.

He quickened his pace. The welcome sight of trees appeared through the open hull of the cave. Elanor's body tensed, and her breathing quickened into frightened huffs.

I must get her into the light.

His foot finally crossed the threshold, and they burst out underneath a sunlit sky. He blinked his eyes, adjusting to the brightness. A slight smile curled the edge of his mouth. He glanced down at Elanor, hoping she, too, felt the sunlight's freedom. But all too quick, he discovered she had gone limp. Her one arm fell behind her—drooping and lifeless.

"Oh, no, no, no, no—" He tsked, delicately tapping her check. Her face was pale; her cheeks gaunt. "Elanor." He pulled her closer into his arms. "Come on. Wake, my love. We made it out. You are free." He rocked her into his chest and knelt to the ground. His magic kindled, and he pressed his fingers to her head. "Iacha—Elanor. Iachau."

Grief swelled in his stomach at the thought of losing her. "Aaugh," he groaned. The pain invaded his heart. But this time—this time, the memory of the stream rolling over his feet came to him. He was not alone.

"Please. Great God," he pleaded. "Help me." Tear tracks wet his cheeks, and he pressed his forehead into hers.

Merlin heard a voice within him say, *You cannot heal her.*

"Then what am I to do?"

You can do nothing.

Merlin whimpered, "What?"

A hand suddenly grasped his shoulder. Startled, he turned. The Man in Blue stood beside him; the sounds of a babbling spring trickled into Merlin's ears.

He gasped. "I know this place."

The cave and the forest had disappeared, and Merlin found he was now in the healing sanctuary he and Elanor had disappeared into long ago. He eyed the Man in Blue with hopeful sorrow.

"We have been here before." Even as Merlin spoke, twinkling waves of light appeared. Echoes whispered over the glassy, still waters of the ethereal pool.

The man knelt, placing his hand on Elanor's arm. "She has been calling out to me every day since she was taken into that dark place. I heard her cry."

"Why did you not go to her—help her?"

"I have been with her, just as I was with you in the forest."

Merlin sniffed in an ache and peered at his beloved.

"The devils of this world have a right to torment those who are eager to believe their lies. Elanor's belief in her own weakness made it easy for her to doubt her own value. Osian's witchcraft effortlessly entangled her mind, confirming to her all she believed true." He turned to Merlin. "You could heal her body, give her food and water, but Osian has broken her mind. This you cannot heal."

Merlin furrowed his brow. "You mean there is no hope?"

"My voice speaks to her even now. The words of *my song* have been playing over the lies. In this place"—he waved his hand around the sanctuary—"there can be no more deception."

"What is this place?"

"This is a piece of my home. I created it for you, and for her." He wrapped his arms around Elanor and lifted her away from Merlin.

Merlin stared agape at the Man in Blue, begging for understanding.

The man smiled. "This is your home." He caressed Elanor's head, cradling it into his chest. "This is how the world changes"—his eyes grew misty—"when the ones I love come to know me as *I Am*." He leaned his head close and whispered in Elanor's ear, "Come now, it is time to be cleansed." He kissed her forehead, then walked her down into the water.

Merlin's forehead creased. He did not understand but watched the man wade into the spring. The gentle ripples of the water called to Merlin, so he scooted over to its edge. He reached his trembling fingers toward the water, eager to touch it and remember its warmth. When his hand broke the surface, peace enveloped his spirit. Joy leapt into his heart, and he lifted his eyes to see the Man in Blue grinning at him with pleasure.

With wide eyes, Merlin breathed, "This is my home."

The man nodded, then turned his attention back to Elanor. His face shifted, and his brows scrunched with heavy concern. He cupped water into his hand. Light dripped from his hand like crystals as he carried the water to her forehead, trickling it over her face.

He pressed his hand onto her forehead and chanted, "Oh, Kingdom of the Sun, renew her with grace. Oh, Kingdom of the Sun, the warmth of your bounty upon her face."

MILK & HONEY

Elanor opened her eyes. Beams of warm light touched the wooden slats of her city flat. She drew a deep breath, taking in the sound of her kettle already bubbling to a boil. The tannins of hot tea floated into her nose. She turned to see her father David collecting clean dishes and putting them away.

Her waking fog lifted, and she picked herself up with a curious smile. "Hey, Dad," she said with a scratchy morning voice. "What are you doing here?"

He shrugged. "Eh…I knew you needed me." He grabbed a stack of plates. They rattled together as he placed them inside a cupboard.

Elanor rubbed her eyes and stretched. "Thank you for dealing with my dishes," she said through a groaning yawn. "I have a problem leaving them to pile up in the drainer."

"I can see that." He chuckled. "I cannot believe you were able to stack so many without them tumbling over."

"I am an expert at dish Jenga," she joked, getting out of her cozy bed.

Her gaze dropped to the fuzzy, red-plaid cardigan discarded on the floor. In one fluid motion, she scooped it up, slid her arms into its welcoming sleeves, and briskly shook off the morning chill. With sluggish movements, she ambled over to the counter, pulled out a stool, and sat down. A content smile spread across her face as she watched her father finish his chore.

He grabbed a steaming mug he had already poured and handed it to her. "With milk and honey. Just the way you like it."

She grinned, sucking in the first scalding sip. "It's perfect." She blew on the steam rolling from the top. "But still very hot." She went to take another sip and squinted; the wispy mist rolled into her eyes. A strange feeling awakened the butterflies in her stomach. Worry knitted her brows. Something was off, but she couldn't put her finger on it. "I—" she started then stopped.

David paused and leaned toward her on his elbow. "What's wrong, sweetie?"

"I…I am not sure." She stared into her tea in hopes the swirl of milk froth would spell something out. "I think I was having a bad dream." A traumatic echo floated through her mind, begging her to remember, but then it eluded her. Her insides turned queasy, and she rubbed her stomach. The more she tried to recall the dream, the more uncomfortable she felt. "Let's talk about something else," she said, flinching and biting the inside of her cheek.

David came around the counter and cozied up on the stool next to her. He patted her knee, then folded his hands into his lap, appearing ready to listen.

She changed the subject. "I am glad to see you. It has been a long time since you came to see me at my flat. Does Helen know you're here?"

"Awe, well," he said, tsking; a sparkle gleamed in his chestnut eyes. "I don't need Helen's permission for such things anymore."

"Really? That's strange. Since when?"

David just grinned, giving her no reply.

Elanor loved the smile lines that formed on his brown cheeks whenever he intently listened. So many days he would give her that same look, sitting on the steps of the Evanses' back garden.

She shook her head; the unsettling sensation leapt back into her throat. "I think there is something—I can't remember." She squeezed her cardigan against her chest. "My heart feels broken." As she spoke, an unbidden tear formed but she swallowed down the growing lump with another sip of tea.

"That's better, eh? The milk and honey helps. Drink a little more down."

Elanor couldn't disagree. The warmth of the tea trickling down through her chest, and the sweetness of the honey on her tongue, brought comfort. She felt safe. She sniffed, releasing a mellow chuckle. "It was just a dream, anyway," she said, peering around her flat. Everything was just as she had left it. Her haven. Small, simple, and contained.

People are always trying to convince me to get out more, she thought sardonically, with a rising patter of her heart. *But I love it here.*

Her eyes settled on the painting she had been working on, and she gasped. "What happened to it?" She jumped from her seat and raced toward it, her tea sloshing over her hand. Her fingers trembled, reaching toward the gray streaked lines. It was a portrait. An important one she had been crafting. Her voice went shrill. "This was my favorite painting. Someone has painted over it."

"What was the painting of?" David asked, his tone less inquisitive and more of a knowing prod.

Elanor's eyes flew across the canvas. Black and gray brushstrokes blotted out the portrait beneath. She couldn't remember who she had portrayed. Her face scrunched as she tried to recall. If it was truly her favorite, why was the image escaping her?

"What is wrong with me?" She searched David's face. His eyes, patient and calm, told her nothing. "Why can't I remember anything?"

David came beside her. His eyes scanned the painting as if he, too, were trying to discern what used to be there, then grabbed hold of her hand. "Elanor, you are here to remember."

Chapter Twenty-Seven

"What do you mean?"

David sighed, then dropped her hand, and went back to the kitchen counter to grab a stool. He returned and set it down in front of the ruined painting. "Here." He patted the seat before placing his hand on Elanor's back, encouraging her to sit. Once she did, he said, "Now, take another sip of your tea. Try to remember."

Obediently, she drank down a little more. Her chin began to tremble. She scanned the gray mess of paint that stained her masterpiece. She wasn't sure why it upset her so much, but she struggled to hold back tears. She took another sip of her tea. The rush of warmth put her mind at ease.

David wrapped his arm around her shoulders and pointed to the painting. "You were the one that wanted to forget. You were the one that grayed out the painting."

"Why would I do that?" A rush of emotion squeezed her chest.

"It didn't feel safe anymore."

A tear dropped. "Why wouldn't it feel safe?"

David dipped his head, and his eyes narrowed. He was holding something back. *Why won't he just tell me?*

He turned to gather another stool. "Something has hurt you." He cleared his throat, positioning the stool next to her. "You are in your safe place, but you are not here to hide. That is who you used to be, Elanor. Instead, you are here to heal. But it is up to you. You must want to get better. All the fragments are here if you want to see them—pieces of hurt along with pieces of hope."

"Why should I want to see the hurt?"

David pressed his lips together. "Because if you do not see it, then you cannot be healed, and you will remain in darkness."

"Darkness?" A sudden memory wrenched through Elanor's mind. A woman on her knees in the dark. Elanor reached to help her, but the woman lashed like a demon—refusing to be saved.

I know this memory.

Then she heard the words, *"All of us have chosen pain, at times, over freedom."*

It was Adhan speaking about Cilaen's mother Efa. Elanor peered at David with her mouth slack. Memories tumbled one over the other, forcing their way to the surface. She pressed her palm against her head and squeezed her eyes shut.

"You have not had a bad dream, Elanor. You are in a fight for your life."

Her eyes narrowly opened, and she whispered, "Is this a dream, then?"

"Parts are like a dream. Other parts are echoes of what is inside your heart."

What if she didn't like what she saw? She inhaled a long breath. If she resisted the pain, could she stay here? Here was nice. Here was safe. Her father was comfortable and warm. But she knew better—staying would not help. She could feel pain radiating—somewhere hidden behind the walls. She couldn't hide from it.

With a resistant nod, she let the first memory of pain in. Another tear welled in her eye. Her voice trembled as she asked, "You are not really here, are you? You—you died."

"I did die." He nodded somberly and rubbed his knees. "But I am not a dream.

No." He shook his head. "I was invited here by someone who knew I would be a comfort to you."

"Who?"

"That does not matter. What does matter is that you are safe. You might feel hurt, but the pain is leading you toward hope if you are brave enough to let it."

Elanor whispered, "I miss you."

"Oh, sweetie. I miss you too." David leaned forward and pulled her head to his shoulder. He rubbed the back of her neck, his touch reigniting her grief. "Let this moment be evidence that I am never far away from you."

Elanor's heart pinched with tight, hot emotion. Tears flooded from her eyes, wetting David's shirt. "What must I do?" she muffled into his shoulder.

David cupped her shoulders, pulled her up, and looked into her eyes. "Follow the signs, Elanor, and drink your tea."

Elanor sniffed, gazing down at her cup. The light brown liquid seemed to remain full and warm no matter how much she drank. She pulled another long draught from her cup. The tea, mixed with the creamy milk, swirled in her mouth. As she gulped it down, a blue spark caught her eye. There on her bedside table was a blue pendant necklace. She abandoned her seat, drawn to the beauty that sparkled from the cyan stone. Hope collided with the suspicion in her chest. Would it reveal more pain? Oh, but she wanted it. She loved it. It was valuable. She could almost remember it now. The desire to put it around her neck pulled on something deep inside her.

"Pick it up," David encouraged.

She reached for it, but stopped, hovering her hand above it.

I am brave, she reminded herself, squeezing her eyes shut for a beat, then grabbed it from the table. While it dangled from her fingers, she instantly knew it. "This was taken from me."

"Why does it matter that it was taken?"

"Because…" She thought hard for a moment. "Because it was given to me." She stared at the stone, struggling to remember. "It was given by someone important to me."

"There is more. Look deeper."

"It was given to me by someone who—who loved me." She turned, glancing back at her father with a smile. "That wasn't so ba—"

Her eyes caught sight of the painting, and it stole her words. Some sallow colors were now blending with the black and gray. As if through a mist, a figure emerged behind the smeared paint.

"You need to separate the lies from the truth, Elanor. This painting is your favorite for a reason. You painted it within the safety of this place. You painted it because you wanted to see it. You wanted to know the one depicted in it."

"Then why am I suddenly so afraid?" She peered back down at the pendant, but instead of a necklace, her hand now held a small blue book. She gasped. "I love this book." Tears gathered in the edges of her eyes, and one corner of her mouth lifted. She swiftly thumbed through the pages. "This book was given to me by…."

Suddenly, she knew him. She lifted her eyes and the painting now bore the face of someone who had hurt her. *Merlin.* She heaved in a sharp breath, and the shock sent her crumpling to the floor. Her arms flailed, casting the tea across the room.

She expected to hit the floor. Instead, she fell through it. The world around her smeared like the paint on her canvas. Trees. Nature. A spring surrounded her. Her body ached, and her stomach churned. She closed her eyes, and suddenly, she felt caught—cradled by a pair of strong arms. She dared a peek and saw the soft features of a man wrapped in light.

"Man in blue," she whispered with a hoarse voice that did not sound like her own. She stared into his eyes. They asked a question that she already knew the answer to. "I-I know he would never hurt me, but I am still afraid. There is another version of him that does, and he never leaves me." Tears brimmed in her eyes. "I sang to you. I called to you for help."

"I heard you," he said, so peacefully that her body loosened. The warm tears dripped unrestrained down her temples. "I have always been with you, but I could not stop you from believing the lies that made the deception real."

She arched her brows, wordlessly begging to know what the lies were.

"I did not create you to fear your own weakness, or to believe you were worthless. Growing up an orphan has taught you to believe you are invaluable to everyone, that you will be easily cast away. You fear Arthur has rejected you, and blame him for your grief. Now, you also believe Merlin does not want you."

She cringed at Merlin's name, fighting within her mind to remember his gentle touch.

"Deep inside, you believe hides a secret weakness. You think once the ones you love discover it, you will become valueless. You think yourself lucky to have found yourself here, surrounded by such a great company of people. You wear yourself thin trying to hide your flaws from them, and you neglect your birthright as a Pendragon." He warned in a low tone, "As long as you believe this, you will not be free from the enemy inside your mind. You will be weak, only because your faith has made it so, and you will *not* fulfill your calling to defeat the strongman."

"I do not know how to stop," she implored softly, holding in a sob. "Even as you speak the lies, I struggle to believe there could be any other truth."

"I know," he said, pulling her closer into his tender embrace. She felt ashamed that her hot tears wet his tunic. But there was such a powerful comfort emanating from him that she leaned closer in. Her heart longed for his answers—for his truth.

"I know you—the sound of you," she muffled into his chest. "It is in Grwyrthrhodd's voice, within my healing magic, and sometimes within my dreams. I have seen you in Adhan's eyes, and felt you within *the song*." Her voice cracked. "You delivered me so many times."

"Elanor," his voice called with a gentle beckoning.

She turned her tear-streaked face to him. His countenance was merciful and kind. Within his eyes, she saw the shape of her own face. Every line and feature wrapped in his acceptance. The tarnished lies did not exist in his version of her.

He said, "Knowing who *I Am* will clear away the lies. Knowing who *I Am* means that you can learn to know yourself outside of the hurt. It will take time, but if you allow me into your heart, I will begin the work."

Elanor gasped with a sorrowful smile. She grabbed hold of his tunic and emphatically nodded her head. "With my whole heart."

The Man in Blue laughed with pleasure. He leaned in closer to her face and said, "Your enemies stand *no chance* against you." Without hesitation, he lifted her, then dunked her under the water. The warm pool bubbled, surrounding her with effervescence. Her arms and legs floated above her as her body sank. Small lights zipped and zagged through the water, piercing different parts of her body. Each time a light hit her, she sensed a tinge of heat, but there was no pain. The sound of the bubbles rolled past her ears, coupled with the echoes of indecipherable words.

One of the lights stopped, hovering just before her face. Her eyes flooded with the reflecting gold light, making her squint. It pierced through her forehead. This time she felt pain. She cried out. Bubbles burst from her mouth, carrying her scream to the surface. But then, the sting quickly melted into tingles that buzzed inside her mind.

"Curse BE BROKEN!"

The voice shattered all sound, and all her pain silenced into a vacuum of light. Her body arched backward—suspended in the glowing shroud of glittering bubbles. The light went out, and like a leaf falling from a branch, she folded forward and sank into the watery depths.

Everything faded, and she shut her eyes.

"I love you, Elanor." Merlin's voice echoed within her mind. *"You are my soul."*

28

THE LAND AWAKENS

Merlin watched the Man in Blue immerse Elanor into the water, and then, as if the sun flashed in his eyes, Merlin blinked. When he looked again, the man was gone. Without another thought, he dove into the water after Elanor. He swam, searching through the clear blue. His fingers brushed her arm. He grabbed hold, pulling her close and scooping his arms beneath her.

With a swift kick, he pushed his feet against the slick stones at the bottom of the pool. His face broke through the surface, and he sucked in a long inhale. He swam a short distance until he could stand. Cradling Elanor, he carefully lifted her face above the water, then waded to where his shoulders were above the waterline. He cupped his hand over her cheek and anxiously scanned her lips and chest for breath.

Cough! Elanor's hands shot up over her mouth, and she gasped through her breaths. Her eyes sprang open and darted around before settling on Merlin. They suddenly flared. She pushed away from him, but Merlin grappled her tightly to his chest so she wouldn't sink in her panic.

"Y-You are safe," he swiftly assured her. "I have you."

He stroked her arms, but she pushed away from him.

No, he begged within himself, seeing her alarm.

Merlin's heart was breaking anew. "Please—I will not hurt...."

His words were cut short. Elanor rushed into his chest, throwing her arms around him. His breath caught in his throat. In relieved surprise, he hesitated, then embraced her. Her arms felt strong, and her bones were not protruding.

He sighed into her wet hair. "Oh, thank the Great God."

"I wanted to believe it was really you," she muffled into his chest. "I was just so afraid."

A healing tear dripped down his cheek. "I am so sorry. It was my fault. I should have been there to protect you."

Elanor turned her doleful, glassy eyes up at him.

Merlin hated to ask but needed to know. "What did he do to you?" He clenched his teeth, awaiting her reply.

"It is not your fault, Merlin," she said through a squeezed whisper.

His frown deepened. He wanted to receive the forgiveness, but the pain was still too fresh. He held her chin, relishing that at least health had returned to her cheeks. But her tender eyes still held a well of trauma. He folded her back into his arms.

"My heart aches. I…" Merlin winced, his jaw tightening. He had been too weak to keep her safe, and remembering how he found her in the cave gutted him. Neither of them were ready to speak, so they just held each other. He pressed his palm against her back, feeling her heartbeat. Each thump filled his heart with remorseful relief. She had beaten death again, but it wasn't because of him. Every time, a miracle. When would the grace run out? Every instinct told him to steal her and Gwendolen away to somewhere safe. Let all else run its course without them.

"*Trust*," a voice said, floating through the warm comforting humidity. The air soundlessly whispered a reminder that he was not alone.

"Osian," Elanor began. Her body stiffened in his hold.

"You do not have to talk about it if you do not want to."

She held her breath as if still considering. Her hand lifted to the vacant spot on her chest where the pendant once hung.

Merlin's voice felt choked, but he forced himself to ask, "Did you lose it?"

She shook her head, then whispered, "He took it."

Merlin dropped his head. An image of Osian's taloned fingers squeezing the pendant against his palm flashed in his mind. His pulse quickened, and he cringed.

"His talisman—it was so powerful. I am still telling myself that everything I saw was not real."

"What did you see?"

"Poison," she snarled, her fingers clawing into Merlin's arms. Her eyes flickered up to his. The water dripped from her hairline, sluicing down her face. Beads of water gathered on her cheeks. "Your eyes—are different."

"I have changed?"

"No. Your eyes are different from his." She lifted her hand to his face, her arm wavering with hesitation. "You were there—with me in the cave. But—" Her eyes welled with tears.

"Sshhh!" His heart stung, not wanting to hear anymore. He could guess what evil Osian had woven into her mind. "Do you still see a monster?" he asked, brushing away the tears soaking her eyelashes.

Elanor shook her head. Her sad brows arched higher. She swallowed, quickly wiping more tears from her face. "The bad is melting away. The Man in Blue helped it become a fading dream. You are not—*him*."

"Good." He sighed mournfully. "Good."

She eased back into his embrace, and he cradled her head against his chest. He closed his eyes, wrestling with regret. Despair lingered on the bank of his soul. But the trickling sound of the water was doing something inside him. It pulled the bitterness away. Each time he opened his mouth to breathe, the sweet taste of nectar rolled across his tongue, stealing away words of sadness. The inviting, mossy earth blanketed the surrounding land, hugging the glistening, oily rocks. In this place, the grief couldn't stay.

Finally, through a long-drawn breath, he embraced the healing atmosphere of the oasis. When he exhaled, an unexpected chuckle bubbled out.

Underneath his palms, he felt Elanor's shoulders lightly bounce, returning his laughter.

"I missed this place," she told him, peering up at him once again, then brushing her fingers down his cheek. "The longer I am here, the less I can be sad." Her gaze drifted toward the banks. Spotting something, she let go of Merlin and lowered her hands to her stomach.

"I am *so* hungry," she moaned with a grin.

She immediately splashed toward the shore, and that was when Merlin noticed what drew her eye. To his delight, he discovered a flat stone with a golden honeycomb, and a bowl filled with milk. Elanor didn't even stop to pull herself onto the bank before a morsel of the honeycomb found its way into her mouth. Her fingers dripped with honey, making Merlin want a taste. He dove in and swam over to her. When he came up for air, she smiled at him, licking the sticky honey from her palm.

"Milk and honey." Her blue eyes sparkled. "I just had some in my tea."

"What?" Merlin chuckled, placing a dripping lump into his mouth. He savored the floral sweetness melting over his tongue. The taste filled every craving with an ethereal satisfaction. Even the hurt that had been pounding inside his chest relented into a blissful calm.

With golden-treacle-covered fingers, Elanor lifted the milk to her lips. A dribble of the precious, nourishing drink dripped from her chin. She wiped her mouth and lifted the bowl, offering it to Merlin. She reminded Merlin of a child enjoying a delectable treat. Purity and innocence gleamed in her eyes. Eager to share in Elanor's delight, he swiftly brought the bowl to his lips. As the creamy milk swished through his teeth, mirth bubbled within him, rekindling his hope.

"I wish we could stay here," Elanor said, placing more honey into her mouth. "Here I am free. All the burdens—stolen away."

With all his heart, Merlin wished for it too. Every part of this place truly was their home. He placed his hand over his heart. It ached at the thought of leaving. But even as he palmed his chest, he felt something else. A newness had settled inside him that wasn't there before. Understanding filtered through his mind like sunlight.

"This time, when we leave this place, we will not be leaving it behind. This home now dwells within us. Inside our very spirit."

Elanor's fingers danced on her lips. "I can feel it inside the water, and within the honey on my tongue. Will it truly never leave us?"

Merlin shook his head slowly. "I do not think it will this time. Not now that we let him in." Merlin lifted Elanor's chin and pointed to his chest. "This is the kingdom."

"I do not understand," she said, scrunching her brow. "But, somehow, I also do understand."

"We must go," he said, holding out his hand.

Elanor took it and he pulled her knees up onto the bank, helping her stand. The spring pool and protected oasis slowly dissipated around them, and then disappeared entirely. Their drenched clothes were now dry. Merlin rubbed his hand over his fresh tunic.

A chilly wind blew through the oaky foliage, rattling the dry leaves above their heads. The yawning black of Osian's cave loomed behind them. Merlin squeezed the fabric over his chest. He closed his eyes, testing if he could still feel the promise of the kingdom in his heart. At the thumping rhythm, warmth spread through his body, nullifying the frigid air. He smiled, feeling a force surge through him, igniting his magic with a new strength.

He surveyed both sides of the ravine that hid the cave. An ominous curse still lay heavy upon the land. The power that pulsed within him could break it.

He turned to Elanor. Her clothing floated on the breeze. Strands of her raven hair blew in front of her face. Her eyes were bright, and her cheeks were flushed with rose. No bitter dirt from the cave remained on her cheeks, and her white gown furled softly underneath her polished leather breastplate. His heart lifted and he smiled. "Now that the curse has been broken in us, it is time to heal the land."

Elanor grinned back, her brows pinching with curiosity.

Merlin walked over to the mouth of the cave and placed his hand upon its accursed stones. He exhaled, then whispered with strength, "Curse, be broken." There was no use for the old words of the druids—at least not in this moment—for now flowing through him was an authority unrivaled to an old practiced tongue. The words fell from his lips, and something older and more abundant sprang to life. This magic, like that of the Crystal Cave, transcended his strength, or understanding. He did not own it, though he felt it coursing through his veins.

With boldness, he declared a second time, "Curse—*Be Broken!*"

Before he even finished speaking, the rocks thundered, splitting apart. Fissures formed, webbing across the stones. The earth at their feet rumbled. Merlin backed away.

What have I done?

There was no time. Rocks would soon bury them. He snatched Elanor's hand and pulled her to the earthen wall on the other side.

"Merlin!" Elanor yelled. "Look!"

He turned to where Elanor pointed and saw the ground shifting above the cave. The earth gave way and crumbled, revealing something that forced its way through. Enormous, gnarled hands emerged, ripping an oak from the soil, snapping one root free at a time. Then it flung the tree to the ground with a *crash*. Legs busted forth next. At least Merlin thought they looked like legs, but they were more like massive tree trunks. A body wriggled free from more tangled roots. The ground grumbled like moaning trees bending in the wind.

An awesome fear widened Merlin's eyes. He pulled Elanor into his side. More earth threatened to tumble away from the now towering tree-like giant. Merlin swiftly kindled a magical shield, just before the giant shook and sent rocks careening down from above.

The creature's shadow rose higher, blocking out the shine of the sun. Branches burst through the treed canopy. The giant behemoth resembled a man made of earth; its limbs and muscles made from tangled tree roots.

It ripped another tree from the ground and wrenched the top branches off, leaving just the trunk in its hand. The giant lifted it above its head, and clods of earth pelted against Merlin's shield. Then the giant hurled the tree like a club on Osian's cave. Lifting it up again, the giant smashed it back down, shaking the earth. The unsettled rock crushed together, creating a dust cloud that smothered the ravine like a fog. The giant pounded and pounded until the hillside collapsed.

The collision unleashed an explosion of dirt and debris in every direction. The echo ricocheted throughout the forest, vibrating the trees. Until finally, the earth settled, and the air began to clear. The sun beamed through the dusty haze in rays, revealing the silhouette of the swaying giant above them. Its shoulders heaved, and it gripped the tree's trunk like a brandished weapon.

The giant's breath echoed like hollow wind through a tunnel. Then it shifted its gaze down to Merlin and Elanor. Its face smirked through the leaves that covered its face like a beard. Merlin hoped it was not considering whether to crush them next.

Merlin raised his hands in surrender, and also prepared to defend with his magic. The giant groaned a deep resounding hum, then moved closer. The sweeping breadth of its movement creaked like bursting timbers.

The closer it came, the more its face emerged out of the shadows, revealing features shaped out of red clay. Lines of moss brimmed its eyes. The wiry hair on its head appeared like a mane of spindly, leafy branches. Its eyes were a deep amber brown, sparkling brightly with green hints around the irises. It stared at them long and hard. Merlin held his breath and clenched his fingers through Elanor's sleeve, grasping her tight.

Then its cheeks rounded with a woody smile.

The giant shook its head, and more clumps of dirt catapulted into the ravine— along with raining leaves. A deep hollow groan quaked from its throat. The sound created images in Merlin's mind of a forest waking to life. The giant nodded a wordless thank you, then rose—its face disappearing back into a shaded silhouette. It took one large step, lifting itself above the ravine, and then stomped away, each step an earth-shaking rumble that dissipated the further it went.

Merlin turned his floored stare toward the cave, which had now become a rubble of rock and stone.

Elanor stuttered, "G-Giant."

Merlin let go of her and stared open-mouthed at where the giant had departed. With a sober chuckle, he dusted the debris from his shoulders and shook his hair, releasing a white cloud of dust. "We awoke the great enaid of the forest." He grinned at Elanor's awed and dust-covered face. "The giant is no longer sleeping. The curse has been broken."

Osian crashed to the ground, his entire body wrenching with pain. Morgan's screams filled his head. Something had broken their power. The curse of the forest was tied to his body, and now his life would suffer the cost. His face turned red, and the veins in his neck swelled. The men from his camp gathered around him. His hideous howls bellowed forth, and his fingers clawed the dirt, tearing out hunks of grass.

His mind swirled into black smokey darkness. Parts of his power were ripped away, one small piece at a time, as though sliced through with the biting teeth of a saw blade.

"Morgan!" he yelled through the abysmal dark, praying that she, too, had not been taken from him. He needed her. She was his source. His plan hinged on her power wielded through him.

"*What is happening?*" he called out to her. All the while, swells of pain slashed through his soul. "*Do not leave me!*"

A blood-curdling scream vibrated through his consciousness once again. It was Morgan's screams. Each one a gong that made Osian's head feel like it was being split asunder. She was hanging on with her nails, pulling on the very blood within his veins. The blood of the murdered that was spilt to conjure her became a vacuum.

Within his mind, he saw his power leaking out through his wrists like tar. If he let it run out, all would be lost. Morgan would be lost. He would die.

"*The chalice!*" Morgan's graveled cry slapped him into awareness. She had helped him find it. It was part of their plan to use it, but this wasn't the time, and it was never meant for him. Its curse would be upon him if he drank from it.

Another wretched scream from Morgan rattled him from the inside.

I am dying anyway.

He snapped his eyes open and stared horrified at the men surrounding him. His face was wet with tears of agony; his pallid cheeks blackened with death. Mucus drained from his nose, and saliva eked from the corners of his mouth.

He strained the command, "Bring me…the box."

The men stood unmoved, gaping at the sight of Osian's supernatural writhing.

"*NOW!*" he screeched.

One soldier turned heel and ran for Osian's tent. He returned with haste and set the box down in front of Osian. Violent tremors wracked his body, but he pressed through, gritting his teeth. With a trembling hand, he reached for the hooked dagger at his hip. His tense fingers slid down the smooth bone hilt. He yelled and, with great effort, grabbed hold of the young man's tunic. Like a viper, Osian ripped his dagger into the soldier's jugular.

"Hold him," Osian commanded. Two men swiftly obeyed and gathered the bleeding soldier by the arms. The man choked with a fast-graying face. Osian mustered himself to open the box.

Inside was a worn, golden chalice studded with round ruby stones. He clutched the stem, then thrust it beneath the young man's slashed throat. He didn't need the man's blood—but it would bring substance to the drink. And the bloodletting satisfied a wicked need building inside him from his own flaring pain.

Blood trickled into the cup. The blood he would need was his own, mixed with Morgan's. Her blood would be the source the curse clung to, granting him the immortal life. Next, Osian pulled his dagger across his palm and, shaking, squeezed a few precious black drops into the chalice.

He tightened his weakening grip on the cup, forced it to his mouth, and swallowed one small sip. The iron-tasting, warm liquid ran over his tongue. Still lying crumpled on the ground, Osian mumbled, "Marwolaeth cymer fi i fywyd celwyddog."

The chalice toppled from his grasp, pouring out onto his chin and down his neck. The golden cup hit the ground with a hollow *ting*. The poisonous curse surged through his veins. Excruciating pain stole any sound he could have made. His whole body seized into one solid plank. Then one last breath rolled from his lips. Death stole over him, and his limbs ran cold.

Instead of the world going black when his life left him, it peacefully stilled. His heart stopped beating and his blood froze. His pain disappeared, and he realized the pleasure of feeling nothing. Soulless. Emotionless. The *nothingness* felt like power.

Slowly, he sat up, looking at his bloody hands, and then over at the *Chalice of Life* on the ground. A growing laughter echoed inside his head. It was Morgan. He grinned with relief. She was still with him.

"Now my power is yours," she said. *"It is as if we are one."*

His smile broadened, and he ran his fingers over his chest, where that blue witch had struck him with her sword. The wound was gone. The slash on his arm and back had also disappeared. He peered up at the horrified men. His face must have appeared frightful with blood staining his pale face. He pulled himself up from the ground and rolled his strong immortal shoulders. Without fear of pain or death, and now no more weakness, how could his enemies stand against him? He squeezed his fists, reveling in his newfound strength. He never wanted to be cursed. The curse of the chalice was meant for the men around him, whose lives were expendable, but now—he felt like a god.

"The cold season of Imbolc is coming," he said to the men around him, enjoying the new strength in his voice. "We will wait for the rest of the men we have called forth to gather. Our strength will be formidable, and then in the season of Beltaine, while new life and hope makes our enemies weak, we will strike for their hearts. And this time—they will have no force to stop us."

SHE CANNOT GO HOME

Merlin and Elanor had long abandoned the forest to return home. The icy weather bit through Elanor's boots, numbing her toes. The cold motivated her steps. With chattering teeth, she peered up at the white sky. A single snowflake fell upon her cheek and melted.

"Snow."

Merlin looked up at the small flurry of white flakes floating down. He squeezed his arms around his middle. "It is unusually bitter this season. Normally only the north sees snow this early into Imbolc." He extended his arm, inviting Elanor into his warmth.

She hesitated a moment. The trigger of pain still haunted her, but then she rushed under his arm, pressing against his side. She kept her eyes glued to the ground, hoping her pause hadn't upset him.

"I do not see us reaching Caer Lial without the aid of shelter, and some horses."

"Are there any villages near here?"

Merlin stared ahead with stark eyes, then nodded to the northeast. "There is a village over that direction. I hate to ask for horses from them—the chieftain was one of the first to come to the Palisade in search of help. It has been some years now—though it is possible that they never recovered from Osian's attacks. It was quite destroyed when last I saw it."

He paused for a moment, his lips drawing thin. "I remember the look in the eyes of the villagers. Everything taken from them—so much death. You have seen the look."

Elanor nodded, remembering the forlorn despair of the refugees. Their somber traipse when she and Merlin led them to the Palisade—all their hope stolen. "Is there another village further north?"

Merlin shook his head. "We must hope there is still a remaining village. If there is not, we will have a long way to go on foot."

"Do you think Arthur and the Cymbrogi are still in Llyonesse?"

"No." Merlin shook his head. "If all went to Arthur's plan, he would have returned to the caer by now to make plans for war. He knew the cold season was coming, and he was not prepared for any major battles. Unless he was given no other choice." Merlin's face twisted with agitation, and he grumbled, "I hope the scouts returned with *something* we can go on. Hopefully they discovered where the enemy encamps, or spotted their ships arriving on the harbor. If there were ships, Arthur would not have hesitated to call to arms all available Cymbrogi to quickly halt their landing." Merlin tsked, walking with more haste. "Holding the lands of Llyonesse hinges on the eldest son of Thul commanding a steady rule."

The foreboding subject set Elanor on edge. The oncoming war with evil pierced her heart with bleakness—it rattled within her spirit like a snake's warning.

She asked, "Why does the Great God allow such death?"

"It happens not because He allows it, but I think—it is because evil men remain free to destroy the goodness He offers. It is a battle"—he patted his heart—"where good men must remember that He is with them, while not fretting about what all may fall. Maybe that is all we need to know."

"The song."

"Yes—its meaning is becoming clearer now. I had always thought the kingdom was something I could create. If I did everything right, I could have it, here and now. Arthur would be great, and all the lands healthy, green, and prosperous."

"Is that not its meaning?"

"It means that we already have it, and it already *is*. That is what was released through the palm of my hand when I broke the curse off the forest, freeing what lay in wait for"—he looked at his hand—"the kingdom. It is more than a time, or a place. It is a tangible authority that means more than palisades or kingships. It is inside here." He brushed his fingers over her heart.

"Magic."

Merlin's eyes brightened. "And so much more."

If the kingdom had come, then why was there still an oncoming war? Though, as Merlin spoke, hope stirred. It was there, right in front of her, and she knew despite her lack of understanding, she could trust it. Peace settled within her, and she wrapped Merlin's cloak tighter around her shoulders. The wool was not quite thick enough to keep out the cold's icy fingers.

The wind picked up and gales blasted Elanor cheeks, making them sting. A sudden dark shadow darted across what little sun they had, and they halted, glancing up. Expansive wings unfurled in mighty golden-green folds across the sky. The gust nearly blew them backwards. The dragon's wings *swooshed*, and Elanor knelt to the ground; Merlin shielded her with his body, blocking the wind. Gwyliwr hovered above them, then lowered to the frosted turf.

"Gwyliwr!" Elanor shouted, the sound of her voice muted by the rush of wind. The giant creature's claws clutched the earth. Her massive wings curled like sails, closing behind her. The beast shook her head, and then she blew a hornlike blast from her throat.

Chapter Twenty-Nine

Merlin laughed, his eyes sparkling with excitement.

Elanor skipped closer, lifting her hand. The dragon lowered her head in greeting. A great, grumbling purr vibrated out of her nose as Elanor stroked her golden scales.

"Well done," Gwyliwr boomed. "You freed more of my kind to retake these lands."

"The giant?" Merlin hollered, running over to join in the greeting.

The dragon purred, "He is Cawr Gwyrdd."

Merlin gasped. "The Green Man."

"He is the guardian of all that is new. He has been sleeping longer than some of the mountains." Gwyliwr lifted her head, and what sounded like garbled laughter rumbled out. Elanor shot her hands up to cover her ears. "But that is not why my master has sent me. The time has come."

Merlin and Elanor exchanged glances, eager to hear what she would say. The dragon tilted her large head toward Elanor. Her image reflected within Gwyliwr's large slitted pupil.

"Come on, dragon. Time for what?" Merlin asked, folding his arms.

"I have hoped for this time to come, but it will not be an easy time for either of you."

Merlin's face slackened. He peered at Elanor, then asked again, "Please, dragon—time for what?"

"Gwenddydd will not be returning with you to Caer Lial."

Elanor gasped.

"Wha—" Merlin moved beside Elanor. "Why should she not return?"

"She cannot." The dragon leaned even closer to Elanor. "My gift of time must now protect her—just for the length of a season."

"Why?" Elanor asked, curling into Merlin's arm.

"But you, Emrys, must go back to the Palisade. You have an assignment there."

"Dragon," Merlin demanded hotly, clearly not loving the thought of being separated from Elanor again. "Stop speaking in riddles. Why is it that Elanor must be protected?"

The dragon's eyes turned solemn. "The promised one will soon be born."

Elanor's brows pressed together, then it hit her. Her mouth fell open. Understanding sank in.

I am to be born?

As if in answer to her thoughts, the dragon said, "The queen has been with child for a while, but now is her final season. You cannot be two, for there is only one."

"I cannot leave her again," Merlin started. "I will go with her."

"You will be with her, but not here. You will watch and guard her within the walls of Caer Lial. I will watch and guard her from the place where time will protect her."

"Where will that be?"

"Wherever it is that I am—she will be protected."

"Dragon!" Frustration sharpened Merlin's voice, and his face reddened. "Where will you be?"

"The cottage and hill where last I saw you?"

Merlin rubbed his head. Elanor stared at him, hoping he had another solution forming that would not take her away from him. She needed him. His nearness healed her. She swallowed down the lump lodged in her throat. Struggling to speak, she stuttered, "H—h…" She pressed her eyes shut to focus. "How long will I have to be away?"

Gwyliwr's voice dropped with a haunting timbre. "Until your parents and Merlin are strong enough to choose."

Elanor knew what that meant. There could not be two. Could she trust that they would choose her? "How will they choose?"

"That remains before them. I do not know for certain."

"But she is here," Merlin fought back. "Has not the choice already been made? There are already two if Gwynevere is with child, and yet Elanor remains here, alive and well."

"Time protects the unborn one while inside the queen's womb."

Merlin grunted, raking his hands through his hair. He paced in circles, creating a ring in the light dusting of snow. Elanor stood frozen, her mind reeling. Her knees buckled, and she folded to her knees, placing her hand on the chilled ground to stop the world from spinning.

"I—I cannot leave her. Not again." Merlin turned, and when he saw Elanor on her knees, he rushed to her side. "I am sorry," he said, kneeling beside her and wrapping his arms around her.

The dragon flicked her head as though annoyed. "There are *no choices*. This is what needs to be done. These emotions that rush within you cloud your mortal minds. You are not being reasonable." She groaned, and it sounded like fire billowed inside her chest. Even the air heated within her proximity. Gwyliwr folded her massive arms in what looked like a pout.

"Dragon," Merlin pleaded, "is there no other way?"

This time she growled, "My *magic of time* will guard her, *Emrys*. It will depend on you to ensure I do not have to do so for very long. The power to hold her may become costly."

"Costly?" Merlin spat, standing up. "Why must it all be so damn costly? Why is there always a price to pay?"

"Because you are changing things," the dragon snapped. Then her voice shifted into a gentler resonance. "You were created for this change, but the cost will be different now that your heart has been filled with the waters that have no end."

Merlin nodded. His eyes dropped and connected with Elanor's. He knelt back down and lifted Elanor's chin with his finger. His eyes—not the ones that hurt her. These eyes loved her. Golden eyes that made her feel found. They searched hers, and then his lips raced to meet hers. His warmth pressed against her, making her heart yearn for more time. Already she missed him. She slid her fingers around his neck and pulled him closer. Without him, would the other Merlin return? She couldn't think that way. No. She had been healed—saved. Osian's trick had ended.

Desperation and fear wrestled inside her, so she gripped Merlin's collar tighter. She wished his kiss could conjure a magic spell to make the rest of the world disappear. For an ephemeral moment, she imagined that it did.

Her heart panged, and she pulled her lips away. "I will be alright, Merlin. So will you. This, too, shall end, and we will be together again. We will never truly be together anyway—not until Osian is defeated." But even as she spoke, a ball of trepidation dropped into her stomach. "I am choosing to trust this time. You too." She nudged him with her nose, seeking to encourage him with her resolve. She could see his eyes wavering—hating to let her go. "We have help now."

He nodded, then dipped his face, caressing her cheek against his. His hands gripped her shoulders. With a tight breath, he lifted his head so her magic could see into his eyes.

Her magic kindled, and she saw his hope and struggle. Then she saw the Man in Blue, and the waters washing over Merlin's feet. She tilted her head. "Yes. Go where you find strength."

Merlin kissed her again before resting his forehead against hers. His lips hovered between her nose and mouth, and she felt the ache within him craving more. Her heart pulsed with the same longing. He bit his bottom lip, took her hands, and stood, pulling her to her feet.

"I will take her to safety," the dragon told him. "And you, Emrys, will not be forgotten. You will be provided for in your journey home." Gwyliwr splayed out her claws, revealing the soft golden pad of her open palm and resting it on the ground. "Come, Elanor."

Elanor didn't hesitate. She knew if she did, she might never go. So, with a nervous flutter in her stomach, she grabbed one of the dragon's black, man-sized talons, and lifted herself onto the padded surface. The thumb and three fingers closed, forming a cage around her. She peered out between them at Merlin, who stared back—his face distraught.

She thrust her arm between the talons and reached for him. But the dragon had already begun lifting her hand from the ground. Everything in her wanted to squeeze through Gwyliwr's fingers and escape. Merlin's eyes called to her. A sob escaped her lips, releasing a cloud of cold breath.

Gwyliwr's claws were now clutched against her chest. Her wings spread wide, and Elanor quickly searched for something to hang onto. She threw herself onto her stomach. It was all happening so fast. The dragon's wings batted the wind, lifting them from the ground. She crawled on her stomach and wrapped her arms around one of the giant fingers. With a steadying breath, she stared down.

Merlin and the earth shrank away.

At each pump of Gwyliwr's wings, Elanor's stomach dropped further to her toes. The terror of being blown through the dragon's fingers consumed her mind, and she forgot all else. She shut her eyes and held on tight.

Merlin watched them disappear over the mountains. Anger swelled inside him, heating his face. He grabbed a stone off the ground and threw it as hard as he could.

"*AAGGHH!*" His scream echoed across the empty plain.

He'd known this time would come. At some point, Elanor would have to be born, but not now. All he wanted was to hold her close. After all they had just been through, he never wanted to let her out of his sight again. His chest pumped as he stared up at the sky, feeling empty and abandoned.

He tried to console himself that at least she would not be too far away. The cottage was only a short ride from Caer Lial. Then a thought crossed his mind, offering him a glimmer of hope. He huffed, and cold air whirled from his lips. "I may not be able to be beside her, but I refuse to let her endure this season alone with a dragon."

A high-pitched whiny yanked him from his musings. He snapped his head toward the sound. There on a hill, not far from where he stood, was a horse. He squinted. The horse galloped in his direction. His eyes widened. It was the horse he had abandoned outside the Forest of Goll. It had not returned home but had likely been wandering the plains.

Merlin clicked his tongue and waved his arms. Relief flooded his veins, quieting his heightened emotions. The horse puffed, approaching him with a happy canter. Merlin reached out his hand in greeting and smoothed his palm over the white patch on the horse's muzzle.

"Oh, my Great God. Thank you for waiting for me, my sturdy friend." He patted the horse's warm jowl. The horse appeared healthy and ready to ride. At least with a horse he would make it home—and soon.

ARTHUR & THE GOLDEN DRAGON

"Merlin has returned!" a herald shouted from just outside the Great Hall. Arthur jumped to his feet, wrapping his robe over his shoulders. "Open the doors," he commanded, rounding the lit hearth at the center of the hall, its blazing heat keeping the frigid air at bay.

The doors groaned open, cracking against the frost. Arthur hurried to the edge of the steps. The herald pointed, directing Arthur's eyes to the rider speeding toward the hill. Arthur sighed in relief, his breath whirling through the chill air. But then his breath caught.

Where is Elanor?

He stared at the empty space behind Merlin, and what little hope he had of her surviving abated at her absence. All at once, his stomach dropped, his knees weakened, and his heart stopped.

My child. He reeled, glancing over his shoulder at the Palisade, considering Gwynevere's growing belly. Somehow, it all felt real now. The idea of being a father had unlocked. Knowing the fate of his own child was a cruel dagger to the heart. He clutched his chest. The pounding hoof beats of Merlin's horse drew closer.

What will I tell Gwynevere?

An immediate instinct to conceal the truth and shield her from pain swept through his mind. Merlin rounded the top of the hill, and Arthur caught a sorrowless brightness in his yellow eyes.

Dare I hope, he thought, shuffling down the steps with his arms outstretched.

Merlin swung down from his horse, hardly waiting for his steed to stop.

The words were stuck in Arthur's throat. He didn't want to ask in case the worst was confirmed. He forced himself to utter, "Elanor?"

Merlin gripped Arthur's shoulders with an exhausted smile. Through panting breaths, Merlain said, "She…she is alive. And she is well."

"Oh—" Arthur moaned, burying his head into his hand. Waves of relief swept over him, and he stumbled backward. "Thank the Great God." He faced Merlin with moisture in his eyes. A smile twitched at the corner of his mouth. The world blurred for a moment, and then he found himself in Merlin's embrace. Arthur had not realized just how much tension he'd held until now. The news that Elanor was alive unwound his emotions like a rope loosening around his throat. He stifled a moan and clutched his arms tightly around Merlin's back.

Merlin pulled back, gripping Arthur's arms. His eyes brimmed with the same raw relief Arthur felt. Then his gaze floated past Arthur to the Palisade, and he asked, "Is the queen with child?"

Surprise knitted Arthur's brows. "How—how do you…?"

"The dragon," Merlin huffed, placing his hands on his knees, catching his breath. "Elanor is with the dragon." When he peered up, he must have seen the confusion in Arthur's rounded eyes. Merlin pointed toward the towering Palisade. "Gwynevere is carrying Elanor within her womb. It—it is a paradox. She must be protected by the dragon's magic until—" Merlin paused, standing up straight, and his face turned rigid.

Arthur shook his head. "I need to sit down." His heart still thumped through his chest. He rubbed his hand over his face and sank to the frozen steps. The iciness bit through his clothes, but he didn't care. "What of Osian? How did you free her? Has he been destroyed?" Arthur hoped Merlin would tell him it was all over.

With another heavy breath, Merlin joined Arthur on the stairs. "No. Osian still lives. He was not there when I found her. If it had not been for the Man in Blue—" Again, Merlin halted with a twinge, seeming unready to divulge the details. "She is only alive and un-spoilt by a miracle. I will tell you all once I have rested and had some food. I am utterly spent."

"I have much to prepare you for as well. Our armies are ready to march before the first flowers bloom." Arthur paused, then asked, "Where is the dragon keeping her?"

"She is at the cottage. The one we found when we first arrived back from the future time."

"Ah." Arthur nodded.

"There is much to be hopeful for." Merlin slapped Arthur's back, then, with a glimmer in his eye, he said, "Elanor is alive, and the curse that abided within the Forest of Goll has been broken."

The resolve in Merlin's words piqued Arthur's curiosity, and he smiled, wanting to know more. "The forest is no longer cursed?"

"I will tell you everything." Merlin leaned forward, resting his arms over his knees. His head hung with obvious fatigue. "First, I want to see my daughter." He chuckled lightly, then glanced at Arthur from the corner of his eye. "And please tell me the kitchens have something warm I can eat. I have been riding two days in this bitter cold, with a mostly empty stomach."

Arthur laughed, patting Merlin's shoulder. "There will be plenty enough hot food for you, brother."

Merlin's eyes turned somber. "I hope Elanor is getting something to eat." He rubbed his forehead, and the muscle in his jaw twinged. "I *cannot* believe I left her in the dead of Imbolc—with a *dragon*."

"Why did you not stay with her?"

"My charge is to keep the Palisade safe."

"So you will not be returning to her, then?"

"No." Merlin shook his head. "My magic is protecting Elanor from here."

Arthur nodded. That made sense—if any of it made sense. "We have told no one that Gwynevere carries our child—save those who must know. She conceals her belly, and remains mostly within her chambers."

"That is wise. The enemy cannot catch wind of this."

"No. Neither can Elanor suffer the cold season alone."

Merlin grinned. "No. She cannot."

The cottage was bleak, with very little firewood left. There was nothing to help Elanor survive the winter but a few mouse-eaten blankets and wet frozen hay. Gwyliwr lay asleep just outside. The sparsely drifting snow settled on the dragon's golden-tinted scales before melting. Her giant breaths rumbled, reassuring Elanor that she was not alone.

Sadness gnawed at her heart. So, she distracted herself by doing what she could to make the empty space more hospitable. At least the fire was warm. She discarded broken furniture—more kindling for the fire—and swept out all the refuse left behind by animals looking for shelter. Then she tore down all the old cobwebbed herbs that remained from whoever used to keep them.

With a sigh, she placed her hands on her hips and considered what to do next. Icy air snuck in from the holes in the thatch, placing frosty kisses upon her cheeks. She shivered, staring at the holes in frustration.

"I have no skill for this," she hissed. "I don't even have tools." She kicked an axe head; the handle had long disintegrated.

The last time she had sheltered here, they hadn't planned on staying long, and at least had the supplies from their packs. "This is no shelter. I cannot live like this all winter." She adjusted her stiff, leather breastplate. She would take it off, but it gave her another layer of warmth, making her wish she had a change of clothes. At least she still had Merlin's cloak. She grimaced at the worn wool blankets.

It's better than nothing.

"How am I going to do this?" Worry pinged her chest. Being out here all alone suddenly felt insurmountable.

She slumped down onto the same old cot that held Arthur a year before and wrapped the blanket around her shoulders. She shot a glare through the crooked door at the dragon and griped, "Your offerings of broken branches and dead animals are hardly going to help me. All you do is sleep. Do you know anything about what humans need to survive?"

Elanor folded her arms and stared at the fire, getting lost in the flame's flickering rhythm. Her chest tightened with rising emotion. She couldn't hold back the tide. She dropped her head into her palms and sobbed.

A jostling noise outside gave her a start. She jerked her head up, sniffing back her tears, and stared out at the dragon who remained undisturbed.

Maybe it was just her tail?

She wiped her wet cheeks. But then, she heard it again. Rhythmic clops, and then puffing pants.

A horse!

Elanor jumped to her feet, dropped the blanket, and raced toward the door. The dragon made no movement.

Does she not hear it?

Elanor cautiously peered across the threshold. She gasped, throwing her cold pink hands over her mouth. There before her eyes was Arthur dismounting from his horse. Furs wrapped his shoulders. His nose and cheeks were red with the cold. He lifted his face, and their eyes met.

Arthur breathed out a long sigh. His shoulders dropped and his eyes misted.

"I," he started, then stopped. "Merlin said you were here. I came the minute he—he told me everything. Are you alright? I am so sorry Osian—"

Elanor let her hands fall to her sides. Unbidden tears streamed down her cheeks. The relief at seeing him stole away all apprehension. She sprang toward him without thought. Her feet stole over the frosted ground.

Someone had come. *He* had come. But then her eyes captured his gaze, and chains of resentment jerked her back. She halted just before crashing into his chest.

"Fa—" she swallowed, stopping the flow of her words.

FATHER, her thoughts screamed, yearning to tear down the wall she had placed between them.

Arthur half whispered, "I am relieved to see you." He lifted his hand toward her face, but then pulled back, clenching his fingers into a fist. "I could hardly believe the report from Merlin. I worried you both might be dead."

Elanor exhaled with relief. "Merlin made it home? I wish I could have come home." Her heart twinged and her chin trembled. Another tear escaped the corner of her eye, clinging to the edge of her cheek.

"There are many who wished you had." Then Arthur rushed to say, "I-I *also* wished you had come home."

"Well," she said, glowering over at the dilapidated cottage, "this is where I stay instead."

"Elanor." Arthur grabbed hold of her hand. "Please." He wavered, quickly letting go when Elanor's eyes settled on him. "Please forgive me. I—" He glanced warily at the dragon, and then back at her. "I have not been very good at being a father. I still do not know what it means to be one. But to have you stolen away rent my heart in ways I cannot describe. Endless worry consumed me, and my entire world threatened to crumble. I only had the one lingering hope that Merlin would find you. As the days wore on, and I continued to stumble through Osian's snares, I found I had very little hope left.

"When Merlin returned to the Palisade, not even a full day ago, and I did not see you beside him"—Arthur's bottom lip curved, and his eyes pooled—"the feeling was…." He shook his head, palming his chest. "I could not breathe."

His words clashed against the small bit of resistance she held tight. She stared at him in awe, her chest warming. She had so desperately wanted his love yet resented him. She never understood how she could yearn to love someone so much, yet also desire to hurt them. He had never done anything to her, really. But deep in her heart, she felt like he had stolen everything. That he had stolen her father David, and her home in the Palisade. She felt abandoned long before she ever knew him, or dared to give him the chance.

But now, he stared at her with eyes full of love, and any trace of hostility she once held melted away. Tearfully, she lifted her chin. "I am sorry. I have been so angry at you. I waited for you my whole life, and then you—you were…." She fumbled, at a loss for a reason why.

Arthur slipped his fingers tenderly around her shoulder and leaned closer. "I was not prepared either. Your enigmatic presence"—he pressed his lips into a thin line—"was so confounding. All I know is, now I cannot imagine a world without you in it."

In the next breath, Elanor found herself pulled into an embrace. She didn't resist. Her mind searched her heart. She wanted to forgive him, to resolve the wound she felt could not be mended. Eyes squeezed shut, she flung her arms around him and pushed all the old feelings away, choosing to accept him. Here he was, embracing her. How could she refuse?

He leaned his cheek against her head. "More of us are coming."

Elanor looked up. "What?"

A subtle half-smile teased the corner of his mouth. "I would never leave you alone without help. I rode on ahead, but there are others who love you that are on their way."

"Who?" she asked, hope rising in her chest.

"They will likely be here before midday tomorrow. Adhan, Gwendolen, and Samara."

Elanor beamed, almost giddy with emotion.

My daughter—Oh, how I have missed her.

"And also, Peredur and Cilaen will come."

"Peredur?"

"Hah! Yes, Peredur. He would not let your little one from his sight. And I trust his strength to protect you." He glanced at the cottage. "There will be more hands now to make this place livable. They will be bringing a wagonload of supplies."

"I guess it helps to have a king for a—for a father." Elanor watched her words ease the tension in his shoulders and soften his eyes. She quickly changed the subject as tears threatened to fall and turned toward the cottage. "I am glad they are coming.

I was about to burn this whole cottage down. Dragons, unfortunately, do not understand what a *human needs*."

At that, Gwyliwr puffed, making Arthur jump. She twisted her giant head away from them.

"Apparently, she is completely unconcerned with my presence. Is she safe?" Arthur asked, his eyes scanning the large glistening side of the dragon with suspicion.

"I do not think so." Elanor laughed, wiping her misty eyes dry. "But she will be to us." She smiled and observed her father's face in a new light. Her heart blossomed with this mended connection between them. "I cannot wait for them to come."

"It will also do their hearts good to be with you."

"How…" She paused, staring at the ground. "How is mother?"

"I did not know when we left for the Southlands that she had already long been with child. She is showing now—the sight of her when I first returned just…" He gazed at Elanor mysteriously. "I knew it was you. Gwynevere knew too."

"She never told anyone. Why?"

"I do not believe she knows the answer to that."

"This is all so strange."

"Yes, well…" Arthur's face grew more serious. "These times are most dangerous." With a huff, he marched over to his saddle and unloaded a fresh blanket. He flung it around Elanor's shoulders, then shuddered, patting his arms. "It is cold these days. I am sure there is plenty of work to be done before we cook our meal tonight."

The thought of a meal got Elanor excited. It had been so long since she had a full one. "Well then, let us get to work."

Arthur blew on the flames of a dwindling fire underneath the darkening sky.

He placed another log into the fire, gladly watching Elanor enjoy its warmth. She took eager mouthfuls from the meat he had cooked. The juicy oil glistened on her lips.

"Squirrel doesn't satisfy like this venison," she said, shooting Arthur a satisfied grin and pulling the blanket a bit tighter around her neck.

Arthur chuckled. The firelight dancing over the dragon's scales caught his eye. "Does she just sleep?"

Elanor nodded. "It is as though she waits to be useful. She did leave a few days ago, and was gone most of the day. When she returned, she brought me some branches, and a few small animals. I think she knew I did not have the ability to properly dispatch a larger animal. We have spoken very little; however, she seems happy I am here. I can see it in her eyes, as though everything is exactly the way it is meant to be. She likes it when I am near her. I can feel her chest rumble like a kitten's purr when I am close."

"I have never seen a dragon until that day on the hill," Arthur said "Many were the stories Bedwyr's father used to tell of great monsters and giant serpents of the sea. Men spoke of dragons as though they were plentiful at one time—many different kinds. But all the stories told of how they were reclusive, stealing away to their caves high in the mountains."

Arthur stared at the dragon's large claws resting beside her long neck. The sheer size of the obsidian talons were like massive telamons burrowing into the dirt. Leery, he turned back to Elanor. Pointing to the cottage, he said, "Tomorrow we will look at repairing that thatch."

Elanor smiled warmly over at the cottage. "It is nice to think that soon there will be a bustle of people making this empty place more like a home. I ache to have Gwendolen in my arms."

Arthur watched her head drop with regret. "What is it?"

"I keep leaving her."

Arthur winced. *The Holy Cup.* Elanor's admittance brought to mind the embittered attrition that still gnawed at him. He left everyone behind for what he thought had been of such high importance, believing so deeply *the cup* was meant for him. The calling the Fisher King laid upon him was coupled with a burning thirst for the supernatural cup. He thought his thirst for it was righteous.

Was it not righteous? he ruefully questioned.

"There is always something important for me to do." Elanor's solemn eyes dropped, then, with a resenting bitter tone, she went on, "I am a chosen one, meant to bring the *New Way.* What if the evil never leaves us? What if I am forever having to fight, leaving my child for others to raise?"

Arthur pursed his lips, his heartbeat quickening. The cries of Cia's death suddenly replayed in his ears.

He shook his head.

The stinging image of an enemy's blade impaling Gwain, his head whipping back with a painful cry, bled through Arthur's memory.

His thoughts darkened, stewing over what Mordred had done. Could he really blame him for all that had happened?

If I had been there, instead of searching—

He cringed, shutting his eyes tight.

"Are you alright?" Elanor prodded, brushing her hand over his arm, pulling him from his dark musings.

Arthur opened his eyes and met her concerned stare. He had not realized how deeply he had fallen into his thoughts, making his anguish transparent. "It is just—"

A large puff resounded from the dragon's nose. First her eyelid flicked open, then a second layer pulled away like a curtain, revealing yellow eyes laced with fiery red and green. Intimidated, Arthur stood to his feet. Gwyliwr lifted her head, rising to her full height as she stretched, fluffing her golden-green scales like feathers. Her head tilted down to Arthur. He gulped in fright, and his fingers reached for his hilt.

"It is alright." Elanor stood, again reaching her reassuring hand toward Arthur.

"She is a guardian. A savior of life, not a destroyer of it. Well, unless you are an animal in the forest begging to be eaten."

"I have killed men." Gwyliwr's voice echoed downward. "Men without heart. Men who had wicked thoughts. Men whose futures would steal the innocent. Those bones I dashed and did not bury. I spat them upon the ground for scavengers to devour. I do not like the taste of human blood. It is bitter and not sweet."

Arthur wondered if she meant to dash his bones. He readied his stance, either to attack or flee. The dragon's eyes targeted him, increasing his alarm. "I have no wish to harm you, Dragon."

The spikes around Gwyliwr's jaw flailed outward, and she threw her head back. Her neck curved, bouncing with what Arthur could only conclude was laughter. With a growling purr, she whipped her gaze downward so fast that Arthur leapt back before meeting her level stare. "I do not threaten you, king. I knew you would come. This is *your* place, and *your* time."

"Wh-what?" He fumbled, still feeling the need to be ready to defend. He had already half-pulled his sword from his sheath.

"You do not need it," the dragon replied. "Though I know you are itching to pull it free. If I wanted to harm you, you would have been cooked the instant you arrived."

"I—I am sorry to have awoken you."

"You did not. I woke because it is the time for me to do so. I do not sleep like you humans do. I am working to protect this place from time." A long groan exuded from her throat, and a huge plume of smoke seeped through her teeth.

Seeing the smoke, Arthur ripped Caledfwlch from its sheath. The sword immediately heated up, glowing with a white radiant light. It shook in his grip, vibrating so forcefully, he had to clutch it with both hands.

The dragon's eyes flashed, and she said, "*The song* wants to be let out, Arthur." She eyed the sword. "You are going to have to set it free. It is what you truly want. It is why you hungered for the cup."

Arthur's eyes widened. "What do you mean?" He risked a glance at Elanor. She was staring up at the dragon, steadily backing away.

With a deep, breathy rumble, she said with pleasure, "Let me show you." The dragon heaved back a giant breath. Her chest grew wider. Inside was a glowing fiery light. She opened her jowls, and fire leapt from her mouth, enveloping Arthur.

There was no time for retreat. The rush of flames blew like wind, whipping past his ears. He expected any moment for searing heat to consume him—for death to take him. But instead, there was an incandescent burst, and a dull silence.

SILENCE AMONGST THE TREES

Arthur blinked repeatedly to recover his sight as though he had stared too long at the sun. Black and green blurry spots hovered around him. He rubbed his eyes, slowly capturing the flickering, leafy boughs with sunlit rays peeking through. A soft breeze rustled the leaves and filled his ears like a comforting song.

He swiftly oriented himself, shifting his footing. He was in a forest, inside a glen of trees.

Am I dead?

He gulped, his nerves still shaken from the dragon's fire. He slapped his cheeks, then ran his hands down his torso, realizing his sword was gone.

"Elanor? Where am I?" His voice echoed strangely in his ears.

He narrowed his eyes, noticing an opening in the trees ahead. He scanned his surroundings before taking his first cautious step. As his foot landed, the crunching leaves reverberated through the eerily quiet forest. The noise was like an alarm sounding at an intruder. Instantly on guard, he peered around, expecting an ambush.

Movement flickered through the trees.

Arthur froze, spotting a silhouette through the opening. He squinted, trying to get a better look. The figure was still as a statue. After a moment of hesitation, his curiosity compelled him forward. Was it a human, or just a carved effigy?

Arthur tried to soften his footfalls, but it was no use. In fact, the closer he drew to the opening, the louder his steps became—like he walked on gravel, instead of a soft leafy turf. He pressed on anyway, and finally, breaking through the wall of trees, he entered a small circular meadow. At the center, a tall, adolescent boy sat on a raised stump. His innocent eyes stared up into the trees, appearing not to have noticed Arthur's noisy approach. The boy's knees were pulled up to his chest, and his serene gaze seemed arrested by something unseen. The breeze tousled his wavey, golden hair.

Arthur took another step closer, entering the meadow, and his footfall echoed like a thunderclap. Arthur winced. He looked down at the ground and saw only grass, then snapped his gaze to the boy.

"You are making an awful lot of noise, Arthur Pendragon," the boy said without turning from the trees.

Arthur scowled, wondering how the boy knew his name. "I am sorry?" Even his voice boomed through the forest. Arthur pressed his palms against his ears and whispered more carefully, "Wher-Where am I? Have I died?"

"Heh." The adolescent lightly chuckled, his focus still on the trees. "No, you are not dead."

"Then why am I here?" Arthur paused and, hearing no response, edged closer. The thunderous noise of his steps was unbearable, so he stopped and carefully murmured, "I do not belong here. I feel I am an intruder. I cannot draw closer."

The boy remained quiet as if he had not heard him. Arthur shifted uncomfortably, spying the direction he had come and wondering whether he ought to retreat, when the boy broke his silence and asked, "Do you let uninvited guests into your house?"

"Oh, I…" Arthur furrowed his brow. "I did not mean to intrude. I only found myself here. I did not understand this to be your home."

"It is not *you* that is unwelcome, but it is your noise."

"My noise?" Arthur gaped, wondering how he could have been any quieter. This place exaggerated every movement he made, attacking him with the offensive tumult.

"This is not a place, Arthur." The boy cast his piercing eyes at him. His blue irises narrowed in a far-too perceiving way, as if peering past skin and straight into Arthur's soul.

Arthur stiffened, wishing he could hide. He felt exposed. Alone. Ashamed.

"Stop!" the boy commanded, springing from his seat. He approached in purposeful strides, his height matching Arthur's. "Those thoughts you are thinking—those fears—that is the noise that does not belong."

"I do not understand."

"Ssshh!" the boy hushed.

Arthur could not look up at him. The boy's scrutiny was overwhelming. The boy did not seem human, but more like a lamp light—bright as a pyre on a hill. Arthur felt stuck: unable to move, speak or even think.

The boy grasped Arthur's arm, and immediately a calm rushed over him. As he tugged Arthur toward the stump, each step drummed, making him cringe. Arthur yanked his arm away and covered his ears. The relentless pounding sent shards of pain through every nerve.

Memories. Noisy memories heated his emotions. He resisted collapsing to the ground, wanting to scream and drown out the beating waves. Out of the depth of his soul, Arthur groaned, "It was not supposed to be this way."

His voice broke through the noise, and he found he was now sitting on the stump in silence with the boy standing beside him.

"Ssshh! Silence. Listen."

Chapter Thirty-One

"But, I—"

The boy held up his finger. "Listen. Not to yourself. Listen to the trees."

"The tr—"

"Ssshhh!"

Arthur's forehead creased but he obeyed, observing the trees with uncertainty. The boughs danced in a tranquil cadence. The wind shifted its tune, whispering breathy sighs.

Where am I? He hoped the trees might answer.

The sweet trill of a singular bird floated through the wind. Its song was so striking through the silence that Arthur searched the branches, as if for a treasure. His eyes bounced back and forth, until finally landing on a small blue bird with a rosy red breast. It skipped and hopped, fluttering from branch to branch, singing its chirrup.

The little bird spread its wings and floated down with a gentle flickering vibrato, alighting on the ground. It tweeted, hopping over the grass. Its small black eye blinked sideways at Arthur. He remained as still as he could, not wishing to frighten the little bird away. It pecked away contentedly at the ground.

Its pecking started a reaction. Each time its beak pierced the ground, a spark of light flashed in Arthur's eyes, and a twinge of pain pulsed in his chest. It pecked again, and Arthur doubled over.

"Ah!" He groaned, lifting his hand to clutch his heart. "What is it doing?"

"It is showing you where you are," the boy said.

"What?"

It pecked.

"Ah! Make it stop."

It pecked again and again.

"Stop!" Arthur said, leaping from his seat. When his feet landed, the ground boomed like cracking earth, frightening the bird away. The crash unleashed a shockwave of pain through Arthur's body. He collapsed and threw his arms over his head.

The boy's voice grew in timbre. "You asked, and it answered."

Arthur gasped. "What?" He rolled to face the boy who stood silhouetted by the sunlight. His head throbbed, and his anger clawed to the surface. He clenched his fists into the earth. The sensation of the grass and dirt felt strange. He looked down at the grass locked between his fingers. With a sedulous gape, he uncurled his fingers.

He lowered one palm back to the soft grass. As his fingers filtered through the blades and grazed the soft dirt, his heart groaned. He dropped his other hand onto the earth, and an anguish arose, reddening his ears and cheeks. "This—this is—this is *my heart.*" His jaw dropped, and he lifted his head up to the boy. Then sudden recognition widened his eyes. The sun highlighted the blond wavy hair. "You are me?"

Everything started to fade at his revelation. His mind swirled, dredging up his own prideful words spoken in the past.

I am the great sovereign of Prydain...

I am the strength of this land…
None could do as I have done…
I am the chosen one…
It is my destiny to find the Holy Cup at all cost…

The arrogant words pounded his ears, making Arthur hate the sound of his own voice. Merlin rippled into his memory. Arthur recalled that day. He did not want to remember, but he couldn't stop the memory from hurling itself though his mind.

"Arthur, you must listen to me. The Holy Cup is gone."

"No," Arthur contended. "Gwalahad held it in his hand. I can have it once again. It is meant to be a symbol of this kingdom. I am supposed to be the one that guards it—just as the Fisher King has done. He passed it on to me. With it, all will know that I am the deliverer of the New Way."

"You? The deliverer? Do you even hear yourself?"

"My men are ready to go with me. They are just as zealous as I am to see it restored. It came to me, Merlin. It is meant to be mine."

Merlin gaped. "It is meant to be *no one's*. You should have never taken it in the first place. There has been nothing but evil working to destroy Prydain's peace ever since you touched it."

Arthur arched his eyebrow. "Are you saying the cup is evil?"

"No." Merlin vehemently shook his head. "But your need to have it is unrighteous."

"How *dare* you?" Arthur slammed his fist onto the table. "You, who was there that day on the lake when the Fisher King told me of the cup. You felt the power. The hunger." He stormed toward Merlin, stabbing his finger into his chest. "Do not pretend you did not feel the Great God's presence. The Fisher King came and healed me with it. It is my destiny to have it."

Merlin pushed Arthur's hand aside, and with a bitter twist in his lips, he stepped away. "You have been warned. The monks of Avalon came to explain the power of the cup, but you would not listen. Now I am warning you. You think too highly of yourself, Arthur. You cannot own the cup any more than you can tame the wild enaid of old."

"ENOUGH! I am the king. Not you, *druid.*"

"*Druid?*"

"You are not *all* wise. You just want to keep the kingdom from expanding because you are afraid. My lack of fear has won us allies and bested our enemies. If I have this cup, other lands beyond our borders could be gathered to Prydain. Many are fading like wax, but there are remnants that could benefit from my leadership. There were so many great nations before the invaders came, but see how I have saved Prydain. Those lands need a new leader—a New Way. The cup would establish this. This is why *I* am the king."

"You misunderstand your destiny, and the New Way. You risk too much. You cannot leave now. This search is futile."

"I have heard that the Gauls have forests—the forests of Broceliande. They say it has hidden secrets. The east is where the cup was made. These lands could hold clues as to where the cup may be found."

"This will all result in death."

"Or glory," Arthur argued.

"Your glory is here. With *your* people."

"None of it matters without the cup."

Merlin stared at him, then, clearly having enough, stormed for the door. He gripped the handle, but before leaving, he turned. "Your stubborn pride will cost you," Merlin said through clenched teeth. "The cup has become your god. Do you not understand? What costs you ultimately affects us all. We will all pay the price for your mistake!"

Arthur jerked his chin up, disregarding Merlin's words. "My men and I leave at dawn. We will only return once we have found the cup."

Merlin shook his head, then left, slamming the door behind him.

"My arrogance and pride." Arthur sucked in the regret with the fading memory. "Merlin was right. I hate that I did not listen. I hate that I—"

"Ssshhh!"

Arthur opened his eyes, twisting toward the voice. There was someone new kneeling before him. Cerulean light glowed around the figure.

"It is very noisy," the Man in Blue said. "It is time for you to have peace."

"But I failed," Arthur said. Tears of disappointment leaked down his cheeks.

"Yes. You thought the *Holy Cup* was the promise of the kingdom. You thought it was what imbued you with the New Way. You thought it greater than God. You surrendered your kingdom for the cup. And now, you believe that you can no longer be trusted to lead these lands to defeat the enemy."

Arthur whispered through trembling lips, "I do not deserve a second chance."

"Arthur." The Man in Blue settled his hands onto the grass. "If you must hold on to this unforgiveness, then it is true—you will not have the power to defeat Osian. Your own self-doubt will become the prophecy of your future. But it does not have to be that way. Kingdoms of this world fade"—he pressed his hands into the earth—"but I have come that you would have a New Way."

"I cannot forgive myself. I deserve to be punished." At Arthur's words, a ringing pelted his eardrums like the gong of a bell.

"Ah—now there is the source of all the noise." The Man in Blue pushed even deeper into the ground. "Who punishes you, Arthur? Your people do not. Gwynevere does not. Not even Merlin."

"My men. I—I failed them. They are dead because of me."

"No, Arthur. Right or wrong, they followed you—proud to serve their king. So, I ask you again. Who punishes you?"

"The Great God gave me a destiny, a task, to bring the Kingdom of the Sun. I failed. He punishes me."

Dong. The ringing ricocheted inside Arthur's head.

The Man in Blue pushed even deeper into the ground, and an immense force catapulted Arthur into the air. As he crashed down onto his back, he felt like his heart was being burned with irons; his body writhed from the pain.

The man's voice boomed, "My love *never* fails. Within it you can never fall short. You were forgiven before the day of your first breath. I can redeem *all* the stolen time. I punish *no one.*"

Arthur gasped, pressing his hands into his chest. Everything else stilled and went silent. Slowly, the radiating in his chest dissipated. He lay there recovering his breath when a quiet voice within his mind said, *"Now you must forgive yourself."*

Through hot tears, Arthur whispered, "I punish myself."

"And it is time for that punishment to end. Only in the light of forgiveness can the enemy be defeated. Only in this freedom, can you selflessly give your life for this land."

"My life?" Arthur sprang up as if waking from a dream and discovered he was alone. Before him was the lonely stump, surrounded by the trees that whispered with the wind. Upon the stump sat the Holy Cup. Arthur gasped. All these years he had searched, and there it was. The ornately carved goblet just as he remembered it.

I never thought I would see it again.

His heart leapt. The cup sparkled with water brimming over the top.

The man's voice uttered inside Arthur's mind, *"It overflows."*

Arthur stared in amazement at the cup he had searched for. The cup he had lost his kingdom for. Died for. Now finally understanding, he whispered, "I already had the cup. It was in my heart all along."

"I placed it here that day by the lake when the Fisher King commissioned you. But after that day, you never partook of it. The cup is not the kingdom, Arthur. I Am."

The water in the cup drew Arthur's eyes, and his lamenting heart squeezed with repentance. He sputtered, "I am—I am so sorry. I did not understand."

"Drink."

Arthur wiped his forearm across his face to dry his cheeks and timidly rose. The leaves on the trees fluttered as though clapping their hands. *The song* played sweetly on the breeze. He took a step forward, and now the grass quietly swished underneath his feet. A lightness lifted inside him, and he took another step. His mouth curved in a penitent smile. His quavering hands reached for the cup, then slipped around the bowl.

"Listen," said the voice.

Arthur closed his eyes and listened. For the first time in many years, there was stillness. His heart came alive with a thrumming beat. He marveled at the sparkling waters inside the cup. Immediately, unworthiness swept over him.

"The forgiveness is in the water. Drink it, and you will find it."

Arthur rushed the goblet to his mouth. The water splashed over his face and down his chin. He drank, and he drank, and it never ran dry. There was always more. His calling and destiny reignited with each gulp. The words of *the song* timbered like a prophecy over him. He saw the young version of himself gripping Aurelius's sword and tearing it free from the stone.

His eyes snapped open, and he was clutching Caledfwlch. The dragon and Elanor were once more beside him.

Everything gradually settled back to the way it was before the dragon's fire.

Arthur heard: *"You will be remembered throughout history, but only as a legend. History will tell of how you fell. All that you do now will be forgotten. Your failings, though forgiven, had a cost. Your redemption, however, will be remembered by those who love you, and renown in my kingdom forever."*

Arthur drew a slow, measured breath. The weighty words hung heavily in the air before settling into his soul. He squeezed the hilt of Caledfwlch. "I no longer care what remains of my name. My kingdom fades. They all fade. Only *one* will last forever. I now understand the *New Way*. I live and die for the one who redeemed me."

32

WINTER WITH THE DRAGON

Elanor was up before the sun. She was too excited to sleep. Soon, more of her family would be arriving, and she longed more than anything to hold Gwendolen, and not let go. She relished the idea of snuggling her next to the fire, allowing her to fall asleep in her arms. She took a deep breath and stared off through the trees, hoping to see them.

Arthur ambled out from the cottage, rubbing his face. His eyes hung heavy, and he leaned his shoulder against the doorframe, sucking in a gigantic yawn. "I feel like I have been trampled by boars."

"Still some lasting effects from the dragon's magic."

"Mm—" Arthur shrugged, giving into another yawn. "Where is that dragon anyway?"

Elanor pointed up the hill. The dragon stood on the top with her wings spread wide, embracing the icy gales as though she were sailing on the wind. "You can almost see a smile on her face. She must really be enjoying those gales."

"Hah!" Arthur chuckled. "She must indeed."

Gwyliwr opened her wide mouth, letting the wind flow over her tongue. She swayed her head back and forth as though dancing to a ballad only she heard.

"It gives me a chill to watch her," Elanor said, standing closer to the newly lit fire. "The wind up there is like ice."

Gwyliwr shook her head, then released a loud, booming sneeze. Both Arthur and Elanor reached for the ground to steady themselves. The dragon peered down at them with a dopey grin, exposing her rows of sharp teeth before licking her nose.

Elanor giggled. "I have never seen her like this. She reminds me of a puppy."

"A gigantic puppy," Arthur said, joining her by the fire.

Elanor rubbed her hands together over the fire; Arthur did the same. A longing for him to stay pinged her chest. "Will you be returning to the Palisade?"

"Yes," Arthur said with reluctance. "I will stay another day and help get things set."

Elanor nodded, masking her disappointment.

"I must be vigilant. The kingdom needs—"

"I know," she cut in, grinning abjectly. "I am glad you came. I cannot wait for the others to arrive." She pressed her lips together, eyeing him sheepishly. "You saw Him last night inside the dragon's magic, didn't you?"

"Who?"

"The Man in Blue."

"I cannot say that I *saw* him, but—" His face scrunched, a corner of his mouth lifting in a sort of crooked smile. "He was there. I caught a glimpse of him. He was right before me, but I cannot quite remember his face." His stare grew more contemplative. "Merlin has told me of him. He also told me that it was *He* that truly saved you."

Elanor made no reply. The whole experience still germinated inside her heart. She was not certain she understood all that took place. But one thing she did know was this: He was with her now, and she would never be the same.

"I did not understand until now," Arthur said. "I have been naïve and foolish in so many ways."

"He makes it simple. Removing all the—" She twisted her mouth, thinking of the right words.

"Noise," Arthur said.

"Yes." Elanor smiled. "Noise." She offered her hand to him, and he took it, giving an affirming squeeze.

"He has prepared us for battle. We have not been left without help. Live or die, I believe we *can now* fight."

Live or die? Her brow pressed together as she looked at him with uncertainty. He stared into the fire, and Elanor saw an orange flicker of hope. Arthur's enemies would meet the one she had heard so many tales of. The one whose battle frenzy none could stand against. The flash of Arthur upon his black horse rushed through her mind. She heard his battle cry rise in her gut, along with the pounding of many horses.

Soon, she would have her own battles to face. Could she face them like him? Could his steel be found in her gaze? She did not know. She only knew this—she wanted that same fury and strength coursing through her veins. She believed if it did, then she could do anything.

At long last the sound of wagon wheels rolled over broken branches. Elanor dropped the armload of kindling she had been gathering and ran for the clearing in front of the cottage. Any moment they would be driving through the trees.

"I wondered if they would be able to pull the wagon through the forest," Arthur said, joining her. "It will be great to have a few more tools close at hand to get some of this *blasted* work done."

The first to appear was Peredur, leading the way on horseback. Then slowly, emerging behind him, came two large steers pulling a wagon driven by Cilaen. Adhan and Samara sat huddled together with Gwendolen between them, wrapped in a cocoon of blankets. Elanor lifted her hands to her mouth. Her heart swelled at the sight of them. She skipped toward the wagon, her arms outstretched, ready to receive her daughter.

"Elanor!" Cilaen shouted.

Gwendolen cried, "Muma!"

Cilaen pulled on the reins, slowing the wagon to a halt, allowing Gwendolen to jump free.

"Muma," she called again, springing into Elanor's arms.

"How I have missed you," Elanor said, covering Gwendolen in kisses. Her daughter's rosy smile beamed up at her as she giggled. "You have gotten even bigger. Your toes nearly hang down to my knees."

"I am growing."

"I can see that." Elanor nodded, tickling Gwendolen's ribs, and making her squirm with glee. Adhan climbed down and reached for her. "Oh, my Great God, I am so happy to see you." Elanor leaned into Adhan's embrace. Samara rushed to Elanor's opposite side and brushed her back with a soft touch. "And you." Elanor kissed Samara's cheek.

Cilaen shouted over, "Well, we could not very well leave you out here to freeze to death on your own. We thought we would join you."

"Ah, well," Arthur countered, "we will have this place warm and hospitable now that you are here to help."

"I am glad you are alive," Cilaen said tenderly, an arch of concern on his brow. He pulled her into his arms. "I told Merlin he needs to lock you away inside the Palisade. He agreed that sounded a much safer way to keep you."

Elanor smiled. "I missed you too. I am really glad you came." His warmness was always a comfort to her.

"Well." Cilaen shrugged toward Peredur. "This place is not much more than a pile of sticks."

"There is enough here to work with," Peredur said, dismounting his horse. His eyes connected with Elanor's, and he bowed affirmingly, almost cracking a smile.

"I am so grateful to all of you," she gushed, squeezing Gwendolen tighter.

Samara screamed, and they all turned. Cilaen's jaw fell open, and he dropped the tools he had just grabbed out of the wagon.

"Dragon!" Gwendolen tried to wriggle free of Elanor's grip.

"Oh. My. Great. God," Peredur muttered, smacking his forehead, clearly flummoxed.

Adhan gripped Elanor's shoulders with a growing smile on her face. "Beautiful."

"Did Merlin not warn you?" She chuckled, baffled at all of them. Elanor clung tightly to Gwendolen's hand. The toddler was working very hard to jerk free. "Hold on, Gwen. It is alright, everyone. This is Gwyliwr. She is my guardian. She will not hurt you."

Gwendolen successfully yanked free and gamboled toward the dragon. Gwyliwr, seeing the little one, barreled down the hill toward her. The ground quaked beneath her strides.

"Wait! Gwen!" Elanor shouted. Her heart leapt into her throat.

The dragon crashed, skidding across the ground, and rolled over onto her back. Her nose flared for Gwendolen. The child jumped before her, eagerly tapping the dragon's lip. Gwyliwr purred and then puffed, playfully blowing Gwendolen down into the grass into fits of giggles.

Elanor gripped her chest, catching her breath. "See?" she called, waving her hand at everyone's shocked faces. "Completely safe." She wiped the panic from her own face and walked toward her daughter. She sat beside her and pulled her close. "This is Gwyliwr, Gwen. She is mommy's friend." Elanor's seeing magic flashed into the dragon's eye, and her heart melted at the joy teeming inside. She reached her hand up to touch the dragon's nose, and Gwendolen did the same.

Elanor said to Gwyliwr, "Like me, you have been waiting all day to see her, haven't you?" She smiled up at the dragon. "Here I am grateful my friends have come, and I have forgotten to thank you for protecting me. Thank you!" At Elanor's words, Gwyliwr's warbling purrs increased, and the satisfied dragon closed her eyes.

"Gwen?" Elanor cooed. Her daughter beamed a smile of pure joy up at her. "I am so happy you are here with me." She pulled a tendril of Gwendolen's dark silken curls from her face. "I cannot wait to hear all you have been up to since I left for the Southlands."

"I can run real fast now, and Granmov'r says if I don' slow down, I might fly." Gwendolen made her fingers flutter like a butterfly. "I helped Granmov'r make pies."

"Wow." Elanor flashed a dazzled smile. "You are getting so big. What else?"

"Um—" Gwendolen grinned, staring up at the sky as she thought. "Oh—I hurt myse'f."

"Hurt yourself?" Elanor asked. Gwendolen offered her hand, and pulled her sleeve up to reveal a linen bandage with splotches of blood that had leaked through.

"That does not look good," Elanor said, turning a distressed glance to Adhan who was heading toward them. "What happened?"

Adhan knelt, grabbing hold of Gwendolen's hand. "We are not entirely sure what happened. Gwen was—"

"I was playing with the hounds."

"Yes." Adhan smiled fondly. "We were in the Great Hall, and I was helping a serving girl clear plates."

"Uri was playing with me," Gwendolen chirped.

Elanor searched her memory for a moment. "Uri the serving boy?"

Adhan nodded. "Well, ever since I have been at the Palisade, he now serves in the stables. Most recently he has started to apprentice with one of the Cymbrogi."

"Oh." Elanor smiled warmly. "I am happy for him. I remember when I first met him, he was so eager and hopeful to become a warrior someday."

"He was sitting with Gwen by the hearth. The hounds were in a pile warming themselves. There is one particular female hound that has taken a liking to Gwen. She follows her everywhere, and Gwen was snuggling with her. Uri was telling her stories. I was busy helping when Gwen started crying, and then Uri shouted for me. I ran over to discover a large cut across Gwen's forearm. Uri thought she might have been bitten by one of the hounds." Adhan paused, concern knitting her brow. "She was bleeding terribly, so I quickly rushed her to Cilaen, and he patched her."

"Do you not know what happened?" Elanor asked Gwendolen.

"I can't remember, Muma."

"That is strange."

Adhan nodded. "Cilaen was certain it was not a bite. He thought maybe she had fallen on a sharp object. The cut was a clean slice, not jagged. He said her arm appeared cut with a blade."

Gwendolen frowned. "It hurted."

"I bet it did." Elanor gently brushed the bandage. "Good thing you had Grandmother and Cilaen to help you."

"Yah." Gwendolen grimaced, then hopped to her feet to go climb on the dragon.

A tiny bubble of worry rose in Elanor's chest. "Were there any knives or daggers nearby?"

Adhan shook her head. "None we could find."

Cilaen shouted over, "We have our work cut out for us." He flashed a smile, then warily glanced over at the dragon. All the while, Peredur loaded his arms full of supplies from the wagon.

Arthur gave Cilaen an affirming smack on the back, and Cilaen's eyebrows shot up in surprise at the friendly recognition. "Hopefully, the women will be sleeping warmly in the cottage tonight," Arthur said.

"Aah," Peredur said with a grunt. "That is the first task of the day. The building of other shelters for these"—he lifted a wooden cageful of bawking chickens—"can wait. Until then, they will be joining you in the cottage to stay warm."

At his announcement, Gwendolen jumped down from the dragon and ran to see the chickens. "Chickies!"

Peredur leapt from the wagon and swept Gwendolen into a twirling spin. Her squeals of delight warmed Elanor's heart. After giving her a tight squeeze, Peredur gently set her on the wagon's edge, where she eagerly poked her finger into the cages.

"Careful now," he huffed. "Sometimes chickens think little fingers look like tasty worms."

Elanor's eyes misted, and Adhan pulled her into her side. "I am glad she has been so well loved."

"Merlin hated to let her go. Both of you have been deprived of her sweetness, but—" Adhan tilted Elanor's cheek toward her. "You need to trust that the Great God has her, just as He has all of us. There was no accident to her birth in such dire times, and there is no accident to you being a mother in these times either. Did you know—" Adhan hesitated, appearing reluctant to continue. The pain of regret swirled in her eyes. Adhan swallowed and shook her head. "I lost Merlin for three years when he was a child."

Elanor's eyes widened; her curiosity piqued. "What happened?"

"It is a long story. One he could tell you better. Though I think he has likely mostly forgotten. He was so young, only six, when the fae stole him away."

"The fae?" Elanor's imagination reeled to the reality of yet another myth becoming real.

What did they look like? Were they evil? Enaid? Why did they take Merlin?

She had so many questions, but not wanting to derail Adhan, she held her questions for another time.

"I did not know it was the fae that had taken him, until he returned to me years later. I thought he had died." Her eyes welled. "My point is—it was the fae that initially helped Merlin discover his natural magic. There are parts of his magic that the druids could have never helped to kindle. His gift is bigger than he is. He still grasps to understand what it is, and where it came from. But the fae taught him how to listen to it, and not be consumed by it.

"If it had not been for my long season of having lost him, I do not believe that Merlin would have become who he is now." She shook her head. "Merlin feels so deeply. His sensitive emotions are what makes him so wise, and yet have also tossed him, so many times, into the pit. Made him run away. Despair. Even use his magic in defiance. When I lost him again after Ganeida's death"—she gasped, clutching her chest—"he came out of that wilderness bold as a lion. Do you understand what I am saying?"

Elanor looked at Gwendolen racing between Peredur's legs as he lifted a large bundle of thatch.

"None of this is accidental, and none of it will be wasted. I know the regret you feel at not being with her all the time, but something *fierce* has been growing in her. She will not be lost because you have been gone. I promise. Just love her with your whole heart here and now. The Great God has ordered Gwendolen's steps, just as He is ordering yours. No one is born to dark days without the ability to become slayers of the demons that haunt them. Though many fail to recognize their worth, she will not."

Everyone's hands were blistered and tired by the day's end, but so much had been done. This night, Elanor would enjoy sleeping in the newly improved cottage. Inside, the hearth blazed, heating the walls and boiling the water for her bath.

After bathing, she slid into a fresh set of nightclothes. Elanor relished the thought of snuggling next to Gwendolen in cozy woolen blankets. Already, the fellowship of those who had come to wait out the winter restored her spirits.

They sat outside around the fire, and Samara untwisted Elanor's braids. It felt good to have her friend's tender fingers weaving through her hair again. Gwendolen would soon need to bathe as well. Her dinner of bread and venison managed to cover her cheeks and ears. She had been begging all day to sleep inside the folds of the dragon's legs, but to her displeasure, it was just too cold for her to sleep outside—even up against the warmth of a dragon. Though Gwendolen swore the dragon wanted her to, Elanor promised maybe an afternoon nap would be better for a dragon snuggle. As it was, Gwyliwr was already sleeping, and her legs were conveniently tucked away from the heat of the fire.

"Let us have a song then," Arthur said, whacking Peredur upside his knee.

Peredur grunted. "I am eating."

Cilaen, sitting crossed-legged and leaning back on his arms, brightened at the idea. "Yes! A song would be brilliant. Come on then, Peredur!"

Peredur glared at him across the fire, a bulge of unchewed food in his cheek.

Cilaen cleared his throat. "So sorry, Lord Peredur."

"Yes, yes, Lord Pe'dur," came the sweet trill of Gwendolen's voice.

Peredur's face softened at her request, and he smiled, gulping down his chunk of food. "Why should I do it? I am not the one qualified to sing a song."

"Ah," Arthur said, lifting his finger. "But I have sat around many a campfire with you, and I know the gift you have with songs. Especially once you have had an ale or two. Did we not bring any ale?" Arthur glanced back at the supplies still left unloaded.

"Horse dung! I have no special gift."

"I beg to differ." Arthur grinned.

Peredur panned everyone's pleading faces, then rolled his eyes. "Eh, fine," he bemoaned, brushing the food from his fingers and clearing his throat. "But this does not become what I do. This is one time only. In the spirit of having Elanor back, and our bellies full, I will sing. But only as long as everyone sings along."

Arthur told him, "You will have to pick one we all know."

Gwendolen shouted, "Sweet Maid O' Plenty." She scrambled over and lifted her grubby hands toward Peredur. In one swift motion, he scooped her happily onto his knee.

"Sweet Maid, eh?"

Gwendolen nodded, bouncing with excitement.

"Very well, but you will have to help me sing it."

She clapped her hands and kicked her legs, ready for Peredur to begin.

"How does it start again?" he teased.

"Lord Pe'dur," Gwendolen giggled, "like this—" She nodded her head to catch the rhythm, then began: "Her dress was torn; tangles in her hair."

Peredur repeated, "Her dress was torn; tangles in her hair."

"With no coin or bread to spare."

"With no coin or bread to spare."

Gwendolen took a deep breath, and everyone sang along with her…

She sang, I am the Sweet Maid O'Plenty, but there is nothing left for me.
So, I come to the king, and tell him my name, to see if he will agree.

She sang, I am the Sweet Maid O'Plenty, but there is nothing left for me.
So, I come to the king, and tell him my name, to see if he will agree.

The silly song continued, and everyone laughed at Gwendolen's enthusiasm. Elanor scanned the smiling round cheeks that glowed from the firelight.

The king gave her a dress, and put flowers in her hair.
Gave her some silver and pheasant on his finest ware.

Elanor's gaze settled on Cilaen's beaming brown eyes. Like always, he had his brown curls tied back behind his neck. He sang of the maid with a glint that caught Elanor's attention. She followed the trail of his eyes to Samara. Elanor gasped, recognizing a besotted stare. Turning to Samara, Elanor was delighted to see a reciprocated blush.

Cilaen stood with his hands on his hips. "Oh, Sweet Maid O'Plenty," he sang, rounding the fire and offering Samara his hand. She eagerly snatched it and rose to her feet. Everyone clapped, and Cilaen whisked Samara in at the waist. They bounded away in a spinning twirl, dancing away from the fire, out under the moonlight.

Elanor chuckled, and with her mouth agape, turned to Adhan, who shrugged and smiled. "I have had my suspicions that he liked her, but this is new. Not sure Samara knows what to think."

"She appears to be smiling." Elanor laughed, watching them spin. Cilaen sang to her with a fond look in his eyes. "I am very happy for them. I do not know why, but it gives me so much hope."

"Love always gives us hope."

"You know," Elanor said in a hushed voice, "I still think of Cilaen's mother."

"Efa?"

Elanor nodded. "There is always a small sadness behind Cilaen's joy. I hoped healing her might take that away, but—"

"Efa is as she has always been." Adhan sighed. Her eyes spun, watching the couple dance. "Cilaen was seven when his father died. Efa did not dwindle away immediately, but neither she nor Cilaen stopped waiting for him to return. All that came back from battle was his cape and brooch. I think Cilaen hoped he was still alive. Having not seen his body, he refused to believe he was dead."

Elanor's heart was immediately struck with remorse.

"When his mom started falling into despair, Cilaen cared for her. He would say, 'Father's coming home, momma, do not worry', as if his promise would encourage her to get better.

Elanor shook her head, and her brows crimped. "That should not have been left for him to do."

"No," Adhan said. "I tried to take that burden from him. It pained me to tell him that his father would never return—he refused to hear it." Her breath hitched. "With tears in his eyes, he would act as though I were stealing away his greatest wish.

"Cilaen came more and more under my care. His mother being ill made him want to learn to heal. For a while it was a good distraction."

Adhan clasped Elanor's hand, and she swiftly enveloped it with her own. The kindled memories misted Adhan's fluttering eyes. Elanor had never quite known the depths of Adhan's relationship with Cilaen until now.

With a solemn smile, Adhan continued, "I sat with him and taught him. He started assisting me when I healed others, and for a while, it helped. But as time went on and his mother fell deeper into despondency, the more an angry flame within him started to grow. He spent more time, quiet and alone, reading the books I would give him, instead of playing with the other children.

"Around the time of his twelfth year, the situation with his mother had grown worse. I came to his home and found him screaming—" Adhan voice cut out, and she shook her head. "He was preparing to strike Efa. I had to grab him and pull him away."

Adhan placed her hand on her heart. Her lips pressed tightly, as if holding back a wave of sorrow. "Cilaen was so angry. After that, his tears did not let up for a long while. His mother had broken his heart. It was that day I knew he could no longer stay in Dyved."

"That must have been a hard choice for you," Elanor said softly. "I can see how much you loved him."

"I had taken him in as my own, but his mother's illness was hurting him. And there were still too many days when I found him on the plateau's edge, waiting for his father to return. I sent him to Merlin then. It was a good choice." Adhan lowered her head a moment, then peered up at Cilaen, who was now laughing and gasping for breath. Samara's hand was still securely in his.

After Adhan's sad story, the delightful sound of Cilaen's laughter lifted Elanor's heart.

Adhan sighed deeply, and the smile now gracing her face held less heartache. "He has grown so strong. So resilient. But—the pain is still there. Sometimes I see it. In the corner of his happiness, hides a boy that was abandoned by his mother and father. That is what makes him fight and eager to heal others. It keeps the tide from revealing the shore."

COLLISION OF FATE

Merlin dolefully stared east out the Palisade window; his brows knitted. This was the second full moon since he had left Elanor. The season would be changing soon. Already the warmer air filtered through the Palisade's walls. Pressure over Osian's next move was mounting.

"They will be alright," Gwynevere said from the comfort of her chair, caressing her belly with a longing smile.

The sight of her grated against Merlin's nerves. He tried not to look at the radiant expectation in her eyes.

Does she not realize what she will have to do? She cannot keep the baby.

There was very little to distract Merlin from constantly thinking of Elanor and Gwendolen. He felt like a chained hound pulling against his binds, pining for the moment he could be let loose.

Arthur's moping irked Merlin even more. He could feel Arthur stewing all the way from the Palisade's council circle. The challenging circumstance kept Arthur planning the approaching march to the Southlands. He was confident, come the change in weather, that Osian would not stay hidden. Merlin agreed. They would have to be ready to move. The gathering armies of the northern areas of Prydain had already begun to camp outside the citadel. King Bram seemed the most anxious to go into battle against the enemy.

Merlin looked toward the closed door of the chamber. Bedwyr guarded the other side. There remained a lingering animosity between them, and they hadn't spoken. Their interactions consisted of only steely stares and cold shoulders. Merlin knew he had created the rift between them the night Osian took Elanor. But too many other things weighed heavy on his heart that kept him from making amends— though he hated the silence. What he wouldn't give for a flash of Bedwyr's friendly smile and courage.

"Will you stop brooding over there?" Gwynevere chided.

Merlin stubbornly tightened his lips and glared, refusing to turn around.

"Really—you men. I tire of the lot of you." She tsked at Merlin's lack of response. "Do you think I am a fool? I know what is happening here."

Merlin cocked his head, peering at her from his peripheral. Gwynevere groaned, arching to her feet. She rubbed her stomach and grinned. "She will be coming soon."

Merlin rolled his eyes, trying to smother the rising emotions heating his face. He was afraid. But of what, specifically? He wasn't entirely sure. Gwynevere's labor, his distance between Elanor, and the unknowns of war. He couldn't stop his mind from imagining the worst scenarios.

What if…

He sighed, stopping his thoughts. He closed his eyes with a shudder and ground his teeth.

Gwynevere waddled beside him and joined Merlin in staring out the window. "Hm? The sun has been melting the ice more and more. Soon the flowers will be singing in the new season." She touched the window. The warmth of her skin formed a foggy circle. Her eyes drifted up to Merlin. "She will be alright."

He did not waver.

"I know it is hard." She gently patted the top of her stomach. "It is hard for me as well."

"Seems you are doing just fine," Merlin mumbled tersely.

Gwynevere glared at him. "What I am doing, despite the horrible attitudes of all those around me, is enjoying what time I have with her." She sucked in a breath, appearing to take hold of her emotions. "I"—she halted—"I am the one who will pay the most dearly. I know you think I do not know what I will have to do. I just cannot—I *will not* waste what time I have with her thinking about the *loss* of her. I am her mother. She—she is mine, whether as a baby or grown. You *must* understand. I cannot fathom the thought of giving her away."

She continued through clenched teeth, "It rips my heart from my chest. But I distract myself. I do have her now. It might be for only a small moment, but I will love every breath she takes where I get to hold her in my arms."

A tear leaked from Merlin's eye, and he quickly wiped it away. Still, he refused to look at her. "I am sorry, Gwynevere. You are right to love her—here and now. I do not know why my heart wants to deny this. As much as I know it *must* happen"—he finally faced her—"I fear it."

She cupped Merlin's cheek. "Arthur is afraid too. So is Bedwyr. All joy left with the ones who are with Elanor in the forest. But we could have it here. *Please*. Merlin, I need you and Arthur to connect with me in this moment. I do not think I can do this alone. She is my daughter, but she is also part of you—part of Arthur. Our Elanor, born to *this world*."

"Have you told Arthur how you feel?"

She shook her head. "He distracts himself in a different way."

"I noticed," Merlin mumbled. "I cannot blame him. It feels as though everything is about to collide."

A pained cry eked from Gwynevere. "Aaah!" She buckled over, gripping her stomach with teeth clenched.

Merlin snapped to her side. "What's happening?"

"Aaah!" She cried again, heaving fast breaths. "This"—she forced through another cringing moan—"This does not—this does not feel right."

Merlin eyes dropped to the floor. Blood pooled around Gwynevere's shoes. Panic seized him. "I will get the midwife." He clutched her shoulders to support her. Already perspiration beaded on her brow.

This cannot be it? I am not ready? He looked down again. *More blood!*

Merlin's stomach dropped. *Elanor!*

"Bedwyr!" Merlin shouted, refusing to leave Gwynevere alone.

Gwynevere threw her head back into a blood-curdling shriek.

"*BEDWYR!*"

Bedwyr burst through the doors, shouting words Merlin's buzzing head could not interpret. His lips went numb, and white sparks danced in his eyes.

Stay present, Merlin commanded himself, shaking his head against the dread gathering inside him. His knees felt weak, but he refused to let them buckle.

Another scream shot ice through Merlin's blood. Gwynevere's face drained of color, and she collapsed. Merlin stood in a stupor, tossing his hands through his hair.

Bedwyr's voice pierced through Merlin's panic. "What are you doing? Help her!"

Merlin shook his head and knelt beside Gwynevere. A lump clogged his throat, but he couldn't swallow it down. His heart was beating too fast. He stuttered to Bedwyr, "G-Get the midwife. Arthur. Quick."

"Gwen?" Elanor called to her daughter, who skipped along through the newly grown grass inside the thicket. Her giggles brightened the morning sunshine that beamed through the branches. "Come and look at what I found."

Gwendolen leapt over some twigs to Elanor's side. "What you find, Muma?"

"Look," Elanor said, kneeling over a freshly bloomed patch of yellow flowers, mingled with small white clover blossoms. "Soon there will be enough for us to make flower crowns. There were two little girls in Dyved that loved to make crowns with me." Elanor smiled as she thought of them. "They are both probably much bigger now." She picked a flower and laid it on Gwendolen's palm. "Careful, do not crush it. It is your father's and my favorite flower. Primrose. Smell it."

Gwendolen lifted it up to her nose with a grin and blew out through her mouth instead of sucking in with her nose. "Mmmm! That smells nice."

Elanor chuckled. "Not like that. Like this." She demonstrated by lifting her hand with Gwendolen and breathed, pulling air through her nose while keeping her mouth tightly shut.

Gwendolen gave it another go, nearly blowing the flower out of her hand. "Mmmm!"

Elanor giggled, conceding to her daughter's inability.

"Your turn," Gwendolen said, lifting the now wilted flower to Elanor's nose.

Elanor inhaled deeply, then reached for another. A warm, numb sting shot through her fingertips as they grazed the stem. Elanor rubbed them, puzzled, then reached again. The tingling surged up her arm, engulfing her body like a wave. Her blood felt constricted, like her body was falling asleep. Before she could comprehend what was happening, she suddenly collapsed.

"Muma!"

Elanor's cheek hit the ground, but she felt nothing. She saw the forest debris, Gwendolen's frantic face, but they seemed distant, like echoes of a fading dream. She wanted to cry out to Gwendolen, but her lips refused to work.

Samara ran to them. "She-sh-she is turning blue." Her words echoed, sounding jumbled inside Elanor's mind. She was lifted from the ground, and the sunlit flashing between the boughs above blinded her sight. An ever increasing swish blared inside her head, coupled with the pulses of a heartbeat. Red and pink light fluttered over her vision. She struggled to breathe or form a single thought.

She found herself lifted onto Gwyliwr's massive palm. The dragon curled her claws, cradling Elanor like a fragile treasure. "E-El-Elan-n-nor." The dragon's deep and resonant voice shattered the silence around her.

She fought through the haze, narrowing her eyes upon the dragon's giant nose. Gwyliwr turned her head, her large, brilliant eye observing Elanor closely.

"Elanor," the dragon beckoned again, more clearly this time.

Elanor's eyes flickered, seeing the worried faces of Samara, Cilaen and Peredur beside her. She still could not speak, but her senses were coming back to life.

The dragon spoke to her concerned friends. "All my magic must be concentrated on Elanor now. This cottage and glen is no longer protected. If anyone were to come—I cannot hold them back. Elanor is slipping out of time. Something is wrong. I am struggling to hold onto her."

"Why is she so gray?" Samara asked, throwing a blanket over Elanor.

"She is dying," the dragon replied. "I can only hold her here as long as her heart still beats."

"What can be done to save her?" Cilaen asked, anxiousness coloring his voice.

"It is in the hands of the ones delivering her into this world."

"She is being born?" Adhan said, her face wavering above Elanor's.

Somewhere, far away, Elanor could hear Gwendolen crying. She wanted to reach for her. Comfort her. There was nothing she could do; nothing but hope she lived.

Gwynevere's agonized screams tore through Merlin's senses, reverberating in his skull. The midwife hustled, working to stop Gwynevere's hemorrhaging and deliver the child. Arthur's face turned pale in horror. The midwife's dire remarks hung in the air like a curse, alluding to the death of both mother and child.

The metallic smell of blood had never disturbed Merlin more than at this moment. He couldn't leave knowing the situation was hanging by a thread's hope, but instinct dared him to run.

She cannot die, he repeated to himself. His eyes, once again, captured the blood that streaked the floor from the window to the bed.

"She's fading," the midwife warned. Gwynevere's once-piercing screams dwindled into whimpers, and her heaving chest slowed. Her lips were white against her damp skin. The midwife glanced sullenly up at Arthur. "I must reach in and adjust the child if there is any hope of delivery. It will cause the queen immense pain."

"Whatever you need to do. Please, just save my wife and child."

Merlin's heart clenched as Gwynevere's eyes rolled up into her head. Her chin and limbs violently trembled.

The exhausted midwife shook her head. "The wee babe may already be lost. I must get it out if we are to save the queen." She looked to Arthur for permission to proceed. "It may be too late for the qu—"

"No," Arthur shouted, his fists clenched at his sides. "This cannot be." His eyes begged Merlin to tell him something different.

Merlin stood speechless, his blood ice-cold. What was there to be done?

What do I do?

He desperately called to the Great God.

We need your help? We need something that will help? Anything?

He waited, hoping to hear a direction. Nothing.

"All of this will have been for nothing if they die," Merlin declared, jumping into action. He had been waiting to use his magic, hoping for a sign that he should. There was no more time to waste. He sprinted across the room, laying his hands upon Gwynevere's body. Her languid eyes peered at him beneath her lashes. Already, her dilated pupils appeared lost and far away. The green had faded, almost black against her ashen cheeks.

No, no! his spirit cried. *Not Gwynevere—not Elanor.* Dread curled its claws into his gut. Tears flooded down his cheeks. *No!*

He closed his eyes, calling forth his magic, and imagined the silver stream of the forest lapping over his feet. "I am not alone," he whispered to himself. "I am not alone."

Magic burst gold in his eyes, and he pressed his hands into Gwynevere's chest. "Byddwch fyw ac nid marw—Bywyd!" He pressed harder. He was not about to lose them. "Bywyd!"

Another pulse radiated through his fingertips into Gwynevere. Sweat beaded on his brow; all his strength fled into his magic.

Gwynevere's eyes suddenly brightened. She launched up on her elbow and yelled, "Save my baby!"

The midwife plunged her finger in to reach for the baby. Gwynevere screeched, and to Merlin, her wail was a haunting melody, drowning out the specter of death that had loomed over them. Hope rekindled within him as she howled. Arthur gripped Gwynevere's hand, his knuckles bone-white. His other hand wrenched her sleeve.

Merlin continued to use his magic, focusing with all his might. "Byddwch fyw ac nid marw."

With a final yank, the baby came headfirst onto the bloodied blankets. Gwynevere sighed, heavy with relief, and collapsed back onto the cushion.

Everyone held their breath, awaiting a cry. The midwife, now tearful, ignored the baby. "I must save the mother," she muttered, almost too timid to hear. Her blood-soaked hands remained steadfast, working on Gwynevere who lay unconscious. "She is still bleeding."

Fear stole away Merlin's short moment of relief. Reluctantly, he lifted his gaze beyond Gwynevere's leg. There before his eyes lay a tiny baby girl, lifeless and blue.

"No!" he cried, grabbing the baby up in his arms. In a panic, he found a clean blanket and quickly wrapped the infant's slack limbs within the folds. "No." He gasped, rubbing his hand over the baby's chest. He lifted the tiny body to his ear and closed his eyes, listening.

No heartbeat—nor sound of breath could be heard.

The dragon's head lifted suddenly.

"What is it?" Cilaen jerked his eyes up to meet the dragon's, then back down at Elanor. Her pale skin deepened into a grayish-blue. He placed his hand to Elanor's throat, feeling for a pulse. Her chest did not lift with breath. Cilaen's eyes flared with alarm. "Is she—is she—" Seized with terror, he shook Elanor's shoulders. "Dragon!" His pitch heightened. "Do something!"

"Get back," Gwyliwr thundered. She hardly waited for Cilaen to stumble clear before white flames burst from her mouth.

The exploding fire sent Cilaen crashing onto his back. The wind escaped his lungs, and he heaved for breath. Coughing, he sat up, clutching his chest. His eyes rounded even wider at the scene before him.

A white orb of fire spun in the dragon's palm, surrounding Elanor.

At the sound, Peredur and Adhan dashed beside him. Samara stood back, pulling a frightened Gwendolen into the cottage. Her cries were barely audible above the whirling flames.

"What is happening?" Peredur shouted above the fire's roar.

"She—" Cilaen gulped. Needles of adrenaline prickled his skin with sweat. "She was not breathing. She had no pulse." He stood to his feet, rubbing the back of his flushed neck.

"What?" Adhan cried, throwing her hands over her mouth.

"Dragon!" Cilaen called, drawing closer. He lifted his hands, mystified that no heat emanated from the swirling sphere of fire. "What is happening to her?"

"I am holding her still," Gwyliwr said. "Time cannot touch her."

Chapter Thirty-Three

"But—" Cilaen gasped. "Is she dead?"

"Yes," the dragon said with a quaver in her voice.

Cilaen's heart dropped. "*No!* That cannot be true!"

"Destinies can be altered because of choice."

"Whose choice? Why is this happening? Can you not bring her back?"

"I am trying. All I can do is hold on to her, and hope. The infant has not been born alive."

Tears were awash in Adhan's eyes. "If the infant is dead—that means Elanor has never been."

The dragon shook her head. "The *magic of time* is complicated." Winds stirred, rustling the trees. Clouds darkened the skies. "The magic I steward was given by one who dwells outside of time. He sees all, and it was *He* who gave me the grace to bestow such magic over Merlin and Elanor. All that has happened since Elanor came cannot be erased. Not our memories. Not Arthur. Not Gwendolen."

Adhan gasped, turning toward the cottage where Gwendolen still cried. Stormy gales strengthened, and the three of them huddled together.

The dragon went on, "Time does not work that way. And since that is true— something more is meant to happen. The infant *must live*," Gwyliwr said, almost as if convincing herself. "Though Elanor—*this* Elanor, may not."

"I do not understand," Cilaen said through gritted teeth. "She cannot die. There is too much that is meant to be done. She is meant to have a life outside these times of evil. To have peace with her family. This *cannot* be."

Elanor was Cilaen's family. He chose to see her as a sister a long time ago. She brought a sense of home that no one else ever had. He dreaded thinking she might be taken from him.

"I cannot explain to you why things are or why things happen. You must *trust,* Cilaen, son of Caden."

Cilaen had not heard the name of his father since he was a child. Bitter tears pooled in his glaring eyes, and the muscles in his jaw twinged. "How do you know my father's name?"

"I hold time." Her words echoed inside his mind, making his body tremble. "I can see you, and I can see him. You wonder why he was taken from you, and why you were left with a mother who fell into despair. She did not care for you as a mother should have, and you *despise* her for it."

Cilaen wiped a fallen tear from his cheek and peeked at Peredur, embarrassed that the dragon had exposed his hidden pain in front of all of them. Especially the battle chieftain.

Adhan's hands curled over his shoulder, and he shrugged them off.

"How is this about me?" Cilaen hollered, anger blazing through his blood. "Elanor lies within your hand, fading from this world, and you prod at me. Why?"

"Because it is time. The *magic of time* is pressing through. Your father hears your pain, and he calls to you."

"What?" Cilaen snapped, the wind stealing the sound of his voice.

A breathy voice called on the wind. *"Cilaen."*

Through the windblown trees an apparition approached. A translucent Cymbrogi appeared—garbed for battle. His flaxen curls tousled in a knot on the back of his head. Brown eyes set above high cheekbones, and a golden-brown braided beard covered his chin.

Cilaen went slack-jawed as the recognition dawned. He hadn't seen his father since he was a small child. He had forgotten what he looked like. Only fleeting images remained in his memory. The ghost hovered before him with forlorn eyes and a tender smile. In awe, Cilaen extended his fingers to touch him, and they fell through his father's discarnate frame.

He swallowed, throat suddenly thick. "Why did you have to die? You could have stayed. You did not have to fight. We could have been a family."

The Cymbrogi frowned as he traced his fingers along Cilaen's cheek, sending cold tingles across his skin. He hated that he could not feel the warmth of his father's fingers. It felt like a terrible trick.

"Cilaen!" The voice pierced through his heart, unleashing his caged emotions.

He let out a furious scream and leapt at the ghost, hoping to feel him, touch him, somehow. To his surprise, he collided against a warm, round shoulder. Still afraid to believe, Cilaen clamped his eyes shut, then wrapped his arms around the torso, and squeezed. Hot tears streamed down his face. The ghost's arms embraced him, enveloping him in warmth.

Cilaen found himself beating his fists into his father's back, screaming out his pent-up agony. All the sorrow came hurtling forth—all the pain he had buried and ignored.

"I miss you, Father," Cilaen sobbed into the ghost's chest. "I wish you had not left me. I needed you. I wanted a father." His confession unexpectedly soothed his heart, and he gripped the figure even tighter. The comfort of his solidity healed something broken in Cilaen. In that moment, he felt like he had never been alone— as if his father had been with him all along, watching over him.

The wind quieted, and so did Cilaen's tension. His sobs turned into steady breaths.

The wild flickering flames of the dragon's magic seemed muted now that the wind had ceased. Cilaen leaned back and looked up. Before him was not his father, but Peredur. He gaped, befuddled, but then a wave of understanding blew through his mind. A gentle smile curved at the edges of Cilaen's lips.

Peredur smiled back, and he gripped Cilaen's shoulders with an affirming squeeze.

Cilaen shook his head. "Why were you here?"

Peredur's eyes glistened. "It seemed that you needed me to be."

Cilaen chuckled softly, then rubbed his sleeve across his face, drying his eyes. New understanding flickered in his heart. He glanced back through the fiery sphere at Elanor, and he said, "I will trust."

SACRIFICE

"No, no, no, no," Merlin whispered, rubbing the baby's chest. "Breathe, you must breathe."

He had dreaded this outcome. It haunted the back of his mind. He never assumed everything would go smoothly. Now Gwynevere and the infant's lives were hanging in the balance. He couldn't bear to imagine how this might be affecting *his* Elanor.

"Gah, breathe! Hanadlu," he murmured, kindling his magic. "Hanadlu! Come on—breathe, breathe." His mind spun, and the dread tightening his stomach kept him from harnessing his magic properly. His heart beat wildly at each glimpse of the blue lifeless baby. He lifted his trembling hand to his eyes, narrowing them to focus. He had no time—no time to waste.

Great God, you must help me. Please.

Then suddenly, another thought occurred to him. *What if this baby is not Elanor? What if the dragon was wrong?* He didn't want this baby to die, but the thought brought him a measure of relief. *If this was Elanor, she would have lived.*

Merlin gently took a corner of the baby's blanket, draped it over her face, and laid the little bundle on the floor. Then, rising from his knees, he turned aside to help save Gwynevere.

"*Yes—yes,*" a voice soothed inside his mind. "*There was nothing to be done for the little one.*"

Merlin nodded, feeling justified for walking away, but then halted. This voice, though comforting, felt unfamiliar. He peeked over his shoulder at the dead baby he had left lying on the floor.

"*She is already dead. You cannot bring her back to life.*"

Merlin inhaled sharply, squeezing his eyes shut. What was the hesitation? Stilling his mind, he reached for discernment. *What if I am wrong, and this is Elanor? Something needs to be done.*

"*What if you are right, and you sacrifice saving Gwynevere—whose life is fading?*"

Out of the shadow of his questioning thoughts, a bright, forceful voice boomed. *"MERLIN! Elanor is dying. There is no time."*

Merlin snapped his eyes open and spun back toward the child. He did not know who the bearer of the first voice was, but he did know the sound of the Great God. He cradled the infant in his arms, feeling strengthened now that he had heard the Great God's voice, and he whispered into his spirit, "What do I do? My magic has not worked."

"You must surrender a piece of yourself, and she will be saved."

"What does that mean?" He shook his head, struggling to understand. But then, a memory sprang into his mind. He remembered taking the pendant he had given Elanor and transferring a small part of his bardic magic into it. It was a specific magic. He did not know it at the time, but it flowed from the magic of *the song*. He desired that a piece of him would always be with her. However, that small act of love had cost him. A portion of his power never returned. At the time, it felt like a minor thing to do.

The voice of the Great God spoke through his thoughts. *"That song belongs to me, Merlin. Not you. It is much bigger than the ancient rhyme of promise I gave your father. He may have handed it to you, but it is not yours to keep. You must give it to her."*

Merlin's mind reeled. What was he without his magic? It would be a sacrifice of all he had ever known.

A sacrifice worth making to save Elanor's life.

Merlin held the child to his chest. Without hesitation, he pulled from deep within. Golden light enveloped him—all his magic focused on the baby. A wordless hum reverberated from his lips, growing louder—lilting higher. It felt as though he had opened a door to his heart. It took all the willpower he possessed to reach in and take out the magic that dwelled there. Not just a small piece like before, but the entirety of it. Only the whole of his life could be exchanged for hers.

"Cymryd fi i gyd," he sang. The unusual lyrics fell from his lips. "Cymryd y cyfan. Duw dwi'n ymddiried ynot ti. Cymryd fi i gyd." Merlin's ears rang with the foreign words. A chorus of voices sang along in agreement. Their faces illuminated in his mind—his ancestors—the ones who had gone before him.

The magic pulled from him. It writhed with excruciating pain, refusing to let go. He pressed not only part of his being into the baby's heart, but the essence of his very spirit. He strained harder, sweat dripping from his brow. His strength waned, but he knew it was not done. The yellow light surrounding him like a halo radiated brighter and brighter. Finally, the last of his magic drained from him.

He hunched over the child—his song now a whisper. "Cymryd fi i gyd."

And his light went out.

Merlin exhaled, his body sagging with fatigue as he bent over the child. His life was slipping away. The baby lay unmoving, cradled within his arms. His hope ebbed and his breathing slowed, but then a radiant light shone from the corner of his eye. He turned, and Arthur's sword, Caledfwlch, hovered in the air beside him.

"The song," Merlin murmured. With his last bit of strength, he gritted his teeth and reached for the sword's hilt. There was a flash like lightning. The searing light cut like a blade, severing him from his remaining magic. Merlin screamed in agony, clinging to the child.

Then it was finished. Merlin dropped the sword with a loud *clang*. He pulled the baby away from his chest. Her skin was flushed with pink, and she squirmed, alive in his arms. Her tiny eyes peeked open. Golden light glowed inside them. Through weakening breaths, he laid the baby down onto the floor. His vision blurred. All faded and he crumpled beside the baby.

Cilaen held his knees to his chest, leaning against the side of the dragon's palm. His head bobbed, fighting sleep, but he resisted. Should anything change, he wanted to be ready, so he forced himself to stay awake even though it was late into the night.

The women were in the cottage trying to get Gwendolen to sleep. Keeping her away from her mother seemed to help ease her distress, but Cilaen could still hear her whimpers. Peredur lay asleep outside, wrapped in furs by an orange flickering fire. Cilaen kept the fire stoked for him, grateful he had a task to keep him awake.

A creaking sound lifted Cilaen's head from his arms. The cottage door eased open with faint yellow light escaping through the widening slit. Samara stepped out from the doorway; her face illuminated against the white of the dragon's swirling fire. She looked like one of the *ellyllon* of the otherworld—a fair people of golden light adorned in flowers. How he wished he could line her hair with the petals befitting such ethereal creatures. He loved how the magical fire highlighted the end of her nose, and shadowed her eyelashes against her lids.

Samara's presence heated Cilaen's cheeks. He quickly turned his face away, hiding his blush as she sat next to him on the grass. Even in the darkness of night, he worried she could see. He had never told her how he felt. There were moments that made him think she felt the same way, but their duties to others always separated them. He never felt it was the right time, but being here in the forest over these long cold days made his heart grow fonder. He struggled to steer his thoughts away from her. Moments of freedom, like when he danced with her, were so fleeting. By the next sunrise, he was too afraid to pursue anything more.

"Are you alright?" she asked, her sweet voice drawing his eyes back toward her.

"I cannot sleep. Not with Elanor like this. What if in the night, she revives in need of a healer's hand? Or worse. What if she truly is—"

Samara shuddered. "Do not even say it. I *refuse* to believe it."

"I could not have her die alone," Cilaen said, shaking his head. "I feel if I stay close, it will keep the worst from happening somehow."

Samara's cold, delicate fingers slid over Cilaen's hand that rested on the ground between them. His heart skipped a beat, and he swallowed his nerves, hoping she did not sense how anxious her touch made him feel.

"I understand," Samara said. Her soothing voice loosened Cilaen's shoulders, and he smiled, cupping his hand over hers. "I have never met anyone like Elanor. She was the first to make me feel like I was more than a servant. She would tell me things." Samara brushed away a tear. "She did not just make me feel like a listening ear, she made me feel like her friend."

"You are her friend."

Samara nodded, peering over her shoulder at Elanor, who remained lifeless and still within the sphere. Samara turned back; her uneasy eyes drifted up to the dragon.

"Do not worry"—Cilaen nudged her arm—"the dragon is safe."

"I saw what happened with you and the dragon earlier."

Cilaen sucked in a sharp breath at her words. Embarrassment prickled his skin, and he jerked his head and hand away, wrapping his arms around his knees once more. With all his might, he wished Samara had not seen what had happened. It made him out to be a weak *idiot*—like a child and not a man. That was the one part of his life he preferred to keep hidden. The one part that made him feel lost.

"I am sorry," Samara was quick to say. "I did not mean to pry. I just wanted to say—"

Here it comes. The last thing I want is her pity.

"That I admire your strength."

What? He turned to her with a furrowed brow.

"Cilaen, every situation you have ever been in, I have watched you face it head on without fear."

"Really?" He couldn't hide his grin. His heart beamed. After what the dragon exposed, she saw strength?

"You are always there—with Merlin and Elanor, supporting them."

This is what she thought? He had never thought of himself as anyone of strength. He was just in the background, doing what needed to be done.

"Cilaen, you believe when others doubt. That is what I like best."

What she likes best? His heart beat faster, and he wished he had never let go of her hand.

"Even now—you support her."

"I guess that makes two of us," Cilaen said, boldly retaking her hand, hoping she would reciprocate. "You came out here in the dead of the cold season for Elanor."

Now Samara's delicate cheeks blushed. Their fingers entwined, and Cilaen leaned closer, enjoying her warmth. He wished for the strength to tell her more. He wanted to tell her that he thought about her every day and looked forward to just one glance from her eye.

If only the days were not so evil, and we had peace. There would be more time for this.

Bitter regret rose within him, stealing his joy. Elanor had to live. This couldn't be the end of her. All remaining hope rested on Arthur and Merlin. Otherwise, it might be the end for them all.

Cilaen set his jaw and said, "I have seen Elanor die. An arrow straight through her chest. I remember feeling so helpless. I was a healer, with a full bag of medicines, and I could do *nothing*. Her lung was punctured—she was suffocating, and all I could do was sit there. Merlin looked at me as if I were his only hope, and still I had nothing." He shook his head, pushing back the rising emotions. "I *will not* let her go this time. I must be ready to do something—*anything*."

"I will be ready with you," Samara said, squeezing his hand and meeting his gaze.

The light from the fire highlighted her tender brown eyes. Her perfect lips parted, like she was anticipating Cilaen's next words. Oh, how he wanted to kiss them. Even her sweet fragrance, like honeysuckle, drew him to her.

No, he thought, shifting his gaze to the fire. *This is not the time. We have been friends—close friends since Elanor came. Helping each other.* He did not want to confuse her attentions. Oh, but he wanted her. The comfort of her in this moment only made his heart yearn for more.

"Cilaen," she beckoned, her fingers moving up his arm.

He faced her, and he could no longer resist the allure of her eyes. With a hesitant pause, he leaned closer, his lips nearing hers. Her fingers tickled the side of his cheek, and just as her lips brushed his, the sphere of white fire encircling Elanor unfurled and went out.

Merlin woke, curling his fingers into his palms. He felt different. His eyelids slowly opened to a silent world. His body ached and his head split. The cold stone of the floor pressed against his bones. The pain radiating through his body confirmed he was not dead.

I am alive, he thought, turning his head.

The baby was no longer there.

Is my magic gone? he wondered, knowing he had given the child everything. He palmed his chest, feeling his breath freely moving in and out of his lungs. Scrunching his face, he tried to recollect where he was.

"Is the child alive?" he murmured, almost unconsciously. "Gwynevere!" His eyes flashed wide. The fear of her death forced him up, and his blurry eyes captured someone on his knees in front of him. "Arthur?" He saw his blond hair first. Merlin rubbed his eyes and looked again. Arthur was on his knees, clutching the hilt of Caledfwlch.

Arthur stared at the sword dumbfounded, his eyes red from weeping.

"What happened?" Merlin prodded, almost afraid to hear the answer.

"The sword—" Arthur paused, appearing still in shock. "It burst with light." His gaze drifted to meet Merlin's, then he swallowed hard. More tears rolled from his eyes, and he said, "It hovered to your side from where I had it kept." He pointed to the corner. "When you touched it, it healed them."

"Them?" Merlin snapped his head toward the bed. The midwife sat gasping on the floor at the foot of the bed, a rag held to her forehead.

"I could hear it," Arthur muttered. "It rang in my ears."

Merlin scrambled to his feet. The world spun. He stumbled over to the bedside, blinking his eyes to properly capture the scene. The queen lay breathing, holding a rosy-cheeked infant against her chest. Merlin smacked his head, collapsing once more to the floor. He looked over and saw Bedwyr clinging to the doorframe.

"I saw," Bedwyr stuttered, his eyes round with awe. "I saw—light."

"It was like *the song,* but it was more," Arthur said, drawing his finger down the flat of the blade.

Merlin sighed. Everything was alright. A chuckle bubbled up through his chest. Relieved tears leaked out of his eyes. Arthur laughed too, and then Bedwyr joined them.

Bedwyr stumbled toward Arthur. "I feel it still in the air. It is like magic."

Arthur nodded. "Tangible. It is *Him.* The Great God."

Bedwyr turned to Merlin. "Brother, are you alright? I thought you had died." He knelt, placing his hand on Merlin's shoulder.

"Merlin, you saved them," Arthur said, gasping. "You kindled *the song.*"

"I did." Merlin held his hands in front of his face, scrunching his brow. "Or at least, it flowed through me." A feeling of loss swirled in his stomach, knowing what he had done. But as he looked at the baby, he was comforted, seeing her tiny palm resting on her mother's chest.

What happened to me? I thought I had died.

He did feel different, yet not entirely changed. Something else happened when he gave all his magic to save her life. His spirit had flooded out of his body into the baby, until he touched the sword. With Caledfwlch within his grasp, the transference was cut, and something new took place. Something that was outside of him, and had nothing to do with him, or his magic.

With a steady breath, he searched for his magic, part of him fearing that nothing would happen. But he felt it kindling inside him. His magic *was* there. Wind swirled throughout the room, tousling their clothes and hair before dissipating.

"What was that?" Bedwyr asked, his eyes searching the room.

Merlin squeezed his hand into a fist and breathed a sigh of relief. He was willing to surrender it all, and in doing so, he had been given it back. All of it. And there was something more. Even in kindling his power, in this small way, he felt it. It was as if his magic were held within the arms of one more powerful. The same way he had felt it when he woke the giant in the Forest of Goll.

"Bedwyr." Merlin faced him with a contrite expression. "Please forgive me. I never meant to—"

Bedwyr waved his hand. "We have bigger monsters to slay."

"We do indeed. But you are my friend—my brother. A man of honor. I should have never questioned that."

"Love can make you lose your mind."

"Yes, it can."

"I never doubted you, brother. Though I did want to pound you."

Merlin chuckled. Another moist tear sprang free. "I wanted to pound you too."

Bedwyr punched his arm.

Chapter Thirty-Four

"Ow!"

Merlin rubbed his sore bicep and smirked. He pushed Bedwyr back, then they both rolled with laughter. The bit of levity breathed a lighthearted air into the tension they'd all faced over the past few hours.

Merlin's eyes shifted to Arthur, who got up from the floor and lumbered to his wife's side. He pressed his forehead against Gwynevere's, squeezing his eyes shut. His hand rested on the baby. And as tears wetted Arthur's face, Merlin heard him whisper, "I will *never* let you go."

# FLIGHT TO THE FUTURE

"What is happening?" Cilaen asked the dragon as he scrambled onto her palm and rested his ear upon Elanor's chest. His eyes widened. He pressed his ear back down again, listening.

"She is not dead," Gwyliwr said, nudging Cilaen aside and knocking him off her palm.

He jumped to his feet. "I can barely hear her heartbeat," he said with panic in his voice.

The others heard the noise and woke, stumbling out to see what was happening.

The dragon closed her eyes and curled her head, resting the bridge of her snout upon Elanor. "Her heart beats, but she is somewhere else."

With a rising edge in his voice, Cilaen asked, "What does *that* mean?"

"It means"—the dragon lifted her head, seeming disturbed—"that the baby has lived."

"Then why does Elanor not wake?"

A tremulous grumble vibrated through Gwyliwr's throat. "There is nothing more I can do."

"What do you mean?" Adhan asked, rushing to Cilaen's side.

"My magic has done all that it is meant to. Elanor cannot exist in two places. One will live and the other will fade."

"Dragon!" Cilaen shouted. "I cannot accept that. Elanor *must* live."

"But she did live," Gwyliwr said, rolling her taloned hand over and setting Elanor down onto the cold grass.

"You just said—"

"*ENOUGH!*" the dragon roared. The burst of her breath sent Cilaen and Peredur onto their backs.

Liquid pooled in Cilaen's tear ducts. "What of the prophecy?" he demanded, red-faced. "She is one of the three. It is her destiny to destroy the enemy."

Gwendolen's whimpering cries carried from the cottage's darkened doorway, capturing their attention. The dragon coiled at the sound of her sobs.

With a calm air, Peredur lifted a staying hand toward Gwyliwr. "We have asked a lot of you, dragon. Your magic has protected Elanor and saved Arthur. We do not mean to demand from you—but is there truly *nothing* else left that you can do to save her?"

A gigantic tear rolled over the dragon's glistening eye and splashed to the grass. "I had my part to play, and I have done so. I—I can only do as the master instructs. I—" Gwyliwr slowly backed away from them. "I have other things I must do." She flourished her golden wings. "I must leave you now."

"What?" Cilaen stormed toward her. "You cannot leave! We still need your help."

Gwyliwr ignored him, turning her head before leaping into the air. Her wings caught the wind, and with a heavy flap, she rose higher and higher—flying from their sight.

Cilaen shook his head, his brows scrunched tight. Hopelessness crawled through his gut like a snake. Elanor lay on the ground lifeless, reminding Cilaen of his own inability. He was a healer. Why was it that when it mattered most, he could do nothing?

Adhan and Samara rushed to Elanor, and with careful tenderness, they carried her to the cottage.

Cilaen turned his listless eyes to Peredur and pleaded, "She is not dead. She lives. There must be something we can do."

Peredur's gaze hardened like steel. "A Cymbrogi never surrenders the fight." With that, he marched to collect his saddle. His horse waited nearby. He heaved the saddle over his horse and started buckling it from underneath.

"Where are you going?" Cilaen asked, chasing after him.

"Merlin—" Peredur grumbled, his brow set heavy with purpose. "Merlin must be told."

Cilaen grabbed Peredur's wrist, stopping his preparations. "I will go. L-Let me go."

"I am a more able rider."

"Please—let me do this."

"No." Peredur shook Cilaen's hand away. "I know you want to help, but you *must* stay. You are the healer—she may need you."

That wasn't good enough. There was nothing he could do for her here. "Peredur, I can do it—"

"No!" Peredur shoved Cilaen in the chest with a stern glare, then turned and mounted his horse.

Cilaen pursed his lips. Angry tears welled in his eyes.

Without another word, Peredur clicked, "Yah!" He launched his heels into his horse's flanks and disappeared into the forest.

Cilaen cursed, grinding his foot into the ground. Frustration fumed in his thoughts. He hated feeling useless, and wished more than anything that he was the one riding to the Palisade. To just sit and wait—

"*Grrhhaa!*" he grumbled, whacking a tree as hard as he could with his open palm.

Frustrated, he tossed his arms over his head. His hand stung, so he clenched it into a fist. He paced back and forth, then caught Samara's gaze. She stared at him from the cottage doorway, her brows curving with concern.

He couldn't handle her compassion. Not right now. He stormed away from her into the thicket.

Arthur never thought he could feel so complete. He stared adoringly at Gwynevere as she snuggled their baby into her arms. Her green eyes sparkled and her fresh satin braids cascaded over her shoulders. With a serene smile, she ran her fingers over the baby's velvet, dark wispy hair.

The child's irresistible sweet coos tugged at Arthur, and he settled next to Gwynevere, wrapping his arm around them. He reached for his daughter's tiny palm, and she snatched his finger, squeezing it tightly.

Maybe they could stay like this forever. In the back of his mind, he knew the baby might be taken away, but maybe not now. Maybe they had a little while. A family like this was something he had always longed for and never truly had. He never had a mother or father to hold him close. But now, having this, replaced that missing piece.

"I hope the time for her to go never comes," Gwynevere whispered, her eyes forlorn.

"Shhh," Arthur hushed. He didn't want to talk about it. Fear wrestled like a leviathan within him, threatening to sink his heart like a doomed ship. And so, he swallowed down all the biting thoughts that tried to poison the moment. Osian and the coming war fought for his attention. He hurled it aside, holding to the false hope that it could all disappear and refocused on the little blue eyes that stared wholeheartedly at Gwynevere's face.

Why do we have to lose her?

His rationale reminded him that it was Elanor sent through time that made this moment possible. Images of Elanor flooded his mind—memories of the first day they met. But these remembrances did nothing to soothe his heart.

How can I willingly surrender my child? How could Gwynevere?

His heart ached to think of what it would do to her.

Merlin knocked on the queen's chamber door. Grief gripped his chest. He had taken a baby away before—Arthur—but this time would be different. He squeezed his satchel, thinking of the letter he had just placed inside it. The letter for David—the man who would raise Elanor.

Merlin was ready to go, and already wore a cloak with everything he would need for his journey. He had hoped there would be more time for Arthur and Gwynevere to hold their child, but they could not delay a moment more.

Arthur opened the door. He gasped upon seeing Merlin's appearance. "No. Please not yet."

Merlin stepped into the room and reluctantly met Gwynevere's eyes. Her bottom lip quivered as she pulled the baby into her chest.

"I am sorry—" His throat clamped with emotion. "Peredur has just come. El-Elanor is dying."

Gwynevere peered down at her child.

Merlin's heart sank. "She may yet be saved if the baby—"

Gwynevere burst into sobs.

"The magic of time is already upon me," Merlin said, feeling the need to hurry deep in his bones. "I know where I am to take her. The dragon will meet me there."

Arthur's eyes were awash, floating in pools of unreleased tears. He opened his mouth to speak but halted. Then, appearing to find his words, he murmured, "There is no way to prepare for a moment like this." He turned to Gwynevere. "I would do *anything* to save the life of my daughter. Even this."

Gwynevere's eyes were locked with his and she agreed with a slight nod.

Merlin approached to take the child, but Arthur put his hand out to stop him. "No." He shook his head, sniffing in a tear. "Let me."

Gwynevere pleaded to Arthur, "Wait—just wait." A deep wail escaped, and she lifted the baby to her lips. "I love you," she whispered to the child and cradled her head against her cheek one last time.

Arthur held out his hands, and Merlin's heart broke as Gwynevere instinctively held her baby tighter. Her trembling hands betrayed her as she handed the baby over to Arthur.

Arthur kissed the child. "I know you. You saved me. I wish I did not have to let you go." Arthur sucked in sharply, letting more tears fall. With a hard swallow, he placed the baby into Merlin's arms, his fingers lingering on top of the swaddle.

"I am so sorry," Merlin said. "I wish I did not have to."

"You must. This is how it needs to be done. She will soon be back in our arms—delivered from the cottage in the forest."

Merlin cringed on the inside at Arthur's words. He hoped that was true. There was no guarantee that taking the baby away meant that Elanor would live. But it had to be done—on the chance that she would be saved.

Merlin gave a hesitant nod, then turned to leave. The rising wails from Gwynevere clawed at his chest.

Keep moving.

He gritted his teeth. He hated taking the child away from her broken-hearted parents.

Time was of the essence. He could not turn back to look at them or else he might hesitate. He crossed over the threshold, relieved to be on the other side of the door. Arthur and Gwynevere's crying echoes haunted his ears all the way down the corridor. Biting his lip, he squeezed the baby tight. The grievous job was done. Now he had to ride full tilt to meet the dragon. The memories given by the *magic of time* led him on.

Merlin's horse pounded the ground as he held the infant close. Worry for Elanor gnawed at his thoughts. She had escaped death before, and he hoped that this time their luck had not run out.

May the Great God be with her, he beseeched, hoping with every fiber of his being that this was all part of the plan. Elanor would live and the enemy would be cast down. The Man in Blue did not save her only for her to die now. No, certainly they had overcome. This was just another obstacle in their path. They were meant to conquer this darkness together, and together they would. Maybe one day he would lose Elanor, but his heart told him it would not be this day.

Oh, how he longed for her and Gwendolen. The separation was unbearable.

Though, since surrendering his magic to save the infant, he had begun to notice a change. He was connected to Elanor in a new way. He sensed her from afar.

She is not dead yet.

He shook his head and let that truth permeate his mind.

Her source of life beat within his own. If Elanor were dead, the magical cord tying them would be broken. His life was connected to her life. This—he now realized—was where her magic had come from. *The song* that was born within him was what brought Elanor to life.

He squeezed the precious bundle to his chest. The horse's gallop jostled her, but not one cry rose from her lips. Her eyes stared at him, as if observing him. She knew him and he knew her. So strange to have Elanor within his arms, yet his connection to her seemed so far away.

Soon, he would be approaching the field where he knew the dragon waited. He needed the dragon's magic to send the child through time and live. How would it happen? Merlin was unsure. The *magic of time* had almost killed Elanor the first time. She did not have the dragon's magic then. It would have killed Arthur without his and Elanor's aid. Something would need to be done to protect the child. But what? He was certain the dragon had the answer.

He felt a *whoosh* before his cloak blew in front of him, unfurling in a strong gust. He whipped his head to the sky. The dragon soared above him. Her massive wings spread across the sky, blazing past. She soared ahead and landed. Her long talons tore into the earth as she slid to a halt.

Merlin kicked his horse, picking up his pace to meet her. She was in a hurry and so was he. He arrived breathless and carefully dismounted with the baby.

The dragon seemed distressed, shifting from one giant foot to the other. She glanced east toward the cottage, then back at Merlin. Gwyliwr made a growling gurgle. "Your little daughter. She was crying. I had to leave them. The humans—they did not have patience."

"Is Elanor alright?"

"I do not know. But I could not fix it. I can only guard Elanor." The dragon pointed with her nose, indicating the sleeping child cradled in Merlin's arms. "She is here now—not there. I could not do what the humans wanted.

"Gwyliwr—" Merlin said with gentleness, reaching his hand to her nose. She puffed through her nostrils, leaning against his palm. "I understand what must be done. Be at ease. Let us send the child to her home."

Gwyliwr's fretful growls diminished to a purr. "Yes, this is what I must do. Stand back." She lifted her head and shook like a hound shaking off water. The more she shuddered, the more the scales on her neck lifted, rattling like shells scuffing together. Then, with a final violent jerk, several scales lobbed free.

They flung off the dragon, careening in all directions. Merlin twisted away, covering the baby with his cloak. One scale barely missed them, hollowly thumping to the ground beside Merlin.

Gwyliwr ceased shaking. She ran her claws down her throat, hissing as the remaining scales flattened. Blood seeped out where the scales had come free, leaving missing chinks on her smooth elegant armor.

"Was it painful?" Merlin asked. Several golden-green scales gleamed like giant emeralds on the ground. Merlin reached down to touch the scale beside his feet. It was hard and domed like the shell of a sea turtle.

"Yes," she whimpered. "Dragon scales come free like roots pulled from the ground. But for this baby, I had to surrender a few—the hardness of my scales will be a protection. When I send her through time, she will not be harmed. Quickly"— she pointed her black talon to the scale Merlin's hand rested upon—"turn it over and place the child inside."

Merlin pushed it over, and it rolled, rocking back and forth like a shallow cradle. He placed the baby inside.

"Now grab another and place it on top."

Merlin raced to the nearest scale. It was unexpectedly light for its size. He was taken aback by its sheen and translucent quality that glittered like a precious metal. He rushed back to cap the baby inside, but hesitated. The baby lay sleeping with her small arms nestled around her head. Her tiny breaths pumped her chest up and down.

"She will be safe—I promise," the dragon reassured, leaning closer to the infant. "No *time magic* will touch her."

Merlin nodded, then settled the scale on top. They fit perfectly together, safely cocooning the baby.

The dragon launched back, her chest rounding with an inhale of fire. Merlin lifted his hands in front of his face. White flames of time encircled them. The memory reignited in his mind. The trail, the forest, and a sandy-yellow dog. The flames raced up his arms, consuming him. The dragon's fire belched forth, roaring around the capsule at his feet.

He could already hear David's voice echoing in his ears. "Brando! Brando, come on, boy!"

36

THE CALL OF THE GUARDIAN

The rush of time swirled around Merlin. Fears of uncertainty filled him, remembering how the last trip through time had cost him. He hoped there would be a way back home again.

This was how it all began. This was how Elanor would get to him in the first place.

The white flames dissipated, revealing the light of a normal afternoon in a shady forest. A warm breeze brushed past Merlin's face as he took in his new surroundings. Lush green ferns nestled beneath a grove of oak and chestnut trees. Patches of blue-violet, fluted flowers sprang over the long grass like jewels. A pebbled trail wove between the trees, and the smell of the sea trickled into his nose.

Aberystwyth, Merlin thought, remembering the views when he and Elanor drove to meet the Evanses.

He heard it again. "Brando!"

The sound of David's voice brought instant tears to Merlin's eyes. How he wished he could speak to him, throw his arms around him—rejoice at seeing him alive. But that was not why he had come. Even as he thought it, the cocoon of dragon scales appeared at his feet. With haste, he uncovered the baby and saw the sweet child sleeping contentedly as if nothing had occurred. He pulled the capsule and lid behind a nearby tree.

David's voice clamored closer.

Merlin quickly flipped open his satchel and pulled out the letter. His heart swelled remembering when David presented the parchment to him and Elanor. David's eager eyes watching him read it for the first time—it seemed like yesterday. What Merlin wouldn't give to have that moment back, even if just for Elanor.

He glanced down at the baby and slipped the letter into the folds of the almond-brown knitted blanket. With tenderness, he slipped his hands underneath the baby and lifted her up into his arms. Merlin darted his eyes around the tree, careful not to be seen. The trail was still empty. His eyes halted at a stump beside the trail—perfectly cupped to hold the baby.

That is the one.

He snuck onto the trail, over to the dead, moist stump that seemed to be lifting itself up to accept the baby. Merlin quickly laid the infant down on the mossy cushion. His heart wrenched in his chest. He didn't want to let her go. Her eyes were open and she stared up at him. Her tiny, plump arms reached toward his face.

"Elanor," he whispered. A tear dropped down his nose and onto the baby's blanket. "You get to meet your guardian. He will take good care of you." The baby's coos grew louder. "Not all your family will love you, but David will." He pressed his lips to her forehead. Her tiny hand gripped a handful of his wavy hair, making Merlin chuckle.

Woof, woof!

A yellow dog bounded around the corner of the trail, bouncing back and forth, as if begging his owner to follow.

"Brando, wait for me, boy."

Merlin's time had run out. A short moment of hesitation gripped him, but then he sprang away, escaping behind the tree where he could not be seen.

Brando's barks became more erratic.

"What is it, boy? What's got you so excited? Is there a squirrel hiding in that stump?" There was a moment's pause, and then, "Oh, my God!"

Merlin closed his eyes.

"What is this? A baby?"

Suddenly, the sensation of hot breath on his knees startled Merlin. He snapped his eyes down to see Brando. His happy tongue hung to the side, his tail wagged, and he stared up at Merlin.

With a nervous smile, Merlin patted his head and mouthed, "Go on!"

Brando only stared at him as though he had discovered a new friend.

"Brando! Brando!" David called, and the dog sprang away.

Merlin released his held breath.

"What are you doing over there? We need to find help."

Woof. Woof.

"No, I am sorry, we cannot chase squirrels. Our little nature walk has come to an end."

Merlin smiled at the youthfulness in David's voice. He dared a look around the tree. And there, with a happy dog bouncing at his heels, was a thin, youthful David. He looked every inch his son Jack. He stood there rocking the baby with the letter unfolded in his hands. He blinked in disbelief at the page as he read.

David's eyes jerked away from the letter. He gaped, looking right, then left, searching for the one who had left the letter.

Merlin pulled his head back behind the tree.

"Who is that over there?"

Blasted!

Footsteps headed in Merlin's direction. Already, Brando had darted back around the tree to give him a friendly yip. Merlin's heart leapt out of his chest.

That was when he felt it. Merlin sighed with relief. The magic of time had ignited. It was sending him home.

David walked around the tree and discovered Brando barking at nothing. He panned back and forth, certain he had seen someone.

"Hello?" he called.

No one answered.

Mystified, David peered at the baby who was starting to fuss.

"Shhh!" he soothed, patting her back and lifting her to his cheek. "Shhh! I am going to take good care of you. Certainly not going to leave you." David grimaced. "Imagine leaving a wee one like this out here."

He lifted the letter in his free hand. "How did they know my name? Or even that I would be out here?" He shouted to the trees. "Oi! Is this a joke? Someone playing a terrible trick on me?" He cocked his head, considering the strangeness of the situation.

How did this writer know about my wooden knight?

"Not even Helen or the kids know about that."

He had almost forgotten about the toy knight. It was a lost treasure from his youth that he had locked away in a box. But now—

"We need to find where you belong, erm—eh—" He read the name on the letter. "Elanor. Maybe Jack and Nancy will be happy to have another little playmate while Helen and I figure out what to do with you. S'pose we'll need to call someone." He grunted. "Helen—what is *she* going to think of all this?"

Elanor's eyes shot open. Disoriented, she lay on her back in the darkness. Dying coals slowly illuminated the room, helping her eyes adjust. She did not know where she was, but she was *not* uncertain about what she had seen. It hadn't been a dream. Like old, repressed memories, she recalled their adoring eyes as they held her. Mother. Father.

She blinked. A tear rolled from the corner of her eye into her hair. The sound of her mother's humming song floated through her mind. She had been with them for such a short time, but it was just long enough to understand who they were to her.

"I will never see them as I once did," she whispered. More warm tears streamed down her cheeks. With all her being, she wanted to return to their loving arms.

She had just forgiven Arthur for everything she held against him—for questioning his love. She had believed more in his rejection than the possibility of his acceptance. Even after she had mended things, there remained a barrier, distancing her from him.

Not anymore.

She'd seen the love in his eyes. Felt it when he lifted her tiny infant frame to his lips. He was no longer the unknown Arthur she had awakened in the future time. He had become another anchor to this world she now called home.

Merlin.

She sat up, wiping her eyes. She longed to see him too. It was over. She could be with all of them now—and with a full heart.

She gazed around the room. Her eyes settled on the faces highlighted by the dying embers. Adhan slept with Gwendolen curled up next to her. Samara lay not far from them, wrapped inside a woolen blanket.

I am in the cottage.

She sighed in relief. A smile pulled on the corners of her mouth. She discarded the blanket covering her and threw her legs over the side of the hayed platform. Her heart pumped with gladness. She couldn't resist sneaking over to Adhan and Gwendolen. Gently, she smoothed her hands over their resting arms.

Adhan woke first, jolting up with a gasp. Her reaction jostled Gwendolen awake. Gwendolen rubbed her eyes. "Muma?"

"Thank the Great God," Adhan cried, throwing her arms around Elanor—followed by Gwendolen.

Cilaen barreled through the doorway and gaped. "You are awake!"

Elanor turned toward him and shook her head with a gentle smile. "I was never asleep. I was just on the other side of time for a while."

Cilaen's shoulders dropped, and he chuckled. "That makes no sense at all. But whatever the reason is—you are alive and well. I do not need to understand. Thank the grace of the otherworld we did not lose you." He wiped his hand down his face, seeming relieved, and leaned against the doorframe. "That dragon would have had us believing you were dying."

"Gwyliwr!" Elanor jumped to her feet. She had felt the dragon holding her—keeping her safe. She wanted to see her.

She stopped in front of Cilaen and softly murmured, "I could hear you." She threw her arms around him, knocking him backward and squishing him tight. "Thank you for fighting for me." She did not know what she had done to earn his fierce loyalty, but she was glad for it.

Cilaen squeezed her back, tilting his cheek to her head. "I made a promise to Merlin a long time ago."

Elanor could only hope someday she might reciprocate all the care he had given her. She turned to Samara with a knowing smile, then looked back at Cilaen. "It might be time for you to take care of someone else."

Cilaen tensed at her words, his eyes drifting toward Samara.

Elanor glanced at Samara. "Both of you."

Gwendolen's small hand slipped inside Elanor's fingers, stealing her attention.

Elanor picked her up and held her close. Gliding her fingers through Gwendolen's hair, she whispered into the folds of her neck, "I am sorry I keep going away."

Gwendolen nuzzled a little deeper into Elanor's arms. "I knew you would come back, but I still got scared."

"Me too," Elanor said, kissing her head. She headed out the cottage door. "Let us go see the dragon."

"Gwyliwr is gone, muma," Gwendolen said, lifting her head.

"Oh?" Elanor halted. Her brows knitted. Even in the darkness she saw the vacant grass pressed flat where the dragon had lain throughout the winter.

Gwendolen rested her head back on Elanor's shoulder. Turning, Elanor glanced up the hill. The sun was beginning to rise and a faint light silhouetted the top of the hill. Without a word, she started walking up the hillside, holding Gwendolen close. The rising sun called to her. A fresh breeze blew across her face. The paradox of time had been unwound and a new freedom lifted her. She had felt tethered—pulled in different directions her whole life. But now the invisible bonds of time had been severed, and she finally felt set free.

Only one bond remained. One clear true north. It was *him*. She felt him stronger than ever. As she pressed up the hill, her heart burned for him. Her love was unfettered, urging her to run. All the things she'd had no control over were gone.

Where is he? Her heart groaned. She knew he was close and climbed even faster. Her urgency to arrive atop the hill was more than a desire to meet the rising sun. Her heart thumped in her chest. Her breath labored. Gwendolen clung tightly.

Finally, she reached the top and frantically searched the landscape. She knew he was there—not far off. She could feel his closeness.

Merlin?

She set Gwendolen on the ground. "Muma?"

"He—he is here. Somewhere." She spun in a circle, but her eyes only captured a dark naked hilltop. Her breaths pumped, recovering from the climb. Maybe she had just gotten herself excited. Maybe waking from the strange dichotomy had confused her. Maybe—

CRACK!

White flames erupted in front of her. Gwendolen squealed with fright, and she clung to Elanor's legs. "It is alright." Elanor smiled, looking ahead with expectancy. "It is only—" her words cut out as the flames dissipated.

Before Merlin had a chance to attune to his surroundings, Elanor ran to him, every piece of her heart aching for his closeness.

"Merlin!" she cried, burying her head into his chest, breathing in his warmth.

"My soul," he gasped. Elanor felt his shock melt into a joyful embrace. He snatched Elanor up into his arms and spun her around with bounding laughter. "Oh, my Great God! I have missed you." He set Elanor down—

"Da!" Merlin's head turned toward the sound of Gwendolen's sweet voice. He crumpled to his knees—Elanor still locked to his side—and flung his other arm wide for Gwendolen to rush in.

"Da! Da!" Gwendolen cried.

Elanor relished the feeling of him holding them both, pressing his lips to their heads. She inhaled his scent—like cedar and sweat—and peered up to see the relief in Merlin's eyes from having his family nestled within the safety of his arms.

She sighed. "We missed you."

Merlin lifted his head, his eyes glistening. "And I you." Without hesitation, he kissed her thoroughly. Elanor felt his eager affection in his unwillingness to let go. His joy bubbled forth into laughter, making his lips a delight to capture with more kisses.

"You are safe," he breathed, his forehead gently against hers.

She gripped his collar with one hand and stole another kiss. "You saved me. When I was born. Merlin—it was *you*." She remembered only fragments, but she knew that the magic that brought her to life was his. His face was the first her infant eyes saw. Already the memory slipped away, but in this moment, she still saw it captured in the spark of his golden eyes.

He brushed his lips against hers. "I could not have made another choice."

"I love you," she whispered with all the passion she possessed. Her first breath was because of him, and she would take every breath, for the rest of her life, alongside the rise and fall of his chest. "I want to go home. I want to see my mother and my father."

Merlin beamed back at her. "Nothing would bring me greater joy than to return their child back into their arms.

LLYONESE HAS FALLEN

Before the sun had fully risen, they loaded what little they needed for the journey and were off toward Caer Lial. Merlin drove the wagon with Cilaen beside him. The three women sat nestled in the back with Gwendolen. Merlin felt emboldened. He could see the anticipation in Cilaen's eyes too. They forged ahead, eagerly awaiting the citadel walls to come into view.

Having returned, once again through time, Merlin noticed a significant change. He felt strengthened with the baby now delivered, and he sensed a stronger clarity in Elanor. Merlin's sacrifice to save her had turned into a blessing. His magic refined like a precious metal. He and Elanor—a formidable force.

But as they approached Caer Lial, his heightened spirits quickly ebbed. Something was wrong. The encampments outside the citadel walls buzzed with activity.

"What is happening?" Cilaen asked. He shifted anxiously in his seat and scanned the fields.

Fully armored Cymbrogi broke down their tents. Some sat ready upon horseback. Others stood restless, awaiting orders in regimented lines, their spears held high.

"Yah!" Merlin shouted, and the oxen sped faster, pulling them toward the gates. He could waste no time getting to the Palisade. The armies were preparing to meet the enemy. Either the field of battle had been set, or the enemy was on the move. Arthur would be doing all he could to keep the enemy's lines from approaching the citadel. Trepidation rose inside Merlin. He could not get to the Palisade fast enough.

Seeing a regiment of Caer Lial Cymbrogi, he pulled the wagon to a halt and handed the reins to Cilaen. "Get the women to the Palisade. I must grab a horse and hasten to Arthur."

Cilaen nodded, taking the reins. Merlin leapt from the wagon.

Elanor reached after him, leaning over the wagon's side. "Where are you going?"

Merlin rushed over to her. "The war has begun."

Elanor's eyes widened.

"Cilaen will get you to the Palisade. I must go ahead. The wagon will move too slow."

Elanor nodded rigidly, her face tightening as her eyes panned the moving field. Standards and flags of different colors pointed high, flapping in the wind. Blue woad-streaked warriors faces. Some donned breastplates upon bare chests with whorls of the cerulean mud covering their skin.

Elanor appeared distressed when she turned her face back to Merlin.

"It is time to be vigilant. Do not give into fear. That is not what enables strength." Merlin gave her a fleeting kiss, then ran his fingers over Gwendolen's head. "Keep her safe," he said to his mother, knowing that whatever was happening would likely soon involve Elanor.

Adhan grabbed hold of Merlin's hand, her gaze cleaving to his for an ephemeral moment before he slipped his fingers away and then was off. Merlin glanced over his shoulder for one last passing look at his family as he rushed away. His mother's stare lingered. He rubbed his fingers together, still feeling her touch.

Merlin wished it could all be over—that this tumultuous time would never have to come. And yet, he knew without this clash, they would forever be chasing an enemy without resolution. "It *had* to come," he said to himself with determination, approaching a serving boy watering a group of horses.

"Lord Merlin!" The adolescent's wide eyes snapped to attention. His jittery fingers fumbled his grip, letting water pour from the lip of his pail.

"Boy, tell me—what is happening?"

"I am uncertain of the details," the boy replied, his pupils dilated. "The orders came an hour ago. We are preparing to leave. I heard the battle chieftains declaring that the enemy is approaching from the Southlands."

"Blasted!" Merlin cursed. "How close is the enemy? What are their numbers?"

"I am sorry, my lord. I do not know. This all happened so suddenly. I think the battle chieftains are awaiting their Cymbrogi to gather before they tell us more."

Merlin clenched his jaw, scanning the field for Peredur. There were too many warriors rushing to and fro; the field was like a blur of swarming ants. He faced the boy. "I need to take a horse."

The boy nodded, running over to gather a horse already outfitted. Scrambling back, he handed the reins to Merlin. Fear rimmed the boy's eyes.

Merlin leaned down to him. "You are amongst the strongest men in the land. Watch and learn." With a reassuring clasp on the boy's shoulder, he added, "You are a man. Do as the men do around you. And remember, you have the Great Pendragon's courage to steer you through. He will *not* lead you astray."

The boy returned a wary nod, lifting his shoulders a mite higher.

Merlin mounted the horse and galloped toward the gates. He was impatient to know what they were facing. Was the citadel in danger? He tried shaking away thoughts of Elanor and Gwendolen being in the midst of a siege. Maybe he should have left them at the cottage. They would have been safer there. Surely the enemy was far enough off and Caer Lial was not yet under that threat.

He crossed through the first gate. The townspeople bustled in the lanes, their fear tangible like thick, oozing sap. Women hustled their children indoors, while men boarded up windows. The wall surrounding the city would be their final protection. He pounded ahead to the second gate, where the Cymbrogi filled out in lines—most on horseback, but some on foot—blocking Merlin's path.

He forced his way against their tide. Many recognized the need for him to get through and yelled, "Let him through! Let him through."

The pulsing march only increased Merlin's urgency. The tumult felt like a vise of heat and dread around his gut. The more Merlin saw the disquiet on the warriors' faces rushing past him, the more agitated he became. Finally free, he bolted past the lines and up the hill to the Palisade.

"Bedwyr!" Merlin shouted, seeing him commanding a regiment of Cymbrogi who were moving horses from the stables. Merlin galloped closer. "Bedwyr!"

Bedwyr turned to him. Steel was set in his eyes.

Merlin leapt from his saddle. "What has called the armies forth?"

"Great God, I am glad you are here, brother. You are needed." The fire that needled at Bedwyr's brows softened. Quickly, he asked, "The baby? Elanor?"

"All is well. Elanor returns as we speak."

Bedwyr nodded sharply, appearing eager to move on to the task at hand. "The report came to us late last night. It was Elian—Battle Chieftain of Llyonesse."

Merlin's brows scrunched together, then lifted with the memory of the loyal Cymbrogi.

"He and a handful of others escaped to warn us."

"Escaped?"

"Llyonesse has fallen." Bedwyr sighed. "Thul's son was killed—along with everyone else we appointed there. The tower is taken. Everyone—" Bedwyr shook his head, biting his lip. "Every one of them was slain."

Merlin's eyes flared. Rage strangled his gut. "Did they not fight back?"

Bedwyr turned his face away. Merlin could tell he did not want to tell the rest of the tale.

"Bedwyr?"

"They fought"—Bedwyr's eyes shook with hateful tears—"but Osian's army came in like a black stain. Elian and a few of his men fled when they realized that the enemy…could not be killed." He paused with a knowing glare. "Our Cymbrogi cut the demon horde down time and time again, but they would rise unhindered."

"The Chalice of Life!" Merlin spat the name of the cursed cup like poison from his lips. He closed his eyes, remembering the dark battle with the undead in the Forest of Goll."

"They now march for Caer Lial."

Merin clenched his fists, enraged. The hope that he held dangled by a thread. "It was Morguese's blood that bound the enchantment last time. When Llenllaewg slew her, it broke the curse's power, and the enemy was destroyed."

Bedwyr appeared to know what Merlin was thinking and said, "Whose blood has bought the curse this time?"

"It could be many," Merlin grumbled. "Where is Arthur?"

"He prepares within the Palisade. He hoped you would come in time."

Merlin turned to go, but Bedwyr snatched his arm, pulling him back. "Merlin."

"What is it?"

"King Croighcat's armies have not joined our forces."

Merlin's jaw rippled with anger. He knew what that meant. Croighcat had likely slithered back into his usual treachery and his army now filled Osian's ranks. Merlin asked, "How many?"

Bedwyr's brow twitched, as though reluctant to say. "We are told at least five thousand. Our numbers are greater, but five thousand unkillable warriors—" He shook his head. "I cannot fathom the bloodshed."

Arthur stood battle ready on the tiled floor of the Palisade. Gwynevere leant against the side of an oak chair near him. She was still weak but refused to not stand with her husband. Her face was pallid, her eyes sunken and red from weeping.

While Arthur lay asleep in his enchanted death, he had dreamt this battle charge over and over. Now that immaterial battle would meet reality. He would take the charge, but this time he would not wake. This time, he would meet the enemy face on. He had little strategy, but there was no other option.

How does one stop an unkillable army?

He had fought an army like this before and would have died within Goll—Morgan gloating over his corpse—if it had not been for the miracle of Gwalahad appearing with the *Holy Cup*.

Arthur gripped his chest. He had a renewed understanding of the power of the cup. It was within him. Would it manifest a dispelling light upon the enemy? Arthur felt a fool to hope, but it was all he had. The power of the *Holy Cup* had broken the spell before—allowing Llenllaewg time to slay Morguese. Would it somehow come through to help them this time?

It had to. The promise of the New Way had to be stronger than the enemy's wrath. Or else, there truly was no hope that could avail them.

I must believe the enemy cannot destroy the power of the great promise.

But how could he stop Osian's hordes? An army from another land had slipped right under his watchful gaze, covered by Osian's shadow. Arthur was unable to stop their arrival. The enemy was coming with corrupted men from the Southlands.

"At least Dyved escaped Osian's grip," Arthur murmured, glaring at the painted tiles on the floor. He brushed his foot over the details of a warrior holding the head of a giant in his fist. It was Peredur who slew the giant—a seven-foot Saecsan warrior—during the early battles of the Western shores. Arthur tightened his lips. "King Croighcat has not come. Likely he is as two-faced as he ever was."

Gwynevere nodded. "Croighcat has always done whatever benefits him best—without a thought for others or these lands. It is all about power and wealth for him. Though I am not sure I believe he has betrayed us. Something has delayed him. I would not trust Croighcat on his best day, but I saw how set he was against Lugh when we held council."

Arthur drew to Gwynevere's side, gazing upon his wife with admiration. He tenderly lifted her chin with his fingers and stared into her dull emerald eyes. He saw pain behind her forced strength. Her body hadn't even recovered from having the baby; they had just lost their daughter, yet here she was at his side, giving him counsel. He would likely not be returning from the battlefield. Not without a miracle, and she knew that.

Arthur breathed a deep sigh. "I do not want to leave you."

She dipped her head and wordlessly clung to his leather breastplate as though creating another shield around him.

The door clicked, and the iron hinges groaned. Arthur snapped his head toward the entrance.

Merlin walked through the door.

A sharp breath escaped Arthur's mouth. He was relieved to see Merlin returned, but a ball of bitterness sat heavy in his chest. Merlin's empty hands were a reminder that their baby was gone.

"My friend," Arthur faintly croaked, emotions squeezing his throat. "The-the baby."

Merlin avoided Arthur's gaze and focused on the floor. "All has been done as it should have been. She is safely in the future." Foreboding spread across his face when his eyes met Arthur's. "The battle is upon us."

Arthur wished to tell him something different, having very little hope.

"I *must* believe that the hands of the Great God offer us an impossible hope—even if we cannot see it," Merlin said, as if trying to convince himself. "We must have faith that he will come through. Or else, what has this all been for?"

Arthur gripped the hilt of Caledfwlch. Even his sword might possess some magic to destroy the death looming over them. He rubbed his thumb over the snaking whorl emblem on the hilt's pommel. "I have hope—though I fear it may come at the cost of my life and far too many Cymry." Arthur's eyes misted. "Have we not lost enough, brother?"

"This is not the end." Hope brimmed in Merlin's voice despite the sorrowful look on his face. "You have come back from the dead. My power is now strengthened. Elanor's—"

Gwynevere gasped at her name.

Arthur swallowed hard, afraid to ask. "Where is our daughter? D-Does she live?"

Merlin's expression softened into a smile. "She is here." He motioned toward the Great Hall. "She is just behind on a wagon with Gwendolen. She is most eager to see you."

Gwynevere burst toward the doors, her hand covering her mouth as if holding back a cry. Arthur ran after her. Gwynevere's limping haste tugged at the strings in his heart. He could think of nothing else. He grabbed Gwynevere's hand and let her pull him through the door. His emotions blinded him to everything else around him. Through the courtyard garden, they stole on an errand that could not wait. His hand could not reach the doors of the Great Hall soon enough. They pushed through into the vacant hall.

Daylight highlighted her silhouette through the large front doorway. Their steps faltered as they caught sight of her. Merlin did not rush past them but halted behind Arthur, remaining on the threshold.

Arthur's heart skipped a beat. The tingle of relieved affection rushed into his eyes and cheeks. He couldn't even see her face. Just her shadowed outline. Her hair whipped through the breeze, then settled on her shoulders as she crossed the threshold.

Elanor stepped toward them. Arthur saw her eyes. The beauty of her. Her life, being as it was—infant then woman—returned to them. The face he and Gwynevere had come to know so well.

Elanor lifted her chin to speak, but her trembling lips stole her words. When finally, she cried, "Mother"—then through a sobbing heave—"F-Father."

THE ENEMY'S FIRST STRIKE

Elanor found herself quickly enfolded in her parents' loving arms. Gwynevere reached her first and pulled her to the floor, then Arthur's arms squeezed them both. Their tears mingled, bringing a new and profound understanding of who they were to each other.

Gwynevere's fingers pressed into Elanor's back, clenching her clothing. Her mother's warm wet cheeks nuzzled Elanor's ear. Her breath, the comforting sound of safety and belonging. The feeling now strangely familiar. Gwynevere's kisses on her cheek felt like home.

Elanor never dreamt she could have this. She had long accepted that this was something she would never have, and grieved the loss a long time ago. The name "orphan" was her banner, knowing she would never know the love of a mother. Not like this. She knew Gwynevere was her mother, and Adhan's gentle hand had been upon her life. But nothing had cracked open that part of her heart—at least not until now.

This is what it feels like to have a mother.

Elanor had returned from exile to another world, to find parents—a true home.

Arthur cupped Elanor's cheeks in his hands, rubbing his thumbs underneath her eyes. "Daughter," he whispered. His words washed over her heart, making her feel whole.

Elanor nodded with a sigh. "I understand now."

"I know—" Arthur keened, his eyes wet with unshed tears. "I know."

He truly was her father. Her heart melted into his arms, finally letting go of the last pieces she had kept from him—the parts that would forever belong to David. There was room in her heart for all of them.

She gripped his wrists. "Please, do not go to battle." She couldn't lose him now that she truly had him.

Arthur's brows curved. Elanor saw the regret in his eyes. "If—if I was only brought back so that I might know you"—he glanced at Gwynevere—"and to see my wife again, that would be enough."

Gwynevere's cries surged.

"I must play my part. I am king. My people must have courage, and *I am* that courage. You and Merlin are also part of that strength."

"Why?" Elanor pleaded.

Arthur pulled the strands of hair away that stuck to her tear-streaked cheeks. "Because we have been given *the song.* The demon that rages against us can never take that from us, and we must remind the people. The song is the New Kingdom. Its bearer is the New Way. Death cannot rob it from us."

Elanor smiled despite herself. To see the hope and understanding in Arthur's eyes meant she could believe it too. She waved for Merlin to join them right as a loud blood-curdling scream tore apart their moment of harmony.

Merlin bolted for the door. Elanor, Arthur, and Gwynevere scrambled to their feet. Merlin's heart plummeted to the floor, knowing who was just outside the door. His mother…Gwendolen.

"Help!" Cilaen's voice called.

More voices started yelling. An increasing commotion resounded from just outside the door.

Merlin pushed through onto the stone terrace. Light blared in his eyes, then he saw it.

Blood!

It pooled on the ground. Cilaen leaned horrified over Merlin's mother. Samara rushed to aid him. Adhan's blood covered Cilaen's hands, which he pressed against her neck. Her pale lips gasped for breath.

"WHERE IS GWENDOLEN?" Elanor screamed. The sound of her shriek shook Merlin to his core.

He didn't know what to do first, but found his knees hitting the ground next to his mother. Shock pulsed through his veins. Merlin gaped at Cilaen, who pressed the fabric he had torn from his shirt against Adhan's throat.

Tears brimmed Cilaen's lower eyelids. "P-Peredur. He has gone after him."

"Gone after who?" Arthur shouted.

Merlin couldn't speak. His mother's eyes already drifted far away. "Mother! No!"

"Who took her?" Arthur demanded, his voice a hollow echo in the background of Merlin's consciousness.

The world slowed—Merlin felt his grip on reality slipping.

Mother. Gwendolen.

Samara told Arthur, "It was Uri. He had a dagger. He was *not* himself."

"He cannot have gone far," Arthur said.

Elanor had already taken off for the stables.

Chapter Thirty-Eight

"Elanor!" Arthur called, running after her.

Merlin couldn't breathe. Everything played out like a disconnected dream. He leaned closer to Adhan and whispered, "Momma?"

Her ageless beauty was slipping through his fingers. Her lips turned bluer through each gasp. He couldn't hang onto her. He didn't know what to do about Gwendolen. The control had been ripped from his hands.

"Please, momma." Groaning wails surged up his throat. He fought with everything in him to calm his unraveling emotions, but he was falling apart.

He pressed his hands on her chest. The warm, slick blood seeping against his fingers flooded his mind and body with horror. His magic stirred in painful prickles. "Byw—"

His voice cracked, and he tried again. "Byw. Iachau."

He swallowed. His grip on his magic was too weak—he struggled to find the flow. "Byddwch fyw ac nid marw." He sputtered through his tears, grasping at hope as a black hole opened wider and wider in his soul.

Adhan wheezed through labored breaths. Her eyes wavered upon Merlin. "S-Son," she choked. "I—s-sorry." Her lips continued to move without sound. The words *love* and *you* tumbled out.

"No! Momma! Please. Do not go." She had been his constant while others had passed on. Her life—never a threat to anybody. He had just gotten everything back. Only Osian—that was all he needed to conquer. Destroy him, and the loss would be over. This was not part of it. This was not what he had been prepared for.

A light sprang past his eyes.

He looked down, and his mother's breaths had ceased—her eyes empty of spirit. The fleeting memory of her fingers touching his just before he left them not even an hour earlier cut like a blade to his heart.

"Momma," he breathed with hardly a sound, stroking her forehead. His bloodied fingers left a mark on her porcelain skin. He had never been very good at loss. The panting of the ghostly wolf heated his ears. Maybe Osian had won. He had ripped open the doors of *Dubnos*, releasing that otherworldly hell upon the living.

"Retreat. Retreat back to me," the malicious wolf's voice beckoned. *"The Man in Blue—he fooled you. Gave you false hope. In the end, it is always me. Come back to me. I am the only place where your pain is kept away from you. This is what happens when you leave me."*

Merlin shuddered. Squeezing his eyes shut, he worked to center himself. He searched to find them—his reasons for not throwing himself into the fire.

Elanor. Gwendolen.

Suddenly, his dire plight smacked him in the face. "*NO!*" Merlin shouted. The release of his cry sent out a shockwave that shook the trees and knocked those who stood nearby off their feet.

He heaved, capturing his breath, then opened his eyes. Trembling, he reached for his mother and kissed her forehead. His lips quivered as he lingered over her. Then, with a strangled sigh, he released her and rose to his feet. He wiped his face, leaving streaks of his mother's crimson ichor on his forehead and cheek.

As if waking from a nightmare, the world sped back up around him. Merlin peered down at Cilaen who lay on the ground, having been knocked down by his power. Cilaen clutched his chest. His watchful eyes blazed up at Merlin. Samara lay next to him, clinging to his arm.

Merlin turned to see Gwynevere on her knees, just past the door's threshold. Cymbrogi in the yard and around the terrace scrambled. Arthur and Elanor were gone.

I have to find my daughter.

Terror gripped his chest, but pushing through it, he unbuckled his legs and chased after Elanor.

"I have to go with him," Cilaen said, rising to his feet. "I have to help."

He stared down in horror at Adhan's blood on his hands, hating the sight of it. All it did was remind him that he couldn't save her. She was like a mother to him.

Why did it have to be her?

She was the one holding Gwendolen in her arms when Uri unexpectedly attacked. Cilaen had been right there. He could have done something.

A regret-filled snarl eked from his lips as he bitterly wiped his hands on his tunic.

I stood there like an idiot watching that boy pull his dagger from his belt.

There had been no sign of danger. It was Uri. He was a friend.

Cilaen set his jaw and started after Merlin.

"No!" Samara yelled, running after him. She grabbed his hand to stop him.

"I *have* to!" He snapped at her more aggressively than he meant to.

"No. No, you do not. You do not have to do anything. *Please*, Cilaen," she begged, her hand clenching his wrist. "Do not leave me. Not now."

His heart softened, seeing her yearning eyes. He could see in them what he had always hoped. She was leaving his heart little doubt. She loved him—but now was not the time.

There is never time.

Regret surged in his chest, but he had to go. "Listen," he said more gently. "I do not mean to leave you, but"—he tenderly gripped her arms—"I am part of this. So are you."

He swept his gaze over her flushed face, his heart beating in his ears. She was so lovely. He wished there was time for them. Her lovely soft lips called to his, and he leaned in, then hesitated. "I am not a warrior. Useless in times like—"

"You have never been useless, Cilaen," Samara said.

"I am going to help. I am going to fight. I will not be left behind to tend all the broken bodies—helpless to do anything else. She was right there in my grasp and I let Uri take her."

"I do not want you to die," she murmured softly, her bottom lip quivering

"I cannot stay." He shook his head with remorse rising in his chest. Her pleading stare created a bitter sting.

Samara reached up, sliding her slender fingers down his neck. A tear rolled free from her eye. "I will not make you stay," she whispered, lowering her hand. She took a sad, reluctant step back, then turned to walk away.

A lightning bolt of longing struck Cilaen's heart. He watched her turn away, and he could stand it no longer. "Samara!"

Quickly, she turned back around, sad hope brimming in her eyes.

The instant he saw her face, he dove for her. He entwined his fingers behind her head and crashed his hungry lips against the sweet softness of her mouth. She pressed back, as if eager to reciprocate, and his heart burst. Now that he let her in—let her close—it was even harder to let her go.

Samara peered up, her eyes full of longing. She whispered one last time, "Please, do not go."

He captured her lips again. This time, he pressed with a gentle ache of goodbye. Then he pulled away, trembling, but he had already made up his mind. He was decided. "I *will* come back to you."

He stepped away, leaving her tearful. His heart was diffident. Clenching his feelings into his fists, he hurried off.

THE MADNESS

"Uri cannot have gone far," Merlin shouted after Arthur, who was rushing to help Elanor saddle Brynn.

Arthur faced him. His countenance burned. "With the Cymbrogi distracted in their preparation, he may have slipped past them."

"Peredur?" Merlin rushed to ask, hoping Arthur could give him some assurance. Though, he realized Arthur knew as little as he did. He avoided Elanor's eyes and couldn't look at her. If he did, he feared he wouldn't hold it together. He already felt like a fragile pyre—easily toppled with the right push. All he could do was bury his reeling thoughts underneath the urgency of finding his daughter. Hopelessness tried to surface, stealing his resolve at every breath.

Gwendolen's screams filled his mind with images of her lifeless body—just like Adhan's—and it crippled his strength. Her screams were far away, calling to him from a hiding place somewhere out of reach.

"Peredur would be on their trail," Arthur confirmed. "Likely calling Cymbrogi to his aid—"

The screams. They blared louder and louder in Merlin's subconscious. He wanted to wring his hands, when suddenly, it connected. His magic kindled and he felt his eyes flash. He knew where the screams were coming from. They were real. A sudden vision of Peredur and the Cymbrogi fighting Osian's hoods unfolded inside his mind.

Hoods! Merlin's heart skipped a beat. It was no longer just Uri. Osian's henchman had joined the fight.

"I know where they are," Merlin shouted, gripping Elanor's arms and looking into her panicked eyes for the first time. "They are still in the citadel."

In one swift motion, he mounted Brynn and pulled Elanor up behind him. They were off at a dart. Arthur and Cilaen followed behind. The clash of weapons rang inside Merlin's consciousness. He rode on a mission down the Palisade hill and circled around the back, where the orchard sloped down upon the training fields in a wild, unmanicured grove.

When Merlin reached the edge of the trees where he knew he would find them, he lowered Elanor like she weighed nothing. His magic flared, amplifying his strength. He leapt from his horse and dove into the trees. Elanor followed close behind.

He hadn't given himself time to grab a sword. He wouldn't need one. Darkness rumbled in the depths of his soul. He had kept this part of him at bay, but no longer. All control burned away like chaff. None would be safe from his wrath.

Metal rang out nearby, but Merlin no longer heard Gwendolen's screams. No more cries. Panic amped his speed.

He saw the first hood dashing between the trees. Merlin scrambled after the perpetrator. The villain was battling with a Cymbrogi. Merlin didn't hesitate. He stretched out his hand and shouted, "Dihenydd!"

In an instant, the fiend blasted backward. His body twisted with a bone-clattering crunch.

Merlin darted over to the body. Blood leaked from the nose and mouth. He would not rise again. Not one of Osian's undead. Empty eyes of death stared stagnant, a stinging reminder of his mother's death. Rage boiled his blood. He growled, clenching his jaw—unable to reason whether what he had done was wrong.

He twisted his head, then burst like a rogue hound toward the next vile snake. Hot coals burned within him at each strike. Every hood he discovered met with the same demise.

"Dihenydd!"

Merlin gave them no time to scream out before he smashed them with the force of his magic's fist. This was why the enemy avoided him—why they never came this close. This was a forbidden magic he held at bay.

Merlin charged through an opening in the trees where the rest of them battled. Nearly a dozen hoods attacked Cymbrogi. Many good warriors already reddened the soft turf beneath their feet, which only further enraged Merlin. From the corner of his eye, he saw Arthur blaze into the fray, bounding between a warrior and a yellow demon. With one slice, the enemy's head was lobbed free, thudding to the earth.

Merlin turned, locking eyes with his next kill. "Dihenydd!"

The flailing body and morbid sound of breaking bones halted the fighting. Several wide-eyed hoods gaped in horror at Merlin's large, fuming frame. His arms extended out with threatening, curled fingers. Several hoods vanished from the fight with a *crack*. The few remaining did not act swiftly enough before Merlin's magic struck, crumpling their bodies to the ground.

Merlin fought to calm himself and took a quick swallow. The untamed magic pulsed in his veins and in his skull, disorienting him with its destructive hunger to smite all in his path. He panned the surroundings. A few awestruck Cymbrogi remained. His eyes fixed on Peredur who stood breathing heavily; his bloody hand wrapped around Uri's throat. Peredur had him pressed against a tree. Uri's feet dangled above the ground.

"*Where is she?*" Peredur roared at him.

Elanor gasped, catching Merlin's attention. The sight of her pulled him back to sanity. His eyes frantically searched for Gwendolen amongst the carnage.

Chapter Thirty-Nine

"Gwendolen!" he called, working to quell his nerves.

"*GWENDOLEN!*" Elanor screamed.

The razor-sharp panic in Elanor's voice wrenched his stomach.

"She—she is gone," Uri choked with a wicked smile. Blood wet the flaxen curls on the side of his head where he had been struck. "He has t-taken her. Lord Osian—has taken her."

"Where?" Peredur commanded, pressing his sword against Uri's throat. Three deep slashes marred Peredur's face. He bled from his shoulder, and his gut—

Merlin's breath faltered. Peredur's gut shimmered with a steady stream of blood.

"He wants you to find her. He wants *you* to come," Uri said, directing a malicious glare at Merlin, "to the Crystal Cave."

"What?" Merlin gasped. The confession sucked the air from his chest.

The Crystal Cave? Evil wasn't allowed there. It was the old magic. The magic that divided darkness and light.

Uri started to laugh.

Peredur scowled before rearing back and thrusting his sword into Uri's gut.

"Wait!" Arthur shouted, but it was too late.

The corners of Uri's mouth drooped, and his pupils undulated. Peredur let him crash to the ground. Uri heaved. He wrapped his arms around his stomach and crumpled into a ball like a writhing insect.

"Why, Uri?" Elanor cried. Her feet fumbled beneath her.

"I—" He panted, tears brimming his eyes. "I did not want to do it."

Merlin noticed a change in Uri's voice and immediately knew. Another one—another mind stolen through Osian's evil talisman. Uri's mind had been taken. Merlin lowered his arms to his sides, his heart softening with pity.

"I am—" Uri grunted, his face reddening. "I am sorry, my lady. I could not stop myself. I wanted to stop." A small sob rolled from his mouth. He groaned, until one final breath eked from his lips, and he was gone.

Elanor collapsed to her knees and dropped her face into her palms. Cilaen rushed to Elanor's side and wrapped his arm around her. Her weeping pierced Merlin like a dagger driven through his rib cage. He doubled over, clutching his knees to keep from falling as his mind spiraled into an endless hole. How had the enemy been so clever—taken advantage of them on every front? And now Gwendolen. He wanted to comfort Elanor. Tell her everything would be alright. But he couldn't get his lips to move. Shock paralyzed him.

His mind raced with plans to rescue his daughter. But he knew full well it was a trap. His knees buckled and he hit the ground, lifting his hands to cover his ears. Alarm bells blared in his head with hissing venom. Visions flashed of the blood pouring out from his mother's neck. The threat of Gwendolen chewed into his spirit. The twisting crunch of his magic breaking bones churned the bile in his stomach.

He remembered this sting. This insanity that sent him running when Ganieda died. He killed so many that day. The same battle frenzy that filled him when his grandfather had died gave him the name Dodwr Marwolaeth—Bringer of Death.

Was this the foul stench he wanted to return to? Was this how they were going to win? His darkness matching Osian's?

The barking, hacking howl of the wolf beckoned to him again. But then suddenly Peredur collapsed where he stood, gripping his stomach with blood seeping between his fingers.

"No!" Arthur cried, rushing to him.

How to stop the madness? Merlin pleaded in his mind. Dread consumed every thought as he stared at Peredur, who lay sputtering in pain.

"No!" Cilaen cried, dashing over to Peredur, unbuckling his breastplate with haste. "Y-You will be alright."

Merlin numbly watched the scene as Cilaen raced to inspect the wound. Blood pulsed out of the gash.

Cilaen pressed his hands against the wound and shouted to Elanor, his voice muffled in Merlin's ears. His eyes drifted to the tears streaming down her horrified face. Merlin knew how she felt. Trapped inside a haze of anguish, the world continued to whirl around them. All the while, they fell inside a chasm of their own collapse.

"Elanor!" Cilaen yelled, but she did not budge. "*ELANOR!* You need to help. You *must* help him. Your healing magic."

She nodded with a choked sob, inching forward on her hands and knees, and touched Peredur's forehead.

The muscles in Peredur's jaw rippled. "I am s-sorry," he said through clenched teeth. "I—I had her. She was within my grasp." He lifted his fist, slick with blood. "Osian flew down in the form of a falcon. His talons tore into my flesh, but still I would not let go of her. No—" He swallowed, his face twisted in pain. "Nothing could pry her from my fingers. I *promise* you."

Elanor listened listlessly. The story painted the terrible scene in Merlin's mind. He was unsure he wanted to hear the rest. Unsure he wanted to know how it ended.

"I ripped the falcon from me, and threw it to the ground. He transformed into a man. I-I had him then." Peredur's face turned sheet white, and he slowly blinked his eyes at the sky. "I put her down behind me and attacked with my sword. I swore I hit him—my blade cutting through him time and again—but he did not falter." Peredur scrunched his brow as if struggling to remember. "He could not keep up with me. I was stronger. He was a weak fighter. I do not know what happened—but his blade caught me. I fell."

Tears streamed down Peredur's temples. "He already had her by the time I was back on my feet. I took hold of her heel. Then he was—*gone*. T...took her." He squeezed a fist above his face, then opened it, gazing at his fingers. "She disappeared from my hand."

Arthur mumbled tearfully, "Ssshh. Be at rest, my friend."

Peredur groaned. Shudders surged through his body.

"Elanor?" Cilaen begged.

Her eyes were squeezed shut with concentration. Her palm pressed against his forehead—her body rigid.

"Please," she whispered. "Great God, help me." She wasn't finding the magic. Merlin had struggled to find his when his mother slipped away.

"You are one of my mightiest," Arthur said, clutching Peredur's palm to his chest.

"I—" Peredur struggled to speak. "Esu calls to me. In his presence, he...he—" Peredur faced Cilaen who sucked in gut-wrenching gasps. "I will be proud to meet the father of such a worthy son."

Cilaen's voice broke as he sobbed. "Do not go. Please...Stay."

Peredur's trembling body relaxed. An ethereal smile gently formed on his lips, then a sigh escaped from his depths. He was no longer with them.

A suffering breath escaped Arthur's lips. He passed his hand over Peredur's eyes—closing them. Another light had gone out—stolen by Osian. They were, yet again, helpless to keep the thief at bay.

INTO THE FIRE

Arthur languidly rose to his feet. Another of his men lost. But this time, there was no sting of guilt. Instead, the grinding, tumultuous grief solidified a resolve in him. Arthur narrowed his eyes. Osian's undead would have no idea what hit them. A newly born righteousness spurred him to fight. He would hack down each enemy until the one whose blood created the curse was spilt.

This is not an impossible fight.

He picked Caledfwlch up from the ground, wiping free the red tar from his blade on the moist grass, then slid it into its sheath. The metallic *click* from his sword rang like a bell in Arthur's ears, signaling the battle had begun. He would lead the land's warriors forth, and he would lead them without fear.

He walked over to Elanor, took her hands, and lifted her to her feet. Her sorrowful eyes drew him in, and he kissed her forehead. "No more tears now, daughter. The time has come." He turned to Merlin who had already risen.

Merlin nodded, lifting his hand toward Elanor. "We must go and find our daughter." Merlin's sober eyes were filled with unfallen tears. The same pain clung to Arthur, but it was time to stuff his grief into a box for later.

Merlin said to him, "I cannot go with you into battle, brother."

"No," Arthur agreed, shaking his head. "You must find Gwen and destroy Osian. Your battle will be on one front, mine on another. Though I will miss having your magic on the battlefield."

"This—" Merlin's voice broke with an edge of regret. "This cannot be what the Great God intended."

Arthur hung his head. "The Great God did *not* intend any of this. Though the enemy's deeds"—he growled between his teeth—"have stolen *nothing* from His authority. It is up to God to win this fight—for we cannot."

A snarl twisted Merlin's lip. "One has to wonder why He has not prevented this."

Arthur nodded. "Yes. I wonder—but it does not strengthen us to think that way."

Elanor lifted her dejected gaze to Arthur. "Have we not already lost?"

Arthur felt the defeat in her tone. There had been little that had gone their way. Every time they had faced the enemy, another loss came to slap them down. He struggled to find the words, but forced himself to speak. "Merlin and I have the blood of many battles on our hands. Scars that sear deep. Each battle we have fought on our own strength. We have conquered all our enemies—until now. Not this time." He paused, trying to keep the faith. "This time is different. This time, our strength fails us, and we cannot force our enemy to the ground. This time, we cannot trust in our own strength. For we have nothing except our resolve. We are meant to trust in something else. That is all."

Merlin's steely eyes met Arthur's with agreement. "There is a piece of the New Kingdom within each of us, and we can only bring it forth as we trust."

Arthur nodded, remembering Marcus's vision of the acorn crushed in the ground, and trees that grew from its death.

"If the Great God does not meet us on the battlefield, then we will lose. Into the fire we go—if we burn, we burn," Merlin said, offering Elanor his hand once again. "I watched you plucked from death many times, and saw miracles where there were none to be had. We may just come out of the fire unsinged once again. We go to find our daughter and see what miracles await us. Arthur will do the same. What have we left to lose? The kingdom will either be lost, or it will be saved."

"Please," Cilaen interjected. "Let me come with you. Let me help you find Gwendolen."

Merlin shook his head, opening his mouth in protest, but was cut short.

"Yes—" Elanor said, letting go of Arthur and taking Merlin's outstretched hand. "If what you say is true, then none of us will be safe from what the enemy intends. Cilaen wants to fight with us—that is a good place for him to be."

Cilaen glanced resolutely at Merlin.

"Of course, my friend. I cannot dismiss you from helping. You have always served me faithfully. This is no less what you have always done." Merlin's voice lowered with a grave tone. "We must go. We cannot delay." He pulled Elanor to him and charged toward the trees. Cilaen did not hesitate to follow.

"We have the *song*," Arthur shouted after them. "I shall sing it in my heart and my blade will echo its truth."

There came no reply as they hastened away, disappearing into the grove. Arthur's heart beat faster at the empty feeling Merlin and Elanor left in the pit of his stomach. He likely would not see them again. Had he said all he wanted to Elanor? What of Merlin?

Arthur lifted his eyes up the hill toward the Palisade. He loathed saying any last words to Gwynevere, but it was time. Bedwyr would be the last of his mighty men to ride out with him. Their last stand would be together, and he hoped that out of the two of them, at least Bedwyr might live to tell of a battle won.

Arthur cast a final melancholy glance back at Peredur before facing the remaining

Cymbrogi standing at the tree line, awaiting him. Their eyes were set with fiery faith. He would do all he could not to fail them.

Arthur turned and knelt beside Peredur.

Honorable. Strong. Friend.

Gently, he folded Peredur's arms across his chest. The leaves on the surrounding boughs undulated in the breeze, lamenting a song of farewell to the fallen warrior. Leaving Peredur without proper mourning felt unnatural, but Arthur did not have the luxury to delay. He could not allow the enemy to get close to the citadel. He squeezed his eyes tightly, mustering the strength to move on.

He called out, "Cymbrogi! Take your battle chieftain upon your shoulders. Carry him to the Palisade and set him down upon the steps of the Great Hall. It will be hard for your fellow warriors to see their chieftain fallen before the battle, but we cannot go without honoring him. And these men"—Arthur pointed to the other slain Cymbrogi—"shall not be left here either. They shall be gathered. Have more men come to collect them. No pyres will be set until we return from battle. They will be honored when we come back conquerors."

Arthur felt like a liar, but he hoped saying it aloud would make it true. None would be honored if they lost. The citadel would be next on the undeads' war path. They would leave no one alive. This would be their end.

Elanor squeezed Merlin's waist as they rode toward the Crystal Cave; the horse's jarring gallop kept her alert. Cilaen's horse raced not far behind them. They traveled wordlessly into the wilds, and Elanor was glad to not be riding on her own. Her head spun with dread. Adhan was dead; her daughter taken. The worst thoughts consumed her mind. She knew what Osian was like—what he was capable of. He moved without regard for life. To think of her little one in the hands of such a wicked villain tormented her every breath, making her skin crawl.

When Osian had Elanor in his clutches, he had made her fear and hate Merlin. If it had not been for the Man in Blue, she was not certain the poison could have ever been removed. So convinced of Merlin's monstrous abuse, she still suffered remnant nightmares.

Now Gwendolen—she swallowed down the anguish. What might he be doing to her mind? Would she know her parents when they arrived to rescue her? Would she even be alive?

Elanor hated to think of it. Part of her would rather find her daughter dead and at peace, than twisted and tortured by a monster. She feared to even hope that they would find her. She knew Merlin was right. This was a trap.

Please, Great God, help us.

She sang the song under her breath. It had kept the evil at bay in the cave, and it was all she could think to do now.

Brynn's hooves pounded the ground. Elanor gripped Merlin's waist so hard, her fingers dug into his tunic, like a cat clinging to a tree. Merlin never flinched or resisted.

They had so far to go. Her heart felt like a cradle without a child. It tortured her every instinct. So consuming was the need to find Gwendolen, she felt like her impatient feet could outrun the horse. She knew it was impossible and sucked in a sob.

Night was darkening the sky, and the light between the trees faded. Merlin would not stop. She knew that. They would ride through the night until they arrived at the Crystal Cave.

I wonder if the morning will ever come?

As night descended, her heart toppled into the pit of her stomach. The pain—the wretched dread—swallowed her like darkness swallowed the forest. Could she escape back to the early hours of the morning, where she and Merlin were united? When Gwendolen was tucked safely in their arms?

Exhaustion made the world spin. She was tired of fighting and her arms loosened. Her mind was slipping—slipping away into the abyss. She let go of Merlin entirely, the bliss of nothingness easing her soul.

She fell, expecting to hit the hard ground, bracing herself for the pain. But instead, she found herself enveloped by a soft and warm embrace. Peaceful. Maybe she really could let it all go.

"Deffro!"

The word pulsed through the listlessness.

"Deffro!"

It came again, and suddenly Elanor remembered Gwendolen. Another wave of darkness pushed her back into the numbing sleep—away from all the pain. She sighed, accepting the spell.

"Deffro!" Merlin's voice demanded with more persistence.

The word annoyed her, unsettling her rest. She shut her eyes tighter and held onto the peace that had evaded her for so long. This…this was silent and comfortable. She couldn't remember all the things that had made her anxious. It felt good to forget. It felt like the shelter of her flat, hiding her away from the world.

"Deffro!"

This time, the word came with light that pierced through the stupor. Elanor felt the urge to speak, but found her voice stolen and lips numb. It was hard to reach for anything. All at once, awareness hit her.

Dark magic!

She writhed, shaking off the false comfort. "Nnnn—nnn!" She tried to speak, but like in a bad dream, her words struggled to come out. Her strength rose and her magic kindled. Blue light burst all around her, and her eyes snapped open.

She shouted, "*NO!* Gwendolen!"

She startled awake. Merlin held her in his arms on the ground.

"Are you alright?" he asked.

Elanor nodded, quickly sitting up with her hand to her head.

"It almost took me as well. Our despair makes it easier for it to take hold." He jumped up from the ground. "Come. Now Cilaen. He is over there. Help me."

Through the darkness, Elanor saw a shadowed lump lying on the ground. Cilaen's horse stood over him—appearing like a blue haunt. Urgency rushed through her and she hurried to her feet, following after Merlin.

"I remember this," Elanor said with wide eyes.

Merlin nodded. "Yes. It is the same dark enchantment we encountered here before. We must be getting close. Osian's shadow is upon this forest."

"How can a man be so powerful?" Elanor asked, placing her hands upon Cilaen.

"Demons are eager to share power with those willing to give themselves over to them. Osian will pay his price in the end," Merlin whispered darkly. "The power is never given without an exchange."

Merlin placed his hand on Cilaen's forehead. "Deffro!" he commanded, his eyes lit with gold.

Elanor ignited her magic and immediately felt a pervasive darkness rush up her arms like icy waves. With each wave, a voice begged her to close her eyes and surrender back into its welcome arms.

Together, she and Merlin pressed, "Deffro."

With a slow flutter, Cilaen's eyes opened. "What happened? I felt—I was—"

"We are under attack. You were enchanted. Osian's dark shadow seeks to keep us at bay." Merlin turned to Elanor. "Which is a hopeful sign. It means he does not necessarily want us getting closer to him."

Elanor gasped. "Gwendolen."

"Yes. We have to keep going." Merlin warned, "Cilaen—the dark magic will only heighten the closer we come. Are you sure you want to continue?"

Cilaen set his jaw and rose, dusting himself off. "I have been trained as a druid of the New Way. Or have you forgotten, teacher?"

"No." Merlin grinned. A proud luster shone in his eyes. "I have not forgotten."

"I know I do not have magic like you, or Elanor. But I still carry something that will defy the enemy. I have not sold my soul and I have my talents. I have the advantage to see my enemy through the eye of Esu."

"Esu?" Merlin asked. "Peredur's God?"

Cilaen nodded. "Peredur spoke to me of Him. He has many names. I did not understand then, but somehow, now I do. He is the same one you have seen."

A glimmer of hope rose inside Elanor at Cilaen's confession. It was like a draught of the hidden waters restoring her soul. How quickly she had forgotten the Great God's nearness to them.

"I am glad you came, Cilaen," Merlin breathed. Then his narrowing eyes scanned the woods. "We must keep moving. There are but a few hours left before morning, and I plan to be on the enemy's heels before the sun rises." He leaned down, his face a shadow in the dark, and said with foreboding in his voice, "We must not let our heart sink into despondency. The evil here feeds on it, and will weaken us." He lifted

Elanor's chin. "We will find Gwendolen. Osian cannot have her. She is ours. Esu will keep her safe."

Elanor wanted to believe. Others had been taken without the hand of the Great God's protection. She felt her healing power had evaded her, but she repeated Merlin's words in her head anyway.

She is ours. Esu will keep her safe.

They climbed back onto their horses and continued ahead.

Morning was breaking when they finally arrived at the two weathered stone edifices guarding the trailhead to the cave. Elanor remembered them. The formless statues may have once been finely sculpted warriors. They were her first sign of hope after a similarly long, scary night when pulling a poisoned Merlin through the forest.

"I had hoped we would arrive at the time between times to enter the cave." Merlin paused, glancing up at the guardian stones. "Yet, the power to enter the Crystal Cave has always been closed to evil. Osian should not be able to access the inside." He turned to Cilaen, who pulled his horse alongside theirs. "We will need to be cautious. Osian could be waiting at the top of this hill, ready to snare us. I suggest we leave the horses and go on foot. We will move more quietly that way. Though it may be that Osian already knows we are here."

Cilaen silently nodded, dismounting his horse.

Merlin held Elanor's arm as she slid off the saddle, then he dismounted also. Now that they were so close, her heart squeezed inside her throat. She feared what she might find. Did she want to see what Osian may have done to her child? She would have to, for she would not leave her little one to the fate of their enemy.

She patted Brynn's neck, seeking comfort as her insides quaked.

"We will leave the horses to roam," Merlin said, hesitating, then continued, "in case we do not return."

Elanor's nerves prickled like needles on her skin. She focused on Gwendolen, and in doing so a fury flourished within her that shook away the fear, helping her feel stronger. She moved with Merlin and Cilaen to the steep trail, leading up the side of the mountain. They stared woefully up at the stone guardian as they passed it on their way through. It was like leaving behind the last place of safety.

At each climbing step, the wind blew hollow against an unnatural silence. The absence of noise, a mute threat, amplified the emptiness. It was as though the ground beneath them was dead. She ran her fingers along the moss growing up the right side of the rock wall. Her magic searched for what she had felt the time before—the magic that permeated this place. But now it seemed gone. An ominous warning twinged in her belly.

Merlin echoed her thoughts. "Something is not right."

Could things get any worse? Carefully, they hastened their pace. Elanor's heart quickened. She wished she could silence her footfalls like everything else. The pounding of her heart was like an audible drum revealing them to Osian. The plateau that held the tall circling stones loomed ahead. Elanor caught her first glimpse of the top of the hill. The dull light of sunrise illuminated its edge.

In her haste to get to the top, she kicked a stone, and it cracked down the hill, ricocheting off the pathway.

Blast!

With a quick inhale, Elanor, along with Merlin and Cilaen, thrust themselves against the ridge wall, glancing up to see if the noise would summon the villain to their position.

Elanor clenched her teeth, waiting for the worst. Anger washed over her for being the one to draw attention to their presence. She tried to control her heaving breaths. Nervous sweat broke over her in hot tingles.

No one came. Nothing stirred.

With a tense nod, Merlin indicated for them to continue.

Now it really did seem like a trap, with Osian waiting patiently for them to walk like rabbits into a snare. The bait dangled through the noose, ready to strangle them. But what choice did they have?

Now at the top, Merlin peered around the edge.

Elanor felt Cilaen's fingers seize her hand. She turned toward him. His eyes were bold, and he squeezed her palm in his.

Merlin gasped.

Fear pounded Elanor's chest, stealing her breath. What had he seen?

He rushed onto the plateau with his mouth gaping. Elanor and Cilaen scrambled to join him.

Now she also saw what caught Merlin's breath. The circle of stones lay in ruins—the tall pillars toppled and pounded into rubble. Elanor stared in stunned silence as she crossed the grass, scanning for Gwendolen. The mysterious doors that sealed the cave had been blasted away, leaving a gaping hole, like a wound in all that had been good.

Careful. Quiet. Elanor and Merlin entered the cave. This would be the trap, and they knowingly stepped inside. They had to.

As their eyes adjusted, they came upon a devastating sight. Every crystal lay in pieces. White powdered shards littered the ground, crunching like broken glass under their feet. The walls, once splendorous and glittering with prisms, were bare and dull.

Merlin cupped his hand over his mouth. "How? What sort of magic would be powerful enough to destroy the origin of truth and balance? This place was the very law of magic itself. Pure, good magic."

Involuntary tears fell from Elanor's eyes. "Wh—" she swallowed, her voice stolen. She tried again. "Where is Gwendolen?" Elanor collapsed to her knees, sinking upon the crystal dust. She lifted her hand. Small shards stuck to her palm like white sand.

"The magic is gone," Merlin said, reeling with palpable distress. "Gwendolen."

Cilaen's voice rang, calling Elanor and Merlin back from the depths. "She is here!" Cilaen pointed. "She is just behind this rock."

The ground beneath their feet rumbled. Earth and stone started crumbling like a waterfall. Elanor spun around. The entrance was caving in, stealing their light source. There was no way through the cascading debris without being buried alive. The cave darkened as rocks covered the last remaining rays of light.

They were trapped in the pitch dark.

41

THE CLASH OF THE UNDEAD

Arthur glared ahead at the horizon; the Cymbrogi of Prydain followed their king to meet their adversaries on an impossible battlefield. Their feet pounded with purpose. The warriors on horseback led the host; foot soldiers marched behind. The horses—their one advantage. The scouts had reported the undead were entirely on foot. The force of their stampede would crush the demons to the ground, hopefully crippling them before the battle on foot raged.

Arthur cringed, recalling the woeful faces of the Cymry at his announcement of the death of their high battle chieftain, and then revealing the horror of the undead.

This is no way to go to war, Arthur ruminated darkly, but what choice did they have? *None.*

Arthur eyed Bedwyr, who rode next to him. Arthur's heart was still shattered from Bedwyr and Gwynevere's lamenting cries when Peredur was placed upon the steps of the Great Hall. Another body to line up with Merlin's mother. The slain Cymbrogi lay one by one on the grassy turf below them.

He gulped down great swells of grief. Gwynevere's wailing rang inside his head—a cadence that matched the marching hoofbeats behind him. Arthur's one consolation remained that Osian's horde was farther off from the citadel than he imagined.

Caer Lial would have time if things do not go well.

He looked to the standards heralded by his Cymbrogi. Not one was lifted high enough. They tilted slightly, as if already defeated.

Surely, this weighty march will only ensure our death.

The Cymbrogi knew the plan. Upon the open field, their sheer number would surround the enemy. His archers would knock their arrows. That was another advantage—they outnumbered their foes. Their thousands would have been more than enough on a common battlefield—their enemy doomed at the onset—but not this day.

Arthur needed to galvanize the Cymry strength. Win or lose, he would convince them they could defeat their adversary. But how? There was only one thing. One vein that had been within his heart since his time waking in the future. He would return—the Cymry's *once and future king*. He would lead them into the battle like he had dreamt inside his sleep of death. *The song* would be on his lips, honoring the one who gave him back a kingdom.

A kingdom, but this time, not *his kingdom*. He understood that now. This understanding broke the burden of his own importance. Arthur knew whose hands held the battle, and it was not his own. He was but to lead them in courage, strength, and fealty.

He turned a more deliberate eye to Bedwyr.

Bedwyr glanced back, then lifted his brow. "What is it, brother?"

Arthur released a deep sigh, then said, "I have to remind the people of what we are fighting for."

Nodding, Bedwyr agreed, "They will need it. I—" He paused. "I will need it. It has become hard to see through the veil of bloodshed. Our strength has not even been a pebble in Osian's shoe."

"I do not believe that. *I cannot*. If that were true, he would not have spent his own blood on demons and unkillable armies. He stops at nothing to destroy because the very idea of a New Way threatens every stone he raises his foot upon." Arthur pulled his sword from his sheath and lifted it above his head. "He cannot muzzle a truth that will linger—even if he successfully tears down this whole land in an attempt to bury it. Our lives *will not* be spent without marking Osian's head with death. He is but a man." Arthur's words lifted his own heart.

With anticipation rising in each breath, Arthur sang above the march:

> *Sweet…Are the healing days, when pain will find no way.*
> *The earth will sing, for the Sun has made it day.*

Never before had the promise rang with more impact than now as the first few words fell from Arthur's lips. The prophecy in opposition of the evil arose before them. The corner of Bedwyr's mouth lifted. Emboldened, he also drew his sword, and his voice joined with Arthur's.

> *Sweet…As it will be proclaimed the new days of the Sun.*
> *Its rays will rise high, setting thrones upon kings' holds,*
> *The New Way coming and the land set in gold.*

Voices, one by one, raised to meet theirs. Swords, spears, and standards lifted. The sound steadily became a roar. For in just this moment, those words transcended the doubt and made them believe *the song* was enough. At the echo of each word, a memory of something more powerful kindled, lifting the tribulation the warriors could not carry on their own. Like an answered prayer, they kept singing—

Chapter Forty-One

Oh, Kingdom of the Sun, renew our land with grace.
Oh, Kingdom of the Sun, the warmth of its bounty upon our face.
Blood will stop dripping, as the oil of gladness is tipping.
The sword no longer killing, but its emblems triumphing.
A new day rising, with the old moons setting.
Sweet…days of the Sun are coming.

It felt as though a mighty hand swept down from the clouds, pushing them forward. The march went from a dragging drole to a brisk pace. Ferocious, the Cymry raised their voices in unison, like a host of trumpets. If there were ones amongst them who did not know the song—*the promise*—they knew it now. Their voices soared, filling their steadfast eyes with hope. They chanted the lines boldly.

What did the enemy hope to gain? Arthur felt strengthened and now viewed *the enemy* as a cornered mouse. How could he have let his faith fail and succumb to doubt? He did not know how they would win, but even if they were all slain, this promise would break the enemy's back.

He saw them. Their enemy's heads rose above the land like blood teeming over a hill. They were garbed in black, and leather clad. The pitted iron helms shone like sharp rocks jutting above the waves. No more yellow hoods. Only black monsters in jagged armor, pouring out onto the open field.

Arthur lifted his arm, halting his army's march. In silence, they stared ahead at the huffing undead. They still appeared as human, which made their dreadful omen of undeath seem a mere illusion. Arthur smirked inwardly, watching the enemy pant at the ready.

Arthur bared his teeth.

They have breath in their lungs—they can be killed.

Then Arthur roared, "The days of the Sun are coming!"

His warriors beat their metal weapons upon their chests, and the pounding rhythm accompanied their voices. The song once again thrummed through the air.

The enemy stood mystified at the raised voices. A stupor descended, making some of them lower their weapons. Confused, the enemy glanced back and forth as if awaiting their leader's command.

But that did not last. One growling voice blazed over their confusion, resolidifying their purpose. In an instant, the enemy found their feet amidst the Cymry's exaltation. In a loud clash of metal, the horde locked iron shields together, pointing their spears forward like splintered spikes. As one unit, they advanced, a wall moving to flatten every Cymry warrior.

This barricade will not last them, Arthur thought, forgetting the undead enchantment, and choosing to fight based on what he knew would knock them off their feet. He swung his sword down, signaling his archers. In trained unison, they unleashed a hailstorm of arrows. His warriors had fought against barricades like this before—nothing but a small wave of the ocean they would quell and put back to sea.

The whizzing arrows plowed into the meat of their enemy, sending shields flying and bodies tumbling over like wheat sliced with a sickle. Arthur did not wait for them to rise again and pull the arrows from their flesh. He roared his next command. The first regiment of Cymry horsemen charged the enemy's vanguard. The foot soldiers spread outward along the flanks, forming the bowl shape that would surround the villains.

"Heads," Arthur called to them. "Go for the heads."

They might be unkillable, but he would like to see them fight headless. Arthur imagined hacking off limbs to repel the enemy. The battle frenzy blazed like fire in his stomach. The hammering hooves of their horses were but a heartbeat away. The Cymbrogi's relentless song melded with the black demons' wretched cries.

In a flash, metal clanged, and bodies collided. Arthur's horse reared onto its shining black haunches and pounded past the spikes, knocking down a shielded devil. The Cymry army barreled through the enemy's front line. Arthur swung Caledfwlch as his horse maintained a wild push through the black throng, crushing bodies under its hooves. The repeated collisions jostled Arthur in his saddle. He squeezed with his thighs to hold steady and continued the barrage. He roared with courage, slicing foes at the neck with his sword. Blood spewed into the air. Screams rang out, quickly deafened by his warriors' fierce battle cry.

Their charge successfully knocked the enemy back, but Arthur knew the stampeding wave would not last.

This battle is far from over.

"Gwendolen?" Elanor called out in the abysmal dark.

Merlin spun toward the sound of her frightened, quavering voice.

"Over here," Cilaen called back. "Sh-she is not awake."

"Is she alright?" Merlin panicked, blinking—hoping it would clear his vision. The darkness was so tangible, it made the divide between them seem infinitely farther. He heard Elanor's scuffling steps through the crystal sand and felt his way toward her.

"I do not know," Cilaen said, his voice filled with concern. "She is warm and her heart beats. But I cannot see if she is injured in this *blasted* darkness."

Merlin swallowed hard, trying to center his magic to conjure a flame of light. Elanor's whimpers disturbed his focus. His head swam in the horror of their situation. The purity of the Crystal Cave had been utterly obliterated. He didn't even know that was possible. This place had been sacred. Far above mortal hands to control.

They were trapped. Gwendolen was found, but it had all gone wrong. Osian, once again, had the upper hand. All of the bad fought for attention in his mind, making it hard to breathe.

"Tan o olau," he finally said, kindling magical light. But his words seemed suffocated, as though swallowed by a void.

Nothing happened. No magic.

He put his hand, palm up, in front of his face. It felt like it wasn't even there in the darkness. He pulled on his magic once again. "Tan o olau."

Still nothing. His magic—something repressed it.

A scratching sound resonated through the cave. Next came a sputtering flash, then the smell of burnt sulfur. The cave flickered with the orange light of a round, hovering flame the size of Merlin's hand. It had not been his magic. He turned, peering at Elanor; his eyes were still adjusting. She stood not far from him with widening eyes. It had not been her magic either.

Where is my power?

He turned his hand back and forth as if it held the answer. Then, a sudden realization chilled Merlin's blood. Had his magic been destroyed with the cave's? Elanor's? Was all good magic gone?

No! He pressed his eyes shut. *Help us.* Merlin's spirit called out to someone— anyone. *Man in Blue.* Had He been destroyed along with the cave? Along with everything that offered them hope? Merlin knew what the magic had felt like in the cave. It had felt the very same as the old man by the silver stream, and the spring—the water that restored his very soul.

Merlin lifted a suspicious stare toward the flame. Whose magic had illuminated the cave with the dull flicking light? The orange flames licked around a black empty orb. The longer he looked at it, the more it felt like a sucking emptiness was eating away his magic. Merlin tore his eyes away and searched the cave. All he wanted was to run to his daughter's side, to see if she was alright—to comfort Elanor. Her erratic breaths unnerved him as she frantically searched their child for injury. His daughter lay alarmingly lifeless on the floor.

Merlin could not let his guard down. Something lurked inside this darkness with them.

Finding his strength, he demanded, "Who are you? Reveal yourself." Merlin balled his hands into fists, readying himself for whoever might reply. Nothing came—just the glint of the hovering flame. The muscles in Merlin's jaw twitched, and he tightened his lips. Slowly, he stepped closer to the flame. The last thing he wanted was darkness shrouding them again, but this flame was not good. He needed to snuff it out.

Refusing to give up on his own magic, he lifted his hand above the flame. "Cael ei ddiffodd," Merlin whispered. He waited, but no magic. The place inside where he found his magic was an empty hole. He felt like a ghost, reaching out, only to discover his fingers could no longer grasp anything.

What he did feel, though, was the flame burning into his palm. Quickly, he snatched his hand away, clenching the pain inside his fist. Just yesterday, he was flinging men through the air like leaves blown in the wind. Now, he couldn't even smother a light. He opened his hand to look at the newly forming blisters. They taunted him like a curse.

He regretted using his magic the way he had. The vision of his magic, tearing through bodies as though they were chaff, coiled his gut. He stared at his blisters, then up at the flame. That magic he used felt dark—just like the burning orb hovering before him. Did he want that dark magic if it meant he could save his family, and the world he loved?

A voice growled from the dark recesses of the cave. "Where has your power gone, Emrys Wyllt?"

Merlin snapped his eyes up. A tall silhouette emerged from a darkened corner. Its dull shadow peeled from the wall in the shape of two sprawling wings then disappeared. The blackness undulated before a pale face appeared, highlighted by graying skin underneath the eyes. He looked like death. His cloak hung from his shoulders like black feathers.

"Osian," Merlin hissed.

Elanor yelled, "What have you done to our daughter?"

Osian stalked toward her, lowering his eyes. "I have just put her to sleep. I cannot have the little thing kicking and screaming. I am keeping her safe and alive. You, on the other hand, I have no plans of keeping alive. Not this time."

Elanor shrank back from him. "What do you want with her? Why did you take her? She is only a child."

Osian's thin lips curved into a devious smile. "Did it hurt? Did people die?"

Merlin launched toward him, but Osian flicked his hand, flinging Merlin across the chamber and into the jagged stone wall. His head smacked hard, making his vision spin. Sharp rock bit into his skin and muscle as warm blood trickled down his neck.

Elanor screamed, jumping to her feet.

Osian flashed a devilish glare. "How does it feel, Emrys, to be without magic? I do not have to fear your power now."

"How?" Merlin asked, his vision blurred.

"It is all about knowing the right secrets. Blood." He drew the word out with pleasure, as though he craved it. "It possesses the power to unlock many doors that remain closed to the weak." He turned his seething eyes to Elanor. "All I need are the right *sacrifices.*"

Osian shot his arm out toward Elanor. His power knocked her onto her back, and his magic dragged her across the floor, seemingly by her ankles. Cilaen reached for her hands, but too quickly, she was yanked away. Her fingers clawed lines through the crystal dust.

"No. Do not touch her," Merlin barked through clenched teeth. An invisible force pressed his head back against the stone.

Elanor skidded to a halt at Osian's feet. He bent down, twisting his finger into her hair. Then he gripped a handful into his fist and lifted her from the ground. Elanor screamed, her face cringing with pain.

Merlin looked on, helpless. With a strained breath, he pulled his arms, his legs— nothing would budge.

All humanity was gone from Osian's eyes. Whatever remained of the foolish boy from years ago had been swallowed up by the evil he consumed. He lifted Elanor until her feet dangled above the floor.

"Hello, Blue Witch," he hissed, jerking her head as he spoke. "You have slipped through my fingers too many times. This time, I have made sure that no magic can save you. Not yours—not his." Osian's eyes flickered over to Merlin. "Not even the ancient magic of this cave can help you. I made sure to ruin it completely. It is gone. Along with your *New Way*." He spat the words out like bile.

Osian pulled a dagger from his cloak. In one swift motion, he pressed it to Elanor's throat. "Emrys," he growled, "the all-powerful has *nothing*. Unable to save his woman. Not even able to save his daughter. And he will not be able to save his king, or his people. You"—he pressed the dagger with sickening pleasure against Elanor's skin, drawing a trickle of blood—"have failed."

"*NO!*" Merlin screamed. "Please." Tears flooded his eyes. Would it be the same as his mother? He watched, horrified, while the blood painted Elanor's porcelain skin. He fought with all the strength he could muster. His whole body tensed against the invisible chains.

The light flickered dim before an ear-piercing scream split the room. Merlin's blood ran cold.

Both of Cilaen's hands encompassed the flame. His eyes flailed wide with pain, but he did not let go of the sorcerous coal. His mouth contorted as he groaned, squeezing to snuff it out. The fire licked up through his fingers, setting his hands aflame.

Cilaen's desperate move distracted Osian, who dropped Elanor, and Merlin's feet hit the floor.

Merlin burst across the chamber like lightning, fury raging from his gut. Quick as a clap, Merlin had Osian's dagger by the hilt, and he fought to pry it free. They grunted with teeth bared, their hands and arms tangling like rope. The battle was short. Merlin seized control and plunged the dagger into Osian's chest.

A spear struck Arthur's horse in the side and he and his steed plummeted. The terrain hit like a battering ram. Stars danced in his eyes, but he quickly shook off the daze. He couldn't stay grounded. He had to get up and fast. The battle raged around him. He glanced at his hands. His sword was missing.

Caledfwlch.

Frantic, he spun around. There it was, just ahead of him, but too late. On his left, an enemy soldier was already upon him, arcing his sword above his head.

Quick, Arthur commanded himself.

He rolled to the side just as the devil's sword swept down—just missing his ribs. He grabbed a discarded shield and covered his head and torso, right as the attacker stuck again—hard and fast. The heavy shield bashed into Arthur's face. He didn't have the chance to resist the strike. Blood poured from the bridge of his nose.

No time.

His opponent reared back, and Arthur gripped the shield, seizing his moment. He shoved the shield's pointed edge into his opponent's chest.

That got him.

The enemy soldier collapsed, heaving from the blow. Arthur rolled onto his hands and knees toward his sword and clutched the hilt. A burst of power filtered through his arm and into his body. He had felt this before. Aided either by the sword, or his own adrenaline, he and the sword were one on the battlefield.

He rolled over just in time to see his recovered rival lifting his broad arms for another strike. His enemy's chest was vulnerable. While still on his back, Arthur swung Caledfwlch. The blade hit its mark, slicing through his enemy's chest. The black warrior buckled forward onto his knees, clutching his chest.

Arthur scrambled to his feet, keeping a clear eye on his mortally wounded foe. As the warrior stretched his shoulders back, exhaling fresh breath into his lungs, Arthur remembered what kind of demons he was fighting.

His eyes flared, and he swung at his foe's neck. The demon faltered, standing momentarily still before his head toppled from his shoulders. Hands flailing, the warrior collapsed to the ground. Arthur would not wait to see a headless warrior rise, but bolted into the battle, scanning the scene.

Bedwyr.

Arthur spotted him not far away. His chest swelled with pride as he watched him knock enemies down—one right after another. His face bore the blood of his kills. Eager to fight at his side, Arthur fought his way forward, hacking through the demons in his way. If any glory came from this battle, it would be he and Bedwyr fighting back-to-back.

Behind Bedwyr, the ground crawled with bodies that were stirring back to life. The unnatural evil unsettled Arthur's resolve—the glory fading from his pumping blood. At least the killing blows slowed the enemy down, but that was all it did. All Arthur could do was swing. His sword guided his path closer and closer to Bedwyr.

Another demon's blade clashed against Arthur's sword. This warrior had more experience. His strikes held power, making Arthur's teeth rattle with every clash. Between the slits of his enemy's helm, Arthur saw two human eyes. A human that willingly surrendered himself to an undead curse. What had Osian offered him? What made him willing to sacrifice his soul? Was his mind taken like so many of the Southlanders?

No.

This snake had been happy to ally with Osian over whatever lies he had offered him.

Fool.

Arthur brought his sword up from underneath his enemy's, attempting to disarm him, but his sword slid free without effect. His challenger's return swing jostled Arthur's footing. He stumbled back, opening himself up for a fatal jab.

But before his attacker could deliver the strike, a silver blade, like a shard of hope, pierced through his foe's chest. The enemy warrior dropped his sword. Arthur gaped.

It was Bedwyr. His teeth bared and his eyes were wild like a ravenous wolf. Bedwyr pulled his blade free, then whipped it through the villain's neck. *Slice*. As the demon's head fell, Arthur's and Bedwyr's eyes locked with grisly triumph. A swift moment of brotherhood shone amidst the violence before they turned, bracing against each other's backs.

"Fight for our brothers," Arthur yelled over his shoulder. "Remember their faces. Let us die with their spirit in our blades."

THE TALISMAN & THE DRAGON

Osian let go of Elanor's hair, and she crumpled to the ground. Trembling, she pressed her palm to her throat. It was slippery with blood. Panic twisted her insides. Her breaths came in short, sharp gasps, and her heart pounded in her ears. The wound did not feel too deep.

Merlin was locked in a gut-churning struggle with Osian—both fighting to seize control of the blood-tipped dagger. Elanor crawled away, clinging to the treasures she had pulled from Osian's neck.

A cry ricocheted between her ears. Elanor snapped her gaze to Osian. Dread widened his eyes as he stared agape at the hilt of his own blade sticking out from his chest. He grunted as saliva dripped down his lip. Painful lines deepened in his forehead.

Cilaen yelped in pain, collapsing to the floor. He splayed his burnt and bleeding fingers. The flame still flickered above him.

Elanor was struggling to shake off her shock when the cave started echoing with devious laughter. She jerked her eyes back to Osian, whose distress had now shifted into a demented smile.

Merlin stared agape in horrified confusion. He reached for Osian's blade once more.

Osian shouted, flinging Merlin back across the chamber. Merlin moaned, rolling onto his side, holding his arm with teeth clenched. Elanor stared in horror at her adversary. His long pale fingers wrapped over the bony blade lodged in his chest. He pulled with a pained grunt, and the curved blade slid free with black blood oozing from his chest.

His body straightened, and he seethed, "You cannot kill me."

"You," Merlin said, a sneer marring his face. "You are cursed."

Osian laughed. Morbid delight sparked in his eyes. "I am more than cursed. Morgan's blood flows within my own. She—" He stopped, examining the tar-like gore dripping from his knife, then he tossed it away. The blade clanged across the

305

cave. "She has given me the power of the otherworld, and I no longer have to pay with my own blood." He curled his hand into a fist in front of his face. "Or pay a price for my magic!"

"There is always a price," Merlin bit sharply.

Osian mildly chortled, dismissing Merlin's words. His deranged eyes turned back to Elanor. She shrank back, goosebumps stippling her skin. "Now where were we? One final task and Morgan will be able to destroy what is left of those Cymry vermin. They are about to understand what little their courage amounts to."

Violet smoke billowed out of Osian, seeping out through his mouth and eyes. He stepped closer to Elanor, his arms wide.

She scooted away in mad desperation, hiding the jeweled objects she held within the folds of her dress. The vapor took shape, reaching for her with whirling bodiless fingers.

Merlin! She wanted to cry out to him, but terror stole her voice. Her body trembled from the inside out. Merlin's shouts rang in her ears, his tone powerless and desperate.

Cilaen?

She gasped. Cilaen was reaching for her. His palms glistened with blood and blistered flesh. Osian's magic held both Merlin and Cilaen at bay. It was too late. Osian was upon her.

The smoke curled around the hand she pressed against her throat. The ghostly vapor became a cord, pulling her hand away from her wound.

"No," Elanor growled, resisting the pull. The smoky cord morphed into a hand and a face burst out from the haze. Elanor screamed in fright, then lost her voice entirely as Morgan's laughter infiltrated her mind. The phantom placed her other spectral hand around Elanor's throat. Morgan's body took shape through the mist and knelt before her.

"There is plenty enough blood," Morgan's disembodied voice echoed through the chamber. "No need to waste it all until we are done."

Elanor stared at Morgan's pale lavender skin. Her lips were white with death, her black eyes empty and soulless. Her black hair hung like liquid strands, flowing into the entrails of her dress and fading into a vaporous blur.

"Come now," Morgan said, pressing Elanor's bloody palm to her face. Rouge streaks from Elanor's fingers lined Morgan's cheek. Morgan licked Elanor's fingers with her eyes closed. Pleasure curled the edges of her mouth as she tasted the blood. Morgan took her other hand away from Elanor's throat and drew it across her other cheek.

A growl buzzed within her mind. The sound heated up her neck and cheeks. She squeezed her eyes shut, recognizing the demonic sound. The buzz radiated a pain deep inside her skull.

Elanor screamed, flinging her hands over her head, feeling like it might crack open.

"See. I told you; you were a wrecker." The harsh words echoed in her mind and soul.

"This is all your fault. If you had never come here, they would all be safe. Now you will watch them all burn. You should be dead, and now you will wish you were."

No. Elanor resisted. She already knew this voice. She would not allow it to rob her of hope. Maybe she was about to die. Maybe they all would, but the only fault lay at the feet of Osian and his evil muse.

Elanor glared up at Morgan, pursing her lips against her teeth. "Your words are powerless. I will crush you." Hot, angry tears welled in Elanor's eyes. "You will lose it all in the end. All your lies will come to *nothing*. Emrys and his Pendragons will crush your head."

"Ha, ha, ha! You think you are strong? You think you can resist me?"

Morgan's eyes flared yellow with flecks of red flame. Her eyes morphed and grew larger. The pupils elongated into vertical slits. The marks of Elanor's blood on Morgan's cheeks transformed into black scales, and rows of sharp teeth jutted out of her gaping mouth. A ferocious roar vibrated the air as the hulking vaporous shadow of a wretched inky dragon dominated the cave. Then it disappeared.

Morgan was gone.

Elanor clutched the stolen pendants inside the fabric of her dress. One of them was Osian's talisman, the other her blue pendant. She had seen them against Osian's chest as she hung by her hair. When Cilaen grabbed the flame, she'd snatched them. Osian didn't even notice them ripped from his neck when she fell. She didn't know what she would do with them, or what power might be gained from them, all she knew was this: she couldn't let Osian possess them.

The tormenting buzz still rang in her head, but she remained determined. What she could do, she would do. Like the snake's head she had crushed on this very ground years before, she would do again to this—*talisman*.

"Now you," Osian shouted, sprinting over and nabbing Merlin by the throat. A fleeting holler escaped Merlin as Osian squeezed.

There was no time. Elanor searched the ground around her for a large crystal or chunk of rock *There!* Just a few feet away lay a crystal big enough to fit nicely inside her palm. If she was swift, she could get to it before Osian stopped her.

She dove forward on her hands and knees. Her eyes blurred. Blood dripped from her throat onto the stone floor. The lying voices pounded like hammers inside her head. She felt the round, rough edges of the crystal. Her mind wanted to fade. She was losing blood. Her fingers shook.

Can I do this?

It didn't matter. None of it did.

There was no time for her to differentiate between the talisman and her pendant. Her heart ached for it, even while she lifted the crystal above her head. She unfurled her dress, letting both pendants drop to the ground.

"What are you doing?" Osian's voice was like a nightmare, calling her back into his nebulous torment.

She brought the crystal down. Again and again, she slammed the crystal into the pendant jewels, praying they became dust. In the frenzied moment, she felt herself weakening. She just kept pounding, and then heard a sound like ice cracking when it slowly melts. A sweet perfume of honey wafted up to her nose. Then there was another sound. Her eyes widened—she knew its sweet melody. It was *the song*.

Osian grabbed her from behind, snaking his arms around her torso. She kicked, thrashing against him, and wiggled free. Tears fell from her eyes, and she scrambled back to hit the pendants a few more times.

This time, Osian plucked her up from the floor, his arms constricting her body like a giant snake. She held onto that crystal. If she could free her arms, she would bash it into his skull.

Suddenly, an earth-shattering *BOOM* deafened all sound. Stones cracked, the ground shook, and Osian dropped Elanor. She tumbled away from him. Now free, all she could think of was getting to Gwendolen—finding Merlin—before they were buried under collapsing rock.

Merlin found her first. His fingertips reached for hers, then he pulled her into his arms. She glanced over and saw Cilaen holding Gwendolen before the demonic flame finally snuffed out.

Arthur steered his mind away from the losing battle. They would fight until they could fight no more. His hope remained that, somehow, the miracle he prayed for would come to their aid before it was too late. He and Bedwyr battled the same undead rising again and again.

A shadow captured his eye, soaring above the battle. He lifted his head toward the sky, and his stomach tightened with dread. Instead of hope, evil had come to rip away what small advantage they held.

A slithering, elongated, pitch-black dragon blazed above the battle. Its wings were pointed and clawed with its oval head surrounded by an array of hair-like spikes.

"This cannot be," Arthur said, dumbfounded.

The dragon's roar halted the battle to a momentary standstill. Both armies stood aghast. The dragon flew over them, the heated gust forcing many down onto their knees.

Is it only an omen? Arthur prayed, watching it fly from the battle.

But then it turned, arching back, its path directed toward the mass of battling warriors. Its red eyes raged and its massive wings spread overhead like a storm of black clouds. The closer it came, the more the dragon's mane flared around its head. Its chest bulged and lit orange with surging breath—a hollow drum filling with death.

Where had this evil come from? The demon heralded doom to the entire battle-field. Arthur braced himself. Iron shields flung above heads, forming a broken wall. Arthur's only hope was that the dragon's fire might also consume the undead.

A cannon of oblivion was unleashed. The roar of fire, like molten lava, belched forth in a stream of death across the battlefield. Screams of terror rose above the clashing weapons. Fear radiated from Arthur's heart and shot down into his toes.

"No!" Arthur screamed, powerless to stop the monster from devouring his men in flames.

The fire sizzled and popped, and the instant stench of cooked flesh hit Arthur full in the face. The dragon flew past the lines of warfare, but it was not finished. Before Arthur could take a second breath, the demon turned for another strike. Men scattered, trying to flee.

Chilling shadows appeared amid the smoky mire. A quiet wind dissipated the smoke in billowing whirls, revealing charred, fleshy skeletons with weapons in hand. The undead seemed re-invigorated by the fire, moaning and growling through the undulating heatwaves. Bits of armor clung from their skulls and hung from their bodies. The fire revealed the monsters' true nature. The undead were no longer cursed humans, but now ghouls of Annwn.

Arthur choked back the bile surging in his throat. His battle instinct squelched his shock, and he yelled for his men to fight before the dragon struck again. His voice sounded disconnected from his conscious mind. The world around him slowed in a steady rage of hateful steel.

The hell dragon swooped for another pass, burning down more men. Arthur's sword was a heavy anvil in his hands, slicing through the bodies of the relentless undead. He fought on, refusing to lose heart.

Arthur screamed. Piercing pain rent the right side of his rib cage. Arthur turned; an undead warrior smiled at him. This one still appeared human. His sweaty hair blew in the heated wind without a helm. A chunk of flesh was missing from his cheek, exposing the clenched teeth underneath. A sword was clutched in his fists with Arthur's blood stained on his blade.

Arthur barely knew what happened next. His mind reeled, and his body took over. Maybe it was Caledfwlch—he wasn't sure. All he knew was that more heads fell from his blade than at any other time during the horrific battle. He hacked them down, one after the other. A baleful cry hurled out from his depths, pure fury igniting every movement.

Where is Bedwyr?

The sudden realization struck Arthur amidst the frenzy. His back was absent of his brother's warmth. He spun around, searching the field. Mangled and scorched bodies lay scattered around. His eyes could not capture their faces or features. He hoped Bedwyr remained among the living still fighting. But Arthur couldn't stop to find him. He wouldn't stop.

The enemy closed in around him. With the dragon's fire avalanching, Osian's undead were quickly outnumbering the living. Another demon blade slashed Arthur's thigh. The dragon turned to dive a third time. Arthur felt Annwn siphoning all hope from his blood. There was no stopping the dragon. Another wave was coming to kill more Cymry.

The cave lay shrouded in darkness again. Their puffing breaths echoed in the stillness. The ground had stopped quaking, and to Merlin's great relief, the chamber had not caved in. He squeezed Elanor tightly to his chest, grateful to have her in his arms. Her body lay limp with heavy breath. He pressed his hand to her throat—fearful of how much blood she may have lost.

The atmosphere of the cave had shifted. Magic dully vibrated through the air. Merlin could feel it, and it wasn't Osian's sorcery. No. It was a familiar magic. The good magic that had been silenced tickled the air—though it remained muted like muffled breath.

"Stay still," he whispered to Elanor. Then, in careful silence, he pulled himself up from the rocky floor. "Tan o olau." An orb of circling golden light appeared on his palm, dispelling the darkness of the cave. He sighed in relief. A slight smile lifted on his trembling lips, but then, he shifted his attention to Osian. His eyes narrowed, discovering him hunched over the shattered talisman.

Osian didn't lift his gaze from the floor. His shoulders shook like a man possessed.

With a drawn, angry tone, Osian seethed, "You—little—*witch.*" His lurid glare shot toward Elanor. "You will pay for that." He whipped his hand out, hurling his magic at her.

Merlin had already stepped between them, and his magic formed an iridescent shield, deflecting Osian's attack. Merlin groaned, struggling to stay connected to the dull stream of magic

Osian rose to his feet and leered. "I am not sure what advantage you think you have. You cannot kill me. You may have somehow recaptured an ounce of your magic, but do not make the mistake of thinking you will live." Osian's power blazed, pressing against Merlin's shield. "I hold the power."

Osian was right. The flow of magic was still stagnated. There was not enough power. Merlin's brow perspired as he tried with all his might to hold onto the threads of magic.

"Rah!" Osian shouted, ripping his hand through the air, breaking Merlin's shield and cartwheeling him through the air.

Merlin slammed onto the ground. Darkness engulfed them once again. A stinging sensation radiated through his hands. His arms burned. Merlin ran his fingers over his arms and felt the wet warmness of lacerations on his skin.

Please. Great God. I am not enough. Your ways must come. Your magic. Your light.

Just then, a voice resonated through his spirit. *"Declare my name!"*

Merlin did not understand. What was his name? Great God? The Man in Blue? Was it Grwyrthrhodd? He had now known Him in all three. The Triple God.

"Declare my name!" the voice commanded again inside his mind.

What is your name? he begged to the voice, hoping to hear an answer. Images raced through his thoughts. Elanor's healing. The Man in Blue leading the way.

Then Marcus's words echoed, *"It is not in magic we find our answers. That is what the dark ones do. Who leads you, Merlin?"*

A painful, stinging light slammed a vision into his mind. He saw the hooded men he had twisted and flung across the orchard. Merlin felt the guilt like a punch in his gut.

The voice drummed, *"Who leads you, Merlin? Magic, or…"*

Merlin's eyes filled with tears. "I am so…so sorry," he whispered.

"Sorry?" Osian's voice shot back. "Do you think your sorrow will stop me from killing you all?" The evil flame burst back, dispelling the darkness.

Merlin swallowed the rising tide within, defying Osian's vile threat with a defiant glare. Inside him, something was shifting. A control he had always held over his world—his own life—was relinquishing. It was not in his own hands to stop Osian, but there was an authority being given him to conquer this darkness. He could feel the pieces moving back together. All that the pain had made him forget. Now he was ready. It was more than a name he needed to declare; it was a name that echoed from the deepest recesses of his heart. The thump of his heartbeat made it ring louder and louder, until it bubbled forth onto his lips.

"Dwi Yn!"

CRACK!

At his declaration, the cave walls split. A small bit of crystalline light emanated through.

Merlin heard the voice again. *"Whose strength?"*

"Dwi Yn!" Merlin shouted even louder. It wasn't a name. It was something more.

"Whose Authority?"

"Dwi Yn!" At the name, the crack burst wider.

"Whose Kingdom?"

The bardic power of the song swirled inside Merlin's heart, and he declared, "Dwi Yn. Y Gorffennol. Yr Awron. Y Brenin Dyfodol." His voice echoed like a wave. The cave wall broke open, revealing crystal prisms like giant pillars, jutting out from inside. White, gold, and blue light danced, making them sparkle with ethereal, incandescent light.

Now Elanor was on her feet. Merlin stood too. Blue emanated through her eyes. The song flowed from her lips. The words—the name Merlin declared—echoed old prophecy: *The king of the once…and forever future king.* The very words that had been spoken over Arthur had new meaning.

Osian's flame was immediately snuffed out. The light from the crystal prisms burst, bathing every corner of the cave as though they stood in the rays of the morning sun.

Osian screamed, tossing his arm up to shield his eyes. "Your words cannot save you." He barreled toward Merlin, tackling him to the ground. He pressed his hand over Merlin's mouth, but Merlin retaliated. His newfound strength hurled Osian through the air—his head whacking like a melon on the ground.

Osian wiped the blood from his lip, then jerked himself onto his feet. Dark blood flooded over his temple. Rage twisted his face, and with a devious gleam in his eyes, he stole toward Cilaen.

Merlin sped after him, his stomach churning. He wouldn't make it in time. Osian was already there, forcing Gwendolen from Cilaen's tightly clinging arms.

"No," Cilaen shouted, kicking against Osian's legs, and pulling the child in with his burnt hands.

Osian growled, "You *stupid* boy." He shoved Cilaen, cornering him against the wall. Then, placing his hand on Cilaen's forehead, he snarled the wicked word, "Marw!"

Cilaen's eyes rolled back in his head, and he collapsed to the floor.

Elanor shrieked. Osian twisted around with Gwendolen hanging limp in his arms.

Merlin stood back. Osian threatened Gwendolen, his hand to her forehead—the same he had done to Cilaen.

Osian panted, smiling through his teeth. "You do not seem to understand. Even with your power, you have already lost. It was Morgan's blood that was poured into the *chalice* that I drank. My life is bound to hers. I will live no matter what you try to do to me. My power will crush you. You're fighting for nothing." His top lip curled, his eyes flicking between Elanor and Merlin. "The undead your father fights," he spat toward Elanor, "is futile. My men drank blood from the *chalice of life*. But it was not my blood, and it was not Morgan's blood that cursed them." Osian shook Gwendolen's flaccid arm, revealing the red scar on her forearm.

Merlin gasped in horror. "How did you—?"

Osian cackled with sinister glee. Elanor covered her mouth, and she crumpled to the floor. "My servants made sure we had her blood. The only way for the immortal curse to be broken is at the sacrifice of your own child. Kill her, and the curse will be broken. But as your child lives—the undead thrive. Morgan is already feasting on the flesh of what remains of the Cymry armies."

43

THE GOLDEN DRAGON

The third wave of the dragon's fiery breath blazed through the battle. This time, the explosive molten flame hit close to where Arthur fought. Hot, burning wind hurled him into the air, along with other flailing bodies. He slammed into the ground, losing his breath. His ears rang. The cries of wounded men sounded muffled in his ears. Searing pain flared in his body. He had been burnt. How badly, he was unsure.

Arthur rolled onto his back and stared up at the sky. It was white with plumes of black smoke unfurling in the wind. The battle fell silent in his ears, and he considered the moment of his death. The stink of burnt bodies consumed him with mournful dread. No one had come. No miracle had saved them. Had it been worth it—marching the Cymbrogi of Prydain onto a field that promised their deaths?

Arthur's gut twisted and his eyes darkened. He closed them tight, shutting out the mire. When he opened them again, he discovered he was standing on the steps of the Great Hall. The blighted field had disappeared. Was it a dream? Maybe a vision? Had he died and stood on the other side of the veil?

Gwynevere was in his arms. Her green eyes filled his heart with peace. She was a healing balm, drawing shut the curtain of darkness. The curve of her smiling lips, over her pearl teeth, called him closer into her comforting arms.

It had to be worth it, he felt now, embracing his wife. For her, for them—all the Cymry of Prydain. The enemy left him no choice. The Cymry would soon all die, and so would he, fighting for the world they loved. But for him, this time he fought without arrogance clinging to his glory. He had met his daughter, and watched her become strong. His legacy was now properly set on someone other than himself. The New Kingdom pulsed in his chest. He was redeemed in every sense. All his mistakes forgiven.

Taking a step back, Arthur opened his palms, letting his people go. He could not save them. But at least he had fought for them—been there for them. This time, failure could not take his ear and run him into the ground.

With tears in his eyes, he pressed his lips to Gwynevere's. He savored her sweetness before it all came to an end.

She pulled away, and with a gentle gaze, she beckoned, "Arthur."

Her eyes stared into his, and within hers, he saw rising tension.

"Arthur," she repeated, lifting her hands to his cheeks.

Her voice sparked something inside him.

"It is not time to surrender," she said, but the vision of her started to fade. Her whisper echoed in his ear. "It is not time for you to die." Then she vanished through his fingers.

He was conscious again, and the agonized cries of battle flooded back into his ears. What could he do? The pain in his body kept him from moving. He swallowed, his throat sticky and dry. The only thing he had left was the promise. He kept his focus on the sky, and through a cracked, stretched voice, he sang—

"Blood will stop dripping, as the oil of gladness is tipping.
The sword no longer killing, but its emblems triumphing.
A new day rising, with the old moons setting.
Sweet…days of the Sun are coming."

The roar of the black dragon's return thundered overhead. He turned his head, and a tear dripped from his eye onto the bloodied soil. The terror was coming to finish them off. How many more attacks would it take before the last of them was consumed?

The dragon's mouth opened wide and its taloned claws extended.

But then…Arthur gasped. Hurtling across the sky, like a streak of gold and green lightning, Gwyliwr Aures dove through the ether. The black dragon didn't have a chance before Gwyliwr's massive jaws collided around its neck, knocking the demon off course. The evil dragon thrashed, and they fell in a tangle across the sky. Then, as a burning ball of fury, they careened into the forest. The crash rumbled the ground. Trees burst, splintering on impact.

The raging roar of the two dragons vibrated the air. The boughs of the forest shook against the wrestling creatures. Arthur sucked in a sharp, painful breath. He shifted onto his side, marveling at the dragons' battle.

A blaze of red and black erupted from the trees. The enemy dragon escaped up into the sky. Gwyliwr drove directly behind. The demon serpent struggled to fly. Holes were torn in the membrane of its wings, making it falter each time it pumped its massive pennons.

Gwyliwr snatched it by its tail. Her teeth sank deep, and the black dragon bellowed. She jerked her head, sending the monster flying like a catapulted boulder. Warriors scattered—the stygian dragon careened toward the field. The sight of its scaled hide grew larger like a raging cataclysm.

The creature slammed into the ground, shaking the earth on impact. Its long neck rolled over the field as men darted clear. The dragon's spiked head hit, cratering the ground. Gwyliwr swooped toward the grounded dragon with her talons flared.

Arthur leaned up on his hands. One silent second passed and Gwyliwr plowed atop her kill. Her claws sank into the black dragon's exposed chest; her jaws ripped into its neck. The monster howled and liquid flames poured from the corners of its mouth. Gwyliwr narrowed her eyes—her teeth bared, dripping with gore—watching the struggling demon's demise beneath her. A sputtered snarl rolled out of Gwyliwr, building to a zenith. She extended her claws, lifting them above her head, then raked them across the creature's chest.

Smoke billowed from its chest like a burst cavern. Arthur flung his hand over his eyes. Bits of flaming flesh shot through the air. When he looked again, the black dragon lay with its fleshy gray tongue sagging out from its wide open mouth. Violet sulfuric smoke billowed from the flayed, cavernous hole in the dragon's chest. The predator's heart rested on the ground beside its corpse.

As the lavender smoke dissipated, Arthur saw her. Morgan's yawning face shrieking up into the sky. He almost thought he could hear her before the wind dispersed her entirely.

Gwyliwr's chest pumped above the dead demon. Her eyes still flared, exposing the white.

Arthur wanted to shout for her. Would she continue to help them fight? But his sight was fading. He collapsed onto his back and his body numbed.

A skeletal demon appeared above him. The remaining seared flesh on his face threatened Arthur with a broken sneer. He had lost his sword amongst the chaos, leaving him with no weapon to defend himself. Arthur thrust his hands out as a shield. The undead soldier lifted his blade, revealing his empty black bones.

A blade swept through the demon, severing its spine. His torso crashed to the ground. Arthur's fading eyes struggled to see a shadowed warrior finishing off his opponent by cutting off his head. The warrior picked up the boney torso and flung it into the fray.

Gasping for breath, the warrior knelt over Arthur.

"Bedwyr," Arthur groaned with a strained smile, seeing his friend's features finally come into view. Relief washed over Arthur. He closed his eyes and drifted away.

Osian buckled forward, dropping Gwendolen like a stone. Her small unconscious form flopped to the ground. Osian wretched, gripping his stomach and stumbling backward. His face contorted in pain. There was no moment of hesitation. Merlin dashed toward Gwendolen—Elanor joining him in a snap.

Merlin didn't know what Osian was up to; he spared the shortest glance at his child's face before setting his eyes back on his convulsing enemy.

"*NO!*" Osian screeched, writhing as though harassed by an invisible foe.

Merlin bounded toward him. Maybe Osian was unkillable, but that would not stop Merlin from trying. He gripped Osian's neck, pulling him up from his worming, and shoved him against the cave wall.

Osian's eyes widened in terror. "Th-this cannot be. She cannot—" His pupils shrank in realization.

"What is it?" Merlin demanded, jerking Osian.

Osian's gaze slowly met Merlin's. A drop of blood leaked from Osian's nose, and he said, "Morgan…she is gone. She has left me. I—" Then, as if snapped out of his trance, he bared his teeth and ripped Merlin's hand from his throat. With a snarl, he flung his arm at Merlin, releasing a merciless burst of his power.

Merlin slid back but remained on his feet. The force had not been strong enough to knock him down.

Osian shrank back, gaping at his hands as if wondering what went wrong.

Merlin struck back with a focused pulse of his magic, knocking Osian off his feet and onto his stomach. His face smacked the gritty ground with a dull thud.

"Ah," Osian whined, rubbing his hand over his bloodied chin.

"Where is your power?" Merlin asked. "Was your power tied to the witch?"

Osian set his jaw, refusing to reply.

"Rwy'n eich rhwymo," Merlin commanded, and in an instant, his magic yanked Osian from the floor and suspended him in the air. "What happened to your power, Osian? Was it not her blood that bound you to the Chalice?"

Elanor's voice rang out in a desperate sob. "He's dead."

What? Merlin struggled not to lose focus. *Cilaen.*

"What did you do to him?" Merlin's heart pulsed painfully in his chest—it took every bit of strength to not rip Osian apart. Maybe now he *could be* killed.

Why shouldn't he die? After everything he has done—all the lives he has stolen. Why should I extend Osian one ounce of mercy?

Osian grunted, fighting against Merlin's hold. "I-I will…I will not stop," Osian said, almost as though baiting Merlin to kill him. "Your New Way—it's weak. You-you surrender your power to the authority of another. That makes you a slave. The old religion stamps out the weak."

"*You* are the slave, Osian. The old religion can only produce death. It cannot give life. It is a *curse*. One that you will go down with. One I told you, you would pay for." Merlin gritted his teeth, wondering how much more he wanted to hear if Osian opened his mouth again. "Can you *not* see? No matter how much power you held, you still could have never quenched the light." Sorrow tightened Merlin's throat as he asked, "How do I break the curse? How do I set my daughter free from the Chalice's curse, and save those who fight against your undead?"

"You can do *nothing*," Osian growled. He twisted his head to where Elanor lay weeping over Cilaen, while also holding her daughter's hand. A devilish grin curved his lips. "But *I* can."

"You—" Merlin glared with mistrust. "You would set her free—saving the Cymry?"

"I…I lost everything. There is nothing left. Morgan is gone." Osian looked away, his face despondent. "Somehow you have robbed me of all I worked so hard to build." His head snapped back toward Merlin. A wicked gleam narrowed his eyes. "But I can still cause pain. So much pain, Merlin. You and your blue witch will lose everything. You will have gained nothing." He flicked his head and commanded, "*Mawr!*"

A white burst, like a blade, flew from Osian's hand, striking Gwendolen. The blast sent her little body tumbling across the floor, ripping her free from her mother's hand. Elanor screamed, rushing to Gwendolen's side.

Dread dug its sharp talons into Merlin's heart.

"WHAT DID YOU DO?" His eyes flamed as he squeezed his hands into fists, intensifying his hold, crushing Osian with his power. *Please, do not have killed my little one.* He gritted his teeth, tears spilling from his eyes.

Osian choked, forcing a smile. "The c-c-curse is broken. Is that not what you wanted? Her death ends the strength of the undead."

"No!" Merlin yelled. A pit opened in his stomach, and sorrow seeped in, crippling his lungs. His knees buckled, but his rage girded him into an unfocused attack. An anguished roar tore from his throat as he flung Osian through the air.

Osian's flailing fingers morphed into feathers, transforming into falcon's wings. They fluttered, saving him from a lethal collision with the cave wall, but he still struck it hard. Feathers erupted, and he tumbled to the floor.

Merlin dashed after him. Osian's discarded blade glinted on the ground; Merlin snatched it up. Osian would not escape.

Osian shook his feathered head and his yellow falcon eyes widened. Merlin stole closer. Osian flapped his wings, fleeing into the air. But it was too late. Merlin caught him mid-flight and stabbed the dagger through Osian's heart, pinning him against the wall.

Osian screeched.

Merlin let go, and the bird flopped to the floor. Through strained breaths, he said, "You should have stayed hidden, Osian." He clutched his trembling hands into fists. Elanor's weeping rent into his ears. He wished he didn't have to turn around. He didn't want to face it. Osian was dead, but what had been left?

He stared at the falcon. The wings splayed out. The sallow hooked beak gaping. Merlin pursed his lips with a feeling of bitter defeat. He killed the source of evil in Prydain, but he had not won. The falcon slowly morphed back into a man. The pallid face of Osian, a stinging reminder of all that had happened. What of the battlefield? How many there remained alive?

Must the triumph over evil always come at such a steep cost? Please, Great God. I cannot face it.

THE RETURN OF HOPE

Bedwyr swung his blade in one hand, Caledfwlch in the other, slicing through one undead enemy after another. He shielded Arthur, who lay behind him, from the onslaught. How bad Arthur fared, Bedwyr didn't know, but he wouldn't give up. The blades grew heavy in his grip, and weariness called his name. But he could not stop—could not surrender to death. Tearing the enemy's bodies to shreds was his only recourse, and it kept them from putting themselves back together. After each beheading, he hurled the head far from the body before another demon rushed in to fight. He did not worry about the crawling arms, or the writhing bodies. Those abominations were no longer the threat. What did worry him was the dwindling numbers of the living. Their odds became more and more dire. The miracle Arthur had hoped for never fully came.

But then, like the light of a morning sunrise, came a blast of reverberating horns. Over the hill, behind the enemy, flew the purple standards of King Croighcat's armies.

Have they come to help? Bedwyr's spirit lifted, hoping. *What has taken them so long? Maybe they have not betrayed us after all. Or, more likely, Croighcat was reluctant—hoping his miserly gold would keep him safe. But no matter. He has come now.*

The undead turned to face the new threat. Croighcat's Cymbrogi flooded down the hill on horseback. The battle cry renewed, and those who had been fighting joined the call. At least their numbers had increased. At least they would have a little more time to hope for a miracle.

And that was when it happened. As Croighcat's men collided onto the field, another opponent clamored toward Bedwyr. He swung at the undead warrior who, unlike Bedwyr, would not grow weary.

Bedwyr wore his weariness like a second skin, his arms shaking from fatigue. But still he fought on. Each pounding strike was another moment that he refused to let go.

His enemy swung. Bedwyr dodged the strike and closed in on his opponent's exposed side, seizing his opening. He pulled his blade back and stabbed his foe through the ribs. Bedwyr reared back, ready to take his head, when he noticed something different in his enemy's fleshless eyes.

Pain.

Bedwyr halted, watching confusion and fear ripple across the demon warrior's wide-open jowls. He appeared, suddenly, human. His eyes rolled as he plummeted to the ground. Bedwyr peered around, ready for his next combatant. His tightened jaw loosened and his face slackened. Enemy warriors dropped all over the field. Those that had been roasted by the dragon's fire, or were already wounded, collapsed to the ground dead—and stayed dead.

An enemy warrior locked his faltering eyes on Bedwyr. With a labored breath, Bedwyr took a step forward to pursue the fight. But the warrior's eyes rounded with horror, and he fumbled back. A Cymbrogi from behind sliced through him, and he toppled over in death.

The miracle, Bedwyr thought, watching the enemy hacked down. With the aid of Croighcat's men, the struggling Cymbrogi of Prydain now had the battlefield. Together, they cut down the retreating enemies.

Bedwyr turned back to Arthur and slumped to his knees beside his king. He brushed Arthur's golden hair from his forehead before surveying his numerous wounds. The left side of his body and face had been burned. How badly, Bedwyr couldn't tell.

"Arthur," Bedwyr beckoned. "We—" He gulped a lump of exhaustion and pain into his chest. "The enemy is defeated. The miracle came. Please…brother." He cradled Arthur in his arms. "The kingdom can be ours once again."

"Ours?" Arthur whispered with his eyes still closed. A slight smile tugged at his lips. "It was never ours."

Bedwyr gasped—tears welled. "We still need you, brother. The kingdom needs you."

"Perhaps."

Arthur said no more. Bedwyr held him as the sounds of battle dwindled. It was over. Bedwyr dipped his forehead to meet Arthur's. Exhausted, he began to cry. The loss of Arthur—it would be like it was before, but even emptier without Peredur.

"You must live," Bedwyr keened. "Do not give up the fight. Not now. Not yet."

"They cannot be dead," Elanor sobbed, clinging to hope. "She is not dead."

Elanor cradled her daughter against her languishing heart, rocking her back and forth. She muttered those same words over and over with her eyes squeezed shut. Maybe she could make all the bad disappear. "It is only dark magic. It can be undone. They will live." The more she confessed those words, the more despair surged back like an unbeatable wave. She couldn't accept it—she wouldn't.

A shadow moved in front of her eyelids. She opened her eyes to find Merlin kneeling before her. His wet cheeks glistened, and as he rested his hand upon hers, she could see his surrender in each shed tear.

She shook her head. "No…no, Merlin. She will live. She must. Cilaen. I cannot—" She choked, swallowing hard. "We can save them. Our magic. We *must* try."

Elanor glanced over at the gleaming crystals inside the cave wall. Their magic pulsed freely through the chamber once again.

"Great God," she cried in desperation. "Please, help us."

Merlin buckled forward, his shoulders quivering with his sobs.

"No—do not give up. *Merlin.*" Her plea felt hollow on her tongue. Merlin's despondence was like a wall of grief she could not tear down.

She started to speak again, but her own despair stole her voice. She reached for *the promise*, but even the thought of speaking it out made her feel abandoned. Powerless. Angry. The promise slapped her across the face with its failed sentiments. But she pushed back anyway, having nothing else to cling to, and whispered, "Sweet…Are the healing days, when pain will find no way."

There was nothing sweet—nothing healing. Pain was all she could feel. She clutched Gwendolen even tighter, and with a warble in her voice, she sang it again. "Sweet…Are the healing days, when pain will find no way." The words choked her, but she couldn't let go—not yet. She tried to say it one more time, but a keening lament fell from her lips instead.

Merlin's hand squeezed her fingers, and he said it for her. "Sweet…Are the healing days, when pain will find no way."

She glanced up at him, nodding through her tears. Hearing Merlin say it renewed her strength and comforted her spirit.

"It is time to wipe the blood from your sword," a quiet voice spoke beside them. Elanor yelped, startled, and both she and Merlin darted their eyes toward the voice.

Kneeling with his hand brushing Cilaen's forehead was the Man in Blue. He looked at them with sorrowful eyes and said, "I am so sorry that this battle has been so dark—so damaging."

"Where were you?" Merlin asked with a somber lilt.

"Merlin," he said, his voice filled with tender, affirming love. Elanor was struck by its warmth. "This battle was more than what you could see with your eyes. But please understand, I have never left you. You were never alone."

Merlin dropped his head.

"There has been death," the Man in Blue said with a nod. "Some of the devastation done by your adversary can never be undone, but some *will* be undone, and all *will be* renewed."

Faith sparked inside Elanor's heart. "What can be undone?"

"That depends on you. Can you believe that all I have given you is enough?"

Elanor's brow scrunched. What had she been given? The song—the promise of the *New Way*? Or her healing magic? None of this could undo what had been done.

Not for Gwendolen. Not for Cilaen. She brushed her daughter's cheek. Another one of her tears slid down her nose and dropped onto Gwendolen's forehead.

As if the man had read her thoughts, he said, "There is so much more. I did not just give you one gift; I gave you it all."

"All of what?" she sobbed.

"All of everything I have." He returned his solemn gaze to Cilaen. "It is not his time. Neither is it time for your little one to enter my kingdom without you."

"I do not understand."

"I do not need you"—his eyes flicked to Merlin—"*either of you* to understand. I just need you to *trust* that what I tell you is true."

"Elanor," Merlin said softly, "you were right. It is within our hands."

"Even death?"

The man smiled. A single tear dripped from his eye. "This day, the authority has been given to you. But you must believe."

Through sobs, she said, "Sweet…Are the healing days, when pain will find no way?"

"That is the promise."

Elanor nodded, then, quietly at first, she began to sing. Each line became bolder. This time, she was determined to believe each lyric. And that was when it changed. Just like the song she sang when the unicorn came to her in the forest—a song she did not know, with words she could not understand, leapt from her lips. Merlin sang also, their voices echoing off the walls of the cave. Soon, the crystals resonated with their voices. Blue light beamed brighter and brighter. Swirls of azure light danced around them, filtering past their cheeks.

Elanor saw Grwyrthrhodd inside the illuminated lights, along with others, whose voices echoed along with the song. The words siphoned poison from her heart, just like it had the demon snake's venom from Merlin's arm.

As she held fast to the promise, the illusion of her flat in the future world faded further and further away. What had been was no longer. Not even the threat of Osian existed to steal it all away. He was gone. Destroyed. The New Way was removing all the dross. The New Way, no longer a future promise, but a realized truth.

The song ended and the light dissipated to a gentle glow. Elanor lifted her eyes. The Man in Blue had vanished. Cilaen still lay upon the floor and Gwendolen lifelessly hung in her arms. But something had changed. Looking up at Merlin, she could tell he understood it too.

She drew a long, confident breath and said—first to Gwendolen, then to Cilaen—"It is time to wake up."

"Muma?" Gwendolen's sweet voice trickled into Merlin's ears, making him gasp. His chin trembled, and he watched mother and daughter smile at one another.

Cilaen. Merlin's heart leapt as he peered behind Elanor.

Cilaen's eyes fluttered open with a confused grimace. He lifted his hands, turning them back and forth. "The burns—they are gone."

Merlin could not spare a single moment. He dashed to Cilaen's side and wrapped him up in his arms. A consoling laugh bubbled forth, and he squeezed Cilaen even tighter.

Cilaen reciprocated the embrace, heartily pounding Merlin's back. "I thought…I thought I had died."

"You had." Merlin couldn't let go. Waves of victory swelled in his spirit. "You are back to us from death. A miracle. The hand of the Triple God brought you back."

"Osian?"

"He is…" Merlin pulled back, patting Cilaen on the shoulder, hardly believing it himself. "He is dead." He indicated Osian's lifeless body sprawled on the floor.

Cilaen gasped, his eyes wide with disbelief.

Merlin wiped his arm over his cheeks to dry his eyes. Now seeing Osian dead felt like victory instead of bitter defeat. Just moments ago all was lost. But now… everything had been given back. The nightmare was over.

"Daddy!" Gwendolen leapt into his arms.

"Oh, my sweet little one," he said, cupping the back of her head and placing a kiss on her cheek. He turned to Elanor, touching her throat in awe. The cut from Osian's blade was healed. Merlin laughed with heavy relief, squeezing a handful of his daughter's silken hair. He cherished her warmth, her small hands clutching his arms. To think he had lost them for even a moment summoned more tears to his eyes.

"We did it," Elanor said, her eyes bright and filled with hopeful expectation. "It—it is done."

With Osian's depraved connection to Morgan severed and the curse broken, the Cymry on the battlefield were hopefully overcoming the enemy horde.

Is Arthur and Bedwyr still alive?

Not knowing soured his moment of triumph. How many had been killed within the clash?

"Let us leave this place," Merlin said, setting Gwendolen down as he rose to his feet. He could not wait to inhale fresh air. This time, the air would come with a breath of freedom. He and Elanor could be together. They could have their family, without threat of the darkness destroying their future. He lifted his hand and plainly spoke, "Agor."

The rocks caving in the entrance toppled free. Daylight pierced through the seams between the rocks. It was almost too good to be true. Merlin had been fighting hopelessness and grief ever since Arthur died. Now, the revelation washed over him. All the pent-up destiny that had been a burden all his years had finally come. He had become the kingmaker to usher in a kingdom that would never end.

As he stepped out over the rocks and the warm sunlight hit his face, he saw a land renewed—saturated with the promised Kingdom of the Sun. The golden light painted the green grass, the trees, and the gray of the crumbled stone pillars. It was a new age.

And though the destruction of the Crystal Cave's surrounding stones was a somber sight, Merlin found purpose in the sacrifice. The crystal ruins became the doorway to hope, paving the way for their victory—the old yielding to the new with a silent grace.

He hoped Arthur had survived to be part of this new day. That the sacrifice of Cymbrogi blood had been worth this world's restoration—just like these stones. He hoped that a victory cup, overflowing with ale, awaited them from Arthur's throne in Caer Lial.

THE ONCE & FUTURE KINGDOM

They rode back to Caer Lial. Elanor's eyes lifted to the hill where the Palisade sat with red and gold flags streaming in the wind. Her mind wandered at the sight. Would Arthur still be king after the raging battle with the undead? Would she see her father again?

Upon the steps of the Great Hall stood Gwynevere and Samara, who bounced on her toes, smiling at Cilaen.

He was the first to dismount from his horse. He ran up the steps, wrapped Samara in his arms, and spun her around. "Marry me," he eagerly asked the minute her feet hit the ground.

Samara laughed, flinging her arms around Cilaen's neck. She repeatedly kissed his lips, cheeks and chin, before finally saying that she would.

Gwynevere's cheeks flushed with emotion as she enfolded Elanor, Merlin, and Gwendolen into her arms. Elanor felt Gwynevere's relief, mingled with worry and grief.

"A rider has come," Gwynevere said, her eyes flicking between Elanor and Merlin. "The battle has been won. There was great loss of Cymry life, but the enemy has been conquered. Arthur"—her eyes flooded—"was badly wounded. They are bringing him home to us. More I can tell you, but first, tell me how you found our little one." She cupped Gwendolen's cheeks in her hands. "What of Osian?"

Merlin released a heavy sigh, his eyes shimmering with joyful tears. "He is dead. All his curses are broken."

Gwynevere laughed as tears tumbled free.

It took another two days before they saw the first lines of Cymbrogi return through the gates. Arthur was aloft on the shoulders of the Cymry guard. Bedwyr led the march from his horse.

Elanor entwined her fingers through Gwynevere's. Both held their breath, standing on the Hall's steps, Merlin beside them.

"So few horses," Elanor murmured, not meaning to say it aloud. A lump formed in her throat, hoping her father was alive, even if just for her mother, but it felt like she was clinging to an unwinding ball of twine. She had only just become his—just accepted him as father—and now she might lose him, just like she lost David.

I can't bear to lose anyone else.

Adhan had been stolen from them. Peredur, a fallen hero. Neither had been honored yet. There had been no time. They were wrapped and prepared, awaiting their unbuilt pyres within King's Tower—the Chamber of the Pendragons. Merlin still wept over his mother's death. Elanor knew that pain all too well.

Please. She pleaded to the Great God. *Please let him be alive.*

The nearer the Cymbrogi came, carrying Arthur on a pallet, the more her heart sank. She didn't mean to squeeze Gwynevere's hand so hard, but her mother reciprocated the tense grip. Arthur's head jostled back and forth, making Elanor want to flee. Maybe it was better not to know. The suspense was killing her. The Cymbrogi marched in a sorrowful cadence that crept far too slowly. Why was there no hurry? If he were alive, wouldn't there be some urgency?

"I have the healing rooms prepared," Gwynevere said, her voice quavering. "They will restore him."

Elanor instinctively nodded, hoping there would still be a need.

The lines of Bedwyr's face became clearer. Elanor searched his countenance for anything that would prepare her. He did not evade her gaze. Instead, his lips parted with a tender smile, his eyes awash without despair. Her heart beat faster—Bedwyr had given her hope.

She lifted onto her eager toes, peering at Arthur. His hand draped over the side of the pallet, bouncing limp at each step. She could see the lacerations on his hand.

Burns. Elanor stiffened, gripping the collar of her dress.

Finally arriving at the steps, Bedwyr dismounted and commanded, "Bring the king to his family, then take him to the healers."

What? Elanor nearly leapt. Gwynevere gasped, clinging to Elanor's arm.

They brought the pallet down onto the stone terrace.

Gwynevere did not hesitate but bolted toward Arthur. Merlin rushed ahead of Elanor. She lifted her hand to her mouth when she saw Arthur's numerous wounds. His armor and shirt had been removed, revealing the blood-soaked linens covering his torso. A tourniquet was wrapped tight around his leg.

He was conscious. A feverish sweat beaded his brow, but he forced a smile. His eyes danced over the three of them.

Through a graveled and strained voice, he said, "Do not fear. I will live. I just"— he coughed—"need some healing medicines."

Gwynevere trembled, letting Arthur's hand go. She rose to her feet and commanded, "Take him to the healers."

"Wait," Elanor yelled, rushing to him. "Let me heal you." Relieved tears streamed from her eyes. She could at least try. He was alive. That was all she needed to have faith.

Arthur looked at her, his face softening. "Of course," he groaned through a spasm of pain, "you are Gwenddydd."

She smiled, turning to Merlin. He nodded for her to try before laying his hand upon Arthur's chest. Together, the light of their magic ignited and their gifts flowed. Arthur's pallid face and darkened eyes slowly enlivened. His lips turned pink and his cheeks flushed with a healthy color. His strained body relaxed. The magic waned, but Arthur's wounds remained.

Merlin squeezed Elanor's hand. She faced him, knowing it was now up to the healers to finish the job.

"Thank you," Arthur uttered.

Cymbrogi quickly carried him away through the Hall's shadowed doorway.

Elanor stared after him, her anxiousness ebbing as her heartbeat settled. A fragile smile lifted her cheeks. Merlin approached, helping Elanor to her feet. He wrapped his comforting arm around her shoulders and squeezed her to his side.

"The king will live," he said, kissing the top of her head.

Elanor slid her arms around his waist and rested her head on his chest. His gentle warmth engulfed her, and in that moment, she truly felt like everything would be all right. Arthur would have his kingdom. She would have her family. A whole family. A home with Merlin and the Great Pendragon—the once and future king.

As the rest of the Cymbrogi returned to the Caer, a crescendo of exultant cries rose amongst the people. With each king's safe passage over the threshold, the jubilation intensified. Elanor, standing with Merlin on the terrace, spent hours immersed in the joyous spectacle. Swells of emotions tingled her skin at the collective roar of victory. The shadow of evil had truly been vanquished, and at last, they reveled in their freedom.

All the kings had lived, yet their return was not without mourning. Pain overshadowed their triumph, the heavy losses evident in their eyes. Thul, in particular, bore the weight of his son's death. Croighcat, who in the end had saved the day, entered the Great Hall with softened features and humility in his stride. Bram's bearing appeared more like a king, while Cormach's tear-soaked cheeks spoke volumes of his sorrow. The people of Dyved mourned Adhan as they would a fallen queen. Her death, a last breath of the old world. Elanor's heart broke at Merlin's lament for his mother. Though it was a grievous pain, she clung to it and did not want it to end. It kept Adhan with them—a tether to her memory, lingering just a little longer.

Days later, after Arthur recovered from his wounds, he sat back in his chair at a table topped with roasted boar and browned bread. The singers were chanting and the dancers were twirling at a feast overflowing with ale. His people's joy multiplied the abundance. The food and drink never ceased to run dry.

Arthur peered down the length of the table. Bedwyr sloshed his ale, laughing and telling stories, his eyes alight with mirth.

Gwynevere's soft fingers rested in Arthur's hand. She rubbed his red scars with her thumb. The left side of Arthur's body was forever marred from the dragon's fire. Scars wrapped his cheek and neck, but he hardly cared. His eyes bounced, following Gwendolen's happy skips as she tried to keep up with the dancers. Her life was a reminder of what the enemy could not steal from them. Her innocence, a reflection of his daughter's echo.

Elanor and Merlin sat on his right. The lilt of Elanor's voice twittering to Merlin over the crowded thrum made Arthur chuckle.

Merlin captured Arthur's gaze. The druid had started it all. His and Arthur's destiny collided into the chaos that had ultimately ushered in something lasting. If Arthur had only known that day, so long ago, when Merlin forced him to pull that sword from the stone—all the pain and grief—the triumph and love that would come.

Merlin gave Arthur a knowing nod, and then cleared his throat and rose to his feet.

Cilaen already held Merlin's harp and handed it to him with seamless timing. A single strum hushed the people, and they quickly shuffled to their seats. The gold sparks glimmered in Merlin's eyes.

Elanor slid her hand into Arthur's. He grasped it firmly. Gwynevere on his left—Elanor to his right.

Merlin lifted his voice, enchanting the room as only a bard could do. The shiver of his magic made Arthur pause in reflection. Merlin's words reminded him of pain, but also enlivened his hope. His heart lifted seeing the world Merlin painted with his lyrics. It was imperfect but filled with purpose.

Arthur Pendragon was atoned. He knew history would never know. But what did that matter? He knew. Gwynevere and Elanor knew. Merlin knew. Arthur smiled up at the bard, then out over his people. Their peaceful eyes sparkled in the firelight. They knew. As long as he was king, they would know that he was Arthur Pendragon, the once and future king of the Britons.

<h1 style="text-align: center">EPILOGUE</h1>

Once Arthur was fully recovered, a company of Cymbrogi, along with Gwynevere, Bedwyr, Merlin and Elanor rode out to the Hill of the Kings. This would be Elanor's first time seeing the stones in their original form within the beauty of the earth as it was in this time—this day. Her heart groaned within her, for a wagon pulled two stones that would be set upon the Hero's Mound.

One of them, she could now read. Time had not erased the lines. Set in ogham and Latin script, she read the epitaph to her father David. It simply read: *David – A kingsman, and guardian of the princess. A worthy warrior of the Cymry.*

Peredur's stone would read the same as Arthur's other mighty men. In ogham the lines would tell of a worthy warrior of the Cymry, who fought beside his king. While passing the lake, Elanor wondered how they had ever found a path to the future Hill of the Kings. In the future time, there was no road lining the hill, and the shape of the lake was smaller and less vast.

Mist rose from the lake, and the early morning sun peeked above the mountains. The beautiful backdrop dazzled Elanor's thoughts, making her think of the Fisher King, his daughter, and the gift of Caledfwlch.

"I wonder if he is still there," Elanor asked Merlin, who rode in silence beside her.

Merlin smiled. "I would love to see one of my kin again." Sadness washed over his face, dropping the corners of his mouth. "No," he continued. "The fair folk have all gone. Their time has truly ended."

Elanor deeply wished he was wrong. She missed the timeless beauty of Adhan's face. Her softness and wisdom. The otherworldliness that appeared in her eyes when she spoke. Adhan's silver hair floating through the wind pricked painfully in Elanor's memory. A deep magic of the old world had existed within Adhan and now only remained within Merlin—within Elanor. She glanced at her fingers, rubbing them together. She was thankful that she had been gifted something so rare and fading. King Cormach would be building a cairn to memorialize Adhan in Dyved. She and Merlin would travel there with Gwendolen soon.

"I am sorry," Elanor whispered to Merlin, fully taking in his ethereal golden eyes.

Merlin held his hand out to her, and she took it. "Mother, and the fair folk, borrowed time. They were meant to fade a long time ago when their world was swallowed by the great flood. But they survived, bringing a treasure that has lasted these many ages within the blade Arthur carries."

"The blue book," Elanor said, thinking of the first thing Merlin had given her. "The stories inside are not faery stories."

Merlin lifted one corner of his mouth. "No. Not faery stories. That history is now a part of your story."

Elanor smiled, loving that she had a connection to a wondrous people through Merlin's magic. She would live to become part of something greater than herself.

"It is hard"—Merlin's brows tightened—"letting go of the past to let in the new. In the past, there was darkness that could not remain, but there was also beauty that never should have faded. Clutching tightly to even the beautiful fragments of our past may cost us the chance to embrace the fresh beginnings and their intended purpose.

"I realize now why Arthur and I struggled so hard. We wanted to keep the old, and reign inside a construct time had done away with. I had wondered why the Great God warned me not to fear time." He soberly laughed. "I thought it meant not fearing your death, or us not returning home from the future. But it was not any of that. It was all about letting go—sacrificing all I hoped to hold onto. It was about having faith.

"I can still have all that was good locked inside my heart. It will never fade. My mother will never truly be gone from me. But I can no longer resent the past, nor carry all that heavy unforgiveness within me. I cannot hold onto things that are meant to fade, but trust that in the end, what matters will be held for me."

Elanor understood what he meant. In her future time, there was pain— loneliness. But there was also her father David. Losing him was a blade to her heart. She wanted to be angry and bitter. And for a while, she was—blaming Arthur for her pain. She had to let it go and trust that the treasure would remain. And it had.

She glanced over at the stone memorializing David, and even amidst the ache of his loss, her love for him endured, a steadfast flame within her heart. Her gaze shifted ahead to Arthur and Gwynevere. She loved them, and they loved her. Time had bestowed many gifts upon her, and though grief was indelible, hope could truly blossom again, defying all the pain and loss once thought insurmountable.

The two hills amongst the mountains came into view. The same two hills that she, Merlin, and David had trekked through to find Arthur. Elanor smiled. She was glad now that David had come with them. Glad his adventure with them had mattered.

A well-traveled road lay between the hills. It had been washed away in the future time, just as Merlin had said. As they passed through the pines, echoes of Jack rang through her mind. He had a chance at redemption too. Elanor hoped he would find it someday when it was his time, and the future world had come again.

She didn't often think about Helen or Nancy. They were forgiven, and she let them go completely, now becoming faded images of her past. They had been catalysts that ignited her struggle to define herself, the dissenting voices she had to silence to discover the truth.

The road opened wider, and there, revealed before her, were two small hills. Her jaw dropped at their diminutive height in comparison to what they would become.

One hill held a small, round burial mound with a stone over its door where the kings were entombed. Aurelius, Uther, and Arthur. The other hill was a little larger, with a ring of tall towering stones clearly visible at its zenith.

Merlin nudged her. "Arthur's inside there, you know."

Elanor laughed, shaking her head. The very idea baffled her. Time played tricks on her mind because, how could that possibly be? Yet there ahead were the stones memorializing the three kings, and the cairn that marked the tomb beside it.

"I will be setting a guard of protection around the tomb. This will make it safe through time."

"Is the Cyhyraeth inside?"

"Heh," Merlin chuffed. "No…that being lives outside of time, and was dispelled when your father died."

"I cannot understand *any* of it."

"Neither can I."

"Arthur is there, but he cannot be—for he is here." She pointed to her father, who was helping her mother dismount from her horse.

"Either way—no one will be going into that tomb until *we do*, someday, in the future time."

"Once and future," Elanor said with a wink.

Merlin nodded. "Once and future."

Waves of time washed over Elanor as her father David's stone was lifted into place. She laid her hand on the marker, knowing that his guardian spirit was there keeping the tomb protected. Merlin set the whorl in the stone in front of Arthur's tomb. The old magic only opened to the one whose name he enchanted into the stone. It would be Elanor, for it would be her hand that broke the seal.

Merlin and Elanor's hands interlaced, and they peered at the hills. The sun sinking low made the stones black silhouettes. Now they could move on. They would build their lives with Gwendolen. She would grow into a world where her grandfather still ruled as king.

"It will not last," Merlin said softly.

"What?"

"Arthur's kingdom."

"Another beautiful thing will fade?"

"The sun rises and it sets. The fruit that will grow because he still reigns will be eaten and replanted."

"What of us?"

"We will live," Merlin said, lifting her hand to his mouth and kissing it. "We will live."

New songs were written that would be sung on the tables of Cymbrogi for generations. Songs that would rewrite the old ways of the past to the New Kingdom of everlasting. This kingdom could not be destroyed, for even as the ancient Cymry ways faded, and eventually the Saecsans returned to take the land, something had been planted that never stopped growing. Arthur's story never stopped being told—though many tales did not contain his return that changed the Cymry world. The story passed through many hands and many tellings, never truly forgotten. The Kingdom of the Sun would fill the pages of storytellers who saw its radiant light shine over the tops of mountains and hills—cascading across the land—always leading the way into its never-fading hope.

THE END

ACKNOWLEDGEMENTS

To my dear friend *Stephanie Cotta*. A huge thank you to you for embarking on this journey with me from the very beginning. Without your support, I do not think that THE ONCE & FUTURE CHRONICLES would have become what they are today. Your investment has made you part of these stories, and your editing super-powers have definitely left your thumbprint on every page. I am so grateful for you. To say that you edited this book, is to not give you the full credit you are due. Thank you for being my friend. Thank you for your support. Thank you for your guidance. And thank you for being fascinated by the fantastic. I love you so much.

To *Brae & Jill Wycoff*. From my first book, to all the stories I will ever write—they will exist because you told me I could. You took the moment to turn aside and blow on the spark that would become a flame. The whole trajectory of my life was changed because you believed in me. Every accolade I receive is because you told me I was a FANTASTIC STORYTELLER. I honor you for every piece I will write from here on to eternity. With all my heart - Thank you!

To my husband *Clay*, my beautiful children *Ezra & Brielle*. Thank you for giving me the time to write, and believing my story-telling was a calling and not just a hobby. The tree that now grows was planted and watered by your belief in me. I love you.

Mom, Dad, Amanda & Audra. I know I have always been the odd one. And now maybe you know a little of the reason why. Thank you for always being the first to read my stories, and support my dreams in so many ways.

Thank you to my fellow Sword-Bearing Kingdom Writer, *Nathan Keys*. Let's keep telling stories and blazing a trail.

And finally, to my superfans *Jordan McFarland* and *Sam Pacheco*. You said it first, and it meant the world to me. I will never forget.

COMING SOON!

A New Book from the Land of Prydain...

In the Northern realm of Orchadés, a cursed kingdom shrouded in sorrow, Duen, a seventeen-year-old outcast marked by both doomed parentage and a crippled hip, embarks on a perilous journey for survival. Fleeing from his village who would have him dead, he crosses paths with Nimwe, a headstrong young woman determined to forge her own destiny amidst the war-torn ruins left by the Saecsans.

As Duen and Nimwe navigate the treacherous landscape, a malevolent witch sets her sights on Duen, seeking to annihilate him. However, a mysterious druid named Merlin senses a hidden power within Duen, sparking a conflict between Duen and Nimwe, challenging their bond and the fate that intertwines their lives.

Set against the enchanting backdrop of the Arthurian land of Prydain, *THE LOST SON OF ORCHADÉS* unveils a tale of resilience, magic, and redemption. This young adult novel serves as a captivating prequel to *THE ONCE & FUTURE CHRONICLES TRILOGY*, the first installment in *THE ILLYDS OF PRYDAIN'S HEROES*. A series depicting the valor and adventures of Arthur's mighty men—weaving a tapestry of heroism and legend.

THE LOST SON OF ORCHADÉS
Part One
The Illyds of Prydain's Heroes

MORE FROM
ANGELA R HUGHES

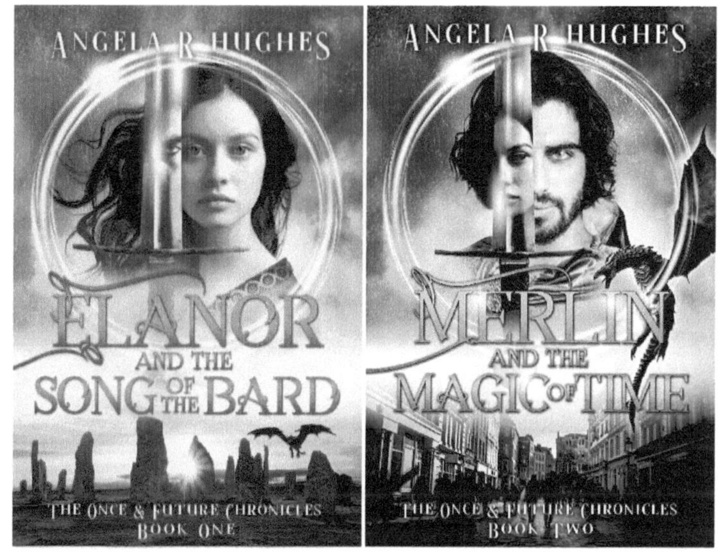

Check out Books One & Two of
THE ONCE & FUTURE CHRONICLES TRILOGY.
Start the adventure with Elanor and Merlin who together become the catalysts to resurrect a dying kingdom, along with an old darkness that wants to destroy it.

Find These books at AMAZON.com, or
wherever books are sold.

For More Information
www.angelarhughes.com

ABOUT THE AUTHOR

ANGELA R. HUGHES

is a historical fantasy author based in Waco, Texas. Her ambition is to write stories that grip and inspire readers, alluring them into her fascinating world of myth and legend.

Angela believes in the power of dynamic, inspired storytelling. She has always been intrigued by folklore and legend, and desired to create her own. Particularly drawn to Arthurian legend and its ancient roots in the history of the Cymraeg (Welsh) people, she has extensively studied Arthurian legend and Celtic mythology.

Much of her fascination with the Celtic world began during her time living in Ireland, where she fell in love with the history and landscapes of Ireland, Wales, Scotland, and England.

In addition to writing, Angela spends her time researching ancient histories and languages—which led her to learn to speak the Welsh language. She also enjoys chatting with fellow fantasy nerds on the podcasts she co-hosts, THE INK MAGES on YouTube and Spotify.

The Once and Future Chronicles Trilogy are the first of her published works. She is currently working on a new book, *The Lost Son of Orchadés*, the first book in *The Illyds of Prydain's Heroes Series.*

Learn more about *The Once & Future Chronicles* by visiting www.angelarhughes.com. You are also invited to follow Angela's author journey on Facebook, Instagram, TikTok and Amazon.

LET'S BE LEGENDARY!

Instagram/TikTok: @angela.r.hughes
Facebook: Angela R. Hughes @onceandfuturechronicles
Twitter: @ARHughesAuthor

IMAGINE NOW PUBLISHING

If you enjoyed this book,
I'd be so grateful if you'd
WRITE A REVIEW....

It's easy and helps my book get into the hands of more readers.
Step 1: Go To www.AMAZON.com
Step 2: Search for my book in Amazon books
Step 3: Scroll down to REVIEWS
Step 4: Leave a Review

I'd love to know your thoughts about my book.
Contact me at *angelarhuges.mythiclegends@gmail.com*
Let me know what you got out of the book.
Join my newsletter for more info on events and releases.
Sign up here: www.angelarhughes.com

Thank You for Your Support